the
dead
survivors

also by KJ Erickson

Third Person Singular

the
dead
survivors

KJ ERICKSON

st. martin's minotaur
new york

www.minotaurbooks.com
www.kjerickson.com

Library of Congress Cataloging-in-Publication Data

Erickson, KJ
    The dead survivors / KJ Erickson
        p. cm.
    ISBN 0-312-26699-5
            1. Police—Minnesota—Minneapolis—Fiction. 2. Minneapolis
    (Minn.)—Fiction. I. Title.
PS3555.R433 D3 2002
813'.6—dc21
                                                            2001048749

First Edition: March 2002

10   9   8   7   6   5   4   3   2   1

For Jack and Dach

Two exceptional southern boys

For every Southern boy . . . there is the instant when it's . . . not yet two o'clock on that July afternoon . . . and it's all in the balance.

—William Faulkner, *Intruder in the Dust*

the
dead
  survivors

CHAPTER

1

At four o'clock on that December afternoon, the dim winter sun cast a shallow light across Joey Beck's apartment. Outside, the sound of heavy traffic was steady as the Friday rush hour began. Joey glanced at his watch, then at the beckoning couch. He had two hours before he was due to meet his dad for dinner. Bone weary, he stretched out on the couch.

It was the darkness of the room and the silence from the streets that wakened Joey five hours later. He sat upright as if shocked, his heart racing. His hand groped in the dark for the stem on his watch. The green light on the watch face flashed on. It was after 9:00 P.M. More than three hours after the time his father had said he'd call.

Joey clicked on a lamp, stretching and shaking as he rose, using physical motion to assert conscious control over the netherworld of sleep. What had he forgotten? *Was* it Friday night? Hadn't they planned dinner for sometime after six?

No message light flashed on the answering machine. Joey punched the menu on the phone to check the call log. Maybe his dad had called but hadn't left a message. Rapidly, he clicked through calls for December 6. Only three calls all day—none from his dad.

He dialed his dad's apartment. Four rings and the answering

machine picked up. Joey hesitated, then said, "Dad. It's Joey. Am I missing something? Thought we were having dinner tonight. I'm at my apartment. Call."

Now fully awake, Joey still felt shocky, like something was wrong. For all his faults, Frank Beck didn't change plans without letting you know. Joey paced, wanting to take a shower, but not wanting to miss his dad's call. It struck him that he didn't know who to call to check on his dad. Six months ago he would have called his mother, and she could have told him with certainty what was going on. Six months ago he could have called any one of a half dozen of Frank Beck's friends, all of whom would likely know where Frank was and what he was doing.

But a lot had changed in six months. A wife of thirty-plus years, friends, an older son and daughter—all had gone on one-too-many roller-coaster rides with Frank Beck. Six months ago when the roller coaster went down—went down steep—they'd all opted off. Everybody except Joey.

Joey hesitated for a moment, then dialed his mother's number.

"Hi, Joey." Mona Beck had gotten caller ID after the separation. She wanted to be sure that when she answered her phone, Frank Beck wouldn't be on the other end of the line. She'd told everybody she knew: "You call and I don't know the number or it comes up 'private name' or 'unidentified'—I don't answer." What she didn't admit to anybody but herself was that she wouldn't answer Frank's calls because she didn't trust herself not to see him again if he did call.

"Mom—I know you don't want to be involved in anything with Dad . . ."

"That's right, Joey." Her voice was hard, just on the edge of mean.

"The thing is, Dad and I had plans for dinner tonight, and he didn't call. I worked a double shift starting at midnight last night and didn't get home until almost four this afternoon. I laid down, expecting to wake up when Dad called at six—we were going to decide when he called where to meet. But I just woke up and he hasn't called. . . ."

Her voice was tight, impatient. "I told you, Joey. Your father is no longer my problem. If you don't expect anything from him, he can't let you down."

"Mom, you know he never says he's going to do something with one of us and then just doesn't show up. He always calls. That much you can count on . . ."

The line was silent for moments. She knew that Joey was right. "You called his apartment?"

"Of course. I left a message . . ." She didn't ask if he'd called his dad's cell phone, which meant she knew Frank Beck no longer had a cell phone. Frank Beck had been the first person Joey knew to use a cell phone, and the cell phone was as much a part of Frank Beck as his right arm. It was when Joey found out his dad hadn't been able to pay his cell phone bills that he knew things were irrevocably bad.

"And you tried the office?" His mother's voice was now a little worried around the edges.

"The office? He still has the office?"

"I ran into Phyllis Quinn at Lund's a couple weeks ago—maybe longer—" She stopped. He knew they were both thinking the same thing. His mother couldn't afford to grocery shop at Lund's. Old habits die hard, and she was feeling guilty. "Anyway, Phyllis said she'd run into your dad coming out of the Dachota Building the day before. She'd asked him if he still had his office there, and he told her that the leasing agent was letting him stay through the end of the year. No phone. Probably no electricity . . ."

"Phyllis said there was no phone?"

She was slow in answering. "I checked. I just wanted to know . . ."

"Maybe that's it, Mom. Maybe he started working on something, forgot about the time, and not having a phone handy . . ."

"Your guess is as good as mine, Joey. Probably better."

* * *

The heater was out in Joey's car, and he shivered all the way downtown. Joey wished his dad's office was anywhere other than in the downtown Minneapolis warehouse district. On a Friday night, the district's bars and restaurants would be full and parking would be at a premium. Then Joey remembered. His dad used to park in the alley behind the Dachota in a space that came with the lease. If his dad's car were in the space it would make sense to go to the trouble of parking and going up to the office.

Joey hit First Avenue North just as traffic from a Target Center concert was getting out. Joey's car crawled, his anxiety building with each traffic light that changed before he made it through an intersection. Couples ran across the street between the cars, women dressed for a night on the town. The women clung to their boyfriends for warmth and to balance themselves on spike heels. These were people his own age, but Joey felt no connection to their high spirits. He resented that any problems they had were easy enough to be obliterated by the energy of a Friday night.

Finally reaching Fifth Street North, Joey swung right, drove a half block, and pulled into the alley behind the Dachota. Without streetlights, it was like driving down a hole. But even in the dark, Joey could see the dim gleam of his dad's silver Jaguar. A wave of relief washed over him—but seconds later he realized the car behind the Dachota didn't explain why his dad hadn't called. All the parked Jaguar meant was that the bankruptcy settlement hadn't taken place yet.

Joey pulled up behind the Jaguar. If you parked here on a weekday during business hours, you'd get towed before your engine cooled. But after ten on a Friday night, with First Avenue traffic backed up, Joey had all the time he needed to get up to his dad's fifth-floor office and back to the car.

Getting out of his car, Joey looked up toward the fifth floor. The windows were dark. Which meant one of two things: that the heavy black blinds in the office were down or that the office lights were out. Joey thought about what his mother had said about the electricity probably being off. If that was the case, what would his father be doing in a dark office with no lights, no phone, no functioning computer?

Walking toward the back door, Joey checked his key ring. The office key—which he hadn't used in months—was still there. Turning the lock, Joey pushed open the heavy metal door. Immediately he was hit with the particular smell of the Dachota's back entrance: unvarnished wood floors, indigenous dust, and uncirculated air that collected under the high ceilings.

Frank Beck had been among the first businessmen in town to renovate office space in one of the handsome old buildings in the warehouse district. He couldn't afford Class A office space for his start-up wireless electronics business, but after he saw the Dachota, it didn't matter. In its first life, the Dachota had been a warehouse that supplied farm implements to the prairies west of the Twin Cities. Beck had signed a lease minutes after opening the door to the vast, derelict fifth-floor space and within a month had gutted the Dachota's top floor down to brick walls and exposed vent work. He'd covered the high, broad windows with heavy black shades. When the shades were up, there was a spectacular 360-degree view that took in the downtown skyline in one direction and the Mississippi River in the opposite direction.

Within weeks of Beck Electronics moving into the Dachota, a half dozen other businesses had signed lease agreements and the warehouse office boom was under way. Frank could have taken an option to buy the Dachota and two other warehouse buildings for less money than a single lease in the Dachota was going for by year end. But as usual, his too-scarce capital was tied up in a venture that was long on concept and short on business plan. So he'd passed on an opportunity that would have made a fortune even Frank Beck would have been hard-pressed to blow.

The back halls of the Dachota were badly lit, and the silence late on a Friday night did nothing to relieve Joey's anxiety. He wound his way through the labyrinth of hallways to the freight elevator, pushed the up button, and heard the immediate clank of the elevator's lifts. The slow grind of the elevator's gears filled the empty corridor, ending with an echoing double thunk as the elevator landed on the first floor. The double steel doors slid back, and Joey stepped forward, pulled the metal gate to the side, and headed up.

Two things were wrong when the elevator doors opened. The first thing was the black lacquer door to Beck Electronics. It was partially open, with no light coming from behind the door. The second thing wrong was the cold air Joey could feel coming from behind the partially open door before he was off the elevator.

The cold hit him with a physical force as he stepped into the office. Without thinking, he pulled the door shut behind him, closing off the single ray of light in the space. Into the darkness he called, "Dad?"

His voice hung in the air for seconds before being sucked into the void. With his right hand, he felt along the wall for the light switches. He flicked all the switches, but no lights came on. He turned to reopen the door to regain the shaft of light, but already the deep darkness had caused him to lose his bearings. He reached again for the wall, finding only empty darkness.

He forced himself to stand still to quell dizziness. Joey thought about the layout of the office. It was open plan with four space dividers and a couple dozen workstations scattered across the polished hardwood floors. The only thing he could think to do was to follow the river of cold air to what must have been an open window. Once he got to the windows, he could raise the shades and let in some street light. You wouldn't be able to read by it, but at least you could see the basic outlines of what was in the office.

Joey started a careful shuffle in the direction of the cold. He had taken a half dozen steps when he struck something. It moved away from him as he reached for it, then swung back at him. He couldn't think of anything in the office that hung from the ceiling. Reaching out, he stabilized the object.

The first shape he recognized was a man's hand.

CHAPTER

2

The message was on his desk when Mars Bahr walked into the squad room of the Minneapolis Police Department Homicide Division.

Call Danny Borg.

He looked at it for a moment before turning to see his partner, Nettie Frisch, come across the room from the direction of the employee lounge. The message wasn't in her handwriting, but he asked her anyway.

"You know what Borg wants?"

"Wasn't here when he called." In front of her computer, Nettie immediately focused on the monitor. She took a big gulp from a partially frozen bottle of Evian water and said, without looking at him, "He probably just wanted to hear your voice."

Mars sifted through stuff on his desk that had come in while he'd been out. Nothing urgent. Things were slow. Minnesota Nice was in ascendance; the city was in danger of losing its hard-earned sobriquet as Murderapolis. He dropped papers back on the desk and glanced over at Nettie. It struck him that something was wrong. It took him a minute, then he said, "You're wearing denim, Nettie. What happened to the black-and-white-only rule?"

"Denim is consistent with the rule. The reason I made the only-wear-black-and-white rule was to keep my life simple.

Denim doesn't make my life complicated. *Plaid* would be complicated. What I want to avoid is having too many options."

"There's no such thing as too many options, Nettie. Not in our business." Mars shifted his attention back to Borg's message, the only thing on his desk with any promise of being interesting. He stretched back in his chair and dialed the downtown command.

Mars had worked with Borg on another case and had been impressed by Danny's hustle. Borg wasn't the most sensitive guy around, but Mars had liked his commitment and energy. Some cops, even good ones, went for the easy answers in an investigation. Borg focused on hard questions.

The duty officer in the downtown command said Borg was out on patrol, but offered to page him. Mars hung up and looked at his watch, making a bet with himself that Borg would call back in less than five minutes. Mars got up to walk back to the lounge for a Coke, but his phone rang before he'd made it out of the squad room.

Danny Borg's voice was breathless. "Special Detective Bahr? I apologize for missing your call."

Mars shook his head. One of Borg's endearing characteristics was a deep capacity for reverence, which was fine except that Mars had become the object of Borg's worship. He'd told Borg to drop the title and call him Mars almost a year ago. Borg's response had been, "Yes, sir. I'll do that, sir."

"Not a problem, Danny. What's on your mind."

Danny Borg's voice lowered. "Do you recall hearing about the guy who hung himself in his office last week? There was a big article on the front page of the Metro/State section on Monday . . ."

"I remember seeing the article. Sounded like a slam-dunk suicide. This is the guy who'd gone bust, right?"

"Yeah. Frank Beck. He'd lost his business, most of his family kind of backed off on him—and the ME's office found out he had colon cancer when they did the autopsy."

"Yeah. I definitely remember reading about it. Homicide

never got a referral—at least, it never came to me. And it would definitely be my kinda case if someone thought it was a homicide."

Borg didn't answer right away. When he did, his voice had dropped another octave. "No, there wasn't any referral to homicide. My sergeant's decision. I was the investigating officer on the scene. Got sent over when the nine-one-one call came in." Borg hesitated again. "The thing is, sir, I did recommend a referral to homicide, but my sergeant said 'No way.' And on the face of it, I can understand that. It's just that there were a couple things I thought merited a second look. But my sergeant is saying to leave things as they are. He's probably right. . . ."

"Tell me why you thought it should have been referred."

"There were two things. A number written on the guy's arm, and I couldn't find anything that connected to those numbers. No bank accounts, pin numbers, nothing. That, and I couldn't find where the guy got the fabric for the noose. For that matter, I couldn't find anyone who knew him who said Frank Beck knew how to tie a hangman's knot. What everybody said about him was that Beck wasn't a detail guy. He was a big idea man. Was sloppy about doing anything that required a long attention span. So I have to ask myself, how'd a guy like that tie a picture-perfect hangman's knot?"

Mars didn't say anything right away. He bounced a pencil on his desk and thought about it. His first reaction was that if Danny Borg had a gut feeling something wasn't right on a death, that in it self was enough to bring homicide in. And he agreed with Borg that questions about the number and the noose should be resolved.

"Let's do this. Send me a copy of your report from the scene, the medical examiner's report, and anything you took from the scene. I'll look it over. If anything comes out of our review, we'll open an investigation. No promises, but I agree with you. It sounds like we should know more than we do about the number and the noose."

"I really appreciate that, sir. The other thing is, Beck's

10

youngest son was pretty torn up about what happened. Either way—it stays a suicide or you find out something that makes it a homicide—the kid is going to feel better being sure. He's a good kid, just started college last fall. The only one who stuck by his dad when things got really tough." Borg hesitated again, then said, "I hate to put you on the spot, but can we handle this without a formal referral? I mean, without the paperwork and everything? Like I said, my sergeant hasn't authorized . . ."

"Don't worry about it. Just send me what I asked for. We'll worry about paperwork if we decide to open an investigation."

Without looking at Mars after he hung up with Borg, Nettie said, "What was that about?"

"Remember reading about the guy who hanged himself in his office—about a week ago?"

Nettie gave Mars a look.

Mars ignored the look, and said, "Borg thinks there are a couple of issues we should review before closing the file."

Nettie put words behind the look. "C'mon, Mars. There was nothing—*less* than nothing—to suggest this might be a homicide. And lots to support suicide. From what I read, this guy had every reason to die and nothing to live for."

Mars nodded. "I agree—from what I read at the time. Nothing that raised any flags, that's for sure. But I also remember from what I read that the family was pretty devastated. First the financial losses, then the suicide, then finding out after the fact that the guy had cancer. And Borg said Beck's youngest son is taking it pretty hard. I don't mind taking a look at the file and talking to the kid. If it'll make him feel any better . . ."

Nettie said, "I know what's happening here. You're projecting."

"I'm *what?*"

"You're projecting. You're thinking, 'What if something happened to me, and Chris needed to talk to someone about what happened?' "

Mars made a face. "So what you're saying, is, I make decisions about work priorities based on stuff that I connect to my ten-year-old son? I don't think so. If my taking an afternoon to look at the file helps a family accept the medical examiner's conclusion, I'd say the public interest is being served. Chalk it up to goodwill. Something the department needs as much of as it can get."

"What I'm saying is the First Response Unit is already having credibility problems, what with the murder rate being down nearly seventy percent since we got the FRU assignment. Chasing around trying to make a big deal out of a case the downtown command has already called a suicide isn't going to win us any friends."

Mars shifted in his chair and turned away from Nettie. "Winning popularity contests has always been my weak suit. If we can't keep our enemies off our backs, we might as well make them happy by giving them something to whine about."

"Project away, if it'll make you feel better," Nettie said.

Mars was on his way out of the squad room when the phone rang. He walked back to his desk, looked at the caller ID, and picked up.

"Hi, Karen. Dinner off?"

"Nuh. Just that I've had a hell of a week. I want to go someplace really nice. Someplace with cloth napkins and good wine."

"Fine with me. As long as they don't water the Coca-Cola. You've got somewhere special in mind?"

"Restaurant Alma. It's new. On University, between Fifth and Sixth Avenue. Ted and I had dinner there a week ago with some of his clients. It was sublime."

"So I'll meet you there at seven?"

Karen was silent for a moment. "Mars, you've got to promise me something."

"Depends on what it is."

"Dinner tonight is on me—" Mars started to protest, but Karen came back at him fast. "I mean it, Mars. I know how much

12

you make and I know what your child support payments are. You can't afford to eat at Alma. And I don't want to stint on what I order because I'm worrying about what you can afford. I want to have salad, an expensive entrée, dessert, coffee—I want to order whatever I want without thinking about it. And the only way I'll do that is if you do the same and I pay. Don't be a bonehead about this, Mars. If it were the other way around, we wouldn't even be discussing this."

"It's my son you should be having dinner with if you're bent on charity. He could bankrupt you in two courses without even ordering a glass of wine."

CHAPTER

3

Mars arrived at Restaurant Alma ahead of Karen Pogue. He understood immediately why someone seeking solace would choose Alma. It was spare, comfortable, friendly, and quiet. Within moments of being seated—and without ordering—the waiter brought him a Coca-Cola in a tall, thin glass. Mars looked up in surprise.

"Compliments of Mrs. Pogue, sir. She said to tell you she'd be a bit late. She's ordered a crostini starter for you, as well. It will be just a moment." The waiter hesitated, and Mars glanced at him, uncertain of what was expected.

"Your Coca-Cola is all right, sir?"

Mars grinned. He sipped the Coke and gave the waiter a thumbs-up. "Good body, not watery. Proper balance between carbonation and syrup. Very acceptable, thank you."

Mars looked over the menu while he waited. Karen was right. Unless he stuck to his Coke and an appetizer, he couldn't afford to eat at Alma. This was not a limitation that troubled him much, except as it affected his relationship with Karen Pogue. Their friendship—which had begun when Karen Pogue had conducted a series of in-service seminars for the police department on the psychological origins of sexual deviancy—had remained professional for a couple of years. Over time, without acknowledging a shift in focus, they'd get together over dinner even when there was no case that needed discussing or a training agenda to develop. Usually they ate dinner at one of a half dozen restaurants that met two criteria: food that was both good and cheap.

Mars didn't like to think that his limited financial resources had reduced Karen's dinner options. As an academic and clinical psychologist who was married to a high-powered tax attorney, Karen didn't need to think much about what she spent. Mars, with maybe one-third Karen's income—not to mention what her husband Ted earned—and a personal commitment to child support payments well above state guidelines, counted pennies. Their financial circumstances being different, Mars knew in the abstract that he should be comfortable with Karen picking up an occasional check. In reality, he didn't like it at all.

Karen and the crostini arrived at the same time. She was, as usual, dressed in what Mars had come to recognize as the uniform of professionally successful women. Carefully cut clothing in expensive fabric, jewelry of precious stones and metal, matching leather purse and shoes. The toes and heels of the shoes were crisp, unscuffed. All symbols of—what?—not so much luxury as abundance. People who had more than enough of everything. People who had extra, who didn't worry when they wrote a check the week before payday if the check would clear before their payroll entry hit the account. People who spent a lot of time dropping off and picking up stuff at the dry cleaners. Mars guessed that Karen spent more at the dry cleaners in a month than Mars spent buying clothes in a year.

Tonight, in spite of the spit-and-polish exterior, Karen looked harried. Sitting down, she scooped up a crust of crostini. "I'm famished," she said. "I've been thinking about this since three o'clock this afternoon."

"And I thought you ordered in advance for me. Now I realize it was just gluttony on your part."

"Never have dinner with a homicide investigator," Karen said. "They see right through all your little ruses. How's your Coke?"

Mars held the glass up. "Good. Especially good for a high-end restaurant where Coca-Cola on tap is usually bad. It gets no respect. So. What made your week so tough?"

Karen started to talk but was interrupted by the waiter. She ordered a forty-eight dollar bottle of wine.

"You know I'm not going to help you drink the wine?" Mars asked.

She nodded. "If you were a drinker, I would have ordered two bottles. And I'm going to order dinner for both of us. Just to keep you honest."

Their dinners ordered—green salads with pear and goat cheese for each of them, served with steamed halibut in parchment for Karen and braised short ribs for Mars—they both settled back. Mars asked again, "Your week. What was the problem?"

Karen exhaled. A lock of short auburn hair fell loose on her forehead, as if in testimony to stress. "More like a bad couple of weeks, really. My research associate screwed up a grant application, and I had to spend the past week getting it fixed. Then, to be absolutely sure the application got to the right office in Washington by the deadline, I had to put a graduate student on a jet to D.C. Just got confirmation before I came over here that he got it in under the wire."

Mars shook his head in sympathy, then waited. He was sure there was more to come.

Karen looked up at him a little sheepishly. "But what really got my streak started was Frank Beck's suicide."

Mars looked up sharply. "You knew Frank Beck?"

Karen nodded. "And you're going to earn your dinner tonight, Mars. I told Frank's youngest son, Joey, to call you . . ."

"Hate to disappoint you, Karen, but just about the last thing I did this afternoon was to agree to review the Beck suicide file. The officer on the scene at Beck's office had a couple questions he wanted me to follow up. Probably nothing, but I agreed I'd take a look. Off the record, not a formal investigation, at least, not at this

16

point." Thinking about it, Mars grinned. "And you've done me a favor. Your asking gives me a good excuse for reviewing the case. Which gets the officer on the scene off the hook. His sergeant told him to leave it alone."

Karen's face softened with relief. "I'm so glad you're doing this, Mars. I mean, everybody who knew Frank accepts that his death was suicide, but Joey is really struggling. I talked to him at the memorial service, and it was clear he just wasn't getting past what had happened. He's such a wonderful kid—smart, affectionate, funny—a huge heart. But he's capable of spending the rest of his life spinning his wheels trying to prove his father didn't commit suicide. Anything you can do to help him accept what happened—well, if he gets past this, he'll do wonderful things with his life. If he can't, he'll turn into one of those guys that wander along Hennepin Avenue talking to themselves."

"How do you know the Becks?"

Karen refolded her napkin, and stared at it as she spoke. "Ted did some legal work for one of Frank Beck's businesses a long time ago. Frank Beck was—*charismatic* wouldn't overstate it. Even Ted was charmed." She looked up at Mars. "And Ted, as you have probably noticed, is not easily charmed."

Mars let Karen's words pass without comment. Karen and Ted Pogue's marriage was one of life's great unsolved mysteries. For all Karen's tendencies toward self-indulgence, Mars had no friend who was wittier, more generous, or more perceptive. Ted Pogue was her opposite. Cold, self-absorbed, and critical, Ted Pogue had none of his wife's social and interpersonal skills. While Mars had rarely seen them together, what he had seen suggested a marriage of convenience. Which didn't, for Mars, explain why an independent woman of means, without children, would stay in what appeared to be a loveless marriage. Mars was always ready to hear Karen out on this subject, but apart from the occasional elliptical comment, it was the one conversational topic she consistently avoided.

17

"Anyway," Karen said, "Ted invited the Becks to buy a share in our lake group. I think I've mentioned the lake group to you?"

Mars, with a mouth full of crostini, shrugged his shoulders. If she had, he didn't remember.

"Ted inherited nearly a hundred acres on Lake Guelph up north. The property had a main—well, I suppose you'd call it a lodge—and a cluster of smaller cottages. Ted anticipated that property taxes would eventually make the property unaffordable, so he renovated the property and sold shares to friends. The covenant on the shares provided that any member of the lake group selling their shares could do so with a two-thirds vote by other members. True to form, when Frank Beck got into a financial bind on this last deal, he sold his share *before* he asked for group approval. Ted was furious. Not that there was any problem with the Morriseys—the family that wanted to buy the share from Frank. But Ted could not abide that Frank had gone off on his own like that. Ted blocked the Morriseys from buying the share. Frank not only did not get the money from selling his interest but the Morriseys sued him for legal costs. The other lake group members pretty much sided with Frank. They were ticked that Frank had been careless, but we all—everybody except Ted—loved Frank and Mona. In the end, to save face with the group, Ted bought back Frank's share before Frank died. So we own the Beck cottage at this point. Which reminds me. I should invite Mona to go up with me—they must still have stuff in the cottage. It's awkward. Ted is still furious about how Frank handled things. Wouldn't go to the memorial service, which I thought was really inexcusable. You go to those things for the family, don't you? I went, of course, and it was at the service that Joey asked about somebody to contact at the police department."

"And there's no doubt in your mind that Frank Beck *did* commit suicide?"

Mars's question stopped Karen. She looked at him, surprised. "Not after everything that happened. Of course not. If it had happened, say, five years ago—yes, that would have surprised me. But Frank's last bust-up was a disaster. People lost a lot of money. And at Frank's age it wasn't clear he'd be able to start over. Then Mona left. I gathered from what was said at the time that she'd given him an ultimatum when he took all their capital and put it into this wireless electronics thing. She told him she couldn't risk their security again. That if it didn't work, she was going to walk. I doubt he believed her—which must have made it just that much harder when she did leave. It left Joey high and dry, too. He was set to go to Princeton last September, but there wasn't any way that was going to happen after Frank filed the bankruptcy petition. The funny thing is, the two older kids were never were much affected by Frank's business failures. They lived the good life when times were good, and Frank always managed to get back on track after earlier disasters. Both the kids went to Princeton as undergraduates. Then Laura got an MBA and Frank Jr. went to law school at Columbia. Frank paid the freight for them all the way. But when this last problem happened, they were the first to walk away from Frank. Joey, who really has been hurt by what happened, stuck by his dad.

"But then, Joey's always been a special kid. We were up at the lake a couple of times when Frank and Mona were there with the kids. They were a lovely family. All of them good-looking and great together. But Joey was a standout, even in that family. Kind of like he got the best of each of his parents. He had his father's joie de vivre and imagination and his mother's self-discipline. I remember being at the lake one year when the Becks were there for Frank's birthday. They invited us to come over for cake and ice cream. The two older kids had written a song for their dad, Mona had made the cake, and Joey presented his dad with a Beck family genealogy he'd put together. Frank's family goes way back. I don't remember exactly, but I think his mother was a Daughter of the American Revolution and his father's family had been in the Civil War. Or maybe the other way around. Anyway, Joey couldn't have

19

been more than twelve or thirteen at the time, but the genealogy was fantastic. I remember feeling bad—Frank didn't spend more than thirty seconds looking at what Joey had done. Typical of Frank.

"Anyway, I'm getting off track. My point is that losing so much money *and* Mona—well, it was easy to believe Frank had gone off the rails. When we found out about the cancer—that pretty much put a wrap on it. Even if Frank didn't know he had cancer, he had to be feeling lousy. I doubt he would have had the energy to start over again, assuming he *had* been able to find the capital. So—do I believe he committed suicide? Yes. Absolutely yes."

"And you can't think of anyone who had a reason to kill Frank?"

Karen looked startled. "You're considering that he was *murdered*, Mars?"

"A case like this, you pretty much have two choices: suicide or murder. You find a guy hanging from a perfectly tied hangman's noose, an accident really isn't in the picture."

Their food arrived and both shifted their attention. Karen moaned with pleasure at her first forkful of halibut, quickly spearing another forkful that she passed over to Mars. It was unbelievably moist and tender. But no better than the fall-from-the-bone, deep flavor of his short ribs. Mars shook his head. "Okay, I'm impressed. And this *is* going to cost me money because I'm going to have to bring Chris here. He's the gourmand in the family."

"How is Chris?"

Mars nodded as he ate. "Good. Ten last month." He paused, thinking thoughts that came to the surface that he really hadn't taken time to focus on. The good thing about Karen was she was a great listener. Mars allowed himself to think out loud. "He's changing. . . ."

"Which ten-year-olds will do. . . ."

Mars nodded again. "It's just that—well, he's always been my

20

clone in a lot of ways. But that's felt more like imitation than character. Now the ways we're alike seem like they're coming from genes and hormones. Powerful stuff. And kind of alarming."

"Some of the things you say about him—like the interest in food—that doesn't really sound like you. He gets that from his mother?"

Mars shook his head. "No. Denise is what I'd call a church-basement cook. You know, hot dishes, stuff you make with a can of mushroom soup and hamburger. Adequate, but no imagination." Mars tapped his fork on the plate while he chewed. "There are things about Chris that are just Chris—as if by combining my genes and Denise's genes you produce something that's like each of us but also totally original. Chris's food thing is one of those."

"How is he like Denise?"

"Organized . . ." Mars hesitated. "Actually, the ways he's like Denise are the ways that are changing the most."

"For instance?"

"Scouts. He started Cub Scouts right off and was fanatical about earning badges, moving from being a bobcat to being a wolf, then a bear—all that stuff. That's Denise. And I was—hard to explain my reaction, other than to say that on one hand it was kind of gratifying to see him get in a groove and stick to it. To be capable of committing to solid values when you're seven years old. But I've always had problems with rigid, moralistic institutions, and part of me wasn't comfortable with that. The same part of me that never feels one hundred percent at home in a police department, I suppose."

"And now?"

"Chris is starting to be bothered by the kind of things that kept me out of organizations like scouts when I was a kid. Part of it might just be that his pack leaders the first two years were good people. The guy he's got this year is a Nazi, and Chris is pulling back. Which is good—that's the reaction I'd want him to have. I think he's got doubts about moving from Cub Scouts to Boy

Scouts. But the funny thing is, I'm realizing that it was kind of comfortable having a kid that fit in to those kinds of activities. I can respect the reasons he's losing interest, but it feels a little bit like he's choosing a harder path in life. A groove can be a comfortable way to live. Not that it ever worked for me. Living in a groove is what drove me out of my marriage with his mother. . . ." Mars held up a finger. "I just remembered. I need to pick your professional brain on something. Chris's mom thinks it's time for a birds-and-bees discussion. She came across some *Playboy* magazines between Chris's mattress and the box spring. . . ."

Karen's brow furrowed. "She's checking out what's under the kid's mattress?"

"You have to know Denise. The original neat freak. At least once a month she vacuums under there."

Karen looked horrified. "You aren't serious."

"Like I said. You have to know Denise. My question is, do you have any professional guidance on how this discussion should go if I want to avoid raising a sexual deviant?"

Karen shrugged. "From everything I've seen of your relationship with Chris, I would have assumed this is something you've covered as part of your ongoing conversations—osmosis, provided your side of the flow is healthy, is really the best way to have it happen." She took another forkful of halibut, then, talking with her mouth full, said, "That's what I remember about the times I've seen you with Chris. The night he came with you when we had dinner at the Village Wok? He was having problems with some kid who was real possessive—what I remember about that conversation was that you didn't give any off-the-shelf answers. You really thought about what you were saying—you let Chris *see* you thinking. When kids get into trouble is when parents give false messages. Kids know a false message when they hear it. Then their fevered little brains invent something that's a hundred times worse than the truth. So just be yourself. Say what you mean. Listen and respond honestly—probably exactly what you've already been doing."

"Well, we've had a conversation about girlfriends. And about the mechanics. But I think what Denise is getting at is attitudes about women. I suppose part of the problem is that I decided when Denise and I were divorced I wasn't going to involve Chris in any of my relationships with women. I didn't want him getting attached to people unless it was a serious relationship. . . ."

"Which we all know isn't very likely. And I'm beginning to understand why you might find talking to Chris on this subject difficult."

"You and Nettie. You give me no peace on this subject."

"So. *Are* you seeing anybody?"

There was an edge in Karen's question that Mars couldn't figure. He played with his water glass as he said, "Nobody special."

"Nettie said you've been seeing a former felon."

Mars made a face. "As both you and Nettie know, I couldn't work in the department and be dating a former felon. Nettie was playing for effect, as usual. The fact of the matter is that I occasionally go to the movies with a woman who was a witness in the Mary Pat Fitzgerald case. She's a graduate student in English at the university. She had some drug problems, but she's never been convicted of anything."

Mars worked hard at taking a long gulp of Coca-Cola, keeping his eyes on the glass. It wasn't his style to talk about women he was seeing. Since his divorce he'd put a lot of energy into avoiding being half of a couple. *Couple.* The *word* made his skin itch. But from the first time he'd seen Evelyn Rau more than a year ago in an interrogation room at the county jail, he'd had a feeling she was somebody that would mean something to him. When they'd connected by accident after that, it felt inevitable. Which was way too dramatic a word. But for the first time, he was having some problems keeping a woman he was seeing separate from the rest of his

23

life. No question but that she meant something to him. Problem was, he wasn't sure what.

To Karen he said, "It's not a big deal."

"Hmmm," Karen said, a smug look on her face.

"Don't give me that. . . ."

"I didn't say *anything*. . . ."

"You said 'Hmmmm.' "

" 'Hmmm' isn't anything. But before I forget—what you were saying about the perfectly tied hangman's knot?"

Mars waited for what Karen was going to say next.

Still chewing and making a jabbing motion with her fork, Karen said, "That's surprising. I've never thought about the specifics of how Frank died. You're sure it was a 'perfectly tied hangman's knot?' "

"I haven't seen it yet myself, but the officer on the scene said it was very carefully tied."

Karen shook her head. "*That* strikes me as odd. Frank was congenitally careless. Not precise about anything. We had this old rowboat tied to the dock at the lake. I can't tell you how many times somebody had to swim out and retrieve the boat because Frank couldn't be bothered to tie a square knot. Unfortunately, it usually happened when Ted was around. It made him nuts, Ted being the original ship-shape guy. In fact, now that I think about it, he might be the perfect match for your ex-wife. He even taught *me* how to tie up the boat with a square knot."

"You know how to tie a hangman's knot?"

"Nope."

"Good. I can cross you off my suspect's list."

"You're seriously considering that Frank's death was murder?"

"Let's just say there are a couple things that bear looking into—with or without Joey Beck's future being at stake."

* * *

24

As Mars and Karen stepped out of Alma onto University Avenue, the cold hit them like a hard slap.

"Jeez," Mars said, pulling his collar up. "Damn cold for December."

Karen folded her arms together, dancing a little in place to stay warm. "It's Christmas in two weeks, Mars."

"Which means it's *not* too cold?"

"Anything under seventy-five degrees is too cold for me." She gave Mars a quick pat on the shoulder. "Take care—let me know what's going on with the Beck case, will you?"

Mars ran down Southeast Sixth Avenue to where he'd parked. Behind the wheel, he pulled out his cell phone and called Denise.

"I'm thinking if it's this cold tomorrow morning I'm gonna swing by and pick Chris up before I go downtown. Too damn cold for him to be standing out on a corner waiting for a school bus."

"Your choice," Denise said. "The cold isn't a problem for Chris."

"If I trusted the school system to get the buses where they're supposed to be when they're supposed to be there, it wouldn't be a problem for me, either. But I don't. . . ."

"The one time they didn't show up was four years ago, Mars. There haven't been any problems since."

"Tell Chris I'll be out front around seven-thirty."

Chris came out to the car the next morning carrying his wool hat, his parka unzipped. He'd shoved his feet halfway into his boots, walking with his heels on top of the back of his boots.

"Hi," he said, the car door wide open, cold whipping in as he unsaddled his backpack and dropped it into the car. Mars said, "Before the car moves, you get your boots on and zip up your parka. And before you get out of the car, your hat goes on your head."

"It's like two steps from where you drop me to the front door. . . ."

"When the temperature's below zero, exposed flesh can get frostbite in seconds. Especially when there's wind."

Chris made a face, but shoved his feet into his boots and zipped his parka. Mars watched him for a moment, noticing how much Chris had changed in the past few months. Chris's soft, round face was giving way to defined angles. Mars could see himself in those angles. It occurred to Mars that *how* Chris looked was mirrored in the sharper edges of Chris's temperament.

"We still on for breakfast Saturday?"

Chris nodded. "Yeah, sure. You wanna make breakfast at your apartment or go out?"

"I'm thinking breakfast at the apartment." Mars looked sideways at Chris. "Your mom talked to you about the *Playboy*s under your mattress?"

Chris flushed. "They were James's. It was no big deal." He shot a glance a Mars, then looked away.

"I agree. Guess I would have less to say about it if you'd just left the magazines lying around. That you felt you needed to hide them bothers me some."

"I was afraid if Mom saw them she'd throw them away. And they were James's. I needed to give them back." Chris's voice was urgent, plaintive.

They drove in silence for a few moments, then Mars said, "For our agenda on Saturday—let's include a discussion about sex—"

"I know about all that stuff. We've talked about it before."

"What we talked about before is mechanics. What I want to talk about Saturday is—well, attitudes. Personal responsibility. How sex and what you think about girls can get confused."

Chris slid down in the seat. "Jeeez."

Mars smiled. "No lectures, I promise."

Pulling up in front of Chris's school, Mars leaned over to give Chris a hug. He stopped short as he noticed a group of Chris's friends watching the car. He drew back, squeezing Chris's shoulder. "See you Saturday."

The Beck file Danny Borg had sent over didn't raise any particular questions about the cause of death—other than the questions Danny Borg had raised. If anything, seeing the facts of Frank Beck's life on paper made suicide seem like a reasonable choice. The guy had assets worth just under two hundred thousand and outstanding liabilities of more than six million. And for the first time in his life, Frank Beck's financial risk-taking had cost him friends and family. At the time of his death, Frank Beck had lost decades-long relationships, including his wife and two of his three children. Statements from friends and family—Joey Beck excepted—made clear that nobody found suicide surprising, especially when people found out that Frank Beck had had cancer.

Mars skipped to the end of the report to see what Borg had written under outstanding issues: "Check numbers found written on inside right arm of victim (2822173631958) against account and PIN numbers. Check source of fabric used in noose."

He pulled the medical examiner's report and frowned. It had been signed by Dr. Charles Resch. If Mars had to pick a doc in the medical examiner's officer in whom he had the least confidence, Resch would be at the top of the list. Resch was arrogant and sloppy. A lousy combination for a medical examiner. Dr. Denton D. Mont, Hennepin County's chief medical examiner and Resch's supervising physician, was the reverse of Resch: a careful, curious man who always second-guessed the most obvious conclusions. Mars knew that Doc D was as unhappy with Resch's performance as Mars had been on many occasions, but firing a doc was no easy task.

What Doc D had been doing was making sure that Resch got the cases where sloppiness would do the least damage. And Frank Beck's suicide was a likely case to be assigned to Resch under that criterion. But in fact, there was nothing in the ME report to suggest that Resch had missed anything. And you had to give him credit. It had been Resch who had found the colon cancer.

Mars dropped the file on the desk and sat back. There wasn't anything that justified further investigation beyond the two questions Danny Borg had raised. Mars sat silent for a long time. Two small details against the weight of a lot of evidence that supported suicide. But not, Mars thought, enough weight to offset the twist in his gut that said Frank Beck had not committed suicide.

Two things cops always said: Trust your gut.

And, the answer is in the box.

CHAPTER
4

It was what homicide investigators always said about tough cases: somewhere in the reinforced cardboard file boxes that held case documentation were the facts that could clear the case. An interview transcript containing something meaningful that had been missed. An interview transcript that didn't include a question that should have been asked. A reference to an individual that hadn't been followed up with an interview. Forensic evidence that new technology could reinterpret.

The box sitting on Mars Bahr's desk wasn't a formal case file as no investigation had been opened in Frank Beck's death. What was in the box were remnants. The noose from which Beck had hanged himself. An address book. The clothes Beck had been wearing when he died. Copies of Danny Borg's case summary, including Borg's hand-written summary of interviews he'd conducted with Beck family members and one friend. An envelope containing a handful of lottery tickets. Mars pulled on latex gloves and started going through the box, beginning with the noose.

"Look at this," Mars said to Nettie. He put the noose back into the plastic evidence bag and tossed it over to Nettie. Nettie caught the bag with two hands and held the bag up, peering at the noose.

"Nice piece of work—the knot, that is," Nettie said. "What kind of fabric would you say?"

"Not a clue. Maybe wool? But kind of a loose weave."

Nettie pulled open a desk drawer, took out a pair of gloves, and after snapping them on, took the noose out of the bag. She looked closer at the noose, then gave a tug at both ends. "Loose, but plenty strong. Tough fiber." She put the plastic bag down on her desk, laying the noose on top of the bag. With her face down close, she turned the noose around. "Looks like the fabric was sewn into a tube shape before tying the knot. . . ."

"Can you tell how it was sewn—by hand or machine?"

Nettie shook her head. "Nope. You're asking the wrong lady. Betsy Ross I ain't." She got up, put the noose back in the bag, and dropped the bag on Mars's desk. She stood behind him for a moment. "So. You're opening an investigation on Beck?"

Mars sat up straight in his chair, held his arms out straight in front of him, twisting his wrists, and yawned. Then, ruffling his hands through his hair, he said, "Just trying to make a decision if there's enough here to investigate." He looked around the box. "I was supposed to get photos from the medical examiner's office. You see anything . . ."

Nettie bent over, picking up the box. Underneath was a manila envelope. "The envelope came up first thing this morning. Whoever brought the box up dropped it on the envelope." She moved away from Mars. "I'm going back to the fridge to get my Evian water. You want a Coke?"

"Not now . . ."

"This is a one-time-only offer, partner. You want a Coke later, you get it yourself."

"As if I didn't know that," Mars muttered. He pulled black-and-white photos out of the envelope. Two of the photos were standard black-and-white shots of Beck's naked body on a stainless steel exam table, front and back. Beck's face was still swollen and dark from the hanging, his tongue protruding between his lips. The noose had left a clear mark around his neck.

Mars flipped through the photos taken in Beck's warehouse office. An overturned chair just underneath Beck's hanging legs.

The office door ajar. An office window open. The last photo was the one he'd been looking for. A close-up shot of the numbers written on the inside of Beck's right arm. *2822173631958.*

From behind Mars came a loud, sharp crack. He jumped, then turned toward Nettie, pissed that she'd caught him off guard again.

Nettie gave him a sweet, false smile. "Sorry."

It was a daily ritual. As soon as Nettie got in, she'd put a half-liter bottle of Evian water into the freezer in the department fridge. After it was partially frozen, she'd take it out, slamming the bottom of the bottle on her desk to break up the ice. And every morning she'd startle the hell out of Mars—and anyone else in the squad room.

Mars passed the photo of Beck over to Nettie. "You've got fifteen seconds. 'You know what I think when I see somebody like that? I think, that was somebody's baby boy.' "

"Ohhh," Nettie said, "I know it, I know it. Give me a minute."

"Ten seconds and counting," Mars said.

Nettie made fists with her hands and pressed them to her forehead, elbows on her desk. As the second hand on Mars's watch jerked, Nettie's voice came out fast and clipped. "*The Conversation.* What's her name—oh, damn—Laverne and Shirley, she played Shirley. Williams! Cindy Williams. She's walking with, uh, Forrest—I can't remember if that's his first name or last name—in Union Square in San Francisco. And Gene Hackman was taping them from a van. God, I loved that movie."

"You got in on that one just under the wire." Mars pulled out Danny Borg's case summary, which was a copy of the report Mars had already looked at. He confirmed the last time Beck had been seen alive—approximately three o'clock in the afternoon on the day his body had been found. Mars looked for an explanation of the open window and door in the office, but didn't see anything. Then he went through the lottery tickets. Geez. Twenty-five dollars' worth of Powerball tickets—five tickets with five chances on

31

each ticket—all for the drawing held the Saturday after the Friday Beck died.

Something clicked for Mars, and he looked closely at the tickets, searching for numbers on the tickets that would tell a date and time when the tickets had been sold. There were a lot of random numbers on the tickets, other than the Powerball numbers, but nothing Mars could decipher as a purchase date and time. He wheeled over to Nettie on his chair.

"Do something for me, will you? In fact, do two things. Call the state lottery office and see if we can find out when the tickets were sold—date *and* time, if they can give us both." Mars rose, pulling on his jacket.

"And?"

Mars stared at the photo that showed the numbers on Beck's arm. "Send out a request for information to the five-state area. Ask for information regarding any hanging deaths where those numbers are found on the victims' bodies."

Mars slapped a magnetic flasher on the roof of the Pontiac and double-parked outside Glen's Handi-Store that was kitty-corner from the Dachota. Borg's notes had indicated that the last person to see Frank Beck alive had been a store clerk, Colette Magnuson.

The store was deserted when Mars pushed in through the front door, except for a heavy-set older woman standing behind a counter next to the cash register.

"Hello!" she called out. "How can I help you?" Mars guessed a woman working a convenience store alone kept one finger on the counter alarm. He pulled out his badge, flapping it open in her direction. Her relief was visible.

"I'm looking for Colette Magnuson."

"Stop looking. That's me. You're asking about Mr. Beck?"

"I understand you saw Mr. Beck here on December sixth. Just wanted to confirm the time he was here and ask your impression of his state of mind."

"I told that to the other young man who came in. That one had a uniform. You have to be on the job a certain amount of time before they give you the uniform?"

A surprising question. Mars suppressed a smile and considered his answer. "Depends on what your job is. I think the other officer you spoke with was a patrolman. I'm in the investigative division. Investigators don't get uniforms."

"Hardly seems fair," Colette said. Mars could see his stock had fallen in Colette's estimation. Clearly appearances counted for a lot with her. She wore a silver blond wig with a high pompadour, a rigid bang falling in little curlicues over her forehead. She was fully made up with eyebrows that flew in a sharp arch over green eye shadow. Her skin was layered with a thick pink foundation, and her mouth was an outsized, startling red. Every finger of her hands—other than the thumbs—was heavily ringed.

"Do you get a gun?" Her eyes dropped down to his jacket, her expression doubtful.

"I do," Mars said. Anticipating that she would next ask to see the gun he did not carry, he quickly asked a question. "I understand from Officer Borg that you saw Frank Beck around three o'clock the afternoon of December sixth, is that right?"

She nodded emphatically. "That's what I told the young fellow in the uniform."

"May I ask how you're sure of the time?"

"Simple. My shift ends at three. I was wondering where the second shift clerk was and had been checking my watch when Frank came in. That was the other thing. Frank usually came in around nine in the morning, bought a *Wall Street Journal*, then would run back to the Dachota. He was the nicest fellow. Always had something to say. Liked to tease. Just couldn't believe it when I heard what happened after he left here. . . ."

"Couldn't believe it because of how he seemed that day—or just what you knew of him in general?"

"Both," Colette said. "He was always in a good mood. Always

pleasant. Same as ever that day. Not that he didn't have his problems."

"He talked to you about that?"

Colette brushed the suggestion away with a wave of her hand. "He wasn't the kind of guy that whined about his problems. No, the first I heard was from a couple of other tenants in the Dachota. Ad agency guys who'd been standing around shooting the breeze one morning when Frank came in for his paper. After Frank left, I heard them talking." Colette paused, "I wasn't eavesdropping, you know. Couldn't *not* hear it, they were standing right about where you are. Anyway, after that, I saw some things in the *Tribune*. Then, couple months ago when he came in for his paper, I said to him, 'Frank, how is it your office always looks dark?' He looked kind of embarrassed and said they were going to be changing locations and he didn't have any staff coming in anymore. Well, I can put two and two together. But Frank didn't complain. He was always a cheerful, considerate guy."

"Even at three o'clock in the afternoon on December sixth?"

"I'll tell you something. I'd say he was even cheerier than usual. I was sold out of *Journal*s by three o'clock, and I offered to call the other Handi-Store that's over on the skyway to see if they had any left. He said not to bother, he had someone coming in to his office shortly and he needed to get back. . . ."

"He said he was going to be meeting someone in his office that afternoon?"

"That's what I just said, wasn't it?"

"You haven't mentioned this to anyone before?"

"Nobody asked, did they? That young fellow in the uniform, he just came in by chance. Was asking around about when somebody might have seen Frank on the sixth. Someone in the Dachota told him Frank always came over here for a newspaper. I told him about seeing Frank at three o'clock, then he went on his way. Didn't seem like he had a lot of time."

"No," Mars said. "He wouldn't have. And in your judgment, Beck seemed to be in good spirits—even better spirits than usual."

"Yes, he was. He even said as he left that he had a good feeling about the day. Felt lucky."

Mars, noticing the little promotional sign on the counter for lottery tickets, said, "He buy any lottery tickets while he was here?"

Colette Magnuson thought about it. "Frank usually did buy tickets. And more than one. Can't remember if he bought any that day or not. Maybe that's why he said he felt that Friday was his lucky day. I just can't remember if I sold him tickets then or not."

"As it happened," Mars said, "December sixth wasn't Frank Beck's lucky day."

Mars was moving and thinking faster based on his interview with Colette Magnuson. There was nothing Magnuson had said that supported a conclusion that Beck had committed suicide, and there was plenty she said that had raised new questions. Number one: who had Beck been scheduled to meet with after three o'clock on the sixth? Number two: it seemed more than likely that Beck had bought his lottery tickets from Colette Magnuson just hours before he was killed. Would a guy who was hours away from committing suicide spend twenty-five bucks on lottery tickets? Back in the car, Mars called Nettie.

"You get hold of the state lottery office yet?"

"Waiting for a call back."

"You can skip it. The convenience store clerk who was the second-to-last person to see Beck alive said she sometimes sold him lottery tickets. I think it's a safe bet that's when he bought the tickets. If we need to prove that at some point in the future, we can get back to the state lottery office then."

"The *second*-to-last person to see Beck alive? I thought the clerk was the last person to see him alive. . . ."

"Maybe not."

Mars had been uneasy about meeting with Joey Beck because he didn't want to raise the kid's expectations. It still made sense not to raise Joey's expectations, but Mars was increasingly confident there was something to investigate. He debated whether to give Joey a call or to just drop by. He decided the drop-by would give him more control over the meeting. If Joey wasn't around, Mars would call and leave a message.

Joey Beck lived in a two-and-a-half-story walk-up apartment near the university. He buzzed Mars up immediately, but was pulling a jacket on when Mars came in.

"If you don't mind, let's walk over to the Dunn Brothers on the corner. I'm finishing a paper that's due day after tomorrow, and I've been in all day. A change of scenery might clear my head."

They didn't say much walking over to Dunn Brothers. Both were concentrating on not feeling the cold, keeping their heads tucked into raised collars, walking with tight, contracted muscles. With a sinking feeling in his stomach, Mars walked a little behind, watching Joey Beck. Nettie had gotten it exactly right. It was going to be real hard not to project Chris into Joey Beck's place.

It wasn't that Chris and Joey Beck looked a lot alike. Apart from the age difference, their coloring was different, and Joey Beck's features were sharper than Chris's were or would be. The similarity went deeper than looks. There was a seriousness, a quiet, active intelligence that Mars had seen from day one in Chris that was also part of who Joey Beck was. An old-fashioned word came to mind: both Joey Beck and Chris had an *earnest* quality that Mars found deeply endearing.

Pushing into the damp warmth of the coffeehouse, Mars and Joey loosened up, simultaneously unzipping jackets as if to release accumulated cold. Mars pulled a Coke out of the cooler while Beck ordered fancy coffee at the counter. Finally settled at a corner table, Joey Beck said, "I really appreciate this. I mean, you being willing to look at what happened when my dad died."

"It's part of the job. But you need to appreciate that as things stand, the evidence supporting suicide is very strong. . . ."

Joey nodded, his head down. He twisted the coffee cup between his two hands. "I suppose you always hear this when there's a suicide. Somebody who's sure the guy wouldn't do it."

"It *is* pretty usual. What I need you to do is to tell me why you feel so strongly that your dad didn't commit suicide."

Joey's face tightened at the effort of explaining. "If you *knew* him—"

"Joey, a lot of people who *knew* your dad didn't find it all that hard to believe. I need something specific. In fact, I need two things. I need specific reasons why your dad wouldn't have committed suicide, and I need specific reasons why somebody would have murdered him."

The kid's head came up fast. Then, shaking his head, he said, "That's it, isn't it. If Dad didn't commit suicide, he was murdered."

"So? Start with specific reasons why your dad wouldn't commit suicide."

Concentration was visible on Joey's face the same way it showed on Chris's face. Joey's color rose, his pupils dilated. "The thing about my dad was that he really thrived on trouble. He was big on adventure travel—you know, where you spend a small fortune to be miserable and risk death in some remote place. He always had the most energy, was the most excited, when there were problems in the business. When things were going well? That's when he'd get sort of down. He'd get restless. As bad as things were with this last business, I never saw him down about it. He was the eternal optimist. . . ."

"Your mother left him, Joey."

Joey raised his eyebrows and nodded. "Okay. That was a blow. But the way it looked to me, it made Dad even more determined to salvage something. He was never ready to give up on getting her back. This will sound weird, but if my dad had been in one of those periods when everything was in equilibrium, it would have been easier for me to believe he would have become despondent. Not when he was facing a challenge."

"And the cancer?"

"Everybody says he had to be feeling bad. But I was the one that saw the most of him the last six months, and I never noticed anything. He seemed fine to me. He was real motivated. Still hustling. Still expecting to pull this one out of the fire."

"Joey, do you know if your dad had any appointments the afternoon of the day he died?"

"Appointments? You mean, at the office?"

Mars nodded.

"I don't really know. But I don't think so. I mean, nothing was happening at the office. No staff, no electricity, no phones. If he needed to meet with someone, my guess is he'd do it at a restaurant." Joey looked closely at Mars. "Why do you ask?"

"Just routine. Back to my original questions. Can you think of anybody who had a reason to murder your dad? How about people who lost money because of your dad's business failures?"

Joey shook his head. "You've got to understand. My dad always paid people back. Maybe they never made much on their investments with him, but sooner or later he'd pay back their original investments. It was the first thing he'd do when he made any money. Which is part of the reason it pisses me off so much that people walked away from him on this last deal. They all talked about how they couldn't go through another failure. Well, the failures never cost them all that much. What they were really ticked off about was that they hadn't gotten rich quick off my dad. They were mad at themselves for buying into his ideas. They didn't want to be reminded of their own bad judgment, so they cut him off. Greedy bastards."

"But this last failure—from everything I've been told—was on

38

a much larger scale. It follows that disappointment among investors must have been greater. . . ."

"So someone murders him to make sure there's *no* chance they're gonna get anything back?"

"You're making a lot of sense, Joey. Problem is, what you're saying really is an argument *against* anyone having a motive to murder your dad."

Joey edged up a little, took a sip of what was now cold coffee, and said, "Something I've been thinking about. When I got to my dad's office, the door was open, and there was an open window in the office. Dad still had a lot of computer equipment in the office. It was on a three-year lease. It wasn't any secret that the office was empty most of the time. Even Dad didn't go in much. What I was thinking was, maybe someone went in to steal the computers. If they'd taken the computers out the front, they'd have attracted a lot of attention. But there's this parking bay in the alley behind the building, five floors below my dad's office. Maybe they were going to rig something up to pass the electronics equipment out the window and lower it down to a truck or whatever—and my dad came in and surprised them. . . ."

Joey's eyes were fixed on Mars's face, waiting for a sign that Mars was caught up in what he was saying. It was almost painful for Mars to say what had to be said.

"What you've described would make a lot of sense if your dad had died almost any way other than how he did."

Joey's brow rumpled. "How do you mean?"

"Your dad's death was clean, precise. If someone was in your dad's office, he was there for one reason: to kill your dad. I haven't been in the office yet—but from what I read of the scene report, the only thing disrupted was the tipped chair your dad stood on to hang himself. All the equipment was in place—if your dad had walked into the office and found strangers there, without them actually being in the process of taking out equipment, there wouldn't have been any need for violence. The intruders could have come up with any number of explanations for what they were doing there." Mars hesitated. He was finding it difficult to speak in clinical terms of the circumstances of a death that had so deeply affected the young man before him.

Joey Beck understood Mars's hesitation, and said, "It's okay. I've already been through the worst. Remember, I found my dad's body. And this thing has played through my mind a hundred times a day every day since then. What you're saying is stuff nobody has wanted to talk about. It feels *good* to be talking about this. Keep going."

Mars cleared his throat. "If your scenario is right, the office would have been in disarray, and your dad would have been shot, stabbed, beaten—thieves wouldn't have taken time to tie a noose and hang your dad. Especially to tie a noose the way that noose was tied. Nothing sloppy. A real work of art."

Joey's face tensed. "The noose was carefully tied?"

Mars knew what was coming next.

"I guess I hadn't noticed. I mean, all I remember is getting my dad down. I don't remember even looking at the noose." He leaned forward, elbows on the table, pressing both hands to his temples. "It doesn't make sense at all. My dad tying a precise knot? I don't think so."

Mars said, "There seems to be a consensus developing on that point." If Joey hadn't been so absorbed in thinking about a precisely tied knot, it would have occurred to him that Mars had just said something that tipped Mars's own suspicions that Frank Beck had not committed suicide.

"Okay. So I get what you're saying about *how* my dad died. But what about the open window and door? Why would he have done that? And something else. My dad would know I'd come looking for him if he missed our dinner date." Joey fixed Mars with an intense stare. "Something I know for absolutely *sure* is that my dad wouldn't have wanted *me* to find him like that. No way."

"I've been thinking about the same things," Mars said. "And

there could be a link between the open door and window and you being the one to find your dad. The fact is, Joey, that at that point in your dad's life, there wasn't much of anybody who would go looking for him, other than you. So the open door and window could be one of two things: your dad anticipated you'd find him and he wanted to make that as simple as possible—which is why he left the door open—and," Mars stopped, then said, "the cold was a way of preserving his body. So you wouldn't find a decaying corpse when you came in. . . ."

At this, Joey's eyes teared. But he didn't flinch. "You said the open door and window could mean one of *two* things. What's the other thing?"

"That you're right. That your dad didn't want you to be the one to find his body. So he left the door and window open to attract attention, hoping that somebody in the building would notice and check out the office."

Mars could tell from watching Joey's face that he accepted the logic of what Mars had said. He could also tell that accepting what Mars said had let the air out of Joey's last hopes. Mars felt a rush of guilt. Because there was a third possibility about why the door and window had been left open. The third possibility was that whoever murdered Frank Beck had left the window open to complicate a determination of time of death and that in the killer's haste to leave, he had failed to shut the door firmly. The door to the office opened out into the hallway. Cold air being heavier than warm air, the cold air behind the door had held it open.

Mars resisted the temptation to offer Joey the consolation of the third explanation. "One other thing, Joey. There was a number written in ballpoint pen on your dad's right arm. . . ."

"A number?"

"Yeah." Mars stopped, pulled out his notebook and flipped back a few pages. He read the number out loud to Joey. "Mean anything to you—either the number, or why your dad might have written a number on his arm?"

Joey looked blank. "No. Nothing. I don't ever remember my dad writing something on himself—that many numbers, it couldn't even be a telephone number, could it?"

"No," Mars said. "It doesn't appear to be a phone number, social security number—anything like that. And we checked your dad's account numbers against the number. Nothing matched."

Joey said, "Which arm did you say it was written on?"

Mars had said the right arm, but he took a second to think back to the photos before he said again, "The right arm."

A *gotcha* look covered Joey Beck's face.

"My dad was right-handed, Mr. Bahr. If he *was* going to write something on his arm, wouldn't it have been on the left arm?"

Back at the squad room, Mars returned to the file box that contained the remnants of Frank Beck's death. He took out two things: The photo of Frank Beck's arm that showed the numbers written on Beck's right arm and Frank Beck's address book. If Frank Beck *had* written the numbers on his right arm with his left hand, the numbers would look misformed. They didn't. Allowing for the fact that human flesh is an imperfect writing surface, the numbers were precisely formed. Mars opened Beck's address book. He compared numbers Beck had entered for addresses and phone numbers in the book with the numbers written on Beck's arm. Frank Beck's numbers were sharp, sans-serif numbers that conveyed an impression of having been written in haste. The numbers on his arm were four-square, with serifs, the seven with a little horizontal line drawn through the rising line. It was less than improbable that Frank Beck had written the numbers on his arm.

Mars pushed back from his desk and stretched out on his chair, legs extended, hands cupped over his head. Nettie came in behind him.

"I recognize that pose," she said. "You're thinking big thoughts."

"I'm thinking," Mars said, "that the critical mass of evidence

in the Frank Beck case has shifted. I'm thinking it wasn't suicide."
With his hands still clasped on top of his head, he turned sideways
to look at Nettie. Her sleek black hair had fallen forward, so he
couldn't read the expression on her face. "I'm thinking," he said,
"that I need to talk to the chief about opening an investigation—
which means I need you to start a file."

Without saying anything, Nettie leaned across her desk and
picked up a black vinyl three-ring binder. She dropped it on his
desk. On the binder's spine in a plastic pocket was a white card
which read Homicide Case 00-48, Franklin Beck.

"The paperwork," Nettie said, "is in the binder."

CHAPTER

5

"What's the big deal, you asking me about opening a homicide investigation?"

Chief John Taylor sat behind his desk, the top of which was, as always, clear. He was a big, dark-skinned African American—a little bigger every year Mars had known him. Taylor talked slowly, dressed with severe neatness, and in public spoke with a formality that suggested a man of few emotions. It wasn't until after Mars got to know the chief better that he noticed that the chief had two personas. In public, playing the role, the chief was formal to the point of rigidity. He spoke the king's English, never using contractions, his diction never giving a hint of an Alabama upbringing. It was after the chief and Mars got comfortable with each other that the chief's second persona emerged. The chief's physical presence and language would relax and you could see the whole man. Even his devilish sense of humor. The chief, it could be said, suffered fools gladly. He enjoyed them no end.

When Taylor had been hired as chief of police more than four years earlier, Mars had read the appointment as a politically correct move by the city to deflect the black community's criticism of the police department. A couple of cases after Taylor's appointment, Mars signed on as a fan. The chief was a quiet man, but when there was something that needed saying, the chief said it— no matter the result. Taylor understood police work—and police politics—better than anyone Mars had worked with. He respected good police work but had profound contempt for lazy cops whose only loyalty was to their own best interests. And he knew that running a police department on the cheap was an expensive proposition in the long run.

"I just thought," Mars said, "given the discussions that have been going on among city council members about the department's budget, that this particular investigation might raise a few eyebrows. Thought you should know the details in case someone comes after you about it."

The chief sat back in his chair, elbows on the chair arms, hands folded over the girth of his belly. "Do tell," he said.

Mars sat down in front of the chief's desk, leaning forward. "The case a week or so back. The guy found hanging in his warehouse office."

The chief glanced up at the ceiling, his lower lip extending slightly. "The suicide?"

Mars shrugged. "Maybe, maybe not. Right now, my guess is maybe not."

The chief raised one hand to his face, covering his mouth. He didn't say anything.

"I just figured," Mars said, "with all the flak you're getting about the murder rate being down but homicide division resources not being reduced—well, somebody could say this investigation was busywork."

"I assume you're gonna tell me why that wouldn't be true."

"After a few hours' work, I've got at least four significant issues. First, there's universal agreement among people that knew the victim that he could not have tied the noose knot—and I can't find his source for the noose fabric. Second, I've talked to a witness who says the victim was planning on meeting with someone shortly before the time we estimate he would have committed suicide. I need to find out who that was and why they were meeting. Third, there was a series of numbers written on the victim's right arm. We can't find anything in the victim's personal records that matches up with those numbers and the victim was right-handed. I figure if he'd written the numbers, they would have been on his left arm—also, I compared numbers written by the victim to the numbers of the arm. They don't look anything alike. The number formation is completely different."

The chief's expression was unreadable. "You said four things."

Mars nodded. "A small detail, really, but I don't think it can be disregarded. We've estimated the time of death as taking place between three o'clock and six o'clock in the afternoon. That's based on a store clerk who talked to the victim at three o'clock and that the victim did not call his son at six o'clock as they'd planned. It's probable the store clerk sold the victim twenty-five dollars' worth of Powerball tickets at three o'clock on a Friday for a drawing that would take place the next day. I just find it very difficult to believe the guy is going to spend twenty-five dollars on lottery tickets and an hour or two later kill himself. Now, if I can find the person he was supposed to be meeting with, and that person tells me something that explains why the victim would have had a material change of attitude in that space of time—okay. But in combination, these are things that need a second look."

The chief nodded. "Agreed. I got no problems you going ahead. Would be easier if your vic was a nice black grandma livin' on the near north side."

Mars hesitated. "One other thing."

The chief's eyebrows went up and stayed up.

"The guy who died—Franklin Beck—was a friend of Karen Pogue's."

The chief's lower lip extended again. He rolled his eyes sideways. "The woman we use for training seminars?"

"The same. She's also very well wired in the community power structure, as is her husband. I started looking at Beck's death after I got a call from the uniformed officer at the suicide scene. He'd told me enough to justify my looking at the file—even without Karen's call. I talked to Pogue after I decided the case needed a little more work—that was the first I knew that she knew the victim and his family. Anyway, you see where I'm going on this. Pogue's connection—to Beck and the department—could make this look like we're doing favors. That someone's getting access to our resources that isn't available to everybody."

The chief pulled himself up. "Long as we're comfortable there's somethin' that needs investigating—and from what you've said, that's clearly the case—we're just gonna have to take those hits as they come. Where do you stand on a motive for someone killing Beck?"

Mars shook his head. "Nada. The guy lost money and cost his investors money. But apparently, he had a history of making good on debts. And people loved the guy. So motive's going to be a big hurdle. In my gut, I've got a feeling those numbers on the arm carry a message. I mean, if Beck didn't write the numbers, somebody else did. And they didn't bother to make it look like Beck had written the numbers himself. Which tells me they were making a point they didn't want to be missed. But I'm a long way off from deciphering what that point might be."

"Any idea who the message might be addressed to? You're saying nobody who knows Beck knows what the numbers mean? What's the point?"

The chief had raised a question Mars hadn't yet focused on. It was a different way of asking what the numbers meant. "Nobody we've talked to so far knows what the numbers might mean. I just think they have to be important."

The chief rose, looking at his watch. "I need to get on over to a ceremony for new recruits. How you and Nettie doing on your cross-jurisdictional database?"

"Nettie's doing great. She's chairing a five-state task force to set up a pilot database. We'll start testing it next summer—provided the FRU hasn't been disbanded under budget pressures by then."

The chief shook his head in admiration. "I will say, Marshall, that bringin' that gal on in place of a partner was a bonafide stroke of genius on your part. I thought you'd gone round the bend when you said what you'd wanted instead of a sworn staff partner was a clerk from the administrative pool, but it's the best damn thing that's happened to the department. Next to my makin' you a special detective specializing in nondrug- and nongang-related homicides."

"If you remember, when my previous partner retired there wasn't anyone I especially wanted to partner with or anybody who wanted to partner with me, for that matter. You might say no one had a sweet tooth for the Candy Man," Mars said, using the nickname by which he was commonly—and without affection—referred to by other police officers. There were plenty of officers on the force who resented Mars's special assignment and his relationship with the chief.

"Anyway. What I was looking for was someone to get me out from under the paperwork. I didn't have a clue Nettie was going to take off like a rocket. I think I told you, she's working on a proposal for automating all the patrol paperwork. It'd mean a big capital investment up front—squads would have fully functioning computers with on-line, interactive formating for reports. And there'd be a pretty significant training component that the union would probably fight tooth and nail. But the time it would save long-term is phenomenal. That, and report quality would improve. She's including a way of using software for filing charge reports that would prompt officers for the correct legal terms."

"She's still working on the interstate information-sharing project?"

"That too. Of course, that was a project we planned on Nettie heading up once we went over to the Bureau of Criminal Apprehension Cold Case Unit, but she's getting a leg up on it now. Spends a lot of time every day fielding phone calls from other jurisdictions, guys picking her brain about automation initiatives.

That's what the city council misses when they just focus on murder rates. A lull like we've had over the past year gives us a chance to do things that will make a big difference to the department over time. Help us avoid murders, help us solve murders that do happen a lot faster, instead of just chasing our tails on cases."

The chief sighed. "Couldn't agree more, but it's still a tough sell. The resources we put into funding Nettie's and your positions almost three years ago are why the cleared case rate is up. And you were right on the mark when you said guys investigating the gang and drug deaths had to be dedicated to those scenes. But try and tell that to a politician. They just look at the bottom line and say, 'The murder rate is down, but you've got the same number of cops as when it was high.' Well, no matter. I got no problems defending the department's record over the past few years to anyone." The chief hesitated, then said, "I take it you've heard the proposal to fund the expansion of the Cold Case Unit over at the BCA is going to be resubmitted next session at the legislature—you and Nettie still committed to moving over there if funding comes through?"

Mars nodded, immediately feeling uncomfortable. He and Nettie had agreed more than a year ago to leave the MPD and join the State Bureau of Criminal Apprehension's Cold Case Unit. But the expansion hadn't been funded in the last legislative session. Mars's reaction had been mixed. It was a perfect job for Nettie since it would give her a great opportunity to develop interagency databases. For Mars, the job had appeal only because he knew the chief would be moving to San Diego sometime in the next year. Mars had no appetite for going through the political and professional upheaval that he knew would follow the appointment of a new chief. And he knew working with Taylor was as good as it gets. Adjusting to a new chief with less skill and character wasn't something he was up for.

"I have reservations, but long-term, I think it's the right move. No doubts about it being a good move for Nettie. Just not sure working on cold cases is gonna be my thing. But then, if this political pressure keeps up, who knows. Especially after you go. Being a special detective could go away, and I really don't want to go back to the old drill, where it's catch-as-catch-can. Which is why I want to be sure you're comfortable with where we're going on this Beck case."

The chief straightened up. "Can't argue with your reasoning. Just think it's too bad the department might lose the two of you. Far as the Beck case goes, you do what you have to do to satisfy yourself. That'll be plenty good enough for me. Anything else I should know?" The chief got up from behind his desk.

Mars hesitated. It was a big leap to move from suicide to homicide to the possibility that the numbers on Beck's arm might mean something to another investigation in another jurisdiction. But if there was one thing the chief insisted on, it was being kept advised of investigations that moved outside his jurisdiction.

So Mars said, "Just to be on the safe side, we've sent out an information request to the five-state area, asking for information on any hanging deaths where the numbers we found on Beck's arm are present."

The chief gave Mars a dubious look. "You are thinking big thoughts." Then he moved out of his office. "Like I said. Do what you need to do."

Walking back to the department, Mars thought about what the chief had asked about who Beck's numbers' were intended for. There was something about this investigation in general that was making Mars feel edgy. And the chief's question in particular made him feel that the five-state information request was justified.

Seeing him come back into the department, Nettie said, "The chief is cool with your busywork project?"

"Ice cold. And you'd better not knock his judgment. He had all kinds of good things to say about you." Mars reached into his jacket pocket and pulled out the pack of cigarettes he always carried. He hadn't smoked since Denise had been pregnant with

Chris. But he found he missed the comfort of the pack more than smoking itself, so he'd fallen into the habit of buying a pack and playing with it until it wore out. Then he'd buy another. Nettie knew that he played with the pack when he was thinking hard about something. Seeing the pack come out of Mars's pocket, she waited for what would come next.

"You sent the five-state information request?" he said.

"Mars. For God's sake. It's Christmas in less than two weeks. No one's going to pay any attention to a request like this. Don't expect to hear anything until after Christmas. After New Year's probably."

Mars hadn't been back at his desk for more than ten minutes when Karen Pogue called.

"I just wanted to thank you for talking with Joey," she said. "He called me to say he'd met with you, and I could hear a difference in his voice right away. I think you've really helped him to see the suicide more clearly, Mars."

"Glad to hear it. Except I've decided to open a homicide investigation. There are some significant unanswered questions. It may have been a suicide, but I'm not willing to put my name to that conclusion just yet."

Karen's end of the line was silent for a moment. Then all she said was, *"Really?"*

"Really."

"Hell's bells. Who'da thunk it?"

"Now it's your turn to do me a favor. On a couple of fronts, actually."

"Anything."

"Give some serious thought to who—and why—someone would have wanted to kill Frank Beck. And some serious thought to other people I should talk to about those questions."

"Yeah, of course I will. But I'll tell you—that's going to be tough."

"That much I already know."

"Mars? There's another reason I called. I thought about it after we left Alma last night. Don't know why I've never thought of it before. Why don't you take Chris up to the lodge? We hardly use it at all, especially in the winter. And it's magical in the winter. You can hear owls and wolves, the stars are brilliant, you can snowshoe in the woods, there's a cove where the ice is like glass for skating...."

Mars thought about why taking Karen up on the offer wasn't a good idea. Not least of which was that accepting a favor from someone with a personal interest in the Beck case would be sensitive for all the reasons Mars had just explained to the chief.

Then he remembered something Karen had said at dinner.

CHAPTER

6

A personal messenger hand delivered the envelope to Mars. He could feel the two keys even before breaking the seal. The keys looked identical, but one was marked Lodge, and the other was marked Beck Cottage.

Karen's note was detailed: directions to the lodge (estimated driving time, five to six hours, depending on road conditions), recommendations as to the best places to stop on the route, a name and phone number for the caretaker who maintained the property year-round, a drawing of the compound with the lodge and Beck cottage marked, and a list of equipment available should they need it. Karen had ended the note by wishing them a good trip, then added in a hastily written postscript, "I'm sure there's no problem your going into the Beck's cottage as we do own it. Out of consideration, though, I know I can count on you not to disturb things."

It was the opportunity to get close to a private side of the Beck family that Mars had found irresistible in Karen's offer of the use of the Pogue's lodge on Lake Guelph. As it happened, the timing was good. Chris would be off school for Christmas vacation in less than two weeks, then would leave with Denise to go to her parent's farm for Christmas. So it would be good to have some time together to compensate for the time Chris would be away.

Their plans changed when Chris asked to bring his best friend, James Ziemer. Mars felt immediate disappointment that he wouldn't have the time alone with Chris. From the first, the time they spent together in the car had been an ideal venue for talks about everything going on in their lives. They'd begin in silence, with no pressure to talk, and let their thoughts lead them wherever. It was time that was particularly important to Mars as Chris's schedule grew increasingly crowded with preteen activities, and Chris's social life drew him away from the intense intimacy of his relationship with Mars. Intellectually, Mars understood the need for this shift. Emotionally, he missed the time when he had been the center of Chris's universe.

But the trip up North would be a good chance to include a friend in Chris and Mars's plans which, given Mars's living arrangements in a small studio apartment in one of Minneapolis's least desirable neighborhoods, didn't often present itself. So he agreed, and Mars found himself looking forward to the trip. There was a sense of freedom that came with a road trip that he didn't get much in daily routine. And not only would he have an opportunity for a close look at the Beck cottage, but he'd be occupied while Nettie pinned down information he needed to go forward with the Beck investigation.

Top of his list was finding a cryptographer to take a look at the number on Beck's arm. Second, he'd asked Nettie to start tracking down sources for the noose Beck had used to hang himself. And he'd given Nettie a list of people to contact regarding times they'd be available to talk to Mars about Frank Beck. Finally, with a little luck, they might have a response to their request regarding deaths in the five-state region where the Beck number was found on the deceased's body. Mars still couldn't say he had a basis for suspecting there might be deaths with related circumstances. But numbers that had no discernible connection to the victim and no meaning to the victim's survivors had to mean something to somebody. Why else would the perp take the trouble to leave the numbers on the body?

* * *

He went down to the Homicide Division first thing on Friday morning to get some work done before leaving to pick up Chris and James. Around nine, looking at his watch, he decided to make two phone calls he'd been putting off.

The first was to Joey Beck. In one sense Mars was pleased to be able to tell Joey that his father's death would be investigated. But there was a fine balance that needed to be maintained in communicating this information. Odds were still on Frank Beck's death being a suicide. The last thing Mars wanted was to raise Joey's hopes only to expose him to more disappointment. Mars decided the best approach was to be specific: to say that he would be looking into three or four questions that were unanswered and to avoid the general statement that a homicide investigation was being opened.

The second call would be difficult for opposite reasons. Mona Beck, from all reports, wanted her husband's death behind her. She would not, Mars guessed, be pleased to hear there would be more questions. But she needed to be told and telling her would also give Mars the opportunity to let her know he'd be going into the cottage the Becks had owned on Lake Guelph. Doing that would leave Mars with a clear conscience—and, if done properly, a clear legal path for anything he might find in the cottage.

As it happened, Joey Beck wasn't in. Mars left a crisp message which defied optimism on the part of the recipient. As an afterthought, he reminded Joey Beck that any suggestions on people who might have a motive to murder his father were welcome. Then he dialed Mona Beck.

"Yes?"

Not Hello but *Yes?* Sharp. Unwelcoming.

"Mrs. Beck, I'm Special Detective Marshall Bahr of the Minneapolis Police Department."

"*Yes?*" Still sharp, but now wary as well.

"Mrs. Beck, I wanted you to be aware that one or two questions have been raised regarding your husband's death last—"

"Oh, *please*. Can't we just leave this alone? What possible questions can there be about a death in these circumstances? We need to get past this. And agonizing endlessly over what happened isn't going to help anyone."

"I understand your concern, Mrs. Beck. My feeling is that if we can answer a few outstanding questions it will help everybody concerned get past the death. And we wouldn't be proceeding unless we felt there was a basis for raising additional questions. I'll do everything I can to make your involvement as painless as possible. For now, I just felt you needed to know we were proceeding . . ."

"Whatever. Just keep me out of it. And don't get my son Joey's hopes up. This is the last thing he needs."

"I'll do everything I can to keep Joey's expectations balanced. But I will need to talk to you at some point in the future, Mrs. Beck. My partner will be calling you to set something up."

"I'm not going to be available for the rest of this week."

The perfect segue. "I'll be out of town myself. As a matter of fact, I'm going to be up at Lake Guelph using a friend's lodge for the weekend." He hesitated. The silence on her end of the line got heavier, but she wasn't going to bite. "I understand you used to own a cottage in the same compound . . ."

"The cottage was sold to Ted and Karen Pogue a few weeks ago."

"That was my understanding. Mrs. Beck, would you object to my just taking a walk through the cottage? It would be helpful for me to be familiar with places your husband—"

"I told you. The cottage no longer belongs to us . . . to *me*. You'd have to ask Ted and Karen about going in."

"It's my understanding some of your personal belongings are still in the cottage, so I just wanted to be sure you wouldn't have any objection to my just taking a look around."

She sighed. "I'll say it once more. It's not up to me to give permission for something that isn't mine."

* * *

It was nearly 11:00 A.M. before the three of them turned north on Interstate 35. A trip up North in December was a dice roll, but after getting more than a foot of snow the previous week, the five-day forecast for northeastern Minnesota was for clear, cold weather.

Peering at the map, James said, "We going into the Boundary Waters?"

"Near the Boundary Waters," Mars said. "The lodge is just off the Echo Trail that runs north of Ely. The trail is more or less between the east and west sections of the Boundary Waters." He smiled to himself. He'd asked the same question of Karen. She'd snorted in response. "Ted own property on federal land, where he's not in control? Fat chance."

"So if it's not in the Boundary Waters, we could ride snowmobiles?" James stared up at Mars with passionate hope, his wild red hair looking electrified with expectation.

"Karen's note didn't say anything about snowmobiles—so even if there are snowmobiles there, we don't have permission to use them." Mars glanced down at James. "Even with permission, James, you on a snowmobile is more than I'm willing to take on."

James smiled, pleased at this tribute to his essential wickedness.

They were headed toward Two Harbors when James said, "I need to pee really bad."

"You're going to have to hold it," Mars said. "Next pee stop is Two Harbors."

"If I wait till then it'll be Three Harbors," James said, which caused both boys to erupt in laughter. James clutched his crotch with both hands, gasping for breath. He crossed his legs and groaned. "How much longer?"

"Maybe half an hour. There's a grocery store just the other side of town where we can pick up what we need, and a gas station just across the street from the grocery." Mars said. "You guys start thinking about what you want from the grocery store so we can get in and out fast."

Chris took the lead at the grocery store. Being his mother's son, he was passionate about getting good deals. And he cared more about food and cooking than anyone Mars knew. Where that came from was one of the mysteries of genetics. Denise cooked out of cans and boxes. Mars was a twenty-four-pack-of-Coca-Cola-covers-it kind of guy. But since learning cooking basics in Cub Scouts, Chris had progressed to being the kind of grocery shopper who knew what season of the year was best for buying avocados and when you should use plum tomatoes instead of regular tomatoes. He had strong feelings about the difference between Alaskan salmon and salmon from Norway. And he could get really upset that the blueberry season was so short.

It was dark by the time they reached Highway 2 and headed northeast toward Ely. Behind them, Two Harbors's lights glittered along the lake, but in the moonless night, the lake was an invisible black void.

The road to Ely was narrow and tree lined. For the most part, the road was clear, but there was the occasional patch of ice, particularly at sharp curves in the road where blowing wind accumulated packed snow. And more than once a deer leaped from the dark to run across the road in front of the car. Mars relaxed a little when they reached the east end of Ely. Rather than turning left to go into town, they turned right, following Route 21 for a short distance, then turning left again to the Echo Trail.

After a slow drive on the Echo Trail, which was plowed but icy, they approached the intersection that was the checkpoint for the last three-quarters of a mile to the lodge gate. Harold Ivings, the property caretaker, had said he'd be in his pickup outside the gate waiting for them at 6:30 P.M. Mars saw the taillights before he could see the outline of the truck. He flashed his headlights, and then saw a plume of exhaust shoot out of the truck as Ivings signaled a left turn into a driveway across the road.

There was a tall black-iron fence all along the property line. The double gate swung open as Ivings approached, which told Mars it operated on a remote control. Ivings idled beyond the gate until Mars drove through, after which the gate swung shut behind them.

"Cool!" James said, on his knees in the front seat, looking backward. Chris was sitting far forward, his chin on the back of Mars's seat. Ahead of them, small lights set along the roadside at ground level illuminated their route. They drove for minutes along the narrow road, trees right up to the road and arching bare branches above. Then the road opened into a clearing with good-sized log structures balanced along each side of the clearing. At the far end of the clearing and near a broad, white expanse that must have been Lake Guelph sat a massive log building. There were lights on inside the structure. Smoke was coming from the chimney. *The lodge,* Mars thought.

Ivings led them directly to the front of the lodge. He jumped out of his truck and walked stiff legged back to their car. Mars was a little stiff himself as he got out of the car and offered his hand to Ivings.

"Marshall Bahr. My son, Chris," Mars pointed at the backseat, "and his friend James Ziemer. Appreciate your coming out to let us in."

"Part of the deal," Ivings said. "You go on in, and I'll bring your things. Then I'll take you around, show you what's what."

Stepping into the front hall, it was obvious that considerable trouble had been taken to make them welcome. A fire burned in the massive stone fireplace that covered one wall in a great room. Lights were on throughout the downstairs and the floors and furniture shone with fresh polish.

The lodge itself was classic log architecture. The ceiling in the great room must have been twenty feet high, with a railed walk-way running around the upper nine feet or so of the room. A massive wood staircase led from the entry hall to the upstairs. There was heavy, hand-built log furniture throughout the downstairs, all upholstered with large, comfortable cushions. The furniture looked like it had been specially designed for the house.

Chris and James stood motionless in the entry hall, jaws slack. After a moment, Chris said, "Oh, man."

Ivings looked pleased at their response. "A fine old house, this one. Not many like it around anymore. Bigger than it needs to be, of course. But a real work of art in its own way. You fellas come on out to the kitchen. My wife was up here to clean and put the linens out, and she made cocoa and left cookies for you. Thought you might be peckish after your drive."

They all sat around a broad pine table in the center of the kitchen. The kitchen was probably twice the square footage of Mars's studio apartment. Ivings still had on his parka and a lined cap with ear flaps tied on top. Mars suggested he take his coat off, but Ivings shook his head. "Get you settled and I've gotta be getting back." But he continued to sit, seeming to enjoy their company.

James said, "These are the best chocolate chip cookies I've ever eaten. You know what I hate? *Oatmeal* cookies. You know what else I hate? People who give you fruit for dessert. My gramma will do that. Like an *apple* is as good as a hot fudge sundae." James chewed ferociously, a cookie in each hand, alternating bites.

Mars looked at Ivings. "Anything else I need to know?"

Reluctantly, Ivings stood. "Couple things I should show you, if you've got the time now."

As they left the table, Chris stood up and held out his hand. "It was nice to meet you, Mr. Ivings. Tell your wife we really like the cookies."

Harold Ivings looked closely at Chris, then took Chris's hand in both of his, shaking it gently. "My pleasure. And I can't tell you how happy it will make my wife to hear you liked the cookies."

"Yeah, thanks a lot," James said, spitting cookie crumbs. "We may need more before we go."

"Ignore him," Mars said.

Ivings walked Mars through the lodge's mechanical systems in the basement, all of which had been updated to state-of-the-art equipment. Mars hadn't the heart to tell Ivings that he didn't understand a word Ivings had said. More than that, Mars didn't *want* to understand anything Ivings said. If Mars had one burning personal ambition it was to live his life without ever repairing anything. With Ivings, it was clear that the possibility of fixing a complicated piece of equipment was what made getting up in the morning worth doing.

"That red-haired kid. He's gonna make a few waves before he's through." Ivings spoke as they walked from the basement of the lodge out a door that led away from the house toward the lake. His voice was amplified in the silent, dark night by the heavy cushion of snow all around them.

"My thoughts exactly," Mars said. "There are some real likable qualities about James, once you get to know him. But I'd have to say the older he gets the more he worries me."

"Well, there are those that just have to push all the limits before they're done. I daresay that red-haired kid will do more than his share of pushing. Your boy, now. Nice manners, real thoughtful boy."

Mars felt a rush of gratitude and pleasure that always came when others saw Chris the same way he did. Those emotions were quickly replaced by a false modesty that Mars put on partly out of natural temperament and partly as a talisman against bad luck.

"Well, I suppose spending time with James makes me appreciate Chris more. Not to say Chris doesn't have his moments, especially as he's getting older. He's pretty stubborn."

Ivings stopped, taking hold of Mars's arm. "Watch yourself here. There's a pretty steep slope just ahead."

They half walked, half slid down the path that led to the skating cove on the lake. The snow had been cleared from the ice, clearly delineating the perfect oval surrounded by snow-covered trees.

"You've taken too much trouble," Mars said, looking at the smooth shine of the ice.

"Doesn't take a minute to clear the snow. Ice always freezes perfect here. Sheltered the way it is. And there's a level granite bottom in the cove which makes a difference. That, and it's not more than six, seven feet deep. And it got real cold, real fast. Ideal for a smooth surface. Cold as it's been, it's darn near frozen solid to the rock."

Ivings turned and walked Mars over to the far end of the cove. "We've got a little warming hut here, and there's a stone hearth for a fire right over there. We've stocked wood on the other side of the hut, and at the back of the hut we've got the snowshoes and toboggans. I haven't had a chance to get a toboggan run built. Didn't know till day before yesterday anyone was coming up. When the folks used to come up here with little kids, I'd build a run from up there"—he pointed up toward the crest of the slope they'd just walked down—"directly down to the ice." His other arm reached out, pointing down to the pond. "Then we'd build a bunker the other end of the ice to stop the sled. Soon as the sled hits the ice, it spins like crazy. More fun than anything your boys have done before, I can assure you."

"This is all just wonderful," Mars said. "And building the toboggan slide is just the kind of thing Chris likes. We'll get at it first thing in the morning."

"Best way to do it, to my mind—especially when you've got this much fresh snow—is shovel down to maybe six, eight inches of snow. Then spray that down with a bit of hot water. Up at the lodge, in the utility room, my wife's got some big spray bottles she uses for ironing. Doesn't take much, couple bottlefuls in this weather will do fine. Just make sure the water's real hot when you fill the bottles."

Ivings left after they walked back to the lodge. They shook hands as Ivings climbed into his truck.

"Don't hesitate to call if you have any problems." He gave a wave as he headed back out toward the main road.

By the time Mars got back into the lodge, it was after eight o'-clock. He could hear the boys upstairs. In a moment, Chris appeared at the head of the staircase.

"Dad! Bunk beds!"

James slid in his stocking feet to Chris's side. "I get the top."

It occurred to Mars that one of the things that clearly separated children from adults was a passion for bunk beds in general and the top bunk bed in particular. He looked at his watch. "Guys, it's getting late. I'm thinking that cooking out tonight isn't a great idea. Especially given all the cookies and cocoa you've had. I'm thinking maybe roast hot dogs in the fireplace downstairs, and call it a day."

"I got bratwurst," Chris said. "Hot dogs are gross."

They made an early night of it after dinner. In his upstairs room, Mars took out the small, hand-drawn map of the compound that Karen had given him. He went to the window and compared the map to his view. In a moment he'd pinpointed the Beck cottage. It was nearest the lake, set back a bit in the woods. It was frustrating to be this close without yet having gone into the cottage, but Mars was tired. And he was reluctant to leave the boys alone in the lodge for what might be a long time. Going through the Beck's cottage would have to wait until tomorrow, probably after the toboggan run got built.

Chris was up before six. Mars heard him come out of his room, then head down the stairs. By the time Mars had showered and gone downstairs, Chris had squeezed orange juice and was making omelettes. He'd placed a glass full of ice and a can of Coca-Cola at Mars's place on the table. Kind of pathetic when your kid knows that much about your personal vices.

"James still asleep?"

Chris made a face. "He didn't go to sleep until really late. He probably won't get up for another couple hours." Chris turned toward Mars. "We don't have to wait for him to start the toboggan run, do we?"

Mars shook his head. "Will he have enough sense to eat something when he gets up?"

"He'll eat Fruit Loops," Chris said. "That's all he ever eats for breakfast."

It was a brilliant morning, with a cold sun and deep blue sky. As they stepped out of the lodge, onto the porch, the full beauty of the site—obscured by night on their arrival—took their breath away. "Wow," Chris said, "How much do you think a place like this costs, Dad?"

"Not more than, maybe, four-five times what I'll earn in a lifetime. Not counting what it costs to maintain the place and pay taxes."

"So more than we could afford, huh." Chris's voice was wistful.

"A bunch more than we can afford. But we're smart. We have friends who can afford it and who are generous enough to let us use it. Best of all possible worlds."

According to the outdoor thermometer, it was eleven degrees below zero. The absence of wind and the brilliant sun disguised that fact at first. But Mars had no doubt after being out for a few minutes, and especially before they started working on the run, that they'd feel the cold.

If there was anything that gave Mars more satisfaction than watching Chris when Chris was fully engaged in a project, Mars didn't know what it was. To begin, Chris never started a project without thinking it through. Mars described what Ivings had recommended while Chris listened, nodding slowly. Then Chris walked to the top of the hill, scoping out the best path for the run. He spent several minutes in the hut, considering what shovels would work best. And when they started shoveling, Chris shoveled more than his share, paying careful attention to keeping the snow level. When they'd cleared the run from the crest of the hill to the cove, Chris turned, looking back up the hill.

"You know what might be really good?" His face was pink from exertion. They were both long past the cold that had penetrated their parkas before shoveling had begun. Chris unzipped the top of his parka and pushed his hood back. His dark hair was matted with perspiration against his forehead. "Maybe we should build, like, a little bump at the middle, so when the toboggan comes down, it'll hit the bump and fly up some."

They had just finished spraying down the run—which immediately froze into a glistening surface—when James came out of the lodge. James's jacket was open, he had no hat on his head, no mittens on his hands.

"Can we slide yet?"

"You don't slide anytime until you get properly dressed," Mars said. Grimacing, James slogged back to the lodge. Chris and Mars took the toboggan to the top of the run for its maiden voyage. Even allowing for the fact that the first slide wouldn't be the best—that each successive slide would make the run smoother and faster—Ivings had got it just right. It was more fun than anything either of them had ever done before.

They lay on the ice laughing with exhilaration after the sled had come to a final stop, having spun maybe a dozen times on the slick ice before butting softly against the snow bunker.

From the hill they heard James yelling, "Hey, I wanted to go down first."

Chris looked up, and saw James about to come down the run. At full throttle he shouted, "Stay off the goddamn fucking run, you idiot! It's not solid yet!" Then, sheepishly, he turned to Mars.

Mars grinned. A couple years earlier Chris's use of profanity had prompted the two of them to work out a set of rules for when it was wrong to swear. Rule number one had been that it was wrong to use any word—swear word or not—without thinking carefully about what you wanted to say. Rule number two was that using a swear word to get attention was bad. And rule number three was that using any word too much was not acceptable. When either of them broke one of the three rules, the other would just say, "Number one," or "Number two," or "Number three." If the number wasn't called, the other judged the use of the swear word to be okay.

Without speaking, Mars got up from the ice and started to brush himself off. At which point his feet promptly went out from under him on the glare ice, and he fell with a thud. "Jesus Fucking Christ!" he said, lying on his back. Then they both laughed too hard to say anything for minutes.

James came barreling down the hill toward them. "C'mon, you guys. I wanna slide, get up! Get the toboggan back up the hill." As he hit the ice, he fell hard. "Fuck!"

Finally gaining enough composure and traction to get the toboggan off the ice, they started back up the hill. James ran ahead of them. "Whoever slides has to take the sled back up," he said.

The second slide, with James's extra weight, and the run getting set, was awesome. They all lay on the ice for maybe five minutes after the slide to catch their breath. And to figure out how to get up without falling down.

"You shoulda put more bumps on the run," James said. "They're the best."

Chris and Mars turned their heads on the ice to look at one another, each rolling their eyes. "I'm thinking," Mars said, "we're going to pour water on the run, lay you on it till you freeze, then run the toboggan over your body a couple times."

"Very funny," James said.

* * *

After a couple more slides, Mars left the boys on their own. He went back to the lodge to get the key to the Beck cottage, then walked across the clearing and back into the woods to the cottage. He was feeling chilled, having gotten warm and sweaty while they'd tobogganed. The heat of exercise didn't last long in the deep cold.

His fingers numb, he fumbled with the key. He couldn't get the lock to open. He unzipped his parka and crisscrossed his arms across his chest, tucking his hands into his armpits. He waited, stomping his feet on the porch to stay warm. The cottage was more shaded than the other cottages and the cold was biting. After a couple of minutes, he tried again. The key went in, but it didn't turn the lock.

Damn. He looked at the key to make sure it was the Beck cottage key. Which it was. He walked across the porch, trying windows. All were locked—as one would expect in a property maintained by Harold Ivings. He walked off the porch and around to the back. Maybe there was a back door lock the key would fit. There was a back door, but once again the key failed to turn the lock.

At this point Mars was seriously cold. He jumped his way through snow back to the lodge to consider his next move in front of a warm fire. Ivings had said to call if there were any problems, but Mars hated to bother him. It would also be awkward to explain why he should be allowed to go into the Beck cottage. On the other hand, the idea of going back without having gotten into the cottage was totally unacceptable.

Reluctantly, he dialed Ivings's number on his cell phone. Mrs. Ivings answered and explained Harold would be out until that evening. Was there anything she could do? Mars declined, although it was possible she'd have a key to the Beck cottage. He didn't want to attempt an explanation of why he needed to get into the Beck cottage more than once. He said he'd call again in the morning and hung up.

All of this was making the Beck cottage seem more important to the investigation than it had any real possibility of being. Knowing that did nothing to ease Mars's sense of frustration.

After a lunch of canned soup and peanut butter sandwiches—acceptable to Chris only because exercise and cold had made him too hungry to complain—the boys sat with Mars in front of the fire.

"Can we skate this afternoon?" Chris said.

"Sounds like a plan to me," Mars said.

"We should build a fire in the pit, first," James said, "so we don't freeze to death."

Give the kid credit for a good idea. "A *better* plan," Mars said.

"Dad? Can we stay up late tonight to watch the Geminid meteor showers? Our teacher said we should look to the northwest after midnight."

Mars winced. The only idea that held much appeal for him at the moment was a nap in front of the fire. The idea of being awake, in the dead of night, out in the cold, wasn't very appealing.

"Sure," he said. "Why not."

"There's a big pile of sleeping bags in the closet in our room," Chris said. "And there're some of those lounge chairs in the hut down by the pond. You know, the kind made out of metal tubes and plastic strips?"

"I know the kind of lounge chairs made out of metal tubes and plastic strips. What I'm having some difficulty with is figuring out how watching the Geminids, sleeping bags, and lounge chairs made out of metal tubes and plastic strips are related."

"What we could do is dig, like, nests, in the snow. Set the chairs up in the nests, put our sleeping bags on the chairs, then get into the sleeping bags. It'd be a perfect position for watching the sky, and it'd be warm, too."

"That," Mars said, "is a real plan."

Before the boys went out to skate, Chris went into the kitchen to start a beef stew in a slow cooker for dinner. Mars and James fell asleep in front of the fire, waking up when Chris stood before them in his parka, holding his and James's skates by their laces. His face was furrowed in displeasure.

"James, you should have gone down and started the fire. I called you from the kitchen fifteen minutes ago."

James sat up, yawning. He rubbed the top of his head. "Didn't hear you." He reached out for his skates. "I'm gonna put my skates on in here."

"You're going to put your skates on out on the porch," Mars said. "You're not going to trek across the wood floors in here on your skate blades."

It had been years since Mars had gone ice skating, and he couldn't remember ever liking it much. But he bundled up again, volunteering to be fire builder and sideline sitter.

This turned out to be good duty. There was something profoundly comforting about sitting in front of a blazing fire in the midst of a deep freeze. Even his frustration over the key-that-didn't-work melted away. And both the boys were good skaters, fun to watch. James was probably better than Chris. His impetuousness and loopy grace served him well on the ice. They skated until sundown, then made the trek back up the hill to the lodge. On opening the front door, they were engulfed by the joint pleasures of warmth and the aroma of beef stew.

After eating, Chris said, "For dessert we're gonna make s'mores while we're watching the Geminids."

The three of them tried to nap again before going out at midnight, but the afternoon's nap had taken the edge off their sleepiness. Around ten-thirty they started gathering sleeping bags, getting bundled up, and putting marshmallows, graham crackers, and chocolate bars into paper bags.

Within forty-five minutes they were set up down by the lake, inside their sleeping bags, eating s'mores on the reclining lounge chairs. The soft warmth of the sleeping bags in combination with the late hour made them all a little dopey, and their conversation was lackadaisical and disjointed. All three of them had fixed their eyes on the skies, almost forgetting to blink.

Suddenly, James shouted, "Moneymoneymoneymoney!"

"Where?" Chris said, sitting up.

"Over there," James said, still encased in his sleeping bag, tipping his whole body to the left to point.

"Saying your wish out loud means you won't get what you wished for," Chris said.

"Nah," James said. "That's blowing out birthday candles. You can say shooting-star wishes out loud."

"I'm not going to say my wish out loud," Chris said. "That way I can be sure." He dug around in his sleeping bag and pulled out a notebook and pencil. Holding the pencil clumsily in his thick glove, he spoke as he printed. "First sighting at . . ." He shoved the sleeve of his parka up and pushed the dial to illuminate his wrist watch. "Eleven oh three. In the . . ." He looked up at the sky, toward where James had pointed. As he looked up, a double shooting star flashed from the west to the eastern horizon.

"Dogdogdogdog!" Chris shouted.

"You said it out loud!" James crowed in triumph.

"You want a dog?" Mars asked.

Chris continued to stare up at the sky. "Mom says no way. Too dirty."

There was nothing Mars could say in response, but he felt bile rising in his throat. A clean kitchen floor should not be more important than rewarding a kid who deserved to be rewarded.

"If your mom won't let you get a dog, you shoulda wished 'Diediediedie.' " James said.

"That's not funny," Chris said.

Eventually even the sleeping bags didn't protect them against the intense cold and none of them had the will to get out of his sleeping bag, trek over to the hut for more wood and rebuild the fire.

Instead, they packed up their gear and went back to the lodge. It was after one o'clock, but they weren't quite ripe for bed. Chris sat down at the dining room table and reviewed his notebook record of meteor sightings. James asked to build a fire in the fireplace, and Mars went into the kitchen to make hot chocolate.

When he came out of the kitchen with the mugs, both boys were sound asleep in their sleeping bags in front of the fireplace.

CHAPTER

7

Light shining on his face woke Mars at eight-thirty the next morning. The boys were still asleep in their sleeping bags in front of the fireplace. Mars's last conscious memory was lying on the couch, watching the fire. He was still on the couch, but the fire was long dead. As this was their last day at the lodge, and they'd need to make an early start the next morning, Mars tiptoed quietly past the sleeping bodies to avoid waking the boys. He went into the kitchen and called Harold Ivings.

Ivings met Mars on the porch of the Beck cottage shortly after noon. The boys were out on the toboggan again, and Ivings smiled in pleasure as he watched them. "You've been having fun, then," he said with satisfaction.

"It's been terrific," Mars said. "Your suggestion about the toboggan run was right on the money. Most fun we've ever had."

Ivings pulled a heavy ring of keys from his pocket. "Let me take a look at the key you used," he said. He turned it both ways as he looked at it. "You got the old key. Not like Mr. Pogue to make that kind of mistake." The words were complimentary, but there was something in the way Ivings said it that made it clear he didn't much like Ted Pogue.

"Actually," Mars said, "I got the key from Mrs. Pogue. Karen Pogue. I've met Ted Pogue, but it's Karen that I know well."

Ivings nodded. "That would explain it. Mrs. Pogue's a real nice lady, but she gets harried from trying to do too much, I'd say."

Mars grinned. "You're right on both points. She is a real nice lady, and she tries to do too much."

Ivings turned the lock with a key from his ring. He swung open the door and he and Mars stepped directly into a living room, without any of the fanfare of the lodge's entry hall. Mars let out a low whistle. The cottage was maybe a third the size of the lodge, but what it lacked in square footage, it made up in charm. The broad plank floor was partially covered by an old hand-woven rug. The stone fireplace was a miniature version of the fireplace in the great room at the lodge. The ceilings were lower by probably ten feet and there was more leather furniture than there was at the lodge.

"What a nice place," Mars said, almost not out loud.

"You thinking of buying the place?" Ivings asked. Mars had not explained to Ivings why Karen Pogue had given him a key to the Beck cottage. Mars turned to face Ivings. He could have just said maybe. And left it at that. But that wouldn't have explained why Mars would need to spend a couple hours in the cottage, why he'd need to go through the contents of drawers and closets. Besides, Ivings was a decent man. Mars had no doubt that telling him the truth wouldn't become local gossip.

"Karen suggested my son and I might enjoy a weekend up here. But I also came up because I wanted to spend some time going through this cottage. I'm a homicide investigator with the Minneapolis Police Department, and we're looking into the circumstances of Frank Beck's death. I'll need to spend a couple hours here—I don't want to hold you up. If you're willing, you could leave me the key, and I'd drive it back to you after I finish going through the house."

Ivings fingered the key on the ring. "What I heard was Mr. Beck committed suicide."

Mars considered what to say next. "Definitely looked that way. But we've found a couple things that bear looking into. Could be when we're through, it'll still be suicide. But for now, we're not as sure as we'd like to be."

Ivings nodded. Then he said, "Won't be necessary for me to leave the key. I've got to do my first security check of the day on the other cottages, and I'm going to be doing a mechanical run-through as well. I'll just come back when I've finished up. You finish here before I get back, just lock the lock in the doorknob when you leave, and I'll lock the dead bolt when I come back. As long as you and the boys are around, I don't think there's any problem doing it that way."

Mars started in the upstairs bedrooms. There were three of them and only one big bathroom. The cottage was easy to explore. Being a vacation property, and a not-much-used vacation property at that, there was none of the accumulated stuff of daily living that could take hours to go through. At the same time, it made the search disappointing. It was a sterile environment with no intriguing finds.

It wasn't until he was back in the living room, going through the built-in bookcases, that he found something that made his throat clutch. But it clutched for emotional reasons rather than because there was something that told him why Frank Beck might have been murdered. It was a photo album, with a child's handwriting on the spine: "The History of Dad."

Mars remembered Karen Pogue mentioning that years earlier Joey Beck had made a family genealogy as a birthday gift for Frank Beck. It seemed unspeakably sad that after all that had happened, this testament of love should be abandoned on the bookshelf of an empty house.

He carried the album over to a leather chair by the fireplace and sat down, opening the book. The album's cover page was a pasted color photograph of the Beck family. Mars stared at the photo. His eyes went first to Frank Beck. The image could not have been more different from the photo Mars had seen of Beck lying on an autopsy table in the Hennepin County Morgue. This Frank Beck was filled with life and joy: his eyes shining, his color high, his arms extended over the family in front of him in a gesture of possessive pride.

Mona Beck must have been in her forties in this picture, but she could easily have been the sister of the three children who sat on the floor in front of her. Her smile was less broad than that of any of the others, but her eyes were focused, direct, happy.

The two older children strongly resembled their mother. Joey, who sat cross-legged at the bottom of the picture, looked more like his father than his mother. While he was undeniably the same Joey Mars had met, there was a difference that went beyond age. Mars looked at the picture for moments before recognizing the difference. In the picture, Joey was untouched by sadness.

The album included detailed profiles of Frank Beck's ancestors going back to the Revolutionary War. The largest section featured a Beck relative who had been a member of the First Minnesota Volunteers at the Battle of Gettysburg in the Civil War. Joey had included extensive historical records documenting the history of the First Minnesota. Minnesota had been a state for only three years when the First Minnesota had formed the first volunteers in the nation to come forward to support the Union's cause. It was a moving story.

Mars was so engrossed in the book that he didn't hear Harold Ivings come in.

"You look like you belong here," Ivings said.

Mars slapped the album shut. " 'Fraid not," Mars said.

"You find what you were looking for?"

Mars stood and stretched. "Not really. It was a long shot, but I couldn't resist the opportunity to have a look. One thing." Mars held the album up. "If you don't mind, I'd like to take this back and give it to Joey Beck. He made it for his dad's birthday a few years back. Seems a shame to have something like this sitting in a deserted cottage."

Ivings took the album from Mars and paged through it. "Funny thing," he said. "I remember Joey working on this. Couldn't have been more than twelve, thirteen years old. Asked me to let him work on it in one of the other cottages so his dad wouldn't see it. We called the cottage owner, and they said no problem." Ivings flipped through more pages, shaking his head. "They were a nice family, and Joey was a good boy. You know, your boy reminds me of him some. Just now, when I was inspecting the cottages, your boy noticed and came over. Followed me around for a while, didn't bother at all, but asked real intelligent questions. Joey Beck used to do the same thing."

An ache that was becoming familiar circled Mars's heart. "I know," he said. "I've thought the same thing. I have to admit that part of what motivates me in this investigation is that one way or another, Joey Beck needs to know what happened to his dad. Being told his dad was murdered isn't going to be good news, but I think he'll feel less guilt if that's the outcome."

Ivings held the album up. "I hate to ask you this, but Mr. Pogue, he's a stickler on this sort of thing. He finds out I let someone take something out of the property, he'll blow a gasket. You mind signing something saying you took it and will return it to the Beck boy?"

"Not at all," Mars said. "Tell you what else I'll do. I'll have Karen Pogue write you a letter thanking you for what good care you took of us and for letting me return the book to the Becks."

"No need to say thanks. Just doing my job. You ready to go?" Ivings started to the door, stopped, and pulling on gloves, said, "Tell you the truth, I'd feel better myself if you found out Frank Beck didn't commit suicide. When I saw him up here the week before he died, I thought he seemed just fine. Felt a little guilty that I hadn't noticed anything was wrong."

Mars stood stock-still. "You saw him up here the week before he died?"

"He'd been coming up here pretty regular the last few months. At first I didn't understand it. Then, after he died, I drove into Ely to pick up the *Tribune*. Wanted to read the obituary and all. Well, there was a big article about Beck. First I knew about all his problems. Of course, nobody told me the Becks had sold their share in the cottage to the Pogues, so I really took exception to Mr. Pogue chewing me out on that. . . ."

Mars held up both hands. "Wait a minute. I'm not following this at all. Why would Ted Pogue chew you out about the Becks selling the cottage to them?"

"Not about selling the cottage. About my letting Frank Beck stay in the cottage after he'd sold the share back to the Pogues. Like I said, nobody told me the Becks had sold out. First I knew about it was when I was up here doing a security check, two, maybe three weeks before Beck died. I ran into Pogue and Frank Beck standing right out there on the porch, having a screaming match. Mr. Pogue sees me, and he starts yelling at me about Beck being there. Beck started to defend me, which just made Pogue madder."

Mars shook his head. "How would Pogue have known Beck was up here? It's too long a drive for him to have driven up just on the chance that Beck would be around."

"I wondered the same thing. What I think happened is that Pogue had gotten the monthly report I put together for him on work done at the compound. Something he insisted on having, mostly because he assumes nobody—me included—can be trusted. I put on that report all the work we do for the association, including preparing the cottages and the lodge for visitors. I suppose he took a look at that and saw that somebody had been using the Beck cottage frequently on weekends. Would have drawn his attention because, as I've said, none of the owners here use the place much anymore. Least of all the Becks in the past couple of years."

"Still not clear to me that he'd drive all the way up here on the chance that Beck would be coming up."

Ivings nodded slowly, hesitating. He looked Mars in the eye. "Not my place to tell tales out of school about the tenants up here, but you being a cop and all, I'm going to say a couple things. I can trust you not to repeat this unless it becomes important in your investigation?"

"I'm not interested unless it is important to the investigation."

"Well, truth is, I didn't really think how Pogue happened to be up here that weekend. But one thing occurs to me that I hadn't connected to this situation until you mentioned it just now. Pogue called here, oh, maybe a couple weeks after he would have gotten the last report. Said association members were considering a new method for assessing association maintenance fees. My understanding is the current method is they assess based on square footage of the individual units. Pogue said they were going to be looking at usage as a factor, and he wanted me to let him know by phone if someone planned on being up, how long they stayed— and to add that information to the monthly reports. What was kind of unusual about his asking was that he made a point of saying he'd reimburse me for the phone charges. Not like him at all. That's the kind of thing he usually nickel-and-dimes me about. Says I should take that kind of expense out of my contract payment. And he was real nice about asking, which isn't usual, either."

"So you called him to tell him that Beck would be coming up the weekend he and Beck had the argument."

"Well, now you're into the business end of things, and that I'd have to check with my wife. She's around during the day, so she takes most of the phone calls. She does the books for the association, too. After I'd talked to Pogue, I told her about Pogue wanting to be notified by phone when someone was going to be using an association property, and I told her we were to include our phone charges for those calls on the monthly statement. That kind of thing, she'd just take care of it. Never occurred to me to ask if he'd been called. I think you can assume he would have been."

"I hate to bother you, but can you get me a copy of your phone records for any calls you made to Pogue in November?"

Ivings looked a little uncomfortable, but he said, "I can do that. Don't even know if we've received those charges yet, but when we've got them, I'll have my wife mail you a copy." Ivings looked thoughtful, then he said, "You know, when you stop to think on it—any normal person, if they found out somebody had been using something without permission, they'd say right off, wouldn't they? I mean, Pogue would have said to me when he got the monthly statement, 'Looks like someone's using the Beck cottage, and that cottage belongs to me now.' Or he just would have made a local call to Frank Beck down in the cities, and said, 'Why are you using the cottage without my permission?' That's what a normal person would do, wouldn't you say?"

"Agree with you on that. But you said Beck was up here after the weekend he and Pogue argued?"

"The weekend before he died. He stayed in the Raymonds' cottage. George Raymond called and said he'd given permission. I wasn't going to be available to give Beck the remote for the front gate, so I told him to stop by the house and pick it up from my wife before he went out to the compound. Told him I'd drop in and say hello when I was making my security rounds. I was glad for a chance to see him. Kind of wanted to clear the air after that scene with Pogue. Wish Beck well and all, in case I didn't see him again."

"And your wife would have called Pogue to say Beck would be staying in the Raymonds' cottage?"

Ivings shook his head. "Thing is, I wasn't really thinking about that. I don't doubt my wife would have called Pogue and said the Raymonds would be having a guest at their cottage that weekend. . . ." Ivings shrugged and made a self-deprecating little face. "I'd told her about the argument at the compound. She doesn't much care for Pogue either. And she liked all the Becks. My guess is, she just would have said the Raymond's cottage was going to be used on such and such a weekend. Left it at that."

"So Pogue wouldn't have know that Beck planned on being here the weekend before he died."

"No," Ivings said, his face furrowed. "But funny thing was, when I pulled into the driveway that first night Beck was going to be staying in the Raymond cottage, there was a vehicle parked across the road from the gate. Looked a little like the vehicle Pogue would come up in, so I have to tell you my heart stopped. Thought Pogue had followed Beck up . . ."

"Why would he park across the road?"

"Well, when I thought it was Pogue, what I thought was he forgot about our putting a remote control on the gate. That he'd locked himself out."

"The gate lock is new?"

"New the week after Pogue and Beck had their argument. Pogue insisted. Called me every day until I told him it was done. That and he wanted the locks changed on the Beck cottage. Which is why the key you had didn't work."

Mars felt like he'd had the air kicked out him. What Ivings said was suggesting a possibility that Mars should have thought of on his own. That he hadn't made him physically ill. "But it wasn't Pogue parked outside the gate?"

"I came up right behind the vehicle, put my spotlight on it. There was snow packed up around the plates in the back, so I couldn't get the number. But I could tell it wasn't Minnesota plates. Other thing, it had those tinted windows. Pogue's vehicle doesn't have tinted windows.

"Could you see the driver?"

"Soon as I put the spotlight on the car, I could sorta see the driver raise his hand toward me, then he pulled on out. Probably just some fella made a wrong turn on the road. Happens all the time. I was real relieved it wasn't Pogue."

Not sharing Iving's relief, Mars paced. "You make multiple security checks on the property every day?"

"Part of the job. I come back twice every twenty-four hours. And I don't do it on any pattern. Somebody gonna try getting in to the property, they're gonna watch to see what the regular activity is. So some days I come early, then come back in a couple hours, other days I'll come midday, then after dark, or in the middle of the night. Pity that it's necessary. Never used to be. But with more and more people coming up here, buying vacation homes, leaving electronic equipment and all in the homes—well, it's gotten to be a big problem. I'm proud to say we've never had any losses on this property. But I've chased plenty people off."

"The remote lock on the gate. Before you put on? . . ."

"Well, the gate was there, and it latched. But there wasn't a lock. Not a bad idea to have the lock. I just don't like how the decision was made."

"So you're sure Ted Pogue wasn't up here that last weekend that Frank Beck was in the Raymond cottage?"

Ivings finished putting on his gloves, and gestured for them to leave the cottage. As they walked, he said, "All I can say for sure is that I didn't see Pogue here, and the vehicle I saw didn't have Minnesota plates or clear glass windows."

Mars slept in fits and starts that night. Around two-thirty, he gave up trying to get back to sleep, got up and started packing. At four, he woke the boys. "C'mon, guys. Something's come up, and I want to get back to the cities as soon as possible."

Chris sat bolt upright and while not fully awake, immediately began to get ready. He was dressed and ready to go in a half hour, sitting on a kitchen chair, yawning and staring blankly. The surest measure of his lack of consciousness was the fact that he hadn't asked Mars why they were going back early.

James remained in deep sleep. Mars pulled a sweatshirt over James's pajamas, put socks on his feet and pulled boots over the socks. He stuffed James's limp body into his parka and carried him out to the car's backseat. As he pulled out of the driveway, he glanced over his shoulder in the direction of the toboggan run. Definitely the most fun he'd ever had.

Driving through the black night with both boys asleep gave Mars a chance to order his thinking about what Ivings had said. He couldn't get past blaming himself for not considering that Ted Pogue might have had a role in Frank Beck's death. Karen had told him at Restaurant Alma that Pogue hated Beck and had been enraged over issues involving the cottage. People had been murdered over less. Mars knew from experience where any number of bodies were buried as a result of personal feuds. And Beck had poured salt on Pogue's wounds by returning to the cottage after it had been sold back to the Pogues. If Pogue had found out that Beck had gone back to the lake after the locks had been changed, it might have pushed Pogue over the edge. Especially if Pogue had not been able to get into the compound because of the locked gate. Without having gotten into the compound himself, all Pogue would have known was that Beck had returned to the compound. He would have assumed that Beck intended to stay in his cottage and had probably enlisted Ivings's help in getting the gate control and a new key to the cottage. Based on those assumptions, he might well have begun a plan to exact revenge on Frank Beck.

As far as that line of thinking went, it was more than enough to establish a motive for Ted Pogue to murder Frank Beck. But as Mars drove, the anxiety that such a scenario gave rise to was eased by reflection on the unanswered questions surrounding Beck's death.

To begin, if Pogue had murdered Beck, it was likely that it was Pogue that Beck planned on meeting the afternoon he was murdered. So you'd have to ask yourself: Why would Pogue make an appointment to see Beck? Doing so would leave a clear link between himself and Beck on the day Beck died. Pogue could have, of course, given another name. But he would have had to have disguised his voice and come up with a plausible explanation for why he wanted to meet Beck. Maintaining a disguised voice for any length of time was not an easy thing to do, particularly when the person to whom one was speaking was someone who knew the speaker well. Pogue could have asked a secretary to call Beck and set up an appointment in another person's name. But doing that just created another link between Pogue and Beck and added a witness to Pogue's plans.

In short, Mars didn't believe that it was Pogue that Beck planned to meet the afternoon that he died. And if there had been no plan for Pogue to meet Beck, the window of opportunity for Pogue to murder Beck between the time Beck met with his mystery appointment after three o'clock and six o'clock when he failed to call Joey was very, very small.

Mars's emotional tension gave way as he considered that fact. It was no less stupid of him not to have considered Ted Pogue a suspect when Karen had revealed the animosity between the two men. But the prospect of being involved in the murder investigation of a good friend's husband—at whose house he had been staying during the investigation and about whom he had knowledge that could constitute a motive for murder—seemed less probable than it had when he had been lying sleepless at the lodge.

The two other unanswered questions in the Beck murder didn't tie in any obvious way to Pogue's involvement either. Play the scenario again. Pogue is enraged that Beck has once again acted in violation of Pogue's rights by returning to the cottage. Convinced of this fact, Pogue returns to the Twin Cities and begins—what?—weaving the noose? Why such a complicated means of killing Beck, if that's what Pogue planned to do? And there were still the numbers on the arm. Mars would have to check out any possible links between Pogue and the numbers, but the possibility that such a link existed seemed more remote to Mars than the possibility that Pogue had made an appointment to murder Beck.

The sun was rising to the left as they approached Duluth. Chris sat up, pulling at the seat belt to make himself comfortable and squinting in confusion. "Where are we?" His voice was hoarse with sleep, but the question indicated he was on his way to being fully awake.

"Just coming into Duluth. We'll be back in Minneapolis in three hours."

"Why'd we leave so early?"

"Remember when I told you about going up to the lake—about how I wanted to look at a cottage that belonged to a guy who may have been murdered?"

"Yeah . . ."

"Well, I found some things I want to check out."

"Ummm," Chris said, letting his head drop back against the seat. His eyes closed momentarily, then opened again. "I'm really hungry."

"We'll do a drive-through breakfast once we get past Duluth and are back on the freeway," Mars said.

Finishing his egg-on-a-muffin with many expressions of distaste, Chris crumpled up the wrapper and tossed it into a bag on the car floor. Mars looked over at the bag and said, "Do me a favor. Get your food wrapper out of that bag. I've got a book in there and the wrapper may be greasy."

Chris bent over, picked out the wrapper and tossed it on the floor in the backseat, below the still-deep-sleeping James. Then he reached into the bag and picked up *The History of Dad*. "What is it?" Chris said.

"The son of the guy whose death we're investigating made that for his dad a few years ago. I found it in the cottage. Thought the son should have it."

Chris started turning pages and was quickly engrossed in the personal stories. "You know what's really good about this book, Dad?"

"I know a lot of things that are really good about that book. Just not sure if I know what you think is really good."

"What's really good about this book is he did it before the Internet. Now you could get all this stuff on the Internet, just like that!" Chris snapped his fingers. "But it says in the front of the book that he did this 1993. He had to get all this stuff from the library or someplace. It would have been really hard."

"I expect he got some of it from the State Historical Society—especially the stuff on the Civil War." Mars paused. Right now the only thing he knew about Frank Beck that was even remotely interesting was that he had an ancestor who'd been in the Civil War. That was something Mars had learned in his years of detective work. When a piece of information surfaces more than once, you should pay attention, no matter how unrelated it might appear to be. And this was the second time in less than a week that Beck's Civil War ancestor had come up.

"Which reminds me," Mars said. "We haven't been to the new History Center building yet, and you said you wanted to go. Should we do that next weekend?" Kill two birds with one stone, is what Mars was thinking.

"That would be good," Chris said. He looked again at the album. "Know what I could do? I have to turn in a topic for U.S. history before Christmas vacation. I'd like to read more about"—he turned pages in the album, then held the album open toward Mars. "I'd like to read more about the First Minnesota Volunteers. It says that they saved the Union at the Battle of Gettysburg. I didn't even know that, and I've lived in Minnesota all my life."

Mars nodded. "Tell you the truth, I didn't know it either. That'd be a real interesting thing to check out. For both of us."

CHAPTER

8

"You're back early." Nettie looked sideways at Mars, holding out a pink message slip. "Which is a good thing. I found a cryptologist at the university who can talk to you about the number, but he's leaving for Iceland later this week. He'll be hard to reach for six weeks after that."

"Thanks," Mars said, staring at the slip.

"How was the weekend?" She gave him a second look. "You look shot."

Mars sat down at his desk, leaning forward on the edge of his chair, elbows on the desk, chin resting on his folded hands. "I feel shot. Too much driving in too short a time. And I didn't sleep much last night, fast-food breakfast this morning on the road. Other than that, the weekend was good. A great place. It made me feel bad about being poor."

"Just think how much worse you'd feel if you really were poor."

"Thanks for that bit of moral judgment. And I do know that I'm not really poor. Just that it's not often I want something that costs a lot of money. But that place was something else. The lodge was—well, luxurious. But there were smaller cottages that were almost better. Don't know when we've had more fun. . . ."

"I take it not a lot of investigative work got done?"

He sat up and spun around. "You're wrong about that. Came up with a red-hot suspect."

Nettie looked at him closely, not sure if he was serious.

"Ted Pogue," he said.

Nettie was still squinting in skepticism.

He talked through what he'd found out from Ivings, purposely not saying anything about his own vulnerability in having failed to consider Ted Pogue's possible involvement.

When he'd stopped talking, Nettie looked at him with an open expression of disdain.

"You thought through how you're going to explain why you were staying as a guest in the suspect's lake house?"

"Let's say the problem has occurred to me. But after thinking it through, I'm pretty sure Pogue *isn't* going to be our guy." He held up both hands in self-defense, anticipating Nettie's response. "Which isn't to say it wasn't damn dumb of me not to consider that Pogue might have been a suspect and that I had some conflict of interest issues." He went through his reasoning and was relieved to see from Nettie's expression that what he said made sense.

"So," Nettie said, after he'd offered his explanation, "how are you going to go about establishing that conclusion as fact?"

"I'm going to start by finding out if Pogue has a credible alibi."

Nettie knew Ted Pogue only slightly. But her vicarious connection to Pogue through Mars and Karen gave her a pretty good idea of how Ted Pogue would treat somebody who approached him on the assumption he might be a murder suspect. She grinned maliciously. "*That's* going to be an interesting conversation."

"I'm going to start with Karen. See if she can give me anything solid on where Pogue was on December sixth. Talking directly with Pogue will be a last resort. I'm not into sado-masochism. What did you say you've got on the cryptologist?"

Nettie nodded in the direction of the message slip she'd

handed him. "Gerry Weiler. Mathematics Department at the university. He gave me some times he'd be available to see you—want me to just go ahead and set something up for this afternoon?"

"Sure. Anything else while I was gone?"

There was just a moment's hesitation before Nettie said, "We had a response on the five-state request we sent out on deaths with the Beck number on the body."

Mars's head came up sharply. "And you're just telling me this now, on an oh-by-the-way basis?"

Nettie shook her head. "It was a nonresponse response. Came from an emergency med tech in Bebloe County, Wisconsin." Nettie leaned over and read from a notebook on her desk. "Dona—with one 'n'—Helmer. Like I said, it wasn't much. What she said was that about seven months ago she went out on an ambulance run to a suicide scene. The victim—Gaylord Rowe—was an older guy whose wife had died of cancer...."

"A hanging?"

"Yes, a hanging. Nobody was surprised. The guy had been depressed, hadn't had much motivation since his wife's death. Had even mentioned that he was considering suicide. A county mental health worker had been visiting him regularly and had listed him as a high suicide risk...."

"And Beck's numbers were found on the Rowe's body?"

"Well, that's what makes Helmer's call a nonresponse response. She was still in training and wasn't in charge of the scene, didn't have much contact with the body. She remembered seeing numbers on the Rowe's arm, but couldn't remember what they were or even how many numbers."

"Still," Mars said, "a hanging victim with numbers on the arm. That's something." He thought for a minute. "Why'd an EMT call? Why didn't the county sheriff's department call?"

"Helmer's got a story on that." Nettie passed Helmer's number over to Mars.

* * *

88

"I saw your request on the bulletin board in the sheriff's department," Dona Helmer said. "What you need to understand is, I'm too short to be a cop. So I did EMT training instead. Every time I mention something to the sheriff that I think should be looked at, he blows me off. Thinks I'm trying to make the point that I'm smarter than cops, even if I am short. Besides which, he's lazier than sin. He's not gonna follow up on anything that means he's got to get off his chair or do something as complicated as dialing a long distance number."

"Do you have a record of the numbers—would anyone else remember specifics?"

"I don't think so. I mentioned the numbers to the EMT supervisor. He said they weren't anything. Said the guy did a lot of carpentry, and he probably just wrote down some measurements on his arm while he was working. I asked one of the deputies about it later, and he didn't even remember seeing the numbers."

"And the body?"

"Gaylord Rowe had a sister in—just a sec, I've got the information right here...." Mars heard Helmer flipping through paper. "Anamosa, Iowa. Her name is Esther Moberg. She'd just had hip replacement surgery when she got the call about her brother. Signed off on cremation, and we mailed the ashes to her. Said she'd come up later when she was on her feet again and go through Rowe's house. Only other thing she asked us for was the uniform he had on when he died. Apparently it was some kind of family heirloom. She wanted her son to have it."

"What kind of uniform?"

"Nothing like any uniform I've ever seen. Looked real old." Helmer was quiet for a moment, then said, "I asked the EMT supervisor about it at the scene. He said something about the vic being a 'reenactor.' Whatever that is. The sister would know for sure."

There was no answer at Esther Moberg's residence in Anamosa, Iowa. Mars was reluctant to leave a message about her brother's death, and he was anxious to get over to the university to meet with the cryptologist. So he left Moberg's number on his desk.

Gerry Weiler was a small man in every physical sense of the word. Not more than five foot five, he was small boned, with small hands, small feet, small features. He was dressed the way central casting would dress an academic, which is to say in a tweed jacket, a button-down oxford cloth shirt, and a miniscule bow tie—all of which was expensive and fresh looking. Nothing like the long-haired, scruffy types Mars saw circulating through the hallways of the Mathematics Department at the university.

"How can I help you, then?" Weiler stood behind a neat desk, facing Mars, his fingertips pinpointed on the desktop. "Your secretary should have told you I'm pressed for time. I leave for Reykjavik in"—he pulled a pocket watch out of a pocket in the pleats of his gabardine pants and clicked it open—"almost exactly seventy-two hours. And I've an awful lot to do before then, so please." He made an expansive gesture toward a chair in front of his desk.

Mars pulled the slip of paper with the number written on it from his wallet, sliding it across to Weiler. "I'm involved in a homicide investigation where these numbers were written on the victim's arm. We've ruled out that the numbers were written by the victim or that the numbers relate to any of the victim's account numbers, personal identification numbers—things like that. So, what I'm looking for is anything in cryptology that might give us a start on analyzing what the numbers mean."

"Hmmm," Weiler said, staring at the numbers. "Hmmm. Yes, yes. I see. Hmmm. Well, yes, indeed." He slid the slip of paper back to Mars, drew up the fabric of his pants at the knees and sat down. "I can tell you this. At first glance, I don't see anything terribly sophisticated at work here. Which is good news, bad news. The good news is, if the writer's intent was for you to find a message in what he's written, it's not likely he'd build many blind corners into the deciphering process. The bad news is, once you've identified a sophisticated enciphering methodology, the message will reveal itself. The message you have here appears to be a very simple correlated cipher. That is to say, the numbers relate to something else. Very probably letters of the alphabet. Sounds straightforward, doesn't it?"

Before Mars could agree, Weiler started off again. "But it's not straightforward at all. The problem is, one really doesn't know—unless there *is* a sophisticated enciphering methodology at work—the relationship *between* each of your numbers. This is particularly a problem if the message is not a simple phrase or whole words. Take your number. If the numbers represent letters of the alphabet, depending on how the numbers relate to one another, you have the possibility that the cipher includes a letter of the alphabet, a combination of letters, a combination of words and numbers, whole words, abbreviations, or a combination of all five. If you're lucky, the cipher will at least be a coherent phrase with whole words—if so, it will start making sense to you as you get parts of it—rather like that television game show where letters are turned or a crossword puzzle. The more you see, the closer you get to the meaning. But, just as easily, you could have a cipher that does not contain a simple message or whole words. Very difficult, that. Give me a sophisticated enciphering methodology any day over these amateur inventions. What I would do if I were you would be to start correlating the numbers to the corresponding letter of the alphabet—in other words, 'one' equals 'a,' and so on. See if anything pops out that relates to your problem. But I caution you. There may be millions of combinations within those—what was it, thirteen numbers?"

Mars was taken aback. He'd looked at the number countless times, but couldn't have said how many individual numbers there were. He looked at the slip of paper, counting. "Thirteen it is," he said.

Weiler smiled. "Something of a message in its own right, wouldn't you say?"

CHAPTER

9

After talking to Weiler, Mars found a student lounge area with a Coca-Cola machine. His weariness was transitioning into a general sensation of being unwell, and even the Coke did little to make him feel better. Looking at his watch, he remembered that he hadn't called Karen to thank her for the use of the lodge and to ask if she knew anything about Ted Pogue's whereabouts the afternoon and evening of December 6.

"Mars! How was it—did everything go okay?"

"Better than okay. It was wonderful. I don't often covet other people's possessions, but I could definitely whip up a little envy over the lodge."

"Oh, good. I feel so much better when it's used. It costs us a small fortune to maintain the place, and we go up less and less."

Mars mentioned how helpful Ivings had been and the genealogy album Mars had taken from the Beck cottage. "So you found something that was helpful?" Karen asked.

"More like I found something I think the Becks should have. I'll see that it gets back to Mona Beck. I need to talk to her later this week anyway." He paused, reluctant to bring up his questions about her husband. There was no other way, short of meeting with Ted Pogue. Reminded of that alternative, he began. "Karen— there is one other thing."

"Which is?"

"I should have thought of it at dinner. When we were talking about Ted's problems with Frank Beck. You understand I need to ask. Do you have a good handle on where Ted was the afternoon and evening of December sixth?"

He expected surprise, confusion. Maybe even resentment. But Karen was fast and firm off the mark. "His office had their annual client reception on the sixth. I was there from two-thirty until five, then Frank and I went home together, changed, and went to friends' for dinner. We got home after midnight."

The line was silent for a moment after her answer. Then Karen said, "Are you surprised I was able to answer that question so quickly and completely?"

"Maybe a little."

"It's only that when you said at Alma's that Frank might have been murdered, the first person I thought about was Ted. Terrible thought to have about someone you've been married to for almost fifteen years. Pure luck that it was the one period of time in probably the last year that I could say with certainty I knew where Ted was. Don't know what I would have done if that hadn't been the case."

"You would have called me," Mars said.

"Yeah. I think you're right," Karen said. "Well, anyway. Glad you enjoyed the lodge. I probably won't see you before the holidays, huh?"

"Probably not."

"So," Karen said, "you'll be the first person I say Happy Holidays to this year—and mean it."

Mars considered going back downtown from the university, but he had no energy to negotiate late afternoon traffic. He went back to his apartment with the intention of calling Nettie to get Esther Moberg's phone number in Iowa, but instead lay down on the bed to catch his breath. He fell into a fitful sleep, getting up just before dawn.

The dull headache and vague gut churning he'd felt over the past twenty-four hours were immediately present. He drank a cold Coke from the can and felt some better. He showered, dressed, and arrived at the department ahead of Nettie.

She'd left a note on his desk. She'd been checking on commercial vendors for hangman's nooses. She'd started by checking with the three states—Delaware, New Hampshire, and Washington—where hanging was currently a capital punishment option. She'd faxed photos she'd had made of the Beck noose and all three states indicated that it did not resemble nooses used in executions. Only Delaware had executed a prisoner by hanging in the 1990s—one of only three hangings nationwide since 1976. "Not," Nettie had written in her note, "much of a market for a commercial supplier." Delaware prisoners held on death row who had been sentenced before 1986 had the option of death by lethal injection or hanging. Prisoners sentenced after 1986, when Delaware had eliminated hanging as an option, got the needle.

Based on what Nettie had been told in her prison contacts, should a hangman's noose be required, the prison would contract with a craftsperson to tie the knot. Nice work if you can get it. Mars wondered idly what the going price was for a hangman's noose. Nettie had added that she thought they should assume that the Beck knot was made by an individual—probably the killer or someone the killer had paid. Mars guessed that the killer would have made the noose himself rather than risk introducing another party to the crime. As soon as that thought came and passed, Mars added a caveat. He was making an assumption that the killer worked alone. Mars was a long way from having a solid basis for making that assumption.

Thinking about the noose, Mars picked up the phone and called Dr. Denton D. Mont. After the call he found the plastic bag with the Beck noose, then went downstairs and out onto Fifth Street. He turned left coming out of city hall and jogged the block and a half to the Hennepin County Medical Center. It had warmed into the 30s and the air was heavier, more humid than it had been for days. Clouds hung low and gray, giving the city a forlorn, unloved look.

The short run, absent a winter coat, had not been a good idea. By the time Mars walked into the Hennepin County Medical Examiner's office, he felt like a candidate for one of the ME's sliding drawers.

"You look awful," Doc D said from behind the cloud of cigarette smoke that formed a permanent haze around his head. He squinted at Mars as he inhaled on his cigarette. Doc D routinely ignored public facility restrictions on smoking, and as the people who cared about such matters made it a point to stay out of the morgue, he got away with it. He and Mars had as close a relationship as was possible for two people who never saw each other outside of work. And while Mars couldn't remember a time when either had complimented the other, the trust between them was implicit.

Mars slumped into a chair. "I *feel* awful. But a little aromatherapy down here with you should set me up. You find the Beck file?" Mars suddenly felt warm, and pulled his sport jacket off, placing his cigarette pack on Doc D's desk.

Doc D's eyes went to the pack of cigarettes. "Let me ask you something. All the years we've known each other, I've seen you carrying that pack of cigarettes around, but I've never seen you smoke a cigarette. Not in here, while I'm smoking, or when we've been out at a scene. How many cigarettes you smoke a day?"

Mars held up his hand, his thumb and index fingers forming a zero. Then he held up the cigarette pack. "My security blanket. I quit smoking when my kid's mother got pregnant. But I missed having the pack. So I buy a pack, carry it around, play with it until it wears out, then I buy another pack."

"What'ya do with the cigarettes?" Doc D said, an idea forming behind his eyes.

"Toss 'em when the pack wears out," Mars said.

Doc D frowned. "Terrible waste. Tell you what I'll do. Fifty cents on the dollar. You keep the pack, I get the cigarettes."

"I buy filters. You don't smoke filters."

"For God's sake, Mars. What difference does it make if you buy filters or not if you don't smoke 'em anyway."

"It matters." Mars said. "Besides, it wouldn't be the same, carrying an empty box. And the box would probably fall apart faster if it was empty. So even getting back fifty cents on the dollar, I'd probably end up spending more money."

Doc D swiped his hand through the air in Mars's direction. "You homicide dicks think too much."

"Why don't you do some thinking about the Beck file."

"You know I didn't cut this one up?"

"So I should have this conversation with Resch?"

Doc D's eyebrows raised and dropped. He flipped through the file, looking for the signature of the doc who'd performed the post. Finding it, he raised and dropped his eyebrows again. "I take your point. What's on your mind?"

Mars stretched out on the chair and rubbed his right hand against his temple. "This case came in to you as a suicide. Since then, some questions have come up, and we've opened a homicide investigation. Which isn't to say it still couldn't end up as a suicide. I'd just like to walk through the file with you and see if, between the two of us, we can find anything that got missed first time around."

Doc D was flipping through the file again, "We released the body yet? Ahhhh . . . yup. Too bad. Well, let's see what we've got here."

He spread the photos taken at the scene and during the autopsy across his desk. Then he sat back and read from the file, occasionally sitting upright to take another look at the photographs.

"Here's something—not sure what it means, but it's worth thinking about."

"Whatcha got?" Mars asked, sitting forward.

Doc tapped the autopsy report. "Resch lists cause of death as 'asphyxiation.'

"So?"

"Well, I agree with that. No evidence from looking at the photos that the guy's neck is broken," Doc said. "Looking at the photo taken from behind, if the neck had been broken, you'd expect to see a bruise behind the left ear. Someone getting hanged, if you want 'em to die fast, you use a hangman's knot, and you put the knot directly behind the left ear. That way, when he drops, the neck is gonna break between the third and fourth cervical vertebrae—provided you've got the right drop depth. . . ."

"The right drop depth?"

"I used to know this down to the foot. Came up in a military case I got involved in when I did my residency at a military hospital. It goes something like this. If you want to break the hangee's neck, you've gotta be sure, first, that you're using the hangman's knot. If you've got the right knot, you've got to have the knot positioned correctly behind the left ear—that way, the knot will deliver the force of the fall to the neck. Now, to break the neck, you've gotta have—I don't remember exactly—something like, twelve, thirteen hundred pounds of force. . . ."

"This is sounding *way* too complicated for your average suicide. . . ."

"Don't disagree—but it pretty much depends on the victim. There are guys out there that will go to a lot of trouble to do things right. But, in general, I have to say your average suicide isn't going to be thinking about any of those things. Probably doesn't even know the difference."

"Okay. So we're agreed that our guy used a hangman's knot, but there's no evidence that his neck was broken. . . ."

"You got a better picture of the knot, by any chance? I can't really tell from these pictures."

"I can do you one better," Mars said. Mars pulled his sports jacket off the chair and took the plastic bag with the noose out of his pocket. He tossed it on the desk in front of Doc.

"Ahhh," Doc said. "Just what I wanted to see." He put on latex gloves and removed the knot from the bag. Nodding slowly, he said, "What you've got here is a gallows knot, not a hangman's knot."

"There's a difference?"

"Makes a big difference in how you die. The gallows knot is a simpler knot—based on a multifold overhand knot. You hang yourself with a gallows knot, you're gonna choke to death. The *hangman's* knot is much more precise in how it delivers the force of the fall—which is how it breaks the neck. A hanging that takes place in a state that uses hanging as a form of execution for capital punishment? They're gonna use the hangman's knot. They don't want their hangee to be dangling around gagging for ten minutes while justice is being done. The hangman's knot is—at least by comparison—far and away the more humane method. Provided you've calculated the drop depth correctly."

"Explain again about the drop depth."

"Didn't really finish explaining before. And it's important to what your looking at with this victim," Doc said, tapping Beck's photo. "You wanna make sure your hangee is gonna break his neck—apart from using the right knot—you've gotta divide the hangee's weight into, oh whatever that number was, say, twelve hundred pounds. That'll give you the number of feet your hangee's gotta drop to break his neck."

"*Way* too complicated for Beck. But then, we already know that's not what he did. He used a gallows knot and he didn't break his neck."

Doc D looked again at the photos. "Not even an option. Say your guy weighed a hundred and eighty pounds. Divide that into twelve hundred pounds and you get something like a drop of seven feet. Your guy—just looking at these pictures, didn't have more than three, four feet to fall from where he hung the noose. Even if he'd used the hangman's knot and positioned it correctly, he wouldn't have broken his neck on that drop."

Mars tapped his cigarette box on Doc D's desk. "Let's say Beck hanged himself. The gallows knot is a simpler knot, you say, so that fits with what we know about Beck—although I'm pretty sure even the gallows knot was beyond Beck's expertise and patience. As far as wanting to make his death easier—I just can't see Beck knowing the difference or taking the time to find out."

Doc was nodding slowly. "So?"

"Let's play it the other way. Assume what I'm looking at is murder. What I ask myself," Mars said, "is whether the choice of the knot means something to the murderer. On the one hand, if I was gonna murder someone by hanging them, I'd wanna be sure he went fast, so I'd know he was dead, and I could get the hell out. On the other hand, if I really hated the guy, if my motive was based on strong emotion, it might be real satisfying to see him dangling there—gagging, turning blue, shit running down his leg . . ." Mars pointed to the picture of Beck's swollen, darkened, distorted face.

Doc D lit another cigarette. Simultaneously shaking out the match and blowing smoke, he said, "Tough choice. But remember what I said. Strangulation might have been his only option if he didn't have a place where he'd get a good drop."

"But he *came* with the gallows knot, Doc. No perp is going to walk in to murder a guy by hanging him and wait to tie the knot until he's measured up the drop depth. Maybe a suicide victim wouldn't have thought that through, but our murderer would have." Mars rocked back and forth on his chair for a moment. "The other thing. How do you get a guy to hang himself? I mean, even if you've got a gun on the vic, if I'm the vic, I'd rather have the guy shoot me than to have a noose around my neck and strangle to death. I mean, what leverage does the killer have to get the vic to go along with a hanging?"

"That's the other thing I was going to mention," Doc D said, tapping Resch's report. "Blood tests came in after the report you looked at. Those tests indicated that Beck had a small amount of alcohol in his system and a large quantity of barbiturates—not sure that works for or against a suicide conclusion."

Mars sat forward, elbows on his knees, rubbing his palms together. "So it could go either way. Beck could have had a drink, washed down some barbs to dull his consciousness, then hanged himself . . ."

"Not at all unusual to find a suicide used more than one method to take himself out," Doc said. "But I'd have to say it would probably be more typical to see barbs used with wrist cutting. A hanging, you might see a guy cut his wrists, then climb up on a chair. Don't ever remember seeing a hanging and barbs before."

"Play it this way," Mars said. "We know from the convenience store clerk that Beck was feeling 'up' shortly before he died. That he was meeting someone at three o'clock. Put those two things together. Someone who wanted to murder Beck arranged a meeting, suggesting he had capital to invest. They meet. Agree to join forces. The guy promises to inject capital, then pulls out a hip flask and says, 'Let's toast our future.' Passes Beck the flask. The barbs are in the flask."

"Believable," Doc D said.

"Once Beck gets dopey, the guy proceeds with the hanging."

"You don't have a clue why the guy wanted Beck dead?"

"I think the clue we have is the number on Beck's arm. I was telling the chief. We know Beck couldn't have written the number—he was right-handed and the numbers were written on his right arm. And the numbers didn't match Beck's writing. So we've got a perp who's murdered someone in a real precise way, and he doesn't bother to cover details like the number? For that matter, why write the number at all unless the perp is making a point."

Doc D took out another cigarette, but didn't light it right

away. "And a perp who makes a point that doesn't have any meaning to anyone who knew the victim. That make sense to you?"

Mars sighed. "No. And it's why this case is making me nervous. We've found another hanging death in Wisconsin where numbers may be involved. Haven't been able to confirm the numbers, but I don't like the way this is shaping up."

Doc D raised and dropped his eyebrows, then lit his cigarette. "No wonder you look lousy."

The meeting with Doc D got Mars past how bad he felt. Energy renewed, he decided to take on Mona Beck. He stopped first at the department to pick up the genealogy album, thumbing through the album again before leaving. The picture of Frank Beck's ancestor caught his eye. It was a portrait shot in a Union uniform. The uniform was crisp, fresh. The picture must have been taken just after he had enlisted in the First Minnesota Volunteers and before he'd gone off to battle.

Then Mars's gut tightened. The hanging victim in Wisconsin had been wearing a uniform when he died. An old uniform. Mars found Esther Moberg's number and dialed again. There was still no answer. This close to Christmas, he had to face the possibility that she was out of town.

Mona Beck's address was a cooperative apartment at 510 Groveland. The 510 was an unusual building in the Minneapolis market. It sat at the top of a low hill, across Hennepin Avenue from the Walker Art Center and just south of Loring Park. It was a building that would have been more in place in Manhattan, where realtors would have described it as having prewar construction. This translated into high ceilings defined by hand-carved moldings, deep windows, and hardwood floors.

Mona Beck opened the door to Mars's knock with a frosty greeting, the tone of which Mars recognized from their phone conversation. Except seeing her as she said it made it altogether different. Years alone don't ravage a face the way Mona Beck's face was worn. She was as beautiful as the woman he'd seen in the pictures at the cottage, but the serenity of that face was gone. In the place of serenity there were sharp lines. More than that, what animated Mona Beck's face—and the expression in her eyes—was a sort of terror. In a moment, Mars knew that the hardness in Mona Beck's voice came from a bitter blend of fear, guilt, and a perpetual grief.

She saw him looking at the apartment, noticing the hand woven rugs, the original artwork, the cabinet that was interior lit to show off a collection of porcelain. "It's not mine," she said. "Not any of it. My sister and her husband are in Germany for the next few months. They're letting me camp out here until they're back or until I figure out where—and how—I'm going to live. Whichever comes first."

Mars walked slowly around the living room, from which he had views in three directions. To the east you caught a corner of the pond in the center of Loring Park. The south view framed the intersection between Hennepin and Lyndale avenues. Walker Art Center's rooftop sculpture gallery and a glimpse of the outdoor sculpture garden filled the west windows.

"Nice place," Mars said in a neutral voice, trying to make clear that it didn't make any difference to him if she owned the place or not. "I'd like to bring you up to date on where we are on the investigation, then just a couple of questions—may I?" He gestured to a couch.

She sat in a chair opposite the couch without speaking. She sat tightly, on the edge of the chair, her arms crossed, each hand cradling an elbow.

Mars spoke slowly. "I told you on the phone a few days ago that we were considering the possibility that Mr. Beck did not commit suicide. That he was murdered. And I'm sorry, but I have to ask you. Can you tell me where you were on December sixth, between three and ten P.M.?"

Without looking at him, and without emotion, she said, "I

suppose that's right. If you're considering murder, I'm a suspect. Maybe your best suspect—I was really, *really* angry at Frank. But I can tell you where I was. I took my sister and her husband to the airport. Their flight was delayed, and I stayed at the airport until it was clear they would be leaving that night. I got back—well, I'm not sure exactly what time, but they got on the plane just before nine P.M. I got back to the apartment just before Joey called to say he hadn't heard from Frank. I looked at my watch while I was talking to him, and it was about nine-thirty. I was here after that— but alone. Do you want my sister's phone number in Germany?"

Mars shook his head. "My partner will call you to follow up on that. Sounds fine. We just have to . . ."

She held up a hand. "I understand. Really I do. What I don't understand is why you think murder is a possibility."

Mars hesitated. Experience had taught him when small details were significant. And his intuition was, at this stage of his career, as reliable as a set of fingerprints. But he considered how to explain the subtle facts of the case to Mona Beck in a way that wouldn't sound like he was spinning webs out of air.

"There are several things. Some of the physical evidence in the case is inconsistent with what we know of your husband's character. Then, we have a witness who says Mr. Beck had an appointment the afternoon he died. We haven't yet identified that individual. And, in spite of the problems Mr. Beck had at the time of his death, we haven't found anything to indicate that he was subject to despondency—in fact, quite the reverse. He seemed to thrive on adversity. . . ."

Mars stopped. He knew what he was saying sounded trivial. But he didn't want to go into details about the gallows knot with a woman who so clearly had not worked through complex feelings about her husband's death. And bringing up the lottery tickets at this point seemed irreverent. So he made a leap that took him where he wanted to be in this conversation.

"I know this might sound like not a lot to go on, but I don't want to go into greater detail until we're further into the investigation. I want to assure you that we wouldn't be proceeding if we didn't feel there were substantial questions. What I particularly wanted to talk to you about was anything you might know about people Mr. Beck might have known or activities he may have been involved in where he might have generated some enemies. What I've heard so far suggests that even his investors didn't hold any ill will toward Mr. Beck . . ."

She shook her head. "They considered the money they lost the price of admission to one of the best shows in town. Until this last failure, anyone involved with Frank had fun. And Frank always paid back his investors—at least, paid back what they'd put in. He did that even when it meant personal sacrifice." Her face tightened. "Even when it meant sacrifice for his family."

"Why was the last venture different?"

Mona sighed. "Oh, I don't know. One time too many. It wasn't fresh anymore. Everyone's getting older. What's fun when you're in your thirties, your forties—well, it isn't as much fun when you're fifty. And the money was big. Bigger this time than all the others put together. When people pulled away, they didn't do it with anger—they were just burned out. And I don't think they wanted to see the wreckage. They weren't prepared to raise capital, so they just wanted *not to look.*"

She sat back in the chair, more relaxed than she'd been since Mars had come in. An expression that resembled amusement crossed her face. "Ted Pogue," she said. "Ted Pogue was the only person I knew who held a grudge against Frank. And over something that really wasn't important. Ted hadn't invested the last time, so he didn't fall out with Frank over money."

Mars decided to be indiscreet. Mona Beck deserved it. "We've talked to Ted Pogue, actually. I'm satisfied he wasn't involved." Mars bent over and picked up *The History of Dad,* which he'd brought in a bag.

"I mentioned I was going to be up at Lake Guelph," he

handed the bag over. "I did go through your—well, now the Pogue's cottage. There wasn't anything, other than . . ."

She took the book out, then closed her eyes. Holding the book against her chest, her arms folded around the book, she said, "Just like Joey to do this. And just like Frank not to be interested. For Frank there's no past, no present, only the future." She opened her eyes and looked at Mars. "There *was* no past, no present—and now there's no future."

CHAPTER

10

"This has been—hands down—the most boring series of interviews I have ever done on any case in my entire career."

Mars and Nettie sat at a table for two, near the window at Eat This! on East Hennepin. It wasn't exactly a Friday-after-work ritual for them, but maybe one out of three Fridays they'd end the week at Eat This! They'd made plans for dinner when they'd talked midday, when Mars was still feeling a little better than he had earlier in the week. Now he felt worse than he had all week. Not even Nettie's caramelized onion and fontina cheese pizza appealed to him.

He watched her eat, his elbow on the table, his head on his hand.

"You're not going to eat anything?" Nettie said.

He shook his head.

"I'm not going to feel sorry for you, Mars. Not if you don't go to the doctor. You're never sick. To feel this bad for this long—something's wrong. Why don't you just go to the ER at Hennepin County? You know everybody over there...."

Mars shook his head again. "Don't nag. It just makes it worse." He picked up a plastic fork lying between them on the table. Tracing aimlessly on the table's surface with the fork, he said, "I'll be okay after getting some rest this weekend. I pick Chris up tonight, we're going to the History Center tomorrow morning—other than that, I'm gonna kick back. Besides, what's really making me feel bad is having spent probably twelve hours over the past three days having exactly the same conversation with people who knew Frank Beck. I got nothing—absolutely nothing—new out of anybody. We've never gotten any responses back on our five-state request, other than Wisconsin, right?"

"Wisconsin was the only one. But I told you. If we're going to get responses, I'm betting it will be after Christmas, maybe after New Year's." She looked at him again, hard, her eyes narrow. "Boring interviews don't make you look green," Nettie said.

"Yeah, they do," Mars said. "I can repeat verbatim what every one of the eight people I talked to said. One: It was impossible to hate Frank Beck. He was too good a guy, too decent, too much fun. Two: Somebody hate Frank enough to kill him? No way. That's it—except it took each interview more than an hour to make those two points. And everybody had an alibi that checked out. How often does that happen?"

Nettie waited. She knew Mars well enough to know there was more to his gloom than interviews that hadn't gone anywhere.

"I'll tell you something else," he said. "What this case is making me realize is that working for the state's Cold Case Unit may not be up my alley."

"Why this case?" Nettie looked genuinely concerned.

"It's making me realize how much I need that *fizz* you get on a fresh murder. Coming in a few weeks after the fact—and on cold cases it could be months or years after the fact—just doesn't generate the same energy, the same kind of forensics. I really need the big fizz you get when the body's still warm. Or at least not already buried. All I'm getting on this case is no sleep, because I can't beat the feeling there's something here a lot bigger than just Frank Beck's death."

"So you're thinking you're *not* going to go over to the bureau—if—and when—the legislature funds an expansion of the unit?"

Mars sank forward, running his hand through his hair. "I'm not making any decisions. I'm just saying it's given me a new perspective. What I've said all along is still true. I don't want to be in the police department when a new chief comes in. I can't stomach the thought of going through all that political crap, watching the union jockeying to roll their agenda over everyone before the new chief gets his feet on the ground. So, when the chief goes, if the legislature has come up with bucks, I'll probably stick to our original plan. But this case has definitely given me pause."

Nettie looked irritated.

"What?" Mars said.

"Nothing." She looked more irritated.

"Nettie!"

"Why is it that women always get accused of being indecisive? I get sick of all your wishy-washing around on this topic. You've known all along what the issues are on both sides, including that the kind of investigating you'd be doing on cold cases is different from the police department. So I think you should just suck it up and stick to what we've talked about. If you don't like it once you're there, leave. Big deal."

"What I really like about you," Mars said, "is your compassionate cruelty. You can, in the space of five minutes, worry about my being sick *and* give me a swift kick to the solar plexus."

"Both deserved," Nettie said.

Mars's original plan had been that he and Chris would stop for groceries, then make dinner at Mars's apartment. Leaving Eat This! Mars knew he wasn't up to grocery shopping. Instead, he bought a frozen pizza and a salad to go at Eat This!

Back at his studio apartment, Mars stretched out on the single bed that served as both bed and couch. Chris put his pizza in the oven, then sat down at the table opposite Mars to eat his salad. His worried eyes remained fixed on Mars. He had not seen his dad sick before.

To divert Chris's anxiety, Mars said, "This is probably the perfect opportunity to have our talk about sex."

Chris made a face, then stood up, went to the kitchen, and came back with a paper grocery bag. Sitting down again at the table, he pulled the bag over his head. "Okay," the muffled voice from inside the bag said. "Talk."

Mars grinned. "All I really want to say is—" What did he want to say? Mars folded his hands behind his head and thought about it. He thought about the teenagers he saw on city streets in the course of homicide investigations. He thought about his own teenage experiences. Both thoughts were unsettling.

"It's just that when you get to be a teenager, hormones can be more powerful than brain cells. And hormones can get you in a lot of trouble. . . ."

"How can a *sound* they make get you in trouble?" the voice in the bag asked.

The question stopped Mars cold. "*What* sound that *who* makes?"

"You said whore moans can get you in trouble."

"I still don't see what that has to do with somebody making a sound," Mars said. This conversation was tough going.

"I thought you said that when whores moan they can get you in trouble."

"*Whores!*" Mars said, sitting up to stifle a howl. "Where do you get off knowing about whores?"

"*Everybody* knows about whores, Dad."

"But everybody does not know about h-o-r-m-o-n-e-s, I take it."

"That's what you said, h-o-r-m-o-n-e-s?"

"That's what I said."

"So, what are h-o-r-m-o-n-e-s?"

"Hormones are—well, I guess they're like a chemical substance that makes your body do things. Like, grow taller, grow muscles. In girls, grow breasts, in boys, grow beards. They make your voice get deeper."

"Oh, *that* stuff," the bag said. "I know about that. I just didn't know you called it h-o-r-m-o-n-e-s."

"Back to my original point. You need to think about *why* you do *what* you do. Whether it's sex or anything else. I don't mind your making a mistake because you've made the wrong choice. You're gonna do that. It's part of growing up. But there are big consequences for sex mistakes." Warming to the topic, Mars said, "That's what's so risky about sex. When you're doing it, it's going to feel like fun. Like, going to a movie or playing a video game. But what you're really doing is making a life choice—you're doing something that could change the way you think about yourself, about another person, something that could be with you for years after the few minutes you spend having sex."

Chris tipped the bag back on his head, clearing his face. "Did you have sex before you got married?"

Oh, damn. In an instant Mars knew why he'd wanted to avoid this conversation.

He reached over and pulled the bag off Chris's head, dropping the bag over his own head. Then he said, "Yes."

"Did you and Mom have sex before you got married?"

Double damn. Mars hesitated for a long moment before saying anything. "Let's make a deal. We won't bring other people into the discussion. There are some issues of personal privacy here that I think we have to respect. I, for one, don't think it's fair to have a conversation that involves your mom when she isn't here to speak for herself."

"That means yes," Chris said. Even with his head in the bag, Mars could hear the big grin behind Chris's words.

Mars slept through the night for the first time in a week and woke feeling almost human. Chris was still deep in sleep on the futon next to Mars's bed, lying flat on his stomach, one arm extended, the other over his face.

Mars got up quietly to get his can of Coke. Walking to a window, he pulled a blind up with one finger for a look outside. The heavy skies that had threatened for the past few days were giving it up. Large, slow snowflakes were drifting down. They'd better skip eating breakfast at the apartment and go somewhere quick, like Perkins.

At the Perkins on Riverside, Mars decided to attempt eggs and bacon. Three mouthfuls into the plate, he thought better of it and pushed his plate away.

"I thought you said you felt better."

"Don't want to push my luck," Mars said. He hoped the dim ache he felt over his left eye wasn't the return of whatever it was that had been plaguing him all week. He looked out the window. The flakes were still big and they were coming down faster. "This is starting to look like serious snow. We need to get over to the historical society sooner rather than later."

As they walked out to the car, Chris said, "Know what I heard the weatherman say on the news?" Chris didn't wait for an answer. "Big flakes make big storms. Look at these flakes, Dad!"

The Minnesota History Center was perfectly sited on a hill overlooking downtown St. Paul. The state capitol sat on a hill to the north and the St. Paul Cathedral rode a hill to the south. Recently built, the History Center had been brilliantly designed to take advantage of its setting, with multistory windows framing the capitol, the cathedral, and the city's skyline. In honoring its history, the state had not made the mistake of cutting corners on materials. Minnesota had built an elegant structure of granite and marble with high, light-filled open spaces. But even as he admired the building, Mars thought there was something in its grandeur that was in conflict with Minnesotans' bedrock modesty.

Chris was elated, skipping ahead of Mars down the long entry hall. "A restaurant, Dad!" he called, pointing to their right. Mars had smelled food before he'd noticed the restaurant. The odor had prompted an immediate wave of dizziness and nausea.

"Hang on a second," he called to Chris. Then he sat down on a bench in the hallway, pulling open his parka and letting his head drop between his knees.

"Are you sick again?" Chris stood in front of Mars. His voice was filled with concern—and disappointment at the prospect that their visit was going to be spoiled.

"Just light-headed. Need to take my jacket off." Slowly he stood again. Taking the jacket off helped, but Mars was beyond hoping that he was over whatever it was that was making him sick.

They climbed a broad staircase that led to the research library on the second floor. After signing in and getting passes, they entered the library. The room gave Mars a momentary sense of well-being. It was bright, clean, and conveyed an impression of competent completeness. Mars immediately sat down at a table. "You talk to the librarian about what you need on the First Minnesota Volunteers. I'll wait here for you—if you need help, give a wave, and I'll come over."

Feeling increasingly sick did not deprive Mars of pleasure as he watched Chris talk to the librarian. Chris had a confidence that was visible at fifty feet, and Mars could read the librarian's appreciation of the kid's seriousness. They talked for about ten minutes, with both the librarian and Chris writing things down. Then Chris turned, a broad grin across his face as he walked rapidly back to where Mars was sitting.

"Dad! They're taking a tour group down to see a flag the First Minnesota captured at the Battle of Gettysburg. I can go if an adult goes with me. Can we? We have to go down to the information desk right away. . . ."

There was no way of saying no to Chris's enthusiasm. Mars

stood, trying to ignore the increasing pain he was feeling in his gut. "How long is it gonna take?"

"I don't know. Probably not very long. And there's a book about the First Minnesota that's for sale in the bookstore. Can we get that?"

Chris stood in line to sign them in for the tour while Mars went into the bookstore. Keeping moving was marginally better than standing still. When he came out of the bookstore, Chris was second in line at the information desk. With effort, Mars completed the sign-in sheet and showed identification. "All your tours take this much paperwork?" he asked.

"No," the information desk attendant said. "But there are special preservation requirements for the flag, so we're taking the tour into an area that's not usually open to the public. That and the controversy over the flag." In a conspiratorial voice the attendant said, "I think they're worried about vandalism, or even someone trying to steal the flag."

Mars had a passing moment of curiosity about what the attendant meant about controversy, but he didn't have the energy to ask. What he really needed to know was how long the tour would take.

"About fifteen minutes in the storage area, then the guide will bring you back here for questions."

There were maybe a dozen people in the group going into the storage area. The guide herded them through narrow aisles between large chests with wide drawers. In a far corner, she organized the group in single file, then pulled open a large, flat drawer. Mars spotted a wooden chair along the wall at the opposite end of the aisle and squeezing by the others went to the chair and dropped down.

The guide's voice wafted through the air at him. In any other circumstances, Mars would have been as spellbound as Chris. The story the guide told was that compelling. But today, fighting back waves of nausea, pain, and dizziness, Mars heard only pieces of the story.

"It is the final day of the Battle of Gettysburg and the future of the Union at stake. A handful of First Minnesota Volunteers stands between hordes of Confederates and the Federal position. Just the day before, the First Minnesota experienced the greatest percentage loss of any regiment in the war. But today, the third day of battle, the remaining members of the First Minnesota are ordered into a battle where death is more likely than life. Against all odds, the First Minnesota holds the line against Pickett's Charge. The Confederates have reached the high point of the war, they will never again breach this far into the Union line. And it is at this historic moment that a member of the First Minnesota captures the colors of a Virginia regiment. Those colors—a bit tattered, even bloodstained—but, all in all, in remarkable condition, lie sealed in the case before you."

Simultaneously, the group stepped forward to get closer to the flag and its moment in history. Chris was closest, his mouth slightly open, his cheeks pink with emotion, his eyes darkened by imagination. The guide was saying something about "today's battle between Virginia and Minnesota," but it was at this moment that Mars was overwhelmed by pain and nausea. Unsteadily, he got up and signaled to Chris to follow him out of the room. Chris's face fell into an expression of intense distress. He held up a hand, asking for another minute. But Mars shook his head firmly, and Chris came toward him, his expression one of intense disappointment. As he came closer, the disappointment gave way. His dad looked awful.

"Sorry, Chris," Mars said, "but I'm feeling worse. Think I'd better get home where I can lie down."

They edged back through the group, and Mars gave a signal to the guide that they had to leave. The guide opened her mouth as if to say something to Mars in protest, but she did a double-take as she looked at him. She let them leave without comment.

114

As Mars passed the flag, he looked down. It was in remarkable condition for something that was almost a hundred forty years old and that had been carried in a bloody battle. Mars felt real regret at not feeling well enough to pay attention to the flag's story, but he was past the point of having a choice about going or staying.

As they returned to the upper level of the building, Chris took his hand, then looked up at Mars, startled. "Dad! Your hand is all cold and clammy."

Mars squeezed Chris's hand. "Pretty much how I feel all over. Sorry to take you away. That was interesting. . . ."

"It was just about over, anyway. I want to ask about what the number fifty-eight on the flag meant. But I can find out later. Can we come back when you feel better?"

"Absolutely," Mars said.

Mars knew as soon as they left the building that his ordeal was far from over. The snow was now heavy, and the wind was picking up. Getting back to Minneapolis would be hard going. Chris volunteered to clear the car off, and Mars didn't argue. He got into the car and turned the heat up. By the time they reached the freeway to head west, the back window had snowed over again.

Trying to combat wooziness, Mars rocked back and forth behind the wheel as the car crept along the freeway. Traffic had narrowed to two lanes and the thick, heavy snow had made the road slick as spit. He blew air to ease his tension. He could feel Chris watching him.

"Maybe we should go to the doctor first, Dad."

Mars had been thinking more or less the same thing. But the idea of finding a place to park at Hennepin County Medical Center, signing in through the ER, then waiting for a doc, was daunting. It probably made more sense to get back to the apartment, lie down for a while, then go to the ER when he'd regained some strength. The right thing to do or not, it was all he had in him to do.

It took them forty-five minutes to get back to the apartment.

So much snow had accumulated in the less than three hours they'd been gone that Chris had to pull hard with two hands to get the outside apartment door open.

Once in, stomping and shaking to clear himself of snow, Mars confronted the final barrier to achieving a horizontal position: two flights of stairs. If he needed any measure of just how sick he felt, it was that he seriously considered just lying down in the front entry hall. As much as anything, it was knowing how that would worry Chris that got him up the stairs.

Walking through the apartment door, he headed straight for his bed, falling down on the bed without removing his parka, boots, or gloves. But within seconds of lying down, his stomach started turning itself inside out and moving up his throat. Pushing himself up, he made a mad dash for the bathroom, getting the toilet lid up and his head over the bowl just in time.

He threw up until there was nothing left to throw up. Then he dry-heaved. He couldn't remember the last time he'd thrown up, but what he did remember was that he usually felt better after throwing up. He looked at himself in the mirror. He still looked awful. And there was something especially demoralizing about throwing up dressed in a parka, boots, and gloves. He pulled off the gloves, kicked off the boots, and stuck his head under the faucet, then toweled down his head. He was beginning to quake with chills, so he left his parka on.

The sense of postvomit well-being he remembered from his youth did not materialize. Within minutes of lying down the pain in his gut became intense and localized. For the first time, rather than just having a generalized gut ache, Mars was conscious that the pain was focused in what Doc D would have described as the lower right quadrant of his abdomen. "Oh, jeez," Mars muttered, an idea forming about what his problem might be.

Chris was at his side immediately. "What, Dad?" Chris put his hand on Mars's forehead. The contrast between Chris's hand—which felt like ice—and Mars's burning forehead, startled them both. Chris's face turned serious. "I'm gonna call nine-one-one, Dad."

"Wait," Mars said, as he tried to gather his thoughts to tell Chris why not to do that. In a state of rapidly advancing mental confusion, reasons were beyond Mars's capabilities.

His last conscious memory was of a ringing phone.

CHAPTER

11

Evelyn Rau sat in a chair at the foot of the hospital bed, feet up on the bed frame.

She felt uneasy about being able to observe Mars so closely while he was unconscious. He was the most private person she knew, and there wasn't any question he'd be uncomfortable being observed under these circumstances.

The past few hours had intertwined their lives in a way neither would have chosen. Not that either had a choice.

When she'd called Mars's apartment, Chris's voice had been terror filled. She couldn't have left a ten-year-old boy on his own to cope with a seriously ill father in the midst of a snowstorm now being described as "the storm of the century."

The ambulance had been in front of Mars's apartment as she'd pulled up. She'd never met Chris. Without saying as much, Mars had made it clear he didn't involve women he was seeing in his son's life. But Evelyn would have recognized Chris under any circumstances. The resemblance between father and son had as much to do with expression and movement as it did with physical similarities. After spending most of the past twenty-four hours with Chris, the similarities went even deeper. Mars's soul was in this kid.

Chris rode in the ambulance with Mars. Evelyn had followed

in the car, grateful for the path the ambulance plowed ahead of her. The Subaru had all-wheel drive, but the snow was so deep that without the ambulance running interference she would have been in serious danger of getting hung up.

Chris had given such a complete medical history of Mars's problems over the past week that the ER docs had sent Mars to the operating room as soon as the blood test results showed a sky-high white cell count. While Mars was in surgery for an emergency appendectomy, Chris and Evelyn had sat together in the OR waiting room. Not sure it was the thing to do with a ten-year-old boy, Evelyn had taken Chris's hand. He'd immediately moved closer to her, reaching for her other hand. Evelyn's heart sank. She was pretty sure that falling in love with an emotionally unavailable man's son would be a big mistake.

Three other people could have been there for Chris under these circumstances: his mother, his aunt Gwen, and Mars's partner, Nettie. But Denise and Gwen were out of town and Nettie wasn't answering her phone. Without the storm, Denise and Gwen could have been back in town in a couple of hours. With the storm, attempting to get back to the Twin Cities would be a life-threatening enterprise.

Chris and Evelyn talked about calling Denise. Chris thought about it carefully.

"I think we should wait till Dad's out of surgery," Chris said. "If we call before we know anything, Mom will just worry. And it'll be worse because she's stuck in the storm."

Evelyn agreed, so the two of them settled in to wait out the surgery. They had cheeseburgers in the hospital cafeteria, Evelyn read, and they talked about movies they'd seen. It was surprising to Evelyn that Chris did not question her presence. Chris probably knew less about her than she had known about Chris. She decided that Chris's implicit trust in his father was automatically transferred to anyone Mars had considered a friend.

After three hours, Chris, exhausted by the tension of his dad's emergency, fell asleep. Evelyn stretched out on the opposite couch, planning to sleep, but instead her mind churned the circumstances of the past couple years that led to her being in a hospital waiting room with Mars Bahr's son.

It had begun when she'd seen a young woman and a man on the Father Hennepin Bluffs on the Mississippi nearly two years earlier—no, it really started before that. It had begun when, as a disillusioned graduate student in English literature, she'd allowed herself to slide into an abusive relationship with a guy named Gary Sehen. Sehen, who'd presented himself as a struggling college student, had been seductively kind—and, Evelyn had thought, refreshingly free of the academic bullshit that had been weighing on her soul in graduate school. But Sehen's real hook in Evelyn had been his true vocation as a small-time drug dealer who provided her with easy access to amphetamines. It was a long time before she realized that Sehen's interest in her had been as someone he'd recognized as emotionally vulnerable and as someone who had natural access to a strong market for his products.

It was months after she'd taken up with Gary Sehen, and long after she'd moved beyond amphetamines and into serious addiction, that she'd been on the Father Hennepin Bluffs to do a drug deal. She'd watched a couple walk from their car to the trails on the bluffs. Three days later, she'd seen the girl's picture in the *Star-Tribune*. The girl had been found dead on the bluffs.

It was information that Evelyn had stored mentally on the chance it would be useful to her at some point. That point arrived when Gary had been killed in an altercation with a supplier, and Evelyn had been taken into custody on suspicion of accessory to murder and possession with intent to sell.

She'd sat in a gray-green interrogation room in the Hennepin County Jail waiting to see the homicide detective who'd investigated the death of the girl on the bluffs. When Mars Bahr had walked into the room, she'd felt an immediate sense of connection. She knew without being able to say why that this was somebody who would be part of her life beyond the circumstances that put her in that place at that time.

She would find out later that the county attorney's case against her was weak, and that she probably would have been released without the identification she'd provided in the girl's murder. But she now knew without a doubt that being held and providing evidence was the best thing that could have happened to her. She had taken the only chance she had to get out of the self-destructive cycle that had become her life and get back on track.

Out of jail, she had reconnected with Mars by accident. They'd begun a casual, tentative friendship. There wasn't any man she liked better, but her expectations for the friendship were limited. Limited because of what she understood of Mars's character and because her own future was uncertain. She didn't spend a lot of time worrying about that. She took what came in the friendship at face value. In a few months she'd be in England doing research for her dissertation, and she told herself the time away would either make or break the relationship.

In a state of reminiscence and half sleep, Evelyn was jolted back to reality by the arrival of the surgeon. He was impossibly young and disconcertingly tired. He walked with an arrogant slouch, dropped to the couch next to her, pulling off the green scrub cap on his head. His feet were still covered in green paper slippers.

Evelyn reached over and put her hand on Chris. He wakened immediately, looking frightened.

"Dad?" he said, his eyes darting around the room.

"The doctor, Chris," Evelyn said.

"You're Mrs. Bahr?" the surgeon said.

"Mrs. Bahr is out of town. I'm Evelyn Rau, a friend, and this is Mars's son, Chris."

The surgeon stretched out his hand to Chris. "I'm Dr. Schmekin, Chris. Your dad was one sick puppy."

Chris's eyes got big. "But he's okay now?"

Schmekin nodded slowly, ruffling his hair. Something in the way he did it made Evelyn think the doctor was not unaware of playing a heroic role.

"One nasty-looking appendix. Got it just in time. Had my hand under it as we were taking it out, and the son of a gun busted right in my hand. An hour later, and your dad would have had a tough recovery. As things stand, he should be just fine in a few days. Lucky guy."

Evelyn said, "When will Chris be able to see his dad?"

"Well, he's in recovery now and should be conscious in another two, three hours." He looked out the window. "Not that you're going anywhere, anyway. This is supposed to keep up until morning. God knows how long after that before roads are open again."

Evelyn and Chris had called Denise after talking to the surgeon. There'd been less snow where Denise's parent's lived, and she said they'd start back as soon as the state patrol said Interstate 90 was open to Interstate 35. It was clear she was almost as distressed about a stranger having to take responsibility for her son as she was about Mars's surgery.

They reached Nettie shortly after talking to Denise. Evelyn had met Nettie a couple of times and talked to her frequently on the phone. She'd always felt that Nettie was a little guarded with her. Evelyn wasn't sure if Nettie was jealous of her relationship with Mars or just being protective. Nettie, of course, knew the story of how Mars and Evelyn had met, and Evelyn could understand how Nettie might think Evelyn wasn't a great pal for a cop.

On the phone now, Nettie's voice was cool and sardonic. But around the edges there was real concern—and relief. "I *told* him to go to the doctor," she said, as if being right counted for something. "I'll be there first thing in the morning. Are you okay with Chris? If not, I can probably commandeer an emergency vehicle to pick him up."

"We're fine," Evelyn said. "And short of an emergency vehicle, I don't think you're going to be able to get here in the morning.

122

They're saying it probably won't stop snowing until then. Don't worry about it. I'll hang in until Denise gets back."

"I'll be there," Nettie said.

Mars woke first around three in the morning. Chris was sleeping on the unoccupied bed next to Mars. Evelyn had pulled two chairs together. When the nurse had come in to check Mars's vital signs, Mars said, "Chris?" Evelyn got up quickly and went to his bedside. "He's right here, Mars. He's sleeping." Mars had looked at her without seeing her and gone back to sleep.

"He'll be pretty fuzzy until morning," the nurse whispered as she left.

True to her word, Nettie arrived shortly after 9:00 A.M. Mars had been awake and conscious for almost an hour.

"How did you get here?" Evelyn asked.

"Cross-country skis," Nettie said. "Tough going between my apartment and the snow emergency route, but smooth as silk once I hit Lake Street."

Nettie had made a number of calls to various people about Mars, and between 10:00 A.M. and noon, Evelyn met everyone of any importance in Mars's life. Karen Pogue drove her husband's Lincoln Navigator. "First time the damned car's earned its keep," she said. "You need a ladder to get in and out of it, but I must admit it went through the snow like melted butter."

Chief of Police John Taylor arrived as Karen was leaving. The squad car that had brought him had gotten stuck in the hospital's driveway and was being dug out while the chief was in the hospital. "And you owe me, my friend," the chief said to Mars. "I called the mayor to let her know about your situation, and she wanted a special vehicle to bring her right over. Told her you wouldn't be in shape for visitors for a couple days." The chief looked around at Evelyn, Karen, and Nettie. "I do hope all of you are next of kin, or I lied to the mayor."

Mars grinned weakly. "I'll adopt all of them if it keeps Her Honor at bay."

"Can I give you a lift?" Karen Pogue asked Evelyn. They looked at each other. Evelyn had the same uncertainty about Mars and Karen's relationship that she had about how Nettie felt about Evelyn. Now, with Karen looking at her, Karen's expression friendly, her offer of a ride considerate, Evelyn felt quite certain that Karen's offer was in part motivated by curiosity. Whether the curiosity was motivated by sexual jealousy or just jealousy of someone who shared Mars's time and interests, she couldn't have said.

"Thanks," Evelyn said. "But I'm driving a friend's car. Think I'd better stay around until I can get it back on the road."

"Good luck," Karen said, her voice less friendly.

Denise arrived midafternoon. She greeted Chris and Evelyn, thanking Evelyn effusively before moving to Mars's bedside. Evelyn excused herself, saying she was going to get something to eat, then try to get the car dug out. As she started to go, Chris came up, gave her a hug, and said, "Thanks. I'm really glad you were around."

Evelyn looked over Chris's head at Mars. He held up a hand and mouthed a single word, *Thanks*.

The whole hospital was in holiday mode, with the patient census down in advance of Christmas and with few admissions over the past twenty-four hours due to the storm. Staff were staying on beyond regular shifts and two unshaven doctors were manning the coffee shop grill, serving up free hamburgers to any takers.

An admissions clerk told Evelyn that a plow was expected shortly to clear the driveway from the parking lot to the street. And an hour later, having cleared nearly two feet of snow off the Subaru, Evelyn headed home.

By sundown, Mars was alone and grateful for it. He was tired and with the effect of the general anesthetic almost out of his system, feeling sore. The nurse had roused him from the bed for a hallway stroll, and he'd been startled by the gravity of the pain in his right side.

"It feels," he said to the nurse, "like the doc left a red-hot poker in my gut."

"They try not to do that," the nurse said with an experienced smile. "But who knows. Docs are human like the rest of us. Even if they don't admit it."

Mars woke at around 4:30 A.M. Against orders not to walk alone and in the face of unwelcome pain, he forced himself out of bed and took his IV rack for a walk. He knew the sooner he was active the sooner he'd be out of the hospital. Already the sharpness of the pain was an iota less than it had been the first time he'd walked. But he was dizzy. He walked to within sight of the nursing station, then wheeled the IV rack back to bed.

He dreaded lying in the bed with nothing to do, but he was irrevocably awake. He went into the closet where his clothes had been stashed and went through his jacket pockets. He found the book he'd bought Chris at the Historical Society and the piece of paper on which was written the number they'd found on Frank Beck's arm.

The number was a find. The idea of lying in bed and doing simple ciphering had real appeal. The only problem was, he needed a pen and paper. He supposed he could push the light hooked on his bed and ask a nurse, but that seemed unnecessarily demanding. Instead he shuffled out again with his IV rack and back to the nursing station.

Expecting a lecture, he was relieved to find the station empty. He committed an act of petty larceny and returned to his bed. It took fifteen minutes of heavy breathing once back in bed until he was ready to get to work.

He began by writing out the letters of the alphabet and corresponding numbers underneath each letter:

A B C D E F G H I J K L M N O P Q R S T U V W X Y Z
1 2 3 4 5 6 7 8 9 10 11 12 13 14 15 16 17 18 19 20 21 22 23 24 25 26

That done, he copied out the numbers from Beck's arm, writing under each number the corresponding letter of the alphabet:

2 8 2 2 1 7 3 6 3 1 9 5 8

b h b b a g c f c a i e h

"Bhbbagseefseeaie," Mars said out loud, looking at what he'd written. Then, muttering, "Not a big help." He looked at the numbers again, deciding to combine them in blocks of two:

28 22 17 36 31 95 8

The problem with this strategy was immediately obvious. There were only twenty-six letters in the alphabet and four of the paired numbers were higher than twenty-six. Mars was beginning to get a sense of the complexity of the problem Gerry Weiler had described. He also remembered Weiler saying that not all of the numbers would necessarily correspond to a letter of the alphabet. Some could, some might not. The code might be a mixed message of words and numbers, and some of the words might be abbreviations or incomplete words. So he left the numbers that were higher than twenty-six as numbers and wrote out letters for the numbers below twenty-six:

28 22 17 36 31 95 8
28 v q 36 31 95 h

If there were a message in that combination of numbers and letters, Mars would need another strategy for deciphering it. It was as nonsensical as the original number. Mars lay back on the stiff hospital pillow. Twenty minutes of not-very-deep thinking had pretty much tired him out.

126

He woke when an aide brought in a breakfast that could make a person sick on sight. A pale bowl of imitation oatmeal, an anemic glass of fake orange juice, and a small metal carafe of coffee. What he really wanted was a Coca-Cola. But he knew better than to ask. He also knew that failing to eat anything might make him a less credible candidate for discharge, so he forced himself out of the bed and into the bathroom, balancing his breakfast tray precariously as he wheeled the IV rack. In the bathroom, he carefully considered what would be a believable amount of food for him to have eaten. He dumped that amount into the toilet and flushed, then wheeled himself back to bed.

"Good that you were able to eat," the nurse said, giving him a smile. "The lab tech will be up shortly. The doctor left orders to remove your IV once you'd eaten solids."

"Alleluia," Mars said.

With the IV out, working on deciphering would have been easier. But Mars quickly became a captive audience to a steady stream of visitors. Only Evelyn and Chris didn't show up. Evelyn didn't come because she knew Mars well enough to know that receiving visitors garbed in a hospital gown wasn't something he'd appreciate. Denise kept Chris at home, not being keen on driving any more than necessary.

Mars was contemplating his dinner tray when a solitary figure appeared in the doorway of his room. "I didn't come to see you," Doc D said, "I came for the singular pleasure of lighting up in a hospital room."

"You wouldn't dare," Mars said.

"Just watch me." Doc D pulled up a chair and sat bedside. He lit a cigarette, then peered over the bed at Mars's tray.

"My God," Doc D said. "Have they taken to putting lab specimens on patient dinner trays?"

"They call it Swiss steak," Mars said.

"I can't believe that fools anybody. It's clearly a macerated piece of your own liver, removed surreptitiously during surgery. Damn perverse, I call it."

"What I'd really like is a Coke, but there aren't any on offer. In fact, *I'd eat* a macerated piece of my own liver for a Coke." Mars peered down at Doc D. "I'll make a deal with you. I won't turn you in to the head nurse for smoking if you go downstairs and get me a can of Coke."

"Let me finish this cigarette, and we've got a deal."

With Coke and cigarette in hand, Mars and Doc D sat in companionable silence for a while. Then Doc D said, "Why didn't you call me when you got sick? You know how irregular my life is. It wouldn't have been an inconvenience."

Mars thought about it. He shook his head, perplexed. "Do you know, it never occurred to me. I don't think of you in terms of living patients. Would you actually know what to do if someone who was still breathing asked you for medical advice?"

"Absolutely," Doc D said. "I'd stretch you out on one of the autopsy tables, get out the saw, and split you open stem to stem."

After Doc D and the smoke had cleared out, Mars picked up the cipher papers. He wasn't sleepy, but the day's social activities had worn down his energy. The frustration of his earlier efforts quickly returned. Putting the papers aside, he picked up the book he'd bought for Chris at the historical society, *The Last Full Measure: The Life and Death of the First Minnesota Volunteers*. He began reading with no deep interest, but in minutes the powerful story—of which he'd heard pieces at the History Center just two days earlier—kept him reading.

What struck Mars immediately was the commitment held by the men who became the First Minnesota Volunteers. They fought not because they'd been drafted but because of their belief in the abstract value of a federal union. And this from a bunch of guys who lived in a place that had only achieved statehood three years before the start of the Civil War. Mars wondered if there would be anything in the new millennium that would move people to put their lives on the line with such a sense of purpose and selflessness.

Out of curiosity, Mars flipped back to the index to see if there was anything about Frank Beck's ancestor. Finding the name in the index, Mars went to the pages listed. Frank Beck's great-great-grandfather, Herman Beck, had been one of the few lucky members of the First Minnesota at Gettysburg in July 1 of 1863. He'd survived the three-day battle.

As he turned pages back to where he'd stopped reading, he came across a photograph of the flag he and Chris had seen at the Historical Society. Standing in front of the flag was the man who had captured it on the third day of the Battle of Gettysburg. The photo caption read: "Pvt. Marshall Sherman with the colors of the Twenty-eighth Virginia, which he captured during General Pickett's Charge at Gettysburg. He was awarded the Medal of Honor for the feat."

Sherman was a handsome man—dark-haired, square-jawed, mustachioed. His arms were folded across the jacket of his Union uniform. Even from the distance of nearly a hundred forty years, you could feel Sherman's satisfaction at his accomplishment. Mars went back to the index and checked for other Sherman entries. He found that, like Beck's ancestor, Sherman had been among the chosen few. He had survived the Battle of Gettysburg. But his luck had run out at Petersburg, Virginia, where he'd lost a leg in action at Deep Bottom. He'd returned to St. Paul after Deep Bottom to sell insurance and operate a boardinghouse. He never married.

Mars stared at Sherman's picture. It reminded him of the photo of Herman Beck in Joey Beck's family genealogy album. And it reminded him of something else: that the Wisconsin hanging victim had been found in an old uniform. That he'd been described as a reenactor. For the first time the word made sense to Mars. There was a small but active group of people for whom Civil War reenactments were a life's passion. Was it possible that the Wisconsin victim had worn the uniform of the First Minnesota? That he, like Frank Beck, had a connection to the First Minnesota?

The book closed with a quote from then President Calvin Coolidge: "By holding the Confederate forces in check until other reserves came up, [the First Minnesota] probably saved the Union army from defeat . . . So far as human judgment can determine . . . the First Minnesota are entitled to rank among the saviors of their country."

Mars dropped the book to his chest. His imagination spun with images of the First Minnesota. He felt genuine anger that this story was not part of every Minnesota school child's education. Kids loved heroism. Here it was, in spades, and the story was untold.

Adding the emotion of the story to physical exhaustion finally brought Mars to sleep. The book slid from his chest into the blankets, then to the floor with a slap. The noise wakened Mars momentarily, but his sleep had been so deep that it quickly drew him back.

It was a single phrase that abruptly wakened him. His heart pounded and he was sweating. He strained for meaning in the words, "Twenty-eighth Virginia," which reverberated from his subconscious mind into consciousness.

He swung his feet out of the bed, ignoring the sharp shift of the red-hot poker as he did so. He found the book on the floor, looked through it quickly, then searched for the cipher papers. His finger traced down over his various attempts at deciphering Beck's numbers until he came to the final effort where he'd grouped the numbers in pairs, then translated numbers under twenty-six to letters:

28   v   q   36   31   95   h

There it was: *28 v.*

Rapidly Mars scanned the remaining two letters and three paired numbers. Nothing. He looked back to the original number. And saw it right away:

```
28  22  1  7  3  6  3  1  9  5  8
28   V  A
```

Twenty-eighth Virginia. And Frank Beck's ancestor had been a member of the regiment that had captured the colors of the Twenty-eighth Virginia at Gettysburg. Was it just coincidence that five of the numbers on Frank Beck's arm could be deciphered to spell out 28 VA? Mars knew that it wasn't enough on its own, coincidence or not. He went back to the remaining numbers. For the first five numbers spelling 28 VA to have significance, he had to find a related meaning in the final eight numbers.

His finger traced back and forth. Nothing. He dropped the pages and lay back on the bed, closing his eyes. Another approach occurred to him. He went to the section of *The Last Full Measure* that covered the Battle of Gettysburg. Rifling through the pages he wrote down any number that seemed significant. July 1–3, 1863, the dates of the battle. July 3, 1863, the date of the battle when the flag had been captured. Two hundred sixty-two for the number of men in the ranks of the First Minnesota on July 2 when the First Minnesota had been successful against Confederate troops that were six times the First Minnesota's strength.

Then he went back to the remaining numbers of the cipher for anything that fit. He tried for July: 10(J) 21(u) 12(l) 25(y). Comparing those numbers to Beck's numbers, he found nothing—until he considered that July could also be written as 7.

The numbers popped. He wrote it out again:

```
28   221        7 363      1   9   5   8
28   VA    July 3, (18) 63  ?   ?   ?   ?
```

Mars knew he was now well beyond the realm of coincidence. He had nine of the thirteen numbers on Frank Beck's arm. He spent another half hour searching *The Last Full Measure* for anything that would link the final four numbers. He looked for 1, he looked for *a,* he looked for 19, he looked for *s*—but the numbers didn't give anything up.

His mind was too stimulated to shut down. What could Frank Beck's ancestor have done at the Battle of Gettysburg that would cause someone—at least four generations later—to commit murder? More to the point, what happened on the third day of the Battle of Gettysburg? While the First Minnesota had played a heroic role on the second day of the Battle, the cipher noted July 3, not July 2. He needed to talk to all the Becks, to push for more details about their ancestor and any connection Frank Beck might have had—however tenuous—to the family's Civil War history.

He may have dozed for a few minutes before other ideas pushed into his consciousness. They were jumbled, but Mars knew his own thought processes well enough to know that he needed to pay attention to nagging half thoughts that on the surface didn't have much meaning. He wrote out the vague images: "The information desk attendant at the Historical Society who'd said something about the Twenty-eighth Virginia's flag and 'controversy.'

"The guide who'd mentioned"—was he remembering this right?—"a battle between Minnesota and Virginia." Mars thought the reference had been to a present-day battle. Maybe it had just been a remark about the third day at Gettysburg.

There was something else. Mars could feel it niggling at his brain. He walked himself through their time at the Historical Society, right up to the time he and Chris had left. He'd promised Chris they'd go back . . .

That was it. Chris had wanted to check the meaning of a number on the flag. *What was the number?* Mars concentrated hard on the moments after they'd left the group. Chris had said—? Then it came. Chris had said, "I want to find out what the number fifty-eight means." Mars didn't have to look at his cipher papers to remind himself that two of the remaining four unidentified numbers were five and eight.

It's the flag, stupid.

And if Gaylord Rowe, the Wisconsin hanging victim with numbers on his arm, had died in the uniform of the First Minnesota Volunteers, it was likely that his death, too, was connected to the third day of the Battle of Gettysburg and the captured flag.

The question was, *why?* What had these two men—with no connection other than the possibility of two ancestors who'd fought in a battle 136 years earlier—done to attract mortal vengeance? There must have been hundreds of First Minnesota Volunteers who'd fought on the third day of the Battle of Gettysburg. And how many descendents of those soldiers, four, five generations later?

That was the question that got Mars out of his hospital bed in the middle of the night.

CHAPTER

12

Nettie was silent after picking Mars up at the hospital entrance. They drove through the brilliantly cold, black night, the road framed on either side by huge drifts of snow. The city was motionless, the only moving things in sight were slowly drifting columns of steam rising from rooftops and chimneys. The night sky was cloudless, each star solitary and hard, the moon just beginning its drop toward the horizon.

Mars broke their impasse. "What's the temperature?"

Nettie made him wait while she turned left on Sixth Street to head east toward St. Paul. The turn signal clicked noisily, the car's heater blasted hot, stale air. Without looking at him, she said, "About fifty degrees below what it should be for any sane person to be out and about at two-thirty in the morning."

They drove on to the Interstate 94 entrance. "Which would be about fifteen degrees below zero?" he asked.

"Close enough," Nettie said. After they were on the interstate, she said, "You owe Kiffenburger, big-time. Me too. And I don't really understand why this couldn't wait until morning— or, better yet, until you got a legal discharge from the hospital."

"Leaving against medical advice is not illegal. It's a bureaucratic device. They would have discharged me in the morning, anyway. And maybe *it* could wait, but *I* can't."

"Tell me again what this is about. I'm not real good at remembering things from middle-of-the-night phone calls."

"I've made some progress decoding nine of the thirteen numbers on Beck's arm. I'm reasonably sure those numbers are related to something that happened on the third day of the Battle of Gettysburg. And if we can confirm that the Wisconsin hanging victim was wearing the uniform of the First Minnesota, I think we've got a strong connection between the two murders. I need you to track down Rowe's sister. I've been in a passive mode on tracking her down—but if we've got two related murders, this is a bigger case than where we started."

Mars stopped, reluctant to say everything he was thinking. Nettie had been dubious about the investigation from the get-go. If he told her that Frank Beck had died only because he had an ancestor who'd fought with the First Minnesota Volunteers on the third day of the Battle of Gettysburg, she'd think Mars had flipped into post-op hallucinations. The logical conclusion that followed that line of reasoning required an even bigger leap of faith: if Beck had died because his ancestor had a connection to maybe ninety seconds of action on that July afternoon 137 years ago, when a Confederate regimental flag had been captured by the First Minnesota Volunteers, anyone with the same connection—whatever it was—could be at risk.

He wasn't ready to say that out loud. Not even to Nettie. So all he said was, "We can't wait for people to get back to us. So if you could start on Moberg first thing in the morning . . ."

Nettie sighed. "It *is* tomorrow morning, Mars. When I get to tracking down the dead guy's sister in Iowa is going to depend on when we finish at the History Center. How long is that gonna be?"

"I'm pretty sure two of the remaining four numbers are on a flag Chris and I saw there on Saturday. So I want to check to be sure—and to ask what they mean. The other numbers seem connected to Gettysburg, but they don't get me close to the perp's motive. There's absolutely nothing to suggest Beck had any connection to that battle other than a relative four generations back. So basically that's it. I need to see the flag, confirm that the numbers five and eight are on the flag, and—hopefully—find out if there's any connection between those two numbers and our victims. If we can get anything that explains what the last two numbers—one and nine—mean, that would be a bonus."

Nettie was visibly thinking hard. "Okay," she said. "I'll give you the benefit of the doubt and say what you've found out about the numbers is important to the case. That still doesn't explain why we have to get the State Director of Capitol Facilities out of bed in the middle night to let us into the History Center."

Mars wasn't ready to answer that question. That his beleaguered gut told him it was urgent wasn't going to cut it even with Nettie.

Burt Kiffenburger was visible through the windows of the entry hall at the History Center as Nettie and Mars pulled into the parking lot. A uniformed guard a fraction of Kiffenburger's size was next to him. This observation did not mean the guard was small. Kiffenburger was a giant of a man, standing nearly seven feet tall, weighing close to three hundred pounds. Kiffenburger and Mars had worked together years earlier when Kiffenburger had been on the Minneapolis police force. Kiffenburger was a smart guy who took an opportunity when the state facilities security job opened up. And he was one of the few detectives on the force who had the temperament and ability to successfully make the transition from cop to administrator.

Kiffenburger grinned as the guard opened the door for Mars and Nettie. "We must stop meeting like this," he said, holding his hand out to Mars. Kiff, as he was inevitably called, was renowned for speaking in clichés.

Mars shook Kiffenburger's hand, then introduced Nettie. Kiffenburger's attention immediately zeroed in on Nettie. He was also renowned for being a ladies man.

"A pleasure," he said, holding on to Nettie's hand a moment too long. "And your reputation precedes you. The gal who's gonna change investigative techniques, is what I hear."

Nettie pulled her hand back, looking like she wanted to crawl out of her skin.

Kiffenburger turned to Mars. "And what I heard about you is that you're under the weather. What're you doin' running around town in the middle of the night?"

"He's AWOL from the hospital, is what he is," Nettie said.

"I'm fine," Mars said. "A little light-headed, but I feel a heck of a lot better than when I was here Saturday."

"Look," Kiffenburger said, "I promised the History Center's director we wouldn't go down to the flag until she gets here. Why don't you brief me on what's going on while we wait." He made a motion to the guard, who opened the doors to the center's cafeteria. "Asked them to put the coffeepot on. Let's sit here while we wait for Linda."

Without Coca-Cola on offer, Mars sipped tentatively at the steaming coffee. "Explain to me," he said, "why the History Center director thinks she has to be here for this."

Kiffenburger shook his head. "Linda VanCleve takes a very proprietary view of the center. And just now, the flag you wanna see is maybe the most valuable artifact the center has. In fact, I met with Linda couple days ago. She's asking for extra security measures to protect the flag. That's part of why I want to hear your story, to see if there's anything you know that justifies extra security."

Mars's brow furrowed. "Why would the flag be so valuable?"

"I only know what Linda's told me. First off, Confederate flag values have been skyrocketing over the past few years. Linda said there's even been a boom in counterfeit flags. And this particular flag, captured at what many people consider to be the most historic moment of the Civil War, apparently has particular interest. Which on its own would probably justify special security. What's gotten Linda all hot and bothered is a flap between Minnesota and Virginia over possession of the flag. Virginia says we hold the flag illegally. Huge movement out there about getting the flag back. Linda's concerned a bunch of guys from Virginia may attempt a raid." Kiffenburger chuckled. "Probably thinks the two of you are wolves in sheep's clothing. I'll bet money she'll ask to see your badges before we go down." Kiffenburger took a big gulp of the boiling coffee. "So. Spill the beans. Why do you wanna see the flag?"

What Kiffenburger had said raised hair on the back of Mars's neck. Kiffenburger had described a situation that raised strong emotions. Maybe emotions strong enough to motivate someone to commit murder? What Mars still couldn't see was how Frank Beck would get caught in those emotions.

Through the cafeteria windows, Kiffenburger saw the guard opening the front entrance door as a small woman with a determined walk came in. "Hold on a minute," Kiffenburger said. "Looks like the director has arrived. Simpler to tell the story once."

Linda VanCleve looked at Mars and Nettie as she said, "What's going on, Kiff?" She had medium-length blond hair that fell into an elegant order as she pulled the knit wool cap off her head.

"Your favorite subject, Linda. The Twenty-eighth Virginia's flag. This is Marshall Bahr, special detective in the Homicide Division, Minneapolis PD, and his partner, Nettie Frisch."

VanCleve unzipped a huge parka. "I don't mean to be rude, but we'll be going into the center's most secure area. Do you have identification?"

Kiffenburger guffawed. "You just won me money, Linda."

VanCleve ignored Kiffenburger, but looked closely at Mars's

and Nettie's badges. "Okay. But I'm going to want you to sign our standard access agreement . . ."

Kiffenburger said, "Linda, Mars was just about to go over the circumstances of a homicide investigation that he thinks may be linked to the flag. Probably helpful all around if he does that before you go downstairs."

"Hold on," VanCleve said. Then she walked away, coming back with a cup of coffee. "Let's hear it," she said, sitting down. She had not smiled since arriving.

Mars began with a brief description of Frank Beck's suicide and of the numbers on Beck's arm. He didn't get any further when VanCleve said, "Let me see the numbers."

Mars pulled his jacket off the back of the chair, reached inside a pocket, and pulled out his cipher papers. He started with the number on Beck's arm, then talked them through his deductions regarding the meaning of the eleven numbers. Linda VanCleve's concentration deepened as she listened. As he explained 58, he could see that she was fully engaged in what he was saying.

"You're right in remembering that one of the numbers on the flag is fifty-eight," she said. "It's a stenciled number, put on the flag sometime in the 1860s, by the war department, based on their numbering system for captured flags. The flag was returned to the war department at some point, although exactly when is a subject of some disagreement. You're probably aware that a group in Virginia is contending that someone in Minnesota—most likely Marshall Sherman, the man who captured the flag on the third day of Gettysburg—borrowed the flag from the war department for ceremonial purposes and failed to return it." She looked around the table with a steely expression. "We have a fully developed legal, analytical"—her eyes narrowed as she fixed each of them in turn with a compelling stare—"and *moral* argument against Virginia's claims. But feelings run strong. Which is why I've asked Kiff for extra security."

Mars said, "What I don't have a good handle on is how my victim may have become a target for someone who has an interest in the flag. I've not found anything to suggest he was active in Civil War historical activities in general—or with the First Minnesota in particular, other than being the descendent of a member of the First Minnesota. Do you think any of the Virginians involved in this dispute might go so far as to murder someone, provided we *can* establish our victim's connection to the flag?"

VanCleve didn't answer right away. When she spoke, Mars was aware that she was balancing strong feelings against a sense of fairness. And maybe a historian's commitment to accuracy.

"I'm not the Historical Society's Civil War expert. There are any number of people I could put you in touch with that could better answer that question." She paused again. Then carefully, deliberately, she said, "I will tell you this. What I know of the passions associated with the Civil War—well, I just don't know of any more deeply held emotions. At the same time, the Civil War enthusiasts I have met are—without exception—reasonable people. More than that, I'd say they're honorable people. And I'm talking about both sides of the war. Those whose allegiance is to the Union as well as the loyalists on the Confederate side. The reenactors are the most active group, of course, and I've met several of the reenactors, including a number from the Twenty-eighth Virginia. They were here just over ten years ago, for a ceremony honoring the hundred twenty-fifth anniversary of the Battle of Gettysburg. The flap about the flag really wasn't a big issue then. They all wanted to see the flag, of course, but there weren't any of them that seemed anything less than trustworthy. Maybe a little nutty about the Civil War, but they care as much about history—about the integrity of *historical fact*—as any professional member of our staff."

"So you wouldn't expect anyone you know who's associated with this issue to be involved in a murder?"

VanCleve shook her head. "Most definitely not anyone I've met."

Mars said, "If they're trustworthy, why are you asking for extra security for the flag?"

"The issue is getting a lot of attention in Virginia. And, from what I understand, there are going to be some major newspaper articles in papers all over in coming months. The people in Virginia who have raised this issue *are* reasonable—whether I agree with them or not. But the issue itself has drawn the attention of other groups and individuals who are not reasonable. We've been told as much by the Twenty-eighth Virginia group that's organized to support the flag's return. ROFers, they're called: Return Our Flag. It's the people who hold rabid personal views about the war—and let me be blunt—racists and antigovernment groups— that concern us."

Mars said, "Do you have names of these individuals—or the groups they're affiliated with?"

"What I can do," VanCleve said, "is give you the names of people we've had contact with in Virginia on this issue. I think they'd be as concerned as you are about the possibility that someone had been murdered because of a connection that person had to the flag."

Kiffenburger rose. "I still have hopes of seeing my bed before dawn." He looked at VanCleve. "Any reason why you need me to ride shotgun from here on out?"

VanCleve shook her head. "No, go on. I can handle things from here. I just hope when the governor asks for your recommendation on the security appropriation we've requested, that you'll bear in mind we may already have a murder associated with the flag."

The storage area where Mars had seen the flag the previous Saturday felt ominous in the middle of the night. It shouldn't have been different from Saturday. Being underground, the light source was the same. Mars decided the heavy foreboding he was feeling was the product of his own expectations about seeing the flag now that he knew it might be connected to a murder. That, and the general sense of anxiety that had risen from his wounded gut as soon as he'd made the connection between Beck's death and the numbers on Beck's arm. The anxiety he felt now was heightened by the real possibility that more than one death was tied to the flag. And beyond that, the possibility that more people could be at risk because of an association with the flag they didn't even know existed.

VanCleve signaled the guard to unlock the case in which the flag was held. They all drew closer as the drawer pulled open. With or without a contemporary link to tragedy, the flag inspired awe. It was in remarkable shape, given its age and that it had been a battle flag. With the exception of a few rifts in the fabric and stains—bloodstains?—its red field looked solid.

And there it was, in the upper left-hand corner, in black-stenciled numbers: 58.

The flag's red field was bordered with a whitish-colored hem. The field was crossed with a white-bordered blue cross, thirteen white stars within the blue of the cross. To the left of the cross's center were the white letters: 28th. To the right of the cross's center were the white letters: Va. Infy. Mars did a quick mental calculation to see if the letters *Infy,* which he took to be an abbreviation of the word *infantry,* connected to the missing cipher numbers 1 and 9. His mental comparison didn't establish any relationship.

Linda VanCleve's voice, affectionate and respectful, softly recited the flag's physical statistics: "The field of the flag is a red wool bunting. The St. Andrew's Cross is dark blue wool bunting. If I'm remembering correctly, the wool bunting used in this flag was issued first in 1862 and was manufactured in England. There was a long-haired breed of sheep in northern England that produced wool that had particularly desirable characteristics for flag bunting. Earlier in the war, silk and cotton flags were used, but it became obvious they weren't sufficiently durable. This bunting has the advantage of being both durable and sufficiently flexible to hang and fly gracefully." Her finger traced over the top of the flag's case. "The border on the flag is also wool bunting. The lettering that you see has been painted directly onto the bunting."

Nettie stepped forward, bringing her face close to the flag's case. She looked up at VanCleve. "Is it possible to remove the case so I can feel the fabric?"

VanCleve's expression fell in horror. "Absolutely not," she said. "The case is opened only under specially controlled conditions—and it's never touched by human hands. When we have to handle the flag, we wear cotton gloves."

Nettie turned back to Mars. "It's hard to say without feeling the fabric. But Mars, does it look familiar to you?"

Mars stepped closer to the flag case. As he stared, Nettie said, "Like the fabric in Beck's noose?"

They sat in VanCleve's office until dawn. With the basic facts of Beck's murder now clearly linked to the flag, Mars explained to Nettie and Van Cleve the need to identify living descendents of First Minnesota volunteers who'd fought at Gettysburg. He was relieved that neither VanCleve nor Nettie viewed the risk Mars had defined as nuts. But VanCleve had other concerns.

"Think about it. There were four hundred and sixteen members of the First Minnesota—counting all ranks—at the Battle of Gettysburg. Let's give ourselves a break and call it four hundred. Assume that of that number, twenty-five percent did not produce offspring prior to or after the Battle, for whatever the reason—death, sterility, whatever. That assumption leaves us with three hundred guys who produced offspring. Let's make another assumption that works in our favor. Let's assume that the average number of offspring produced by that generation—and each of the succeeding four generations—is three. And bear in mind that three is a conservative number until after the Second World War. Then just do the math: three times three hundred is nine hundred," Linda VanCleve ticked the numbers off, counting generations on her fingers. "So. By the time you get to the fifth generation—ostensibly our target victims, although there may still be some fourth-generation descendants around—you're looking at a population—conservatively—of more than seventy thousand descendents. You see the problem?"

Mars leaned forward, elbows on his knees, and rubbed his head with both hands. While it felt great to be rid of the vague feeling of sickness that had plagued him over the past few weeks, there wasn't any question his stamina was limited. Faced with the complex problems of the investigation at hand, what he really needed was a clear head. And for a clear head, he needed sleep.

He sat upright abruptly. "Let's do this. Nettie, I need to split our work on the investigation. I'm going to focus on identifying suspects and doing what we can to prevent future deaths. I need you to take over pinning down the facts of the case that will support a conviction once we have a suspect in hand. Meaning, I need you to follow up on the Wisconsin victim, to keep working on identifying the fabric source on the noose, and doing what you can to find out what our final two numbers—one and nine—mean."

Mars turned to Linda VanCleve. "Anyone on your staff who can serve as a liaison if Nettie has questions about documents that may be helpful on the last two numbers?"

VanCleve nodded. "I'll give you the contact information before you leave."

"What I really need from you," he said, tipping his head at VanCleve, "is your best judgment as to what it would take to identify living descendents of the First Minnesota soldiers who fought at Gettysburg. If there's even a chance we can get that done in a reasonable amount of time—and provided we can establish the Wisconsin victim's link to the First Minnesota—we can try to come up with some financial support from Minneapolis PD and begin a process of notifying jurisdictions where those individuals are resident. Can you get me your best guess in the next twenty-four hours?"

VanCleve nodded, starting to look tired. "I'll get back to you with a time and people estimate before close of business today. The only way to do it is to take a couple of the First Minnesota soldiers and see how long it takes us to get from 1863 to present descendents. I've got three or four top-notch genealogical researchers who'll be in today—I'll get them started on it as soon as they show up. Then I'll extrapolate from what they do today to the current descendent population of the First Minnesota."

Mars gave VanCleve a small smile of appreciation that included implicit recognition that he knew how much he was asking. "And can you get me names of people who'll have a handle on where I can start looking for my suspect?"

VanCleve nodded again. "That'll be easy."

Mars had a hard time staying awake as he and Nettie drove back to Minneapolis.

Nettie said, "Sleep. I'll wake you when we get to your apartment."

"I'm not going to the apartment. I need to get downtown and start making contacts with other jurisdictions, other agencies— what I really need to do is get in touch with the chief. As soon as you confirm our Wisconsin victim, we need the chief to get behind our contacts with other jurisdictions. Without that, I'm just not sure people are going to pay attention. It's what you said before. This time of year—with an investigation that is as bizarre as this one—people just aren't focusing. If the chief makes contacts at his level, we might get this thing off the ground. . . ."

Nettie shook her head. "The chief left yesterday, as soon as the airport opened. Alabama—for the holidays. He won't be back until after New Year's."

Mars groaned. "Geez. I think I even knew he was planning on being out of town. Damnation. This is a big deal. He needs to be involved. . . ."

"Look, Mars," Nettie glanced down at the clock on the dash.

"It's not quite seven o'clock in the morning. You go back to your apartment, shower, change, catch a nap. I'll go downtown and call the chief in Alabama, brief him on what's going on. Give him a couple hours to think through what he can do from Alabama. I'll have him call you at the apartment around noon. You can decide then when to come downtown."

Mars started to protest, but Nettie interrupted him. "Stop being so damned pig-headed about this. You're exhausted, and you're worthless to us if you end up back in the hospital. I'm not saying 'Get some rest' out of consideration. Right now, it's the best thing you can do for the investigation."

He knew she was right.

The apartment seemed like a relic from another century as he opened the front door. It was hard to believe that it had been only three days since he'd been carried out on a gurney. What he'd known then about the case and what he knew now were light-years apart. His blood pressure rose when he thought about the time they'd already lost.

Before taking his parka off he called Denise to tell her he was out of the hospital and doing well. Chris was still sleeping, but Mars promised to get over to the house before Chris and Denise left town for Christmas at Denise's parents. After hanging up with Denise he stared at the phone for a moment. Then he dialed Evelyn's number.

"I'm out," he said when she picked up.

"How do you feel?"

"For somebody who spent two nights in the hospital and last night at the History Center, I feel pretty good. I just wanted to say thanks for hanging in with Chris at the hospital."

"You spent the night at the History Center? What was that about?"

"Look, I need to shower and catch some sleep. Any chance you could pick up some takeout and get over here around noon? I've got no appetite, but I should be eating something if I want to develop some stamina. I can tell you about the History Center while we eat takeout."

"See you at noon."

CHAPTER

13

"Listen to this," Evelyn said.

She was lying on Mars's couch. Mars was at the kitchen table, directly across from Evelyn, working through the files Linda Van-Cleve had given him. It was almost three o'clock in the afternoon and the chief still hadn't called. Mars had called Nettie just after one to ask what was going on. Nettie assured him the chief would call and that it was probably just taking the chief longer to make his contacts. So Mars kept on the files, waiting for the call.

He had been distracted from the paperwork by the opportunity to watch Evelyn without her knowing she was being watched. Evelyn was like Chris in her ability, when seriously interested in something, to concentrate so hard that the rest of the world fell away.

Since they'd first met in an interrogation room on the third floor of the Hennepin County Jail, Mars had been fascinated by the elliptical and complex attractions of the woman now lying on his couch. He had begun with her by being off-balance, something he wasn't used to when dealing with a witness in a murder case. Even at their first meeting when she was bruised, drugged out, and bloodied—she'd been within splattering range of the head wound that had killed her boyfriend—she'd had an unnerving serenity at her core. She'd been *still*—still as in quiet and still, as in motionless. Everything had been in her eyes, and in the small smile that was on her lips more often than not.

In their first few minutes together he'd missed the fact that she was beautiful. It took looking at her awhile to see it. Like trying to find a shot through a camera lens before you've focused, the image sharpening once you take time to find what it is you're looking for. It had been the simplicity of her appearance that had misled him. Straight brown hair, smooth—almost translucent—skin, hazel eyes that went green depending on the light, and fine, well-balanced features. It had been her hands—long, graceful fingers with clean, square-cut nails—that had made him look at her again and consider that she was in fact beautiful. But more than any single physical feature, from the first it had been her intelligence that had caught his attention. The penetrating perception, the sharp wit, the eyes that saw and understood everything.

This afternoon, on his couch, reading, she was dressed in a gray sweatshirt and jeans, her shoes off, her head propped on a folded pillow, an ankle balanced across a raised knee. He liked that she looked good just like that. Liked that when she got up in the morning she washed her face with soap and water. Liked that she bent over, head down by her knees, to brush her hair and that when she straightened up, tossing her head back, her hair fell into a natural, shining order. He liked that from bed to fully dressed took her—at the outside—maybe three minutes.

She'd been reading the news clippings that VanCleve had pulled together for Mars on the controversy between Minnesota and Virginia over the Twenty-eighth Virginia regimental flag. Evelyn's clear, smooth voice read out loud: " 'The battle colors of the Twenty-eighth Virginia were carried by Sgt. John Eakin. Eakin was struck three times by Union fire before dropping the flag. A private raised the flag again but was immediately shot. Then Col. Robert Allen raised the flag—only moments before he was mortally wounded, but not before he passed the flag to John Lee, who stepped up on the wall and waved the colors in the face of enemy fire. The flag's staff was hit by a shot, knocking the flag from Lee's hands. Lee retrieved the flag before he fell wounded, still struggling to keep the colors of the Twenty-eighth Virginia flying.' "

After she'd read the passage, she'd dropped the article to her chest and stretched her legs, raising her heels slightly, then dropping them flat to the bed. "My God," she said, "there's passion for you. I'm not sure there's anything anymore that people care that much about."

"That," Mars had said, "is the question we need to answer."

Evelyn twisted to her side, bending her elbow and resting her head on her right hand as she looked at him. "Tell me how you're going to do that."

Mars stood, walked to the fridge for a Coke, calling back to Evelyn, "You want anything?"

"No. So, tell me. What *is* your strategy for figuring out why the flag would get Frank Beck killed?"

Mars walked back into the living room, dropping down on the bed at a ninety-degree angle from Evelyn, his feet on the floor, his back up against the wall. He picked her feet up, dropping them on his legs. "The first order of business is to be sure that Beck didn't die for the simple reason that he had an ancestor who fought for the First Minnesota on the third day of the Battle of Gettysburg. If that's all it is, we've got big problems. It means that the universe of potential victims is more or less unmanageable. What I'd like to find is something that lets us significantly narrow the potential victim pool. Couple of possibilities there. The most obvious one would be that Frank Beck's ancestor captured the flag. But we know that isn't true. All accounts of the flag's capture are consistent. Marshall Sherman, a private in the First Minnesota Volunteers—"

"*Marshall* Sherman?"

Mars grinned. "No relation. And I don't think anyone ever called him Mars. Anyway, Marshall Sherman captured the flag.

He received the Medal of Honor for the capture. There's some disagreement over the circumstances of the capture, but no disagreement that it was Sherman who captured the flag. So the only possibility left is that Beck's ancestor—Herman Beck—had some link to Sherman we haven't figured out. That's a particularly good possibility because Sherman never married and didn't have any children. If someone today wanted to take revenge against *Sherman's* descendents, they'd be out of luck. Nettie's going over war department records that are on-line at Cornell University, trying to find a link between Herman Beck and Sherman. But we're not kidding ourselves. The kind of records that are available more than one hundred thirty years later aren't going to have much of the personal detail that would show the kind of relationship we're looking for. . . ."

"How about personal correspondence? I'd think the Historical Society would have a fair number of letters, primary documents, from Minnesota soldiers who'd been in the Civil War."

Mars nodded, with a little side glance of appreciation at Evelyn. You wouldn't think a graduate student in English and a homicide detective would have much in common professionally. But this wasn't the first time in discussing an investigation with Evelyn that he found they used similar methodology to do their very different jobs. "It's what a liberal education is all about," Evelyn had said when he'd mentioned to her that he was surprised by how much compatibility there was between how they did things. "Looking at details to reach a larger conclusion, finding relationships between seemingly unconnected facts, moving from the specific to the general, from the general to the specific. . . ."

"Nettie's got Historical Society staff checking that now. So far, nothing."

"What's your backup plan?"

Mars frowned. "Option number two is a real long shot: that Beck had done something to attract the perp's attention."

"Like?"

"That's what's hard to figure out. Maybe making a contribution to the Historical Society or supporting something connected to the First Minnesota Volunteers. Nettie checked both those possibilities out pretty thoroughly with the Historical Society this morning. Nothing there. And besides, neither of those possibilities is consistent with Beck's style. He wasn't a philanthropist and didn't give a crap about anything other than the deal he was involved in at any given moment. Maybe there's something else, something we haven't found yet—but finding whatever it is, *if* it exists, doesn't look real promising right now. When we know more about this other guy who died in Wisconsin, we might find something that matches with Beck. . . ."

Evelyn rolled over on her back, readjusting the pillow under her head. She wiggled her toes, and Mars took hold of her stocking-clad feet, massaging them gently between his hands. "So," she said, "options one and two are in process and not looking very good. What else?"

"Nettie's busting her butt trying to figure out what the final numbers—one and nine—on Beck's arm mean. The other numbers gave us the links to the flag, the third day of the battle and the twenty-eighth Virginia. I'm hoping those last numbers will give us the link to Beck or other victims. And Nettie's got a number of irons in the fire to locate the source of the fabric used in the noose. We find the source, we might be able to find who was accessing the source. So far, nothing on the noose or the last numbers."

"This is really bothering you, isn't it," Evelyn said.

Mars tried to draw a deep breath, but tension tamped down his intake. He continued to rub Evelyn's feet without knowing he was doing it. "I'll relax when I've got a better handle on who's out there we should be worried about. Guess I'm really counting on those last two numbers—one and nine—to tell us what we need to know."

The phone rang. "And there," Mars said, leaning across Evelyn to pick up the phone, "is my other main chance."

Mars could hear the sound of people talking behind the chief's voice on the other end of the line.

"Sorry to interrupt your holiday, sir . . ."

"Apologies all on my side, Marshall. Sorry to interrupt your convalescence."

"I feel great. Especially now that I've gotten a little sleep. Nettie briefed you on what we think we're dealing with?"

"In detail. Want you to know what I've done since I talked with Nettie this morning. . . ."

Mars interrupted. "Just want to make sure you're comfortable proceeding with other jurisdictions before we've confirmed our Wisconsin case. . . ."

"Nailing it down will be useful, but based on what Nettie said, I think we're on pretty solid ground. You've got doubts?"

"No. None. Just wanted to be sure you're aware that there are still questions that have to be answered."

"I appreciate that. But based on what we do know, I think we need to move sooner, rather than later. And remember, all we're asking for at this point is information. We're asking if there have been other hangings. Which is why I've been in touch with five chiefs—Kansas City, Baltimore, Phoenix, Atlanta, and Richmond. I've got good working relationships with all five of them. They'll go the extra mile for us, even this time of year. All five promised to take the lead statewide on checking out hanging deaths. And John Durr at Kansas City is currently head of the National Association of Chiefs of Police. He's gonna follow up at that level. I'm still trying to track down chiefs in Milwaukee, DesMoines, Sioux Falls, and Fargo. Would guess the five-state region is still our prime target area. Lots of descendants will have moved out of the Midwest, but I'm willing to bet the majority are still around Minnesota."

"That's great—any idea on when we can expect to start hearing back?"

"Sooner than if we didn't have these fellas pushing from the top. But not as soon as we'd like. You know the problem, Mars. If

153

there've been hangings where the number is involved, and the deaths weren't investigated as homicides, there may not be any record of the number. It's even possible that the number would get overlooked in a homicide investigation."

"I know. Pure serendipity we made the connection here." The words were barely out of Mars's mouth when he realized they weren't true. They made the connection between Beck's hanging and homicide because Danny Borg had taken the time and trouble to consider that there was more to the death scene than met the eye.

"Something I've been thinking about, Chief. Should we be going public on this yet? My feeling is no—but we've got people at risk. And we don't have a clue who or where they are."

"I had more or less the same thought—and came to the same conclusion. Talked about it with the other chiefs, and they're in agreement. We put out a general notice that there's a killer going around hanging descendents of a Civil War regiment, and we're going to create a general panic. Most folks won't even know if they have relatives who fought in the Civil War, much less with the First Minnesota. What I'm going to say next is gonna sound real cold, but truth is, I think the only way we have of getting this guy is to figure out his method of operation. We go public, he's gonna change his MO. It'll make catching him almost impossible. And like you said, until we've confirmed the connection with the Wisconsin death, there's not enough to go on. Nettie said you're working with the Historical Society to identify the descendent pool?"

"Yeah. I should be hearing back from Linda VanCleve at the History Center anytime now. She wasn't encouraging, but she was going to get me an estimate of man-hours and costs to identify the pool. If we go forward with that, it may cost us some bucks. . . ."

"Uh-huh," the chief said. "Not gonna worry about that now. Comes to that, we should be able to get other jurisdictions to pitch in. Not like we're the only ones at risk here." The chief was quiet again. Then he said, "One other thing. John Durr suggested it, and I agreed. There's a guy from the FBI's Forensic Science Unit out at

Quantico. He's done a lot of work on domestic fringe groups. Knows who's involved in what, how they think. Durr was gonna put in a call and request that Boyle Keegan be sent out to Minneapolis. Got a call back from Durr just before I called you. Keegan'll be in Minneapolis day after tomorrow, Christmas Day."

Mars grimaced. He didn't want to have to waste time and energy managing the investigation with some hotshot from the FBI. But he understood that the chief couldn't turn down assistance from Quantico on a case where this much risk was involved—especially when the risk extended beyond the chief's jurisdiction. And there was always the possibility that Keegan might actually be helpful.

To the chief, Mars said, "I understand."

Mars heard a wave of laughter on the chief's end of the line. The chief said, "Appreciate your making Keegan at home. Think I'd better join the party."

"Right," Mars said. "Sorry to have bothered you. Just thought you should know how this is shaping up."

"Not my party, Mars. I'm comin' back to Minneapolis. Joinin' your party."

Linda VanCleve phoned seconds after Mars had hung up with the chief.

"I've got some rough estimates on what would be involved on our end identifying the First Minnesota's descendent pool."

"Good news or bad?"

"Worse than bad."

Mars winced. "Isn't there any way—"

"If it's okay with you, I'll just talk you through this. But be prepared, it gets complicated . . ."

Mars looked at his watch. "Linda? I hate to ask, but I think you understand how important this is. I was just about to head downtown. Could you meet me at city hall? I'd like to spend some time looking at this and developing some options."

*   *   *

It was after 5:00 P.M. when Mars walked into the squad room. Nettie was hunched over the computer in concentration so deep she didn't hear him come in. Mars tiptoed up behind Nettie, lifting her bottle of Evian water off the desk. He held the bottle over her desk for a moment before bringing it down hard with a resounding slosh. Water spat out of the bottle like a geyser.

Nettie flew off her chair. "You turkey! You scared me half to death. And you've got water all over everything."

"I am *so* sorry," Mars said, grinning.

She stuck her tongue out and gave him a little push. Then she sat back down, twisting back and forth on her chair. "Progress on two fronts."

Mars scooted closer to look at Nettie's computer screen. The screen was dense with small script. "That looks like fun," he said.

Nettie rubbed her eyes with the heels of her palms. "Army records from the Cornell University database. It's god-awful. My big mistake was starting. I don't dare stop for fear that the next file will tell me something worth knowing. The more time I put into it, the less I'm willing to waste that time by quitting. But this isn't what I wanted to tell you about. First off, I got hold of Esther Moberg in Iowa."

Mars held his breath. "And?"

"Her brother was a fifth-generation descendent of the First Minnesota Volunteers."

Mars gulped. "She have any idea about why somebody would have wanted to murder him? Especially any reasons associated with the First Minnesota or the flag?"

Nettie shook her head. "She never considered that he'd been murdered. He'd been depressed since his wife died."

"She say anything about the uniform he was wearing when he hung himself?"

"As it turns out, it was a Civil War–era uniform—which makes it pretty valuable. But it wasn't the ancestor's uniform. The

156

brother had bought it several years back to use in reenactments. Here's what's interesting. She'd talked to her brother on the phone just before she had her hip surgery. He sounded a little more 'up' than usual. She said as much, and he said something exciting might be coming up related to the First Minnesota. She pressed him about it, and he finally told her—in confidence—that he'd been contacted by someone who was interested in doing a documentary about the First Minnesota. Rowe told his sister the person didn't want anyone to get wind of his plans until he had financing in place. . . ."

"Ahhhh," Mars said. "So it could have been the same scenario that we worked out for Beck. The perp figured out what the vic's hot button was and pushed it."

"Exactly. And it could explain the uniform. Rowe might have put the uniform on to meet with the perp. . . ."

"Must have given the perp an extra thrill. The sister never talked to Rowe after the meeting? Do we know if Rowe's death coincides with the timing of the meeting?"

"No to both questions. All I could pin down was that Rowe's last telephone conversation with his sister occurred four days before his body was found. When she found out about the suicide, she figured the meeting wasn't what her brother had been expecting. Kind of like the last light at the end of his tunnel went out. So he hung himself."

Mars sat in silence before saying, "So what we've got is our nightmare scenario. A perpetrator who's killing descendants of the First Minnesota. And we've got zip on identifying who those victims might be."

"That's how it's looking."

"You said you had two things."

"Oh. Right. I've found out some stuff about the fabric on Beck's noose."

"Do tell."

"Come with me." Nettie stood up, stretching as she walked,

arms extended straight up, twisting her wrists. Mars followed her to the lounge, a small, windowless room populated by the kind of furniture you find curbside on garbage pickup days. A steel-tube-frame couch with cracked plastic cushions, a matching chair, a wobbly-legged table, couple of lamps, and an old black-and-white television set sitting on a badly dented file cabinet.

There had been an addition to the room since Mars had left. Taped on the wall were three large posters of sheep. A poster of rare English sheep breeds, a poster of major English sheep breeds, and a map of England with little sheep symbols dotting the map showing where in England various breeds were raised.

"Are you interested in cool coincidences?" Nettie asked.

"Those are a few of my favorite things," Mars said.

"Julie Andrews, singing to the Von Trapp kids during a thunderstorm in *The Sound of Music*."

Mars stared at her blankly.

"You just used a movie line, Mars. Wake up."

"I don't think I've ever seen *The Sound of Music*. I *hope* I've never seen *The Sound of Music*."

"You've really led a sheltered life. It's an okay movie. Except for a scene where a nun who looks like Barbara Bush in a habit sings 'Climb Every Mountain.' "

"Skip the promo for *The Sound of Music* and tell me about the coincidences."

"Coinc*idence,* to be precise. I've been doing a lot of research on the Internet on sheep breeds and wool production—I should warn you. I sent Chris some sheep jokes. I looked at a couple and thought they were okay. Turns out they were pretty bad."

"Thanks a lot."

"Oh, my God. They were so awful. Anyway—apart from the jokes—one of the things I found was the origin of the surname Sherman."

"As in, Marshall Sherman?"

"Exactly."

"And . . ."

"And it comes from the word *shear*, as in 'shear sheep.' It was an occupational surname for people who sheared sheep."

"How this represents a significant coincidence escapes me."

"I should probably tell you about the sheep first."

"Start with where you got the posters."

"Like I said, I was searching on-line for sources of information about wool production and found a guy with the British Wool Manufacturers' Association. Told him what I was looking for, and he sent me these. Better yet, I think there's a good chance he's going to be able to link the fabric in the noose to a specific farm in Yorkshire, England, that's been producing wool since the sixteenth century—including wool that was used by the Army of Northern Virginia for flags and uniforms. The Twenty-eighth Virginia—if you haven't already figured it out, was a regiment in the Army of Northern Virginia."

Mars sat down, propping his feet on the table in front of the couch. "How's he gonna do that?"

"I air-expressed a piece of the noose fabric to him. They're going to do a chemical and microscopic analysis of the fabric ASAP—which may not be until next week, what with the holidays and all. He said some key staffers are out until then." Nettie sat down next to Mars. "But the really extraordinary thing is how they know about this sheep farm in Yorkshire. Mr. Janes—that's my contact at the BWMA, Piers David Janes—was involved in research several years ago with a British museum that was putting together an exhibit on British naval history. They were researching an English frigate that was sunk off the coast of Massachusetts during the Revolutionary War. Janes said sheep wool was mixed with tar to caulk the hulls of English ships during the period this ship was built. They knew—because the Yorkshire farm had records going back to the sixteenth century—that the ship they were looking for would have caulking that contained wool from the sheep on that farm. Herdwick sheep," Nettie said, getting up and moving to the posters on the wall.

She pointed to a sheep on the rare breeds poster, "This guy," she said. "Handsome devil, wouldn't you say?"

Mars rose, moving next to her. A serious-minded critter stared back at them, horns curled over his ears, prodigious amounts of long, grayish white wool hanging all over his body, with the exception of the face and below the ankles—or whatever you called sheep's ankles.

They continued standing in front of the posters as Nettie said, "To confirm that the sunken frigate was the ship they were looking for, they separated the wool fibers from the tar and analyzed them. As it happens, most wool produced by sheep is indistinguishable from one breed to the next—but the Herdwick breed produces a fiber that is distinguishable. So they were able to prove that the sunken ship off the coast in Massachusetts was the ship they were looking for because they could tie the wool in the caulking to wool sold by the farm in Yorkshire to the shipyard that built the frigate...."

Mars turned, pacing slowly around the lounge. "And Janes is saying that the farm has records documenting that wool from their Herdwick sheep was sold to the Army of Northern Virginia for regimental flag production?"

"Not quite," Nettie said. "In fact, it's better than that. The wool produced by the farm in Yorkshire was sold in bulk to a cloth manufacturer in Bradford, England. The weave used by that manufacturer is also quite distinct. Janes E-mailed right after he got the fabric sample I sent him from the noose. He said that even without doing the fiber analysis, he recognized the weave pattern as being the same as the Bradford manufacturer...."

"So the Bradford manufacturer has been producing wool all these years?"

Nettie grinned, shaking her head, pleased at the complexity of her research. "No. They've been out of business since the end of the nineteenth century. What Janes said is likely is that the farm in Yorkshire has sold its wool to a manufacturer in the United States that specializes in manufacturing fabrics for historical reproduction purposes. Those manufacturers would try to replicate the fiber and the weave. I've been talking to some vexillologists in Philadelphia—"

"Whoaaa—some what?"

Nettie smiled her Cheshire Cat smile. "I've learned a new word. Vexillology is the study of flags."

"This case may give you your first and last opportunity to use that knowledge."

"Probably true," Nettie said. "Nonetheless, the *vexillologist* with whom I spoke in Philadelphia said there are a number of cloth manufacturers in the United States that specialize in producing cloth for historical purposes—and that Civil War reenactors are among their biggest customers. She also said that flag reproduction is big business, particularly Civil War flags. Both for legitimate historical purposes and for the counterfeit market. The difference is the customers who buy for historical purposes have a limit in terms of what they're willing to pay. For the counterfeiters, the sky's the limit. She said that a couple years ago a legitimate flag collector paid over twenty thousand dollars for what he believed was a brigade flag for the Army of Northern Virginia— turned out to be a counterfeit made out of fabric made by one of these outfits. And the prices for Confederate flags are going up dramatically every year—which creates incentives for the counterfeiters."

"Have we started contacting the manufacturers yet?"

Nettie gave him a look. "I love this *we* stuff. No, *I* have not started contacting manufacturers yet. I think it makes sense to wait until we get the fiber analysis back from England. One problem we're going to run into in contacting these manufacturers is that they're going to be protective of their customer information—

in part because they make a lot of money from the counterfeiters. So I think we should be pretty sure about what we're looking for and why before we approach them. The other thing to keep in mind is that they could—intentionally or not—tip a customer that inquiries are being made. Maybe a customer we'd prefer not to know that inquiries are being made."

Mars continued to pace the lounge. Rubbing both hands through his hair, he said, "Agreed. Let me just walk through this once more to make sure I get what we've got. We are fairly confident that our noose fabric matches a weave used by an English manufacturer who produced cloth for the Army of Northern Virginia during the Civil War. . . ."

"Yup."

"And your contact at the BWMA is going to be able to confirm—or disprove—that the fiber itself comes from a breed of sheep that is unique with respect to being identifiable from other breeds. . . ."

"Yup again—only because the farm on which the sheep are bred has—"

"—kept records going back to before the Civil War."

"Exactly."

"So. If we can establish that the fiber comes from that breed of sheep, we can trace the farm's records of wool sales to U.S. manufacturers and identify which ones are using that wool to manufacture cloth for historical reproductions purposes."

"That's it," Nettie said. "And it's at that point that I think it makes sense to start the manufacturer contacts to try and get a look at their customer records."

Mars turned in a tight circle, tossing his cigarette box between his hands. "Right. But I don't think we'll have enough legally at that point to subpoena the customer records if they don't volunteer them. Probably need to get Glenn Gjerde from the County Attorney's Office involved in thinking this through. My guess is, we're going to have to have a firm suspect in hand when we go for the customer records." He blew air through his lips, frustrated because he knew that being able to look at the customer lists was their best bet for picking up a name that rang bells.

Nettie said, "Will you please sit down? You're making me nervous, pacing around like that."

Mars dropped to the couch, still playing with the cigarette box.

Nettie frowned. "What *is* bugging you, anyway? Last week you were complaining that this case didn't have enough 'fizz' to keep you interested. Now you're like a guy who hasn't peed for a month."

"You've known guys who haven't peed for a month?"

"Probably more like guys who haven't pooped in a month. Tight asses."

"It's just that there's so much risk here. And our hands are tied right now. We just have to keep putting pieces together until we've got something that gets us to either a serious suspect or a manageable number of target victims. And it doesn't feel like we're anything like close. Which reminds me." Mars looked up at the wall clock. "Linda VanCleve is on her way over with bad news."

Mars and Nettie sat down at their desks; VanCleve stood opposite them. She looked exhausted. And for the first time since Mars had met VanCleve, her perfectly cut blond hair was messed up.

"I'm sorry to have to say this, but our plan isn't going to work."

Mars was looking up at VanCleve. "You're gonna give me a crick in my neck. Sit down and tell me what your problems are."

She sat on the edge of the desk. Mars shook his head and flapped his hand at her. "Lower. I want you on eye level." VanCleve pulled over a chair, leaning forward, elbows on the desk, resting her head in her hands as she talked.

"It's just too slow. Based on our trial run, I'd say to get to the fifth generation for each of the First Minnesota Volunteers is going to be—minimum—seven or eight hours. And that's just to get to a current generation name—like a marriage or property record. To actually *find* where an individual is currently living—well, that could be at least another couple hours' work per individual. So, we're talking about more than twenty thousand manpower days to go through all seventy thousand descendents." VanCleve rubbed her hands over her face. "Plus, I made a big mistake. I said we could eliminate twenty-five percent of the original four hundred and sixteen because not all of them would have reproduced. Problem is, we'd have to spend a fair amount of research time identifying that twenty-five percent. . . ."

"But we're going to have a bunch of people doing the research," Mars said.

VanCleve shrugged. "Okay. So divide the twenty thousand days by twenty-five—and I really can't come up with more people than that who I'd have confidence could do the job right—and you've got twenty-five people working twenty-four hours a day for eight hundred days. More than two years. I can't support that commitment—and I would guess you can't wait eight hundred days for us to identify the descendent pool."

Mars started making popping sounds with his mouth. Then, sitting up straight, he said, "No. You're right. This isn't going to work. We need to come up with some way of narrowing—significantly narrowing—the descendent pool." He looked at his watch. It was approaching 7:00 P.M. "Any bright ideas?"

Nettie said, "What if we came up with some specific criteria—like, specific things we know about Beck and the guy in Wisconsin. . . ." She stopped herself. "I was going to say, then we could select descendents based on that criteria. But that doesn't really get us anything—we'd still have to identify the descendents to do the match."

They spent another hour spinning out dead-end possibilities. When the city hall chimes pealed eight o'clock, Mars said, "We're burning ourselves out. This just isn't productive. Let's pack it in for tonight and hope that one of us will have a brainstorm during the night." To VanCleve he said, "You're going to be reachable by phone for the next couple of days?"

VanCleve rose, yawning. "I have four house guests arriving tomorrow afternoon and another dozen people coming for dinner Christmas day. So, yeah, I'll be in town." She suddenly grinned broadly. "If you could come up with some sort of emergency that got me out of the house Christmas morning, I'd forever be in your debt."

"I'll work on it," Mars said. "One other thing. The chief and I have agreed that this investigation needs to be confidential. So please—come up with what ever explanations will work for what you're involved in. But nothing that tips our hand on a broad-scale murder investigation related to descendents of the First Minnesota."

Mars and Nettie spent another half hour wrapping up loose ends after VanCleve left. Turning off her computer, Nettie rose, then bent over and touched her toes. Straightening slowly, she said, "Speaking of Christmas, do you know that Chris thinks he's getting a dog?"

Mars turned and looked at Nettie. "He told you that?"

Nettie nodded. "Is he?"

"You know Denise, what do you think?"

"What is he getting?"

"A computer. From Denise and me together." Mars made a face. "This is the first time Denise and I have had a serious disagreement involving Chris—apart from my insisting that Chris not wear secondhand clothes that Denise bought at garage sales. The only reason Denise doesn't want Chris to have a dog is because dogs are messy. Which they probably are. But I know—and Denise knows—that Chris would take good care of a dog. He deserves to have a dog."

"Denise and Chris in town for Christmas?"

Mars shook his head. "No. They're going out to Denise's parents tomorrow morning. They'll be back next Monday."

"Is he still awake?" Mars asked as he walked into the house.

"Barely," Denise said. She was wrapping Christmas packages at the dining room table. "Every time I look in on him, he says, 'Dad here yet?'" Denise gave him a close look. "You look okay. Tired, but okay. You've been at work all day?"

"I stayed at the apartment until late afternoon. Went down for a couple hours tonight. When do you leave?"

"Tomorrow morning. Soon as we're both up and ready."

Chris's eyes flew open when Mars opened the bedroom door. "Dad?"

"Hi. Just wanted to wish you a Merry Christmas before you leave."

Mars sat down on the bed next to Chris as Chris punched a pillow in place behind his head. "So you're okay?" Chris asked, his eyes serious.

Mars nodded. "Better than okay. I think that grungy appendix was poisoning my system for a long time. I get tired pretty easily, but overall, I feel a lot better than I did before the surgery."

"Have you found anything else out about who hanged Mr. Beck?"

There was a question worth thinking about. "We've got a better idea about what motivated the killer. It's about the flag you saw at the History Center last week. But there's still a lot we don't know."

"Nettie's found out some real cool stuff about sheep. She found this Web page on the Internet that's got like a million sheep jokes. You wanna hear one?"

"I don't know. Do I?"

"Where do you get virgin wool?"

"I'm thinking I don't want to hear any sheep jokes."

"From ugly sheep!" Chris rolled over on his side, gasping with laughter.

Mars picked up a pillow and punched it on Chris's head. "Sounds like a joke James would appreciate."

"I gave James the Web site address. He printed all the jokes out. There were more than forty pages. The one I told you wasn't the worst. Some are really gross."

"Just what James needed," Mars said. Then he bent over, pulling Chris toward him in a hug. "I've gotta get going. You and Mom have a good Christmas with Gramma and Grampa. Mom and I are giving you a gift together this year, so you'll get my gift on Christmas morning."

"Give me a hint."

The first hint in Mars's mind was that his gift would give Chris access to more sheep jokes. Not happy with that thought, he said, "It's useful."

Chris frowned. "But is it fun, too?"

"One hint is all you get."

CHAPTER

14

Mars woke abruptly. It was dead dark in the apartment and deeply silent. He rolled over and squinted at the illuminated alarm clock face. Only 3:34 A.M.

He fell back on the bed with a sigh. He was too wired from the tension of the investigation to sleep for a long time. He might as well get up, shower, and go downtown. There was a lot to get done to organize his thinking about how to identify potential victims and begin the process of putting together a suspect list. And he'd like to be well along on both those fronts before Boyle Keegan arrived in just over twenty-four hours.

He pulled into the city hall parking garage less than an hour later. Mars frowned. He was early, but he hadn't beaten Nettie in. Her car was parked near the elevator.

She was still in front of her computer, almost exactly where he'd found her yesterday. She noticed him as he came in, raising an eyebrow in his direction. "Glad you're taking it easy."

"I slept like a rock for as long as I did sleep. Would have just raised my blood pressure if I'd stayed in bed. You're still plugging away on the Cornell records?"

Nettie rolled back on the wheels of her chair, rubbing her face with the heels of both hands. "Aaargh. I'm going to give it another two days. If I haven't completed the search by then—or found something that relates to one and nine or Beck that's worth knowing—I'm going to pack it in. What are you up to?"

Slapping down the Beck case binder, Mars dropped on his chair. "I'm going to plow through everything we've got so far and try to come up with a profile on our killer."

Christmas Eve, Mars found, was an ideal day to work without interruption. The phone didn't ring, and only a couple of detectives came in briefly, leaving without the small talk that was typical on a normal workday. Nettie was almost silent, except for the soft clicking of her keyboard and an occasional expletive after she'd completed a particularly fruitless search.

As Mars went through the Beck file he made notes of a word or two. When he reached the end of the file, he looked through his notes and began building associations around the words. It was at this point that his concentration was broken by the canned music piped in through a ceiling sound system. It was on twenty-four seven, but the normal activity in the division usually relegated the sound to white noise. In the silence of the holiday, the tinny Christmas carols were more than usually annoying.

"Damn," Mars said, wadding up a piece of paper and tossing it toward the ceiling. "Any way we can get that crap turned off?"

It took Nettie a moment to break out of her concentration and focus on what Mars was saying. "The music?" she said, looking up.

"Imitation music, at best."

Nettie picked up her phone. "I'll give maintenance a call. But they're union. Doubt we'll get anything other than . . ." She hung up. "A recorded message." She shoved back on her chair and walked in the direction of the lounge.

She came back with a dirty plastic sandwich box and a stack of paper napkins. She opened a desk drawer, pulling out a roll of duct tape, which she slid over her wrist. Then she reconnoitered under the ceiling music speaker. "Let's move this desk under the speaker. . . ." When the desk was moved, Nettie got on top, taped a wad of napkins over the speaker, then taped a Styrofoam box over the napkin muffler.

Mars stood in admiration as the music was muted into oblivion. "You are a genius," he said.

"And I trust that genius is being put to the best uses of the investigation at hand," said the chief's voice. The chief stood just inside the division entrance, a garment bag over one arm.

Mars's and Nettie's faces turned a bright holiday red. Mars managed a lame grin and tapped his head with an index finger. "Concentration," he said. "Critical."

The chief looked tired as he dropped his bag over an empty desk. "Tell me where we are with this business—Keegan still on track to be here tomorrow?"

"Haven't heard otherwise." Mars pulled up a chair and sat. "If you've got time, I'd like to run through my thoughts on how a profile on our perp might look."

"Time is exactly what I've got," the chief said, sitting down heavily opposite Mars.

Mars pulled out his notes, thinking about the conclusions he'd drawn from them. Then he stopped himself. "Something Nettie's confirmed since I talked to you last—the Wisconsin hanging victim. His sister has verified that Rowe was a descendent of a member of the First Minnesota Volunteers."

The chief's expression froze. He did something that was uncharacteristic of him. With effort, he got up from the chair and began to walk in a small circle. One hand was clenched in a fist, punching softly into the palm of the other hand. Watching him, Mars realized that he'd never before seen the chief look worried. If anything, when things got tough, the chief tended to become physically still, as if forcing all his energy into his skull.

"So we're confident we have more than one death tied to this Civil War event?"

Mars nodded. "I don't think there's any doubt about it. We're not going to be able to confirm the specific numbers, but we can confirm that an EMT noticed unspecified numbers on Rowe's arm."

"And still no idea why *this* descendent, or how Rowe and Beck might be linked beyond the First Minnesota connection?"

Mars shook his head, and the chief began to pace again. He stopped abruptly and looked sharply at Mars. "Doesn't seem to me—given what we do know—that we've pulled out all the stops. What we've got working on this—which could very well be the biggest case of both our careers—is you and Nettie. And the two of you seem to be pretty busy tapin' stuff to the ceiling."

It was the closest the chief had ever come to an outright criticism of how Mars was handling a case. Mars felt stunned. In part, the chief was right. But in larger part he was wrong. Mars gave himself a moment to recover from what had felt like a blow.

"With all due respect, sir, I think we've come a long way in the past few days. Less than two weeks ago we didn't even know we had a homicide, and we certainly didn't have a connection to the flag the First Minnesota captured, much less a second death. We've sent out a five-state information advisory, you've got chiefs in other jurisdictions involved. We've got somebody from Quantico coming in tomorrow. The History Center has been helping and will help more—once we know what we need done. And we're trying to keep the investigation confidential at this stage—which also affects what we do and how we do it. . . ."

The chief heaved a sigh and pulled his suit coat off, sitting down again. A deep furrow took shape between his brows. "I'm tuckered out. Never was one for flying—especially back and forth to Birmingham in two days. And I had too much time to think on the plane. Got myself all worked up thinkin' about this thing." He glanced over at Mars, then over at Nettie. "Nobody knows better than I how much you've done. I'm just concerned about our exposure here, and I don't see how we're gonna resolve some of these questions. All I meant to say is, if more people would help, speak up."

Mars pulled his chair closer to the chief, leaning forward slightly. "That's going to come, no question about it. We will be asking for more help. But right now, I've got to get inside the perp's head. And I don't want the noise of more people to block out what I'm hearing while I pull all this information together." Mars grinned. "Which is why it was necessary to tape over the ceiling speakers. I need maybe another couple days of working with what I know. Nettie's making good progress on tracking down the last two numbers. . . ." Mars was careful not to look at Nettie when he made reference to her work on the Cornell database. "And she's found out a lot of useful stuff on the fabric used in the noose. I'll be happy to work with the guy from Quantico—he may have a fresh perspective that will be helpful. But if we pull in a bunch of people at this point—without knowing what we're looking for—I'm going to spend all my time managing what they're doing instead of figuring out what it is we're investigating."

"Can't argue with that," the chief said, looking remorseful. "You'd started telling me about where you are on a perp profile, before I went off the deep end."

Mars wheeled back to his desk and picked up his notes again. "Based on what we know about Beck's plans to meet someone the afternoon of the day he died—and that the store clerk said Beck seemed upbeat about the meeting—I'm assuming that Beck thought he'd identified an investor to bail him out. So this guy has to present as a businessman. A well-heeled businessman. That's number one. A related aspect: whoever Beck was meeting must have been the one to suggest they meet in Beck's office. Beck wouldn't have suggested the office—there was no electricity, no phone—it wouldn't have impressed a prospective investor. But our perp must have known something about the site and recognized it would make an ideal murder scene. Which means he'd been conducting surveillance on Beck. If we identify more target victims, that will be useful information. Any recurring appearances of an unfamiliar person or vehicle, any approaches from a stranger tailored to the targeted victim's special needs—well, that's going to be our guy."

The chief nodded slowly. "So far, so good. We heard anything back on the contacts I made yesterday?"

Mars shook his head. "Nothing yet. But it's still early." He turned back to his notes. "Point two. Clearly our perp has the financial resources and flexibility to spend time pursuing his targets. So we're looking for somebody who has independent sources of income—maybe somebody who's self-employed, or owns his own business. . . ."

"Maybe somebody who doesn't have a family who's going to ask questions about what he's doing when he's gone?"

Mars thought for a moment, then jotted down the chief's point. "Hadn't thought about that—worth considering. The next point is related to the first thing I said. Our perp is well organized. He picked, in both the cases we know about, an appropriate time and site to kill his victims. He prepared a complicated hanging knot, he'd researched what the victims' vulnerable points were, and it appears he used alcohol and barbiturates as a strategy. So I think he's educated, probably successful at what he does, may participate in highly disciplined recreational activities, like sailing—which would also tie into the knot. No pun intended. Maybe a military background, the kind of guy who'd been an Eagle Scout as a kid." Mars paused, his last statement confirming that he was relieved Chris had decided to drop Scouts.

"Sounds like the perp from hell," the chief said.

"Wouldn't argue that," Mars said. "This next thing is important. Clearly our perp is motivated by some personal sense of justice and the need for revenge. He's going to be someone with a history of strong attachments to Confederate causes. Probably has been involved in past efforts to recover the flag—so we need to look at those people real carefully." Mars stopped. "But here's the thing. Given his planning and organization, I don't think he's been involved in a public way with those groups for a long time. I would guess that he disassociated himself with the flag issue well in advance of beginning the hangings—both to make himself harder to find and to avoid tainting that effort if he's caught."

"You said he's motivated by a *personal* need for revenge—by that you mean something other than his commitment to the Confederate cause?"

Mars took out his cigarette box, turning it in his right hand. "I'm not sure yet. When I look at what I already think about this guy—a disciplined, successful businessman who's used to having his own way—a guy like that gets told he can't have something he's passionate about, well, that might be all it would take to set him off. But I think we need to look for anything that might be more personal than that. The way his victims are dying is ugly. He's stringing them up and letting them turn blue. I'd be willing to bet he stays and watches while the vic struggles. Then he writes the number—not making any effort to make it look like the vic wrote the number. Damned arrogant. I don't think that kind of behavior has an intellectual basis. Looks to me like raw personal emotion. We find something personal that motivates revenge, that would be a big help."

Mars stretched and stood, talking as he moved slowly around his desk. "It goes without saying I think our perp is a male. Physically, I don't think there are many women who could hang a man. And I don't think you're going to find many women who develop these rabid, visceral commitments to Civil War causes. Not saying they aren't out there—just think it's less likely to be a woman."

The chief rose awkwardly from his chair. "What you're saying makes our vic out to be a pretty formidable fella." He gestured to Mars to follow him. "C'mon. I sat too long on that airplane. Need to move around some. Nettie, you mind we leave you on your own for a bit?"

Nettie waved them off, and Mars and the chief walked slowly out of the division office, into the marble-floored, silent hallways.

Silent, that is, except for the recurrence of the canned Christmas music.

The chief looked up without moving his head, then looked sideways at Mars. "You wanna bring along a couple plastic boxes and tape while we walk?"

"Won't be necessary," Mars said. Then, in a careful voice, "I've never seen you so upset before. I've never seen pressure get to you."

The lines in the chief's face thickened and drew together. "Don't think I've ever had a case before with so much riding on it. At every level. That we almost missed a homicide bothers me no end. Especially because if we hadn't made a determination of homicide, we'd be exposing an untold number of innocent people to untimely deaths." He looked sideways again toward Mars. "Not that all my worries are so noble. If there are more deaths, we could end up covered in mud. That's not gonna do you and Nettie any good over at the state capitol when the funding proposal for your positions comes up. Didn't want to get Nettie upset, but it's been on my mind."

"What happens, happens. I really don't worry about that."

"Well, that's to your credit." The chief drew in a deep breath, patting his gut. "Truth is, stress is hitting me harder these days because I'm out of shape. That, and maybe something like this coming up around Christmas bothers me."

They wandered down a marble staircase that led into a multi-storied street-level lobby. Dominating the lobby was a massive sculpture of the Father of the Waters, honoring the city's debt to the Mississippi. Alone in the center court, they leaned against the base of the statue, Mars playing with his cigarette box, the chief rocking back and forth between his heels and the balls of his feet.

"It just aggravates me no end," the chief said, "that these murders happen because of a battle that took place more than a hundred years ago. The damage caused by these personal vendettas goes on for centuries. Northern Ireland, the Middle East, the Civil

War. When are folks gonna figure out that you honor the dead by stopping the dying?"

Mars nodded, too tired to say anything eloquent in response.

"Worst of all, most of these situations are religious in nature. Even this Civil War thing comes close to being a religion for some. Just don't see how you reconcile religious beliefs with terrorism and murder. Not that you can't find plenty of murder and mayhem in the Bible—Old Testament especially. Me, I'm a New Testament man. Old Testament is law, New Testament is love. That's what I was always taught. But I can't tell you how many folks who call themselves Christians only know the law. 'An eye for an eye, a tooth for a tooth'—that's what some focus on."

Mars smiled at the chief. "Strikes me a chief of police should be an Old Testament man."

The chief smiled back and shrugged. "Well, I guess I'm getting tired for sure. When I start quotin' the Bible is a sign it's time to head home." He slapped Mars on the shoulder. "One thing I need for you to do—then I want you and Nettie to get yourselves home. That's an order. I'm gonna call building security later tonight, and if you're still down here, I'm gonna assign a squad to escort you home. It is Christmas Eve."

"What do you need?"

The chief reached into the inside pocket of his jacket and pulled out a slip of paper. He passed it over to Mars. "An encrypted fax number at Quantico. Write up a summary of your suspect profile and fax it on out to Keegan. He'll be leaving there around noon tomorrow. Durr promised Keegan we'd send out a file for him to review on the plane coming out."

"What are you doing tonight?" Nettie asked after Mars faxed the encrypted file to Quantico. There was something in her voice that let Mars know she had a hunch what Mars would be doing.

"I don't do Christmas," Mars said.

"*Who* aren't you doing Christmas *with*?" Nettie said.

"I'll probably have dinner with Evelyn. Rita's going out of town, and Evelyn said something about grilling salmon."

"Rita's the secretary in the English department who took Evelyn in after she got out of jail?"

"Yeah." Mars pulled on his jacket, making it a point not to look at Nettie. "How about you?"

"Over to my sister's—as soon as I get through these last three files for 1863."

"C'mon, Nettie. Orders from the chief. We've gotta be out of here tonight."

"I want to enjoy Christmas Eve when I get to it. If I haven't finished 1863, I won't enjoy it. It won't take me long to finish."

"A couple of merrymakers, you and me."

Nettie said, "Did I tell you Chris said if he doesn't get a dog, he'd like a sheep. The sheep could stay outside and it would keep the grass trim. Chris wouldn't have to mow the lawn—which he hates doing. Perfect solution to the dog dilemma."

"Sheep shit on the lawn? No way that's getting by Denise."

"You're missing the point, Mars. With sheep, there wouldn't be any lawn left."

"Suits *me* right down to the ground. Merry Christmas, Nettie."

"You can save that for tomorrow."

CHAPTER

15

"*Jackie Brown* and Chinese takeout on Christmas Eve," Evelyn said. "I think tonight confirms us as fully fledged heathens."

She and Mars had just finished watching the *Jackie Brown* video while eating garlic green beans and beef in black bean sauce from Shuang Cheng. Evelyn had called him at his apartment and asked if he'd mind getting takeout instead of having salmon. So he'd stopped in Dinkytown on his way over. He thought by arriving at the restaurant just after five, he'd beat the crowd of Asian and Jewish families who showed up at Shuang Cheng on Christian holidays. But the restaurant was already almost full, and there was a line at the takeout desk. There was something reassuring about finding so many secular souls gathered together on Christmas Eve.

"Next to any character written by Elmore Leonard," Mars said, "I don't feel at all like a heathen. I feel like Frances McDormand playing the sheriff in *Fargo*. The actor who played the bail bondsman in *Jackie Brown*? A perfect Elmore Leonard antihero. I liked Travolta and Hackman in *Get Shorty*, but I liked them the way you like movie stars giving good performances. The bail bondsman was just—in his skin. It was like the camera found him by accident. Perfect."

Evelyn, sitting next to Mars on the couch, stretched her legs, carefully propping her heels on the coffee table between the white

178

cardboard takeout boxes. "I don't remember the first Elmore Leonard book I read—I just remember that I read fifty pages before I realized this slimeball character I kept waiting for someone to arrest was the book's hero. But what was really kind of amazing was that by the end of the book, I absolutely accepted him as the hero. I've wondered ever since if reading Elmore Leonard hasn't changed my moral compass in some fundamental way."

They sat silent for minutes, both of them in identical positions, feet up on the coffee table, staring forward at the wall in front of them, against which a gigantic thirty-seven-inch television and VCR were centered. There were bookcases on either side of what Rita called "the entertainment center." The bookcases were filled with Rita's romance novels and Hummel figurines that Mars recognized as being identical to those in a foster home where he'd lived in the third grade. Over the bookcases on either side of the television were intensely romantic prints of houses in snow-covered woods, golden lights shining through curtained windows onto the snow. In one of the pictures, a sleigh filled with fur-robed people approached the brightly lit house. A wreath hung on the door of the house and the colored lights of a Christmas tree were barely visible behind the window.

For Mars, the juxtaposition of the Hummel figurines that he associated with one of the four foster homes he'd lived in growing up and the idealized houses in the framed prints that were perfect images of his boyhood dreams of what a home should be, raised two questions.

First, why was it that this house—which in its style and contents was so like the house he and Denise had lived in when they'd been married—didn't give him the same, breath-suppressing, walls-closing-in sense of horror that his and Denise's house had given him from day one?

Second, why was it that the houses in the prints, which came pretty close to matching his boyhood ideal of 'home,' should be something that as an adult he would find so unappealing? He made a mental note to give more thought to those questions in the future, with no real expectation that he would in fact do so.

To Evelyn he said, "Explain to me how it is that you and Rita manage to get along so well as housemates. I can't see that you've got anything in common."

Evelyn considered the question for a moment before saying, "Well, the easy answer is, 'Beggars can't be choosers.' But it's more than that. I've told you before, when I was released from jail, I didn't have any place to go. And of everybody I knew, the only person I felt comfortable calling was Rita. She wasn't part of the set I'd fallen into..." Evelyn looked sideways at Mars. He'd known from the first the gruesome details of Evelyn's "set."

"... And Rita wasn't really part of the academic world. I mean, she was the senior secretary in the English Department at the U, but she made it a point of not being part of the academic world. It's really how she's always managed to maintain her control of everybody in the department. She has a real genius for making pointy-headed academics feel like bungling idiots. And she's so good at what she does, the whole department depends on her. You get on Rita's bad side, and you're not going to get copies of stuff made when you need it, she's not going to put in a good word for you on conference appointments, she won't go the extra mile in scheduling meetings with students and advisors—there're just a million ways she can make the life of an assistant prof or a graduate student harder or easier.

"With me, she recognized on sight that I hadn't bought in to the whole academic *thing*. I started by having this stupidly romantic view of what being an academic meant. I thought it was all about forming young minds and achieving greater understanding of Self and the World We Live In..." Evelyn rolled her eyes. "Man, was I off base. Once I realized how far off base I was, I got real cynical, real fast. It was my cynicism about being a graduate student that appealed to Rita. I think she saw me as an ally. She certainly recognized that I didn't need to be reminded every day how insignificant a thing a graduate student was. But I owe her. Without Rita, I would never have been kept on as a graduate student after I crashed and burned year before last. . . ."

"And living here?"

"For Rita, I'm not sure. I think her prickly personality has kept her a little isolated, a little lonely. I'm company. She has a very maternal streak, actually—'controlling' is what people in the English department say. But I think she likes having somebody to take care of. And while you're right—we don't have the same tastes in much of anything"—Evelyn glanced up at the framed prints over the bookcases— "we respect each other and are considerate of one another. Which is a lot—more than you get in most relationships."

Her words hung in the air. Then she said, "For me, of course, it's cheap. I genuinely like Rita, and given that I go to England in less than two months, finding a place on my own doesn't make a lot of sense. Which reminds me—I dropped the ball on grilling salmon tonight because it took me forever to pin Rueben down on my recommendation letters to the University of Sussex. By the time I got that done, the grocery store was closed. So, no salmon."

"Rueben being Rueben Gill, your—what'ya call him, your thesis advisor?"

"The same," Evelyn said, her voice tired. "Rueben is pathologically disorganized. I've given him letters to be sent twice before. All he needed to do was sign them. He lost them both times. So I had to wait until he came in—which wasn't until after four—then hang around until he could focus long enough to find his glasses and a pen and sign the letters. If I hadn't gotten them mailed before he left on holiday, I might be leaving without approval for library access in Sussex."

Mars felt twinges of something uncomfortable at the prospect of Evelyn's leaving. He put the discomfort on the list of things that required further consideration, along with why Denise's house gave him the heebie-jeebies and Rita's didn't and why his childhood definition of "home" had no meaning in his adult life. For now, he said, "How does Rueben get away with it?"

Evelyn grinned. "In academia? Like, somebody's going to notice?" She was quiet for a bit before saying, "That isn't altogether true—or fair. I think Rueben has paid a price for being sloppy—although my guess is sloppiness is the least of his problems. He's one of a roving band of itinerant academics that move from university to university, never getting a tenured appointment, taking what's available, wherever it's available. I suppose it isn't surprising that someone like Rueben wouldn't be motivated to do much more than show up. What is it that Woody Allen said— and I don't think this is from a movie—'Eighty percent of success is just showing up'? That could be Rueben's motto."

"It's looking like that's all that mattered with our victims in the Beck case. They had ancestors who 'just showed up' at Gettysburg one hundred and thirty-seven years ago."

"You haven't found anything else that explains why these guys would be the victims—I mean, as opposed to any other descendent of the First Minnesota."

Mars shook his head. "If I could find out why Beck, why Rowe, this investigation would take off like a rocket. I'm still hoping Nettie will find out something about the last two numbers on Beck's arm."

Evelyn gave a self-conscious shudder. "The idea of someone just cruising silently around, stalking victims—and the victims having no idea they're vulnerable. Terrifying."

"Everyone's spooked on this one. The chief went totally off the rails when he got back today. And I've never seen him lose his cool. By the end of the day he was quoting the Old Testament: 'An eye for an eye, a tooth for a tooth . . . ' "

"Meaning these are revenge killings?"

Mars nodded. "I think that's a sure thing. But knowing that doesn't explain how the perp is selecting victims. I somehow can't believe he's going after just anyone who had an ancestor fighting at Gettysburg with the First Minnesota."

Evelyn shifted on the couch. "Anyway. What I meant to say before. I apologize for screwing up our grilled salmon dinner."

"Well," Mars said, "I hold no hard feelings about missing our salmon dinner. Shuang Cheng's hit the spot."

Evelyn pulled herself up. "I know what we need. A little Christmas music." She walked over to the entertainment center and sorted through a rack of CDs. She smiled, pulling one out. "This is incredibly hokey and just right. 'The Three Tenors Sing Christmas Classics.'" She bent over and looked in the cabinet again. "Or, an equivalent emotional experience would be to watch Rita's only video, which is *The Sound of Music*."

"I can't believe this," Mars said. "Just last night, Nettie asked me if I was interested in hearing about 'cool coincidences,' and when I said, 'Those are a few of my favorite things,' she played our movie-line game. You've heard us do it—we remember a bit of movie dialogue that fits whatever it is we're doing, then the other one has to name the movie and scene the dialogue came from . . ."

"I've heard the two of you do it. I've never been exactly sure what it was all about."

"The point is, as soon as I said, 'Those are a few of my favorite things, Nettie said—"

"Oh—I do get it," Evelyn said. "Then Nettie said, '*The Sound of Music*, the scene where Julie Andrews sings to the Von Trapp kids during a thunderstorm.'"

"You got it," Mars said. "And now, for the second time in two days, *The Sound of Music* comes up. Maybe one of the only movies ever made that I haven't seen. Your bringing it up now is a coincidence because Nettie mentioned it last night, and the first mention of *The Sound of Music* was related to a coincidence. Which, I think, means that this is the third coincidence in two days related to *The Sound of Music*."

"Life is strange," Evelyn said. She held up the three tenors CD and the video. "Which is it?"

"I can't handle any more coincidences related to *The Sound of Music*. Let's go for the tenors."

They were in the kitchen doing dishes when the three tenors swung into the John Lennon, Yoko Ono song, "So This Must Be Christmas."

"I *love* this song," Evelyn said. "It makes me want to waltz."

"You're in luck," Mars said. "I went to a Catholic boys' school in the eighth grade. Among my many personal accomplishments attributable to Our Mother of Perpetual Grace is my ability to waltz."

"You can't be serious." Evelyn looked startled.

"Just watch me." Mars put the dish towel down and walked into the living room. Surveying the room, he said, "Space is an issue. Waltzing properly requires space. Would Rita freak out if I moved some furniture?"

"She would if she were here to see it. But if we move everything back, so she never knows it happened, I think she'd survive."

Mars moved all the furniture back against the walls of the living room, while Evelyn reset the CD. At the first strains of "So This Must Be Christmas," they began a slow, swooping waltz around the room.

Mars was about to waltz Evelyn through the kitchen and back into the living room when his cell phone rang.

"Ohhhh," Evelyn said. "I have the worst feeling that I've just had my first and last waltz with you . . ."

"*The Last Waltz*. Robbie Robertson is being interviewed by Martin Scorsese, and Robertson explains how they chose *The Last Waltz* as the name for the final concert." He looked at the caller ID screen on his phone, then punched the talk button.

"Another musical," Evelyn said.

"Not a musical," Mars said, "a concert movie. Big difference."

To his cell phone he said, "Nettie, why the hell are you still in the squad room?"

"And ruining my waltz," Evelyn said to no one in particular as she walked back into the kitchen.

Nettie said, "I think I found the last two numbers, Mars. One number, really. It's not one and nine. It's nineteen."

"I'm listening," Mars said, forgetting to be mad, his heart pounding harder and faster than it had when he'd been waltzing.

"Okay. I'm looking at the Cornell University records for the Gettysburg Campaign. There's a table that shows 'killed' and 'wounded' during the three days of the Battle of Gettysburg for the Army of Northern Virginia. It breaks the figures down by command—meaning it shows corps, divisions, brigades, and regiments. Under Pickett's Division, it shows Garnett's Brigade, and the Twenty-eighth Virginia was under Garnett's Brigade. The table shows that nineteen members of the Twenty-eighth Virginia were killed during the three days of the Battle of Gettysburg. I know that's not just the third day, when the flag was captured, but—"

"No," Mars said, "I agree with you. It fits. It makes perfect sense that someone would be looking to avenge the members of the Twenty-eighth who died. The flag represented all of them, not just the ones who died on the third day. I think you've got it . . ."

"Rex Harrison to Audrey Hepburn in *My Fair Lady* when she pronounces 'the rain in Spain' correctly."

"What is it with all this musical stuff? We're in a rut, here."

"So you're okay that we *have* figured out the last numbers."

"Yeah. Good to go. It was maybe even worth it that you worked on Christmas Eve."

"I thought you'd be more excited."

"I am excited. It's great to have this resolved. It's just that I was hoping it would help us explain why Beck was the victim. We'll just have to keep working that."

"Are you and Evelyn having a nice Christmas Eve?"

"Yeah. Great. We were waltzing when you called."

"Oh, right," Nettie said, not considering for a minute that he was serious.

After getting Nettie's call, Mars began some serious pacing.

"What is it?" Evelyn asked.

Mars stopped. "I really can't put off any longer figuring out why Beck was the victim. I'd hoped that would fall out of the numbers, but it didn't happen."

"Explain again what the numbers meant . . ."

"Nettie found records documenting that nineteen members of the Twenty-eighth Virginia died during the Battle of Gettysburg. So, what we've got, when you put all thirteen numbers together, is a message that commemorates the Twenty-eighth Virginia's participation in the Battle of Gettysburg where nineteen men died and where the Twenty-eighth regimental flag was captured on the third day." Mars resumed pacing.

"You're so tense," Evelyn said. "Relax. Ideas come when you're not trying so hard." Evelyn lay down on the couch in the living room, putting her stocking feet up on the back of the couch, watching Mars. Then she said, rising up to balance herself on her elbows, "It's what the chief said, Mars."

He looked at her without understanding.

Evelyn said, "An eye for an eye, and a tooth for a tooth . . . your perp is going to kill nineteen descendants of the First Minnesota Volunteers who fought at Gettysburg."

The knot in Mars's stomach tightened and a chill swept over him, running lightly over his neck and down his back.

"My God," he said, dropping down to the couch. "It makes perfect sense, especially as our guy is into ritual." He leaned back, clasping his hands behind his head, staring up at the ceiling. "But, damn it, we're still left with the unmanageable question: how is he selecting the nineteen victims?"

Evelyn closed her eyes and concentrated. "Couldn't you look

186

for similarities in Beck and Rowe, then match that to other descendants?"

Mars guffawed. "Let me tell you about that option. The director of the History Center has calculated that there's something like seventy thousand descendants of the First Minnesota at this point in time. Just to identify that population—not to mention matching characteristics to the two known victims—would take twenty-five researchers working twenty-four hours a day more than two years."

Evelyn stretched her lower lip in a grimace. "I see the problem." She continued to think. "So what you need to do is come up with known criteria that will narrow the population of potential victims to a manageable number."

"That's it," Mars said. "But I'm not sure what you mean by 'known' criteria."

"Well, as an example, that the killer is only going to target males. I think that would be a pretty reasonable assumption. In my mind, racists are often chauvinists—and given that we think he may be doing the eye-for-an-eye bit, it would make sense that he's going to go after men, not women. And besides, Mars. Your perp is going to have the same victim selection problem you're having. And he probably has a lot fewer resources to solve the problem than you do. He's going to have to start with some really simple rules of selection. Those rules should be as obvious to us as they are to him."

"That is absolutely right," Mars said, getting up and pulling on his jacket. "It's been there all along. Staring me in the face. While I've been eating Chinese and waltzing to Christmas carols."

CHAPTER

16

Mars, Nettie, and the chief formed a loose circle in the squad room. Mars had run through Evelyn's suggestions about narrowing the descendent pool. The chief and Nettie had the same immediate rush of recognition that had struck Mars.

"What we need to do now," Mars said, "is start identifying descendents of the First Minnesota based on that criterion." He looked at the chief. "I need to get Linda VanCleve and some of her researchers in as soon as possible. You okay with that? It's probably going to cost an arm and a leg—I don't think we can ask the History Center to do this on their dime."

The chief was impassive. "We will spend—and do—whatever needs to be spent, whatever needs to be done."

Mars stood. "When we have the descendents identified, we're going to have to put together a major cross-jurisdictional push to get those folks protected while we track down the perp." Mars looked up at the clock. Not quite midnight.

At just after two o'clock on Christmas morning, Linda VanCleve, two young women with brush cuts, and a young man with a long ponytail arrived in the squad room. Mars took a half hour to cover the bases with the folks from the Historical Society, ruing every minute that he was spending on old business. By prior agreement, what they were telling the researchers was that they were looking for a murder suspect who was a descendent of the First Minnesota Volunteers. It was enough to get them started without blowing the confidentiality of the investigation.

Linda VanCleve's face was stony. But for her three younger associates, even the cover story was dramatic enough to burn off the sleep fog and make their pupils dilate.

When Mars stopped talking, Linda VanCleve asked to talk to the chief, Mars, and Nettie privately. "I agree with everything you've said about focusing on male descendents. And using simple demographic statistics, we can assume it will reduce our research by something more than fifty percent. But that's still too big a population. I'm going to make another suggestion for narrowing this thing. It's a riskier assumption, but I think it's reasonable."

"Shoot," Mars said.

"Primogeniture," VanCleve said. "I think from what you've said, your killer would pick eldest-son descendents."

Mars thought about it. "I think that's fine—but am I wrong in thinking that criterion would be useful in narrowing down the current generation population, but wouldn't save us any research time getting to the current generation?"

VanCleve squinted, not getting what Mars was saying.

"Let me state this as a question," Mars said. "Are you saying we'd eliminate any First Minnesota descendent who didn't produce a male in the first generation or in any succeeding generation—or that we would look at our current generation population and eliminate any males who weren't the eldest sons?"

VanCleve blinked hard. "I see what you mean. What I had in mind was this. Say there is a descendent who had four male offspring. I'd say, just track the descendents of the eldest boy. If that son had a daughter, but no sons—" VanCleve hesitated. "That's a problem. But to be safe, I think we need to track the daughter to see if we end up with a son in the target generation. When we get to the current generation we can eliminate any descendent who is not an eldest male." She sighed. "So it might help some, but not a lot."

Nettie said, "Isn't it possible we'll have more than one eldest son living? Like, a father and son—even a grandfather, son, and grandson?"

Another long sigh from VanCleve. "Of course," she said. "Maybe even probable."

They sat in silence. It was discouraging, but Mars felt they were close to something. He twisted slowly on his chair, thinking. The chief's phrase—'an eye for an eye'—kept coming back to him. He thought about revenge in connection with the number nineteen, and it came to him at once.

"Just the survivors," he said. "An eye for an eye—our perp is just going to track First Minnesota Volunteers who survived the Battle of Gettysburg."

The statement went *click* for him. He would have wagered his life he'd just nailed it. To VanCleve he said, "Can we do that? Can you tell me how many of the First Minnesota survived the Battle, a ballpark number?"

VanCleve scratched her scalp hard with both hands. She covered her face with her hands. "Let me think." She was silent for a moment, then she dropped her hands.

"In some sense, what the First Minnesota is best known for is the casualty rate at Gettysburg. They suffered the highest rate of casualties—after the second day of battle—of any unit in any American war—at least, that's one point of view. The exact numbers have been challenged . . ."

"Number of survivors?"

VanCleve took a deep breath. "Let me back into this. I kind of know these numbers by heart, but I need to go through it in order." She bent over and pulled up her purse, a large leather satchel. She rummaged in the purse for a moment, finding a notebook and a pen.

Writing as she talked, she said, "Okay. Four hundred and six-

teen members of the First Minnesota in all ranks on July 1, 1863."
She hesitated, closing her eyes. Writing again, she said slowly, "At
the end of the first day there were, like . . ."

"Try to be as exact as you can."

She grimaced. "I think at the end of the first day of the battle
there were two hundred and sixty-five members left—" She
stopped. "What I can remember—off the top of my head—is going to be the number of troops that were available for muster on
each day following the previous day's battle. Which means the
number I'm going to come up with for 'survivors' after the third
day will exclude guys who did survive, but were too badly injured
to be available for battle. . . ."

"I understand."

"I'm not saying it would be impossible to break the data out by
killed, wounded, and uninjured, but you'd need someone other
than me to get it for you. Tee Tucker, one of our senior historians,
said he'd help later today. His specialty is Minnesota's involvement
in the Civil War. It's just that sorting that out will take some
time."

Mars said, "We may want to get to that later, but for now, let's
look at the number you come up with that just shows guys available to muster." He looked around at the chief and Nettie. "If our
assumption is right, our perp probably would consider that revenge has already been delivered if someone was injured too badly
to fight the next day." Nettie nodded silently in agreement. "And
once we know your number, we'll have a good idea if we're on the
right track."

VanCleve picked up her pen and paper again. "So, after the
first day of battle, two hundred and sixty-five men were available
for muster on the second day. . . ." She looked around the room.
"The second day was the killer—literally and figuratively. In
terms of casualties, that's the day that lives in legend. After the second day's battle, there were only sixty-two guys available for
muster on July third, 1863."

"And of the sixty-two, Linda. How many were available for muster on July fourth, 1863?"

"Well, the battle was over by the fourth, of course."

"But you know how many would have been available for muster?"

"There's a bit of disagreement . . ."

"A number, Linda."

"It's generally agreed that on July fourth, 1863, there were seventeen men available for muster."

Mars looked at the chief, Nettie, and Linda.

"The dead survivors," Nettie said, her voice quiet.

Mars smiled at her. "Okay. The dead survivors are the source for our descendent pool." Looking especially at the chief, he said, "We're making some pretty big assumptions here. You okay going forward on this basis?"

The chief said, "I like it—but it seems a little risky to me. We need to start by checking to see if Beck and Rowe match the assumptions—I mean, that they were eldest sons in their generation and that their ancestors at Gettysburg survived the battle. Then we need some kind of quality control as we move forward to make sure that identified targets match the criteria."

"I know that Beck's ancestor—Herman Beck—survived the battle," Mars said. He glanced at his watch. "Too early to call Joey Beck, but he'll know if his dad was an eldest son. Not sure Rowe's sister will know about the ancestor, but . . ." He looked at Van-Cleve. "I assume you can verify that?"

VanCleve nodded. "What I don't understand," she said, "is how you're going to end up with a target descendent pool of nineteen when you're tracking only sixteen guys?"

"I thought you just said there were seventeen guys available for muster on July forth, 1863?"

"Marshall Sherman didn't marry, didn't have descendents. To my knowledge, he's the only one of the—what did Nettie call them, the dead survivors?—anyway, Sherman's the only one who wouldn't have descendents. So you're tracking sixteen guys, and you need to come up with nineteen targeted victims."

Mars sighed. "I agree. It's not perfect. But I think it's a fit. It just goes click for me. We're gonna have to hope that something surfaces while we do the research that will fill in the three blanks."

"Big enough fizz for you?" Nettie said, looking a Mars with a smug smile on her face. She'd just wheeled in a big white board on which they'd track their progress in identifying the names of First Minnesota survivors of the Battle of Gettysburg and their male descendents.

He looked back at her with raised eyebrows, not getting it.

Nettie turned full toward him. "You said this case didn't have enough fizz."

"I may have been wrong about that." He looked at his watch, frowning. Probably another six, seven hours before Keegan arrived. He stood and began a slow pace, fiddling with his cigarette box. Then stopped and smiled.

"You've got fifteen seconds. 'I'm a little wound up.' And you say . . ." Mars pointed at Nettie, giving her the cue.

Nettie made a face. "Mars, for God's sake. I've been here going on forty-eight hours."

"The clock is ticking. And you are going to feel like a complete fool if you don't get this one."

"No, I'm not."

"One more chance. 'I'm a little wound up,' and you say . . ."

Nettie closed her eyes, concentrating. "Well, *The Fabulous Baker Boys* is always a good guess. . . ." Nettie opened one eye to check Mars's reaction.

Mars frowned, causing Nettie to smile. "It *is The Fabulous Baker* . . . oh, I know. Beau Bridges says, 'I'm a little wound up,' and Jeff Bridges says, 'You're a fucking alarm clock.' "

Behind them, the fax machine rang, followed by the piercing, hollow sound of the connection. Mars and Nettie looked at each other. Nettie walked over to the machine and stood as it chugged out three pages. She read each page as it flopped out, then, without saying anything, walked back, handing the pages to Mars.

The fax came from Salina, Kansas. The first line read, "In response to your request for information concerning deaths by hanging where the deceased was found to have the numbers 2822173631958 written on the body, the Salina Police Department can confirm such circumstances. . . ."

Mars looked up at Nettie. *"Now,"* he said, "we're talking big fizz."

CHAPTER

17

By noon, all sixteen of the First Minnesota Volunteers who'd survived the Battle of Gettysburg and who had produced offspring were in the left column on the whiteboard.

Tee Tucker, the History Center's senior specialist on Minnesota and the Civil War, had stood before the board upon his arrival, not troubling to remove his immense parka nor the incongruous golf hat squashed down on his balding head. He hummed softly as he wrote each name on the board, interrupting himself to make the occasional comment about one of the survivors. When he finished, he stood back, considering what he'd done.

"I've ordered this by date of enlistment. That okay?" Tucker asked Mars.

Mars shrugged. "Why not." Then he stepped forward, and in the right column, entered Frank Beck's and Gaylord Rowe's names opposite their ancestors. As he wrote, he had a morbid thought: the more deaths they identified that they could link to a First Minnesota Volunteer, the less research they'd have to do. They didn't yet have the name of the Salina, Kansas, victim's ancestor, but Mars didn't have any doubts the ancestor's name was in the left-hand column.

Linda VanCleve joined Mars and Tucker in their appraisal of the white board. "It just occurred to me," she said, echoing Mars's thought. "We don't have sixteen names to research. We only have thirteen—sixteen minus the three deaths we know about. Unless you think living descendents from different generations might be at risk—you know, the question Nettie asked?"

Mars had been troubled by Nettie's question about living descendents from more than one generation. He'd even considered assigning protection to Frank Beck's eldest son. But as he'd thought about it, he decided the likelihood that their perp would hang multiple members of the same family was less than zero—unless there was a compelling reason to do so. And uncovering what that compelling reason might be was their best hope for finding the three missing target victims.

Mars explained his thinking to VanCleve, who nodded slowly in agreement as he talked. "The only remaining question is," he said, "where there is more than one eldest male alive, how does the perp pick the victim? Based on what we know about Beck, my guess is he takes the oldest generation. Nettie got hold of Joey Beck earlier, and Joey said his dad was the eldest son and other than Joey's brother, there were no other surviving eldest sons in Herman Beck's line. Once we have more information about Rowe and our victim in Kansas, we should be able to establish a clear pattern of victim selection. Like I said, the one thing we've got to keep an eye out for is something in the descendents' backgrounds that will give us our three missing targets." Mars turned to Tee. "Can I ask you to follow up on that? See if you can find anything in the backgrounds of the sixteen survivors that suggests more than one victim might come from their descendent line?" To Linda he said, "The same for your researchers. Have them watch for something that suggests someone other than the oldest surviving eldest son would also be a target."

Tucker said he'd work on it on his own. It became obvious that Tucker had left his coat on to make a quick escape. As he edged toward the door, Mars thanked him for his help, shaking his hand. "What's 'T' stand for, anyway?" he asked.

196

"It's T-e-e," Tucker said. "And what it stands for is, if this were May instead of December, and the snow was off the golf course, I wouldn't be here."

By early afternoon, the squad room had become chaotic. Nettie was bringing in and setting up extra computers for the researchers to work on as more researchers were coming in. Linda VanCleve moved among them, giving assignments and guidance and answering questions.

Mars and the chief had worked through a new confidential wire to members of the National Association of Chiefs of Police that would be sent out by John Durr from Kansas City.

"This one's gonna scare the shit out of them," the chief said with a smile. He read out loud, " 'The Homicide Division of the Minneapolis Police Department in cooperation with the Forensic Science Division of the Federal Bureau of Investigation and law enforcement officials in Wisconsin and Kansas, urgently request your assistance in connection with the hanging death of—and so on, and so on," the chief said, searching for what he'd called the "off-your-butt-fast" line.

"Here it is," he said, reading with malevolent pleasure. " 'It has been confirmed that this death is connected to other deaths where the victim has a genealogical connection to members of the First Minnesota Volunteers who fought at Gettysburg during the Civil War. . . . ' "

The chief paused, looking at Mars over the top of his glasses. "This next part is in bold, upper-case type: '**BASED ON AVAILABLE INFORMATION, IT IS BELIEVED PROBABLE THAT OTHER VICTIMS MAY BE TARGETED AND AT RISK**. The Minneapolis Police Department is identifying other potential victims and will be in contact with affected jurisdictions at the earliest possible time. The MPD requests your assistance in identifying deaths where the following circumstances exist. . . . ' "

The chief put the message down with satisfaction. "The underlying message is, 'You have a death in your jurisdiction after receiving this message, and you're in deep trouble.' Some of these guys, they don't see anything in it for them, they're not gonna put forth the effort. This message says, this is big-time; pay attention. For that matter, it should get them worrying about whether they've misclassified a previous death. At some point this thing is gonna have to go public, and when that happens, if they haven't already taken action, they're gonna look mighty lame."

Feeling the need to find peace and quiet—and to stir his bones, pump some oxygen into his brain—Mars left the squad room shortly before 2:00 P.M. He wandered back down to the first floor courtyard, where he once again used the Father of the Waters as a backrest. It was surprisingly quiet after the hustle upstairs, the peace disturbed only by the faint sound of the occasional passing car from the street outside and the distant, tinny noise of Christmas carols piped in through speakers three stories up.

A squad car with flashers rotating pulled up at the Fourth Street entrance. A uniform hopped out of the driver's seat and opened the trunk. From the passenger side, a guy in a spring-weight trench coat got out, flinching at the cold, moving awkwardly to lift out an obviously heavy file case. Gloveless, he held out a painfully exposed hand for the bag offered by the uniform.

"Boyle Keegan," Mars said, half out loud, as he headed toward the door.

He couldn't have said why, but on sight he liked Keegan. The word *rotund* came to mind in looking at Keegan: big, as in tall, and rotund. Keegan was partially bald, with what remained of his hair making him look as if he'd stuck a finger in an electrical socket. Impossible to guess Keegan's age—anywhere from Mars's age to fifty would have been Mars's guess.

"Marshall Bahr," Mars said, holding open the door and reaching for the heavy file case Keegan carried. "Boyle Keegan?"

Keegan drew back the case Mars had reached for. On second glance, Mars realized the case was attached to Keegan's wrist by a plastic cord. "Take this one," Keegan said, handing Mars an overnight bag.

In the elevator, Keegan said, "You're the fellow that sent the fax?"

"Yeah," Mars said, suddenly self-conscious about Keegan's appraisal of the profile.

Keegan's expression gave nothing away, but he said, "Good piece of work. Very helpful. As far as it goes. Couple of things you need to add. Liquor stores closed here on Christmas Day?"

Mars blinked in surprise. "Not my area of expertise, but my first guess would be yes."

"Damn," Keegan muttered as they walked into city hall.

Keegan had a surprising affect on people working in the squad room. None of the researchers knew who he was, but Nettie and the chief seemed almost self-conscious. Mars guessed it was a combination of Keegan's demeanor—which was unreadable—and his association with the FBI's fabled Forensic Science Unit. That unit was one of the few divisions in the Bureau that had distinguished itself with both the public and the law enforcement community in recent years.

Keegan looked around the room at the frenetic activity, then at Mars and the chief. "Is there someplace where we can talk?"

Not wanting to go far from the action in the squad room, they led Keegan back to the lounge. He looked at the disreputable furniture and gave a small smile. "I trust this means you spend your money on important things."

He sat down on the couch, which rocked treacherously on its uneven legs. Then he keyed a number into the combination lock on the case that had been attached to his wrist. Simultaneously, the case opened and the wrist lock came free.

Keegan shook his wrist after the lock was off, as if the lock had been too tight. Then he said, "I reviewed the material you faxed before I left Quantico. Which was good. It allowed me to pull together some file information that I think will be useful. I was saying to Bahr," he tipped his head in Mars's direction, "that his profile was especially useful. But I don't think it goes far enough. At first sight, I see at least two things that are missing. . . ."

"Those being? . . ." The chief said.

"There's an element of the crime scene that I think is key and then a point on the suspect that's important."

Mars sat forward. "Go ahead."

"I think you've missed something on the noose."

Nettie said, "Actually, we're doing quite a bit of work on the noose. We're expecting lab results from England that should allow us to identify where the fabric was manufactured. Once we've done that, we're hoping we can get customer lists—"

Keegan shook his head impatiently. "Fine, good. My point was something else. I don't think the perpetrator's choice of hanging is arbitrary. If all the perp cares about is killing the guy, why not just load more barbs into the booze and let them go out that way? Helluva lot easier for the perp. No, I think the choice of hanging is significant in itself. The carefully knotted noose, the special fabric—I think you should be looking for a link between hangings and your perpetrator. The only reason he's gonna go to the trouble of hanging is if it has special significance. I'd look at things like one of the First Minnesota stringing up somebody from the Twenty-eighth Virginia. Along those lines."

Mars blinked hard, like something dangerous had just come at his face, fast. Keegan was right, and Mars was embarrassed. Interpreting the symbolic significance of the method used to commit a homicide was Investigative Techniques 101. He'd been so preoccupied by the numbers that the meaning of the noose had slipped right by him.

"You're right," Mars said. "Missed it altogether."

"The other thing." Keegan said. "Your perpetrator profile is spot on—as far as it goes. But you're missing a key element. You've noted the importance of ritual and symbolism in the perpetrator's actions. But you've limited that analysis to the crime scene. Your perpetrator is going to look for closure after each death, something that symbolizes his achievement."

"Something more than completing nineteen murders?" Mars said. "For me, that would be his focus."

"That will be the grand finale. But with each murder, there's going to be something that marks progress toward the final goal. You aware of anything taken from the victims?"

Mars shook his head. "Haven't found any evidence of that. What you're saying is, the perp would take something to create a—display, something like that, to mark his progress."

Keegan sat back on the couch, causing it to lurch. Keegan paused until he was stable, then said, "My guess would be that he's bringing something back to a site that has symbolic significance. Say, the spot at Gettysburg where the flag was captured. Can you put your finger on that location with any precision?"

Mars nodded. Then shook his head. "There's a copse of trees where the flag was captured. My understanding is it's still there. But I don't think that's where the perp would go for closure. That's a spot no Confederate loyalist wants to go back to."

Keegan held both hands up in a gesture of indifference. "Wherever. My point's the same—I'm betting there is a place that is significant to the perp, and he's returning to that place after each murder to make some kind of symbolic gesture, to leave something. . . ."

"I understand," Mars said. "Let me pursue that . . ."

"If you don't object," Keegan said, "I've got contacts with the National Park Service." His face twisted into an expression of weary ruefulness. "You would not believe the number of per-verts—especially these radical, redneck, right-wing groups—that commit violent acts in national parks. What I'd like to do—just to cover our bases—is have a video cam hidden near this copse of trees at Gettysburg. I'll arrange to have the film mailed to Quantico on a periodic basis and reviewed for any activity that looks significant or—" He hesitated, then said, "Or that follows one of our hanging deaths."

They were all silent for a moment, taking in what Keegan's statement meant. It was the chief who said, "I'd like to think it won't come to that. That we can get this guy before we have another death."

The rueful expression returned to Keegan's face. "With this guy? With a killer who has demonstrated superb organizational skills and who doubtless views himself as doing God's work? A killer who obviously has significant financial resources at his disposal? With a broad and as-yet unidentified population of potential victims?"

Keegan shook his head, then looked them in the eye by turn.

"There will be more deaths. The only question is, how many before we stop him?"

Keegan wanted to review with Mars the files he had brought on radical domestic groups and their individual members. Nettie said, "I think you should move into the conference room. I'll stay with the researchers and get you if anything comes up."

As they moved through the squad room, Mars explained in a low voice what was going on with the researchers and the assumptions they'd made about the killer's selection of victims.

Keegan stood in front of the white board, reading through the sixteen names, nodding slowly. "This is good," he said. "I didn't realize you were this far along." He turned toward Mars and the chief. "I wondered when I was reviewing the information you faxed out—how *did* you figure out Beck was a homicide, not a suicide—I mean, what made you question the suicide in the first place?"

The chief put his hand on Mars's shoulder, but Mars shook his head. "A uniform assigned to the downtown command who was the officer on the scene at Beck's hanging raised the questions about the noose and about the numbers on Beck's arm. Without his raising those questions, the possibility of homicide never would have been considered."

Keegan continued to nod slowly. "A guy like that, worth his weight in gold." Keegan looked at the chief. "What's he still doing in a uniform? Why haven't you got him working investigations?"

Mars laughed. "If Danny Borg heard you say that, he'd carry you on his back for the rest of your life."

"Well, at a minimum, when this is over, he should get some sort of commendation. You don't do it here, the Bureau will come up with something."

Before the chief left, Mars took him aside. "Something else. There's still a lot of risk here. One thing that might help would be if we could get the History Center to give the flag back. At least on a temporary basis. It might slow our perp down, even if he doesn't stop altogether. Buy us a little time. Thought I'd ask Glenn Gjerde in the County Attorney's Office to try and work something out with the Attorney General's Office."

The chief shrugged. "Worth a try, as long as we can maintain confidentiality. I just don't want to see a headline about giving the flag back to save lives because the police can't find the killer."

As Mars and Keegan walked out of the squad room, Keegan made a backward motion with his head toward the researchers. "How much do they know about what they're working on?"

"They've been told they're looking for a murder suspect who may be a descendent of one of the First Minnesota Volunteers. And they've been told it is a criminal offense to divulge information regarding an ongoing investigation without police department approval. We had all of them sign confidentiality agreements—so for now, I think the lid is on. Longer this goes on, the harder it's going to be to keep the lid on. These are smart people, capable of putting two and two together."

"You know why I ask," Keegan said. "This is a sad thing to

have to say, but maybe the strongest thing we have going for us is that we know a lot about how the perp is operating. And he doesn't know we know it. He gets wind that we're onto him, he could alter his MO. That happens, and he'll drop this orderly, ritualistic business and just start trying to take out as many targeted victims as he can, as fast as he can. Knock on the victim's door and blast him. His bottom line is nineteen deaths. If he thinks we can stop him before he gets to nineteen, he's going to go wild."

Mars hadn't thought about it in just those terms, but he knew as soon as Keegan said it that Keegan was right. That realization was followed by another thought. To Keegan he said, "Assuming of course, that he hasn't already completed his mission. All that we know at this point is that three deaths have occurred. The first was the Salina, Kansas, hanging a year and a half back. Gaylord Rowe died seven months ago. I think it's safe to assume he hasn't had time to kill again since Beck, but we have to hope those weren't deaths numbers seventeen, eighteen, and nineteen. Until we've gotten responses to our latest information request, we can't be sure there's anyone left to save. That, or we complete identification of our targeted victims and confirm who's still alive."

"The *temporal* aspect," Keegan said. "I've completely neglected that point." He sighed. "Well, the best you can say—if Beck was the nineteenth victim—is that it simplifies what remains to be done. All you need to do is catch the bastard. Much easier than keeping him from killing again."

Mars looked sideways at Keegan as they walked. There was nothing in Keegan's voice or face that suggested Keegan had made this statement with a sense irony. But Mars didn't believe Keegan was as coldhearted as his remark suggested. A man who didn't value preventing death over solving murders wouldn't have traveled a thousand miles to spend Christmas Day in a cold, strange city.

CHAPTER

18

Keegan spread his files across the conference room table. Then he picked them up, one by one, giving Mars a careful narrative about each group, its key members, the group's purpose, and past criminal activity. When he'd gone through all the files but three, he shoved the other files aside.

"These two," he said, "the Recover Our Flag members—ROFers—and the Pure Blood Boys—those are your prime targets. The ROFers were organized for the express purpose of recovering the Twenty-eighth Virginia's flag from Minnesota. Problem with them, they're pretty much a bunch of straight shooters. I can't imagine any of them being involved in these murders. All their activities have been political: trying to get the Virginia legislature to support resolutions in their favor, petitioning the Virginia Attorney General's Office for legal remedies, fund-raising—things like that. Their principal guy is Phil Stern." Keegan took a photo from the ROFer file and slid it across the table to Mars.

"Stern is decent down to his bones. Early on, some of the Pure Blood Boys tried to join the group. I'm sure their idea was, Minnesota won't give the flag back, we'll go get it. Stern saw to it the Pure Blood Boys were kept out of ROF. He's smart enough to know that if ROFer's activities are tainted by white supremacists, they'll never get the flag back. Stern is an amateur history buff, a descendent of a soldier in the Twenty-eighth Virginia. His interest in the flag is purely historical. I wouldn't even say he cares much about the Great Lost Cause. But he may know of people that fit your profile that aren't on our radar because they haven't been openly subversive—so I'd start with him. And in confidence I'd tell him what the investigation is about. He'll want to be sure the ROFers are on the right side of this problem—he'll do whatever he can to help."

Keegan gave Mars a look as he moved the second file forward. "These guys—the Pure Blood Boys—they'll do whatever, and if violence is involved, so much the better. The problem is, as far as your profile goes, they don't have what it takes to pull it off. Pretty much a bunch of tattooed, pickup-driving racists who spend most of their time in bars bumming cigarettes and in bar parking lots picking fights. We track them because they've been involved in a number of racial harassment cases. Nothing organized, but they've caused their share of trouble. And they're the kind of guys—given a couple bucks to rub together—who might decide to bomb something. I mention them special to you for two reasons." Keegan moved another photo over to Mars. "This guy, Junior Boosey, is their leader. Now, Junior—if he had any serious education or any money to back him, he'd be a force to contend with. Junior has a plan—he just doesn't have the means to carry anything forward. At least he doesn't now. . . ."

Keegan picked up the third file, tapping it on the table. "If this guy were still alive you'd have a perfect match with your profile. Hector Lee Macintosh. Killed in a hunting accident in West Virginia, oh—I'm not sure exactly when. Couple years back, just before I joined the unit at Quantico. Hec was from an old Richmond, Virginia family with more money than General Motors. Married a Richmond woman with money of her own. Both of them—flaming racists. Hec was financing the ROFers until Stern decided Hec was doing more damage than good. That, and Hec was tied up with the Pure Blood Boys. Apparently Hec and Junior had a very close relationship—almost like father and son. So Hec and ROF split. My guess is, while Hec was still alive, he was working with Junior on a plan to take the flag by force. And God knows what else."

Keegan sat back, rubbing his eyes. "When I first read your profile, I thought about what I'd heard about Hec right away. He had the means, the passion, and the craziness to pull something like these killings off. And he was an educated southern boy who could play whatever role was called for in approaching victims. What we need to look for is someone like Hec who hasn't surfaced, who has the brains to keep a low profile. My guess is there's somebody out there that was hooked up with Hec but who kept his head down. Maybe an old fraternity brother of Hec's from UVA. Somebody who had the discipline not to mouth off about his views. Which for sure Hec didn't."

Mars stared at the files on the table. "I'm thinking I need to go to Richmond."

Keegan rocked back on his chair. "That's exactly right."

They were on the way back to the squad room when they ran into Nettie. "We've got two more descendent matches. An eldest son now living in central Illinois. . . ."

"He's alive?" Mars asked.

"He's listed in the telephone directory that will be published next month. Got that straight from the phone company. And we've got a current address. We're still working on a current address for the second guy. That's turning out to be a bigger job than tracing the descendent line. And the chief said he'd meet you in the conference room."

Mars and Keegan turned around. "So now we see how well the notification procedures work," Mars said.

They began by calling John Durr in Kansas City. Durr had agreed that in his position as president of the National Association of Chiefs of Police, he'd make all police contacts regarding targeted victims outside of Minnesota.

Boyle Keegan put in a call to FBI headquarters, which would take responsibility for contacting the special agent in charge at the appropriate field division office. That agent would be responsible for establishing liaison with the local police force and providing any surveillance or protection assistance needed.

They'd spent a long time figuring out what the targeted victims would be told when contacted. No one thought it would be productive to knock on a stranger's door and tell him that a mad killer was looking for him. Once that message got out, it would spread like wildfire, causing panic and jeopardizing the investigation. On the other hand, the target needed to know he was at risk.

It was Mars who said, "Look. Everything we know about the killings that have taken place tells us that the killer is proceeding methodically. He's not breaking into houses in the middle of the night and clubbing victims to death. He's not shooting them from a distance with a high-powered rifle. He's making contact with them in advance and arranging a time to meet when he can be confident he'll be alone with the victim. So the message we need to get to the targeted victims is that they need to be alert to any contacts from strangers—especially if the stranger requests a confidential meeting. Our suspect is going to propose something to the target that is personal to that individual. With Beck, we're pretty sure our perp posed as a venture capitalist. In Rowe's case, we know from what the sister said that the perp knew Gaylord Rowe would be receptive to someone who proposed a project connected to the First Minnesota Volunteers. Nettie—what was it you said you'd found out about the victim in Salina?"

"His wife had died of ovarian cancer, and his daughter had just been diagnosed."

"Right. So it's likely the perp's approach would be that he wants to fund research, a foundation, wants the target to participate in a public education effort—something like that. My point is that all of those strategies fit with a fraud crime. So what we tell the targeted victim, at least initially, is that it's come to the FBI's attention that he may be subject to a contact by someone engaged in fraudulent activities. That he needs to contact the FBI immediately if a stranger contact is made and that under no circumstances should the target agree to meet the person making the contact. Meanwhile, local police or the FBI can be maintaining surveillance on the target. . . ."

The chief said, "That sounds fine, Mars. Only problem—some of these jurisdictions are going to have pretty short staffs to provide the kind of protection you're talking about. Can we give them some idea how long surveillance might be needed?"

Mars thought about it. There was nothing. Not yet. To Nettie he said, "How about this. We know our perp is operating in a ritualistic fashion. For the three murder dates we know of, there's no discernible pattern. What about dates of Confederate battles, something like that? Can you check the murder dates against battle dates, see if anything matches? We'd really be ahead of the game if we could identify specific times when the targets were at risk."

Nettie nodded. "That'll be easy."

The squad room of the Minneapolis Homicide Department had no exterior windows, so Mars was surprised when he realized it was nearly 8:00 P.M. He was tired but not sleepy. A bad combination.

Nettie, who'd been grinding away for days, with no relief other than an occasional nap on the lounge couch, was showing definite signs of wear. The chief had left an hour earlier, asking to be called in if anything came up.

Linda VanCleve came over to Mars at his desk. She sighed heavily and dropped down on a chair, facing him. "I know how important what we're doing is to the investigation—but I've got to let my people go home at some point. Day after tomorrow, I'll have enough people available to set up shifts. But if we keep working these people, they're going to start making mistakes."

"Go ahead," Mars said. "You've been great. When this is over, we'll see that you and your staff get some kind of special recognition." Then, sheepishly, "Any idea when you can get back in tomorrow?"

"I'll be here by seven," Linda said. "I've asked everybody else to be back by eight. We got a current address that we were missing and we're real close on two of the remaining eleven." She looked at him. "Mars, they're starting to ask questions about what they're doing. They're hearing bits and pieces of conversations and picking up on the tension. If I could tell them what's really at stake here, it would be a real motivator."

Mars was too tired to even think about an answer to Van-Cleve's question. "Let's talk about it with the chief tomorrow," he said.

Just before nine, Nettie said, "Good news, bad news."

Mars tilted his head back and looked at her.

"I've found dates on-line for every battle that was fought during the Civil War."

"Don't bother to tell me the bad news. No matches with our murder dates."

"You're so smart."

"Go home, Nettie. I need you smart tomorrow. Especially I need you to work what Keegan said on the significance of the hangings. We've got a long row left to hoe."

As she left, he called after her. "Nettie?"

She turned to look back at him.

"Merry Christmas."

Nettie said, "I think we can punt on Merry Christmas. Happy New Year is the new objective."

Boyle Keegan walked toward Mars, jingling change in his pockets. "I think I've shot my wad," he said. "Still no idea where I can find a jar of one-hundred-proof liquor on Christmas night?"

"Try the minibar in your hotel room," Mars said.

Keegan gave Mars a close look. "You about to head out?"

Mars moved out of his slouch, straightened up, and stretched. "Problem is, I'm too tense. I'm gonna stay here until my head starts to drop. I go home now, I'll just toss and turn. Won't be worth diddly tomorrow."

After Keegan left, Mars turned the overhead lights out in the squad room, which meant the only light sources were the glow of the computer screens and the perimeter lights in the hallway. He sat back on his chair and let his mind wander, staring at the white board, which appeared to glow in the dim room.

He rose and walked over to the board, looking at the dates of death that had been written by the names of three identified victims. Absolutely no discernible pattern. At some level, Mars had known all along that he'd need to go to Richmond, Virginia. Reading Macintosh's file, Mars thought consciously about the need to go to Richmond, to check into Macintosh's background. To look for someone who might have been a silent partner in Macintosh's mission.

Then Mars thought about what he needed to do before he went to Richmond, including something he needed to do first thing the next morning.

Glenn Gjerde was having breakfast in the cafeteria in the lower level of the Hennepin County Government Center.

On sighting Mars, Gjerde said, "Here comes trouble."

Glenn Gjerde was the worst and best prosecuting attorney in the Hennepin County Attorney's Office. The worst because he'd never take a case to court unless the evidence was perfect. The best, because once he was convinced you were giving him a case with solid evidence, you could be sure justice was right around the corner.

For that reason, cops had a lot of confidence in Glenn. The confidence came from Glenn's record of convictions, not from Glenn's personal style. He routinely dressed in a bizarre mix of exercise clothes and what might be described as workplace casual. Today that meant a pair of polyurethane windproof pants, running shoes, an oxford cloth shirt, and a plum-colored sports coat that was at least one size too small. A tie hung out of the lapel pocket of the jacket.

"What's up?" he said, chewing and not looking very interested.

Mars gave Glenn a quick run-through on the Beck case. Glenn got interested. He stopped chewing. "Jesus," he said. "So what do you need me to do?"

"This is feeling too loosey-goosey to me. I think we've got to take action to get the killer to stop—then focus on finding him. I want us to give the flag back to Virginia."

Glenn grinned. "And while I'm at it, do you want me to achieve peace in the Middle East?"

"Only if it doesn't slow down getting the flag back to Virginia. Start by talking to whoever from the State Attorney General's Office represents the Historical Society. Keep Linda VanCleve out of it at this stage. We're working together at this point, and I don't want to get her all riled up. Get it expedited. We need some time here, and I don't want anyone else dying while we're looking for the killer."

Dana Levy called Mars in the squad room right after he got back from talking to Glenn.

"Hate to spoil your holidays," she said. Not sounding sorry. Dana and Mars had history. Brief, a couple years back, but definitely—at least in Dana's mind—history.

It started when Dana joined the department as the public information officer. To be good at that job you needed three things. You had to understand how the media works, you had to be tough enough so that cops trusted—and respected—you, and you had to be willing to spend time learning about everything from how blood spatters to criminal procedure.

Dana'd been good at the job right off. Early on she'd said to Mars, "It'd be helpful if we could talk off-line about how the department can do a better job of working with the media, especially on big investigations where we have to withhold information."

Mars had agreed, and Dana immediately invited him for dinner at her house. Not what he'd had in mind, but not a definite uh-uh. Dana was smart and cute. He was willing to give it a try.

Things started to go wrong as soon as Mars pulled up in Dana's driveway. Her car, parked in the driveway, had two bumper stickers. How's My Driving? 1-800-EAT-SHIT. And, I Drive Way Too Fast to Worry About Cholesterol.

Then she opened the door. She was wearing a T-shirt that read, On the Advice of My Lawyer, My Shirt Has No Comment at This Time. She was carrying a coffee cup that read, Give Me Coffee and No One Will Get Hurt. Mars was prepared for the refrigerator. He just didn't have time to read all the magnets. But he couldn't miss You Can Tell a Guy Is Lying When His Lips Are Moving.

The woman was noisy even when *her* lips *weren't* moving. Which wasn't often. She talked like a repeating rifle, stopping only long enough to look at caller ID on her cell phone and punch "talk." And her cell phone rang a lot.

It was Mars's cell phone that saved him. Before dessert, he got a call. He begged off on urgent business and made his escape. "Something I should be in on?" she'd asked.

"I'll call if we need you," he said.

A week or so later, he felt guilty and invited her to a movie. Not to start anything, but to do a better job of finishing. She talked nonstop until the lights went down, after which she was silent for seconds at a time, leaning toward him like clockwork with a running commentary on the movie.

Mars leaned toward her fifteen minutes into the feature, and said, "I don't talk during movies."

She'd laughed and poked him. "So, listen." And she'd kept up the chatter.

He drove her straight home after the movie. When they'd pulled into her driveway, behind her double-stickered car, she said, "I think I still owe you dessert." She was actually quiet for a moment as she gave him a meaningful look.

Mars looked back and said, "No. Thanks, but no."

Not really a better finish.

So they had history. She was too much of a pro to let it affect how they worked together, but she never missed a chance to put a little knife-twisting spin on their conversations.

"Not much of anything left to spoil," Mars said.

"Got a call from the news director at Channel Twelve."

"And?"

"They're running a story tonight on the ten o'clock news. Near as I can tell, it's a fishing expedition. A bunch of stuff about the money being spent on the First Response Unit at a time when homicides are down. Something about spinning a sure-thing suicide investigation into a big-deal homicide. Good news is, I don't think they've got much. If they had something solid, they'd be holding it till sweeps and they'd be running promos a week before air."

"You've seen it?"

"They're sending a messenger out to my house with the tape. I'll let you know if I think we should comment. What I'm expecting is they'll raise a bunch of questions. You know, is the special unit in homicide earning its keep, what is the Candy Man doing with the suicide—like that. Nothing that'll stick."

"Sounds like someone in the police union has been running his mouth. You've alerted the chief's and the mayor's offices?"

"Of course. Mars? Is this something I should know about?"

"Yeah. But I'm going to have to ask you to sit on it for the next couple of days. I need to get out to Richmond, Virginia, and I'm totally jammed up between now and the time I leave. Something else. What we're working on is highly confidential. At the risk of sounding like a drama queen, it's not overstating the issue to say lives may depend on keeping a lid on this one for as long as possible. You get wind of any specifics on this story, get a hold of me, the chief, or Nettie right away."

CHAPTER

19

Mars hated the way airplanes smelled: dry, artificial air laced with the scent of fabric gone stale from being sat on by hordes of unclean travelers.

Anticipating the odor, Mars's stomach clutched as he entered the cabin of the 757. Nettie, who'd found subtle means of coddling him since his surgery, had pooled division frequent flyer miles to wrangle Mars a first-class ticket for his flight to Dulles International. Mars was both disappointed and gratified to discover that first-class smelled no better than coach.

The first-class stewardess moved toward Mars with a warm smile. "Let me take your jacket, sir. What can I bring you to drink?" Only another woman would have noticed the slightly seductive sway of the stewardess's hips and that the stewardess had, in a seamless glance, taken in that Mars wasn't wearing a wedding band.

"Coca-Cola. Lots of ice."

"I *am* sorry, sir, but we don't stock Coca-Cola. Will Pepsi be alright?"

Mars had known the answer to his request before he'd asked for Coke, but he wasn't going to let Northwest Airlines off the hook. "Skip it, then."

She looked wounded, backing off with his jacket. Moments later Mars noticed her in deep conversation with another attendant, after which they both huddled over the passenger manifest. The second stewardess was fingering a small piece of paper, which she passed on to the stewardess who'd taken Mars's drink order. Then they both looked over at Mars. The stewardess shrugged and moved back into the galley. When Mars next looked up, the stewardess was standing next to him holding a small tray, covered with a white linen cloth. There were two objects on the cloth. A heavy glass tumbler filled with small, square ice cubes. And a red-and-white can of Classic Coca-Cola.

"Mr. Bahr," the stewardess said, "I apologize for what I said earlier, but as it happens we received preauthorization to carry twelve ounces of Coca-Cola as per your physician's order."

Mars barely suppressed a grin. Nettie's fine hand was in evidence here. What he couldn't figure was the "physician's order." As the stewardess set the tray on the arm rest he noticed a prescription form under the glass. Sliding it out he deciphered Dr. Denton D. Mont's signature.

The pair of them were a piece of work.

The positive benefit the flight offered was that for maybe the first time since he and Nettie had made their middle-of-the-night ride to the History Center, he'd have time to think through all the evidence that was coming together in the Beck investigation. Now, with an early morning ice storm just ended and departing flights lined up in an endless queue, it looked like Mars would have four or five hours of uninterrupted contemplation. He was probably the only passenger on the flight who welcomed the delay.

His immediate problem would be finding Junior Boosey. The FBI didn't have a good handle on where he was at any point in time. Mars was going to have to do some backwoods rambling just across the Virginia border in West Virginia to track Junior down. The most recent information available suggested he might be living with a sister—no name for the sister—near a spot on the map called Green Springs. Mars was hoping that when he showed up at the spot on the map he'd find someone who could point him to Junior.

After he finished in the western part of the state, Mars would drive to Richmond. The chief had arranged for Mars to hook up with the deputy chief of police in Richmond.

"Gordon Ball is a man you can trust to keep information under his hat until you say otherwise. We were at the academy together years ago and have been friends ever since." The chief smiled. "He's not from Richmond, so you don't have to worry about his being a partisan, if that's on your mind. Married a Richmond girl, is how he ended up there. And who knows, down the road you might want to have a personal contact out there."

The drive from Dulles International to Salem, Virginia, was as pretty as anything Mars had seen in a long time. To his left, the Blue Ridge Mountains rolled off into a haze. On his right, the Appalachians, shrouded in bare hardwoods, were silhouetted against the sunset. But when the road dipped, the fog would get thick and traffic would slow to a crawl.

Tired from the long flight and the stress of driving in fog, Mars reached Salem before 9:00 P.M. It made no sense to move up into the mountains toward West Virginia after dark, so he pulled in at a Quality Inn just off the Salem exit that would take him west to West Virginia first thing in the morning.

Mars slept the sleep of angels that night and on waking felt fresh and full of energy. After showering and getting dressed, he walked across the street to a café that served a big, hot, greasy plate of fried eggs, potatoes, and toast. He ate all of it, then headed back to check out of the motel.

He took Route 311 west out of Salem and immediately began an ascent into the Appalachians. If anything, the fog was heavier than it had been the previous day. But as he continued the ascent toward West Virginia, the fog broke and Mars drove out into sunshine. Given the hairpin turns of the narrow road, clear weather was welcome.

At several points Mars noticed signs off to the left indicating access to the Appalachian Trail. Until seeing the signs, Mars really hadn't focused on the fact he'd be traveling in the vicinity of the trail. Chris had been reading a book Nettie had lent him about two crazy guys who'd tried to walk the Appalachian Trail. Since he'd started reading the book, Chris had developed a fascination with the trail, and Mars felt a deep pang of regret that Chris wasn't along. At the third directional sign for trail access, Mars signaled a left turn, parked along the road, and walked up the hill until he reached the marked path. He walked slowly for a time until he found a handsome, pocket-sized rock. He picked the rock up, dropped it in his pocket, and headed back to the car—confident there wasn't anything he could bring home to Chris that would be more appreciated.

Green Springs, West Virginia, was just the other side of the Virginia/West Virginia border. The town sign said Green Springs had a population of 267. Looking down the road all Mars could see of Green Springs was a gas station, a bar, and a couple of houses. He decided the gas station would be the best place to check for where he might find Junior Boosey. He had almost three-quarters of a tank of gas left, but decided to fill up, hoping that a paying customer would get more cooperation than a curious stranger.

He'd no sooner killed the ignition than an old guy in a wool jacket and a baseball cap came through the station door and toward the car. "Fill it up for ya?" he said, not looking at Mars.

It had been so long since Mars had someone fill his tank that it took him a second to know how to respond.

The old guy considered the car. "You got your tank on the wrong side from the pump."

"Right," Mars said. He'd parked as if he were filling the tank on his car. "Rental car. Want me to move?"

The old guy squinted at the car. "Should reach," he said, then performed heroic contortions to make it happen. He stood next to the car, hand on the nozzle, eye fixed on the gas meter clicking off the sale. It shut off at 2.3 gallons. Mars winced.

"Hardly worth the trouble," the old guy said. "You up here lookin' for someone?"

The old guy had him dead to rights. Didn't make any sense at all to fool around at this point. "Junior Boosey live around here?"

The old guy resaddled the hose and motioned for Mars to follow him into the gas station. The interior of the station had a hot, kerosene-ish smell. Crude shelves against the wall were lined with cans of Halvoline oil, spark plugs, and boxes of candy bars. The paper wrappings on the candy bars were covered in dust. In the corner, a half-full gumball machine stood, shrouded in cobwebs. Just behind the gum machine was a curtained entry to what appeared to be living quarters.

The old guy said, "Junior Boosey, huh? Well, I just guess I got it in one."

"Got it in one?" Mars said.

"Some stranger shows up, wanderin' around bumpin' into things, well, ten times out of ten, who he's lookin' for is Junior. You pulled up, I say to myself, I bet a dollar he's looking for Junior. So I got it in one, didn't I?"

Mars smiled. "You did indeed. Question is, did I pick the right place to ask the question?"

"Well, you didn't have all that many choices, did you?"

Junior Boosey's sister lived about eight miles from the station, off the main road, down a side road, then off the side road to a two-track rut. The old guy had told Mars that *if* Junior were around, he'd be at his sister's, where he kept a trailer. The old guy hadn't seen Junior himself for sometime, but that didn't mean Junior wasn't around. As the old guy explained it, Junior had times when he did have transportation and times when he didn't have transportation. When Junior had transportation, the old guy would see him at the bar or passing through Green Springs. If he didn't see Junior around, it probably meant Junior was in a phase where he didn't have transportation. "Easier to get hold of then," the old guy said. "He'll be sittin' in his trailer at his sister's, most likely."

Which was exactly where Mars found Junior Boosey. Mars pulled into a clearing at the end of the two-track rut. Directly in front of him was a pin-neat double wide. Bright white vinyl siding with fake black shutters. Couple hundred feet behind the double-wide, near the woods, was a small, silver Airstream. Junior, Mars guessed, belonged to the Airstream.

He got out of the car and walked up to the double-wide. Cool as it was, only the screen door was closed. Mars shaded his eyes with one hand as he peered behind the screen. Before he could say anything, a young woman emerged, carrying a toddler on her hip with one hand, the other hand holding a bowl of what looked like small red pebbles. The barefooted toddler was dipping into the bowl with deep concentration, his mouth and fingers stained deep red.

"Yes?" the young woman said, pushing the screen open, her voice wary, eyes guarded.

Mars quickly flashed his badge. "I'm looking for Junior Boosey. That his trailer in the back?"

She shifted the child. Mars reached up, gently squeezing the kid's toe. The kid pulled his shoulders tight and turned his face quickly into his mother's neck, then peeked back at Mars.

"A beautiful kid," Mars said. Meaning it, but knowing at the same time that the way to most mothers' trust was complimenting their children. "He likes candy, I'd say."

"Not candy," she said. "Don't let my baby have candy. These are wild berries I picked out back last summer. Then I dry 'em in a dee-hydratin' machine I got."

The child was staring at Mars, his head resting on his mother's shoulder. Then he pulled away, leaning over and picking a single dried berry from the bowl. With exquisite delicacy, the child tipped forward, holding the berry toward Mars. Mars held his hand out, but the child pulled back, shaking his head and grinning. Then he leaned forward again, the berry between his thumb and index finger, pushing it toward Mars's mouth. Mars opened his mouth and stuck his tongue out. The child dropped the berry on Mars's tongue, then squealed at his accomplishment.

The berry was both tart and sweet. The drying had made it chewy and had changed the texture of the seeds, which were no longer hard, but had gone hollow and crunchy. "Ummmm," Mars said. "Good. Thank you. You're a generous boy." He squeezed the child's toe again which produced another fit of shyness.

Junior's sister gave it up. "That's Junior's trailer, all right. Haven't seen him yet today, but he'll be back there. Whether he opens the door—that's another matter."

Mars walked on a worn path behind the double wide to the Airstream. Before he got up to the Airstream door, it opened. A small, thin kid with a shaved head stepped out.

Junior was a stereotype. Lean, hard-boned, the shaved head. Narrow jeans, a white T-shirt under a warm-up jacket. Not a big kid, but dangerously fit. From his early days as a patrol cop, Mars had developed the ability to judge when an individual would be a handful if you needed to subdue him. Big was the least of it. What you needed to watch out for was the buff body in combination with something in the eyes. Junior had the combination.

"Junior Boosey?" Mars said, approaching the door. Junior didn't answer. He stood on a cement block that served as a step into the trailer. If Mars had learned anything on this trip it was that trying to be subtle about what he was looking for didn't get him anything. So he said, "Junior, I'm Marshall Bahr from the Minneapolis Police Department." He paused, pulling out his badge. "I'm investigating the death of an individual in Minneapolis that we think may be connected to the controversy over the

Twenty-eighth Virginia's regimental flag. I'd like to talk to you, if you've got a minute."

Junior still didn't speak, but he stepped up and held the door open for Mars to enter. One of the big myths about police work was that all cops worked in daily danger. What cops knew was that it was the street cops, patrol cops, who were at risk. An investigator, like Mars, faced less risk than a big city taxi driver. Mars had almost forgotten what it felt like to come within a hair's breadth of danger, but passing Junior in the trailer's doorway reminded him. As he stepped into the trailer's single room he was momentarily blinded by the change from daylight to the trailer's dim interior. Being blind didn't make him feel less threatened.

When his eyes adjusted to the change, what he saw was a carefully ordered universe. Taking up almost half of the space was a weight-lifting machine that had been bolted to the trailer's floor. Bolted to the walls of the trailer were raw wood bookshelves, with books lined precisely from top to bottom. Mars caught a glimpse of the titles: *Aryan Nation Arise!, The Truth about Human Intelligence, The Citizen's Guide to Firearms, How the Government Is Destroying the Bill of Rights*. Most surprising of all, there was a computer sitting on a narrow counter between the small refrigerator and two-burner stove. Mars guessed Internet access to other right-wing nuts made the computer necessary to Junior. And there was another possibility: that Junior used the computer to research descendents of the First Minnesota.

"Minnesota?" Junior said.

Mars turned. Not sure what Junior was asking.

Junior said, "Minnesota—Minneapolis is in Minnesota, right?"

Mars nodded. "I understand you worked with Hec Macintosh on getting the Twenty-eighth Virginia's flag back."

Junior dropped to the narrow, built-in couch and considered Mars. He flicked his fingers against his knee. "What of it."

"You still involved?"

"Hec's dead," Junior said.

"So I've heard," Mars said. "Doesn't mean you care any less about getting the flag back, does it?"

Junior sat forward, elbows on his knees. "I still care plenty. But I don't even have wheels anymore. What am I gonna do about the flag, sittin' out here in an Airstream?"

"Hec couldn't have been the only one with money that cared. You haven't stayed connected with anyone else?"

"There's a bunch of guys down in Salem still fuckin' around. But they don't plan to do nothin' that's gonna get the flag back. Do-gooders. Hec, he put his money and his mouth on the line. Hec would have done what was necessary. No one else around with balls like that."

"What's necessary to get the flag back, Junior?"

"I'll tell you what ain't necessary. Fuckin' around in courts and stuff. It's ours. We should just take it." Junior fixed his eyes on Mars. "I wouldn't worry none if I was you. I'm about the only guy left standing that'd try something like that, but I've got no backing. If I did, I wouldn't be talking to you now."

Mars looked at Junior in silence for a while. A kid like this didn't come to bigotry in a vacuum. He'd been born and bred to it. Was there a father, an uncle who might have been involved with Hec?

"What's your given name, Junior," Mars said.

"My *given* name?"

"The name on your birth certificate."

"What's on my birth certificate is Baby Boy Boosey. People got tired of calling me that, so they just started calling me Junior. It stuck."

"So your dad's first name isn't your first name?"

"Could be," Junior said. "If I knew my dad's first name I could say. But to know my dad's first name, somebody'd have to know my dad. Never met anybody that did. My ma included."

224

* * *

If you've been born and raised in the Midwest, you can smell salt in the air a hundred miles from the ocean. As he approached Richmond on Interstate 64, the difference in the air—a bite and texture that was distinctly *not* Minnesota—hit Mars with a physical force.

He looked at his watch as he dropped off the interstate, heading toward the city. He'd be just in time for his four o'clock appointment with Phil Stern, chairman of the Recover Our Flag organization. In minutes, the James River appeared to his right. Mars guessed the river was a tidal estuary, which might have accounted for the punch in the air. But given how little water was running in the James, Mars thought it was more likely that a contrary breeze was bringing up ocean air from the southeast.

One thing Minneapolis and Richmond had in common was that they owed their existence to rivers. The guidebook Mars had bought to help him find his way around Richmond had noted that the Falls on the James had been an early source of power for the city's industries. And like St. Anthony Falls on the Mississippi in Minneapolis, economic change and geology had eroded the Falls on the James River's significance to Richmond.

The reception area of Phil Stern's office was the kind of place that gave clients confidence that nothing bad could happen to them or to their money. Which was probably just what a certified public accountant like Stern had in mind. Even in the gloom of an overcast afternoon, the soft patterned pastels of the carpet, the carefully framed prints of idyllic rural scenes, and the young, sweet-faced receptionist combined to deny the existence of anything other than ordered prosperity.

"You're Mr. Bahr, Phil's four o'clock?"

"Marshall Bahr," Mars said.

"Jus' let me tell him you're here, okay?" She picked up the phone, pushed a single button as if it took talent, and in a moment said, "Phil, Mr. Marshall Bahr is here. Okay. Sure thing." She

225

hung up the phone carefully and smiled at Mars. "He'll be right out, Mr. Bahr."

Phil Stern came out of his office and at Mars with an outstretched hand. "Detective Bahr. Sorry to keep you waitin'. C'mon in." He stepped back, holding open his office door. The interior of his office was more masculine, in a planned sort of way, than the reception area. There was lots of wood-grained furniture that had the look of plastic veneer, framed photos of Stern with local political types and third-tier sports figures. And on every level surface, on bookshelves, on the walls—Civil War memorabilia.

On the floor at the side of Stern's desk was a gleaming chrome object with a stiff red brush at one end. Stern paused at the object, tapped a switch with one foot and held the other foot to the now swirling brush.

"Like to keep a good shine on my shoes. Once a marine, always a marine, I guess. Wife got me this for Father's Day last year. Fantastic. Give it a spin, if you want."

"Never was in the marines," Mars said, taking a chair in front of Stern's desk. He managed not to smile as he considered the possibility that his never-shined shoes might fly into a million pieces if subjected to Stern's mechanical brush.

Stern sat down behind his desk, leaning forward with hands folded in front of him. "You said when you called you were interested in knowing more about folks that might have been involved in getting the Twenty-eighth Virginia's flag back . . ."

Mars had been purposely vague on the phone about his reasons for wanting to meet with Stern. He wanted to get a better feel for Stern before letting him in on the details of Beck's murder. Now, after Stern's reference to the marines and his obvious shipshape style, Mars decided to continue to hold his cards close. Stern was showing some promise of matching up with his perp profile.

"We've had a case in Minnesota that looks like it might be tied to the controversy. So we're talking to people who may know of individuals whose interest in the flag has gone off the edge a bit."

Stern shoved back a little from his desk, put a newspaper on top of his desk, then propped a foot on the desk. Looked like about a size 13. Stern was a big guy, starting to go soft, but powerful. His hands cupped behind his head, he looked at Mars directly.

"What kind of case we talking about here?"

"A suicide," Mars said.

Stern made a small guffawing sound. "Man. You trek all the way out here to find out why some guy commits suicide? I've always heard taxes in Minnesota were sky high. Now I know why."

Stern was making it clear that unless Mars was forthcoming about his purposes, Stern was going to play a standoff.

"There are other possibilities. Evidence at the scene links those possibilities to the Twenty-eighth Virginia's regimental flag that was captured at Gettysburg."

Stern dropped his foot to the floor, then hunched forward. He picked a paper clip up from his desk and began twisting it. "You think one of the ROF members may be involved in a murder?" He looked up sharply at Mars, his eyes narrowing slightly.

It was very clear that Mars wasn't going to get anything from Stern without being candid. Maybe not even then. But he was going to have to take a chance or accept that his trip was a wasted effort. For all of his good-natured courtesy, Stern was not a pushover.

"From everything I've heard from the director of our State Historical Society, you're not a likely suspect. But it has to be considered."

Stern lifted the paperclip to his mouth, still staring at Mars. He rubbed the clip back and forth on his full lower lip for a moment, then said, "Who'd you-all think *would* be a likely suspect?"

Mars didn't answer immediately, and Stern said, "Look at it my way, Officer. You come all this way to solve a murder that you say may be associated with a cause I've been involved with for the past three years. Any way you cut it, I don't get a lot out of this. At a minimum, it holds the prospect of discrediting a cause I care deeply about. Worst case, I—or one of my associates—could become the subject of a murder investigation. We both know I don't need to talk to you at all. But the fact is, if a murder has gotten tangled up in this mess, well, I view that as being unfortunate. And I'd be as interested as anyone in resolving that. But I'm only willing to participate if we proceed on the assumption that I am operating on good faith. That we share the same motives." Stern stopped, gave the paperclip a little toss toward the wastebasket. Mars heard the clip land in the basket.

Mars said, "My profile for the killer is that he is a male who presents as a financially secure businessperson. He is well organized—but passionate to the point of rage regarding his cause—which, based on forensic evidence, is the captured flag. He may have a military background, be a sailor—someone who enjoys precision and discipline . . ."

Stern broke into a broad grin. "Well, I guess I'm getting a pretty good picture of why you came looking for me. What's the date I need an alibi for?"

"December six."

"This year?"

Mars nodded.

Stern hollered, "Hey, Deb. Print out my December calendar, will you?"

The door to Sterns office opened. Deb's head poked inside. "You called, Phil?"

"Yeah. I need my December calendar. Print it out and bring it on in, please." To Mars he said, "Used to keep all that stuff in a little notebook. Now it's on a computer, and I've gotta bug Deb all the time to find out where I've been, where I am, and where I'm going."

Since noticing the computer in Junior Boosey's Airstream, Mars had been considering the likelihood that access to and expertise in using a computer would be essential to anyone involved in the hanging murders. Phil Stern had just made the point that he wasn't that guy.

Deb walked in with pages of paper she'd printed out. Stern looked at the pages quickly, then his finger landed in one spot. "Oh, geez," he said. "My fifteenth wedding anniversary party was that night. Don't ever tell my wife I didn't remember right off. I can give you about forty-five witnesses to where I was from five-thirty in the afternoon until just after eleven. Will that cover it?"

Mars nodded. "I meant what I said. You might fit the profile in some respects, but I haven't heard anything to suggest that you've got blood in your eye. I'd appreciate your thoughts as to anyone that matches up on that point—within or outside your organization."

Stern nodded slowly. When he looked up, he smiled. "I'd say you're a couple years too late."

"Meaning? . . ." Mars said.

"Hector Lee Macintosh. Hec would have fit your profile to a T."

"His name has come up," Mars said. "Died in a hunting accident a couple of years ago, if I'm remembering right."

Stern gave a sly smile. "You're remembering it right. Died huntin' wild turkeys. Lots of people called that poetic justice."

"He was a member of your group—Recover Our Flag?"

Stern swiveled back and forth a bit in his chair. "Hec founded the group. Funded it. Which was real helpful. That was before I joined ROF. He recruited me. Knew of my interest in the war, knew I had relatives that fought at Gettysburg, in the Twenty-eighth Virginia. At first, I thought he was the salt of the earth."

"At first?"

Stern picked up another paper clip. He played with it in the fingers of his left hand. It made Mars want to take out his cigarette pack.

"A group like ROF," Stern said, "attracts people other than

guys who are interested in history. When I joined, I got real uncomfortable with some of the members. We had a lot of out-and-out racists involved." Stern shook his head. "I wasn't gonna be any part of that. Told Hec that if those guys stayed, I was out. He didn't object in any way—which kind of surprised me. He personally told the Pure Blood Boys they had to go."

"The Pure Blood Boys. That's the group headed up by a guy named Junior Boosey?"

"You've heard," Stern said.

"I've met with Junior," Mars said.

"Easy to underestimate Junior," Stern said. "No education, no polish. But he's a shrewd cookie. Hec appreciated that. And I think Junior was one of the few people Hec knew who had the same passion for the Lost Cause that Hec had—I mean, somebody willing to wear his passion on his sleeve. Which is why I was real surprised when Hec went along with telling the Pure Blood Boys they weren't welcome in ROF. Hec had an almost—" Stern shook his head and started again. "Hec and Ruth never had kids. No one to carry on that great old Macintosh name in Virginia. For Hec, I think Junior was a surrogate son. His feelings for Junior were more than just respect for an associate. He cared about that boy."

"And there hasn't been anyone that's come forward to play the role Hec played, somebody who's kept up an association with Junior?"

Stern made a blowing sound through his lips. "Now you're running into another form of prejudice. I give Hec credit for one thing. He was capable of seeing beyond Junior's rough surface. Anyone else from Hec's background and class—and we are talking class here, it's still part of what goes on in Richmond—might take advantage of someone like Junior. Use him for their own purposes. But they'd never be seen in public with him, never treat him like a friend. Hec did that. I think he bought the boy a computer. Junior would visit Hec at his house in the West End, have dinner there. But no one else wanted to be publicly associated with what Hec and Junior were up to."

"You did eventually split with Hec, isn't that right?"

"Had to. Hec got the Pure Blood Boys out of ROF, but he kept up his association with the Boys. Especially Junior. Which was almost as bad for what we were trying to accomplish as having the Boys in ROF. It meant we had to do without Hec's financial support, but that was easier to replace than the credibility we'd lose if we had any association with that bunch."

"So there's no one you know of—an old friend of Hec's, maybe somebody who didn't appear to be associated with groups like the Pure Blood Boys—but who had the means and the disposition to be playing a role offstage?"

Stern shook his head. "Lots of people who haven't changed their opinions one iota in a hundred years are smart enough to keep their ideas to themselves. That's where Hec was different. I think it came with having so much money. 'Most everybody else was afraid being a racist might cost money. Hec didn't worry about money."

"How did Hec react to the break with ROF?"

"I didn't even talk to Hec. Just sent him a registered letter saying I was terminating his association with ROF. Sent a letter to the editor of the paper here announcing the same. And it was a critical time, as it was just about then that the Minnesota Attorney General's Office ruled that Minnesota holds the flag legally. We really needed to get a new strategy in place. With Hec, I think it's pretty clear the new strategy would have been to take matters into our own hands, so to speak. Stop working the legal and legislative channels."

"You weren't aware of anything specific Hec was up to?"

Stern shook his head. "It was just a few weeks after that Hec died over in West Virginia hunting turkeys. Solved my problems altogether. Not that we've made a lot of progress on getting the flag back, but at least we've got a like-minded bunch of fellows involved. And no Junior Booseys in sight."

Mars said, "I hate to keep hammering at this—but there's no one you can think of who'd start taking personal revenge as a consequence of not getting the flag back?"

Stern smiled broadly. "Hec's wife. Ruth Palmer Macintosh." Stern shook his head. "Ruth was something else. Perfect match for Hec. Old Virginia money—although small stuff compared to what Hec had. Not a liberal molecule in the woman's body. Thought Hec was a prophet. Never even complained about Hec's womanizing, which pretty much everybody knew about. She married a good ole boy and was more than willing to put up with the consequences. Got a big check from Ruth after Hec died. I felt a little bad about sending it back, 'cause I'm sure Hec's death hit her real hard. But taking the check—well, Ruth would have been on my back forever, once she got her hooks in."

"She still around?" Mars said.

"Oh, my, yes. See her picture in the paper every now and again. Keeps up with the social scene. Can't believe she's happy about doing it solo. Widda's weeds was never Ruth's style."

Stern walked Mars to the door as he was leaving. Shaking Mars's hand, Stern said, "One thing I want to be real clear about. Our wanting the flag back's got nothing to do with keeping alive the glorious spirit of the Confederacy." Stern made a face to make clear he used the phrase ironically. "Quite the contrary. Personally, I see bringing the flag back as a way of ending the war. Doing away with winners and losers, so to speak. From the Federal troops' perspective, the war was fought to preserve the Union. Can't do that if Minnesota insists on hanging on to a symbol that says you won and we lost. That just emphasizes our differences. I'm willing to do anything necessary in taking the flag back in a way that will honor the First Minnesota. No one's denying they were heroes. But Minnesota needs to respect our ancestors who were in the Twenty-eighth Virginia. Needs to show 'us' and 'them'

232

is over. No better way to do that than by giving the flag back to those whose folks died carrying it."

"That's a philosophy Junior Boosey would subscribe to?" Mars said, knowing the answer.

"Hell, no. Not Hec, either. And with Hec dead, I would guess Junior's more rabid than ever."

"Did Junior attend Hec's funeral?"

Stern hesitated. "Yeah. He did. The memorial service. Stony-faced. I was expecting some emotion from him. He worshiped Hec. If anything he looked kind of like he'd won some kind of victory. No way he's ever gonna admit he's beaten. Hard kid to figure out. Just a hard kid is maybe the way to say it."

CHAPTER

20

It was dark by the time Mars reached his Richmond motel. But not, Mars decided, too late to check in with Gordon Ball, Chief Taylor's pal who was a deputy chief in the Richmond Police Department. Ball had promised to have suggestions for Mars on contacts to make in Richmond.

"Where're you staying?" Ball asked when Mars called. When Mars told him, Ball said, "My wife's outta town, and I haven't had dinner yet. You can get from where you are to the Fan real easy."

"The Fan?" Mars said, assuming Ball was going to suggest meeting at a sports bar.

"The neighborhood where I live." Ball gave Mars directions to a restaurant called Not Betty's in the Fan. "Get you started on a little Richmond culture," Ball said.

Not Betty's was the kind of place Mars liked. Casual, decent food, and cheap. Quiet enough for a solid conversation. Gordon Ball was already in a booth when Mars arrived, and in the subliminal language of cops, each recognized the other without asking.

Ball was a big guy, trim but not especially fit. His face was deeply lined, probably too much sun rather than too many years. Mars guessed Ball wasn't much beyond his mid- to late forties. "I appreciate your being willing to come out tonight," Mars said.

Ball shrugged. "Happy to do it. The wife and I live couple blocks over from here. And like I said, I haven't had dinner yet."

"What's 'the Fan'?" Mars asked.

"Couple ways to answer that question," Ball said. "The name comes from the shape of the district—streets in the district radiate from Monroe Park out to the Boulevard in a kinda fan shape. The character of the neighborhood is a real mix—architecturally, racially, economically. There's Monument Avenue, which is the high-end part of the district with lots of historic mansions. At the other end of the scale is the street my wife and I moved to when our youngest went off to college. Bought an already renovated town house. One neighbor is on the faculty at Virginia Commonwealth University, another neighbor is an artist who's married to a vice president at the Federal Reserve Bank—middle-class professionals, like the wife and me."

Mars took a sip of his Coke. "Probably not a lot of cops."

Ball raised and dropped his eyebrows, shrugging. "No, not a lot of cops. That's a universal, isn't it? Richmond or Minneapolis—or any of the other cities where I've been on a police force, for that matter. Not many cops have a liberal bent and a neighborhood like the Fan tends to attract more liberal types. To be fair, most of our guys—and women, for that matter—are raising young families. They want the convenience and space they get in a house in a suburban subdivision. Can't say I blame them. The wife and I lived in the suburbs for almost twenty years. You married?"

Mars shook his head. "Divorced. A ten-year-old son."

"Your ex lives in the suburbs?"

"No. I'm a city guy. Bought a house in a residential part of the city when I was married. My wife stayed in the house after the divorce."

"What's your ex do?"

"She stays home with our son."

"Whooaa," Ball said, "that must be a stretch on a cop's salary—maintaining two households."

"My expenses are minimal. Your wife works?"

Ball nodded. "Does real well as a financial advisor with one of the investment firms here in town. But her real passion is art. She does some work on the side for a local fine arts consultant who buys for corporations and the hoity-toitys who live out in the West End."

Their food arrived, and Ball sat back. When the waitress left, Ball said, "Tell me about this case you're out here on."

Mars talked through the Beck case, focusing on his interpretation of the numbers on Beck's arm and how those numbers linked to the Twenty-eighth Virginia's flag.

"So what you're looking for," Ball said, "is someone involved in this flag issue who'd care enough to kill descendents of the First Minnesota."

"In a nutshell," Mars said, "That's it."

Ball smiled. "You're two years two late."

"Meaning," Mars said, "Hec Macintosh?"

Ball nodded. "How'd you hear about Hec?"

"FBI. Phil Stern, one of the ROFers who was involved with Macintosh. Stern said pretty much exactly what you just said when I asked him about likely candidates. What we're thinking is that there was someone else involved with Hec who maintained a much lower profile. Anybody you can think of that'd fill that bill?"

Ball chewed slowly, shaking his head. "I expect you know about Junior Boosey?"

"Met with him in Green Springs. No question he was involved, but he's not who we're looking for. We're looking for someone slick. Someone who could pass as a businessman. Junior might have all kinds of virtues, but slick isn't one of them."

"No one's gonna disagree with you on that," Ball said. He reached over and pulled his jacket off the back of the booth. Reaching into an inside pocket, he pulled out a sheet of folded paper. He smoothed it open on the table, holding it open with one hand while he forked in mouthfuls of food with the other.

"What I've got here is mostly people affiliated with organizations that have an interest in the flag—some folks from the Museum of the Confederacy, the Virginia Historical Society. I'm afraid there's not anyone here that's gonna be able to point you in the direction of a suspect—but they should be real helpful in answering any questions you may have about the flag. As far as troublemakers go, sounds to me like you were on the right track with Junior."

Mars was disappointed. He'd hoped Ball might have some ideas about specific individuals. Mars hesitated, then said, "What about Ruth Macintosh? Any possibility she could be tied into this. From what Stern said, she and Hec were soul mates."

"Could Ruth Palmer Macintosh be involved in a *muhdah?*" Ball said in mock horror. "Good god, yes. She could drop a guy at thirty feet with a *look*. A killer, that woman. And meaner since Hec died. She doesn't fancy herself as a widow lady."

"You know her then?"

"More like, know *of* her. She still has a fairly high profile in Richmond society. Palmer and Macintosh money together are pretty hard to ignore. The only direct contact I've had with her—no, I should say the only *in*direct contact I've had with her—is through my wife. My wife worked on acquiring some artwork for her. One of the first contracts my wife worked on. Just about drove her out of the business. Ruth changed her mind about what she wanted every other day, whined about prices, damaged one of the artworks and denied it was her fault, disputed her bill—the woman is seriously cheap. Putting Ruth in jail would be a public service, to my mind."

"I'd like to try and get in touch with her."

"Let me make a suggestion," Ball said. "If I were you, I'd try talking to her sister first. Bunny Palmer. Lives down on Cary Street Road—west end, but wrong side of the Road. Bunny and

Ruth may be sisters, but they're a powerful argument against genetic determination. As different as—well, I can't say there's any two things that come to mind that are as different as Ruth and Bunny. Least, what I know about Ruth. Bunny—Bunny I actually know personally. She's an artist, and my wife's bought things from her from time to time. Bunny's been over to the house for dinner any number of times. Good people, is Bunny."

Mars pushed his plate to the side. "Why talk to Bunny first?"

" 'Cause Bunny is shrewd, hated Hec, and will tell you great truths. She knows Richmond society backwards and forwards and may even have more ideas than I do about somebody who'd be mixed up in a deal like this. That, and it will make Ruth crazy that you talked to Bunny first. Will set her up for agreeing to talk to you."

"Anything else I can do to make Ruth willing to talk to me?"

Ball cast a cynical eye on Mars. "Send her your picture, and when you go on over to see her, bring a bottle of old scotch."

It was after eleven when Mars got back to his motel. Too late to call Chris, but not too late to call Nettie. He punched in her home phone and got Nettie's answering machine. He tried her number at the department, and she picked up on the first ring.

"Nettie. It's after ten P.M. in Minneapolis. What are you doing in the office?"

"I'm helping with the target victim research. We've got two more identified down to current address and the contact process in motion. We've got two identified without a current location. So, making progress."

Mars did a quick tally in his head. "Okay—so we've got Beck, Rowe, the guy in Salina—that makes three plus the two you had before I left—I'm assuming the two you just said included two that didn't have current addresses when I left?"

Nettie made a long "uhhhhh-ing" sound, then said, "Right."

"Okay. So when I left we were at five down, eleven to go, and you've got two more identified down to current address, which makes nine to go. Great news. Slowly but surely . . ."

"How about you? Met any southern belles?"

"Gonna try to get to that tomorrow. Too soon to tell whether what I'm finding out is going to help or not. Anything else going on?"

There was a moment's hesitation before Nettie spoke. Mars paid attention to the hesitation. Nettie didn't do hesitation.

"Nettie—what? You sound like there's something you're not saying."

There was another hesitation. Then she said, "There was something in the paper today about city negotiations for state funds at the legislature. You know, one of those prelegislative session outlook pieces . . ."

"And?"

"They quoted the president of the police union on the topic of police department funding. . . ."

"*And???*"

A big sigh. "He said the union was willing to support cuts in selected areas."

"So surprise me. One of the areas was us, right?"

"Wrong. We're the *only* cut the union would be willing to support." Then she hesitated again.

"Nettie?"

She continued without further hesitation. "A reporter from Channel Twelve called the PIO here for a reaction on the union's quote, and in the course of that conversation, the reporter asked what you were working on now. It looks like there's going to be a story—probably in the next few days—about our taking on a sure-thing suicide and that you are following the case in warmer climes."

It was Mars who sighed next. "Dana Levy already gave me a heads-up on that. Thought they were going to run it last night, actually. This whole thing is stupid. To begin with, the state legislature gives precious little money to the Minneapolis Police Department, so why that becomes part of a presession budget story . . ."

"It doesn't matter. You know it doesn't matter."

"It matters," Mars said. "It just doesn't matter that it matters."

The line went silent, then Mars said, "I suppose it would be good, given these developments, if I could bring home a head on a platter."

"That would be good," Nettie said.

"Except it isn't going to happen. Heard anything from Keegan since he left?"

"He called this afternoon. Nothing special. Just that the field agent contacts are going smoothly. It really is helpful to have him coordinate that end of things. You still planning to be back day after tomorrow?"

"Sounds like I'd damned well better be."

Mars got a call from Ball before nine the next morning. Ball had called Bunny Palmer to ask if she'd meet with Mars. "Not a problem," Ball reported, "except she's not free until after one o'clock. Said you should drive out to her house around then."

Mars took advantage of the free time to drive around Richmond. He went back to the Fan, wanting to see it in daylight. It was, as Ball had described, an eclectic mix of grand southern architecture and charming decadence. He thought about that some. Why was it that in Minneapolis urban decay looked run-down, while a neglected property down here had character?

He drove slowly along Monument Avenue, going west, passing intersections where handsome statuary reared, honoring Robert E. Lee, Jefferson Davis, Stonewall Jackson, and other luminaries of the Confederacy. He tried to remember something he'd read about the significance of the position of the feet of riders' horses in military statuary. What was it, all four feet on the ground and the rider survived the war? One foot up, injured? A good question for Chris to figure out.

The houses along Monument Avenue were unrelentingly grand, although some were less well maintained than others. At the intersection of Monument and Boulevard, he started to turn left on the Boulevard to head toward the James River. Then he caught the No Left Turn sign beside Stonewall Jackson's statue. Mars grinned. Appropriate. Jackson, would have approved. Mars swung around the block instead, then headed south on the Boulevard, which according to his map would take him to the Downtown Expressway. He had wanted to walk along the James, but gave that up as it wasn't clear there was a pedestrian path. Instead, he took the Downtown Expressway to Seventh Street, where he immediately found his path to the river was blocked by the Federal Reserve Bank. After another couple of blocked paths, he found his way to Tenth which took him to the Kanawha Canal where he headed west. He drove along the canal and the river to the Tredegar Ironworks, just east of Hollywood Cemetery. Finally, he found a place to park the car and was able to get out for a walk.

The James struck Mars as having a southern character. It was defiantly indolent, with more rocky outcroppings than water visible. Like the rest of Richmond, it had a self-confident grandness that defied any possible shortcomings. Ball had mentioned the previous night that there was a whitewater run along the Falls of the James. The energy of whitewater was hard to imagine from where Mars was standing.

With the Tredegar—soon to be a Civil War Museum according to postings along the old ironworks—behind him, Mars made his way up a grassy hill, past a grand-looking old white building. Not far beyond, he found himself in what looked like it might have been a working-class residential area in the past century. He noticed sign postings designating the area as Oregon Hill. At this point he was near the massive iron gates to Hollywood Cemetery. Looking at his watch, he hesitated. He really didn't have time for the cemetery now. He needed to get back to the car, then out to Bunny Palmer's Cary Street Road house.

Just beyond the I-195 intersection, Cary Street became Cary Street Road, and the neighborhood transitioned from trendy commerce to elegant residences. He remembered what Ball had said about Bunny Palmer's house, that it was on the wrong side of Cary Street Road. The houses on the north side of Cary Street Road looked just fine to Mars, as long as you didn't look at the houses on the south side of the road. Houses on the south side of the road—the river side—were grand, in some cases full-fledged estates, while the houses to the north were comfortable, often handsome, but rarely grand.

He watched the intersections carefully. Ball had warned him that Palmer's house was hidden behind a privet hedge, and Mars wouldn't be able to see the house number from the street. He needed to turn right at a road that intersected with Cary Street Road and park to the side of Palmer's house, which was on a corner.

Mars felt like Alice in Wonderland falling into another world as he stepped through an obviously artist-designed wrought-iron gate in the privet hedge. If you just looked at the house—a smugly solid saltbox shingle with a precise, gray slate roof—you'd miss that this was an artist's home. It was the lawn that betrayed its owner's soul. The grass was cut as finely as the greens at a world-class golf club. More than that, it had been cut in an undulating, circular pattern that shifted and changed depending on how light hit it. Set among the lawn's various sheltered and luxuriously landscaped nooks were stunning pieces of modern and traditional sculpture.

Mars couldn't help remembering that it was when he'd bought a lawnmower that he'd known with a fair degree of certainty that being married wasn't going to work for him. He'd bought the mower after he and Denise—Denise being almost six months pregnant—had moved into the house in south Minneapolis. Mars wanted to pay a neighborhood kid to mow the grass. There was no way Denise was going to spend their money to cut grass, any more than she would have paid anyone to sweep their floors. So they'd gone out to Lyndale Lawn and Garden Center and bought a hand mower.

That it was a hand mower pleased them both. It pleased Denise because a hand mower was cheap. It pleased Mars because a hand mower seemed like less to think about than a gas mower. You get a gas mower, and you've got to get a can to keep the gas in. You've gotta take the gas can to the gas station. You've got to be careful where you keep the can. Then you've got like a hundred parts of the mower that need maintenance. And Mars, being pretty sure he wouldn't do the maintenance, had visions of hauling a gas mower back and forth to whoever it was that fixed gas mowers that weren't maintained.

So they got a hand mower.

The hand mower was no trouble at all, primarily because Mars never took it out of the trunk of the car. Denise did not nag. She did killer looks, but she did not nag. When Mars was around the house, which was as little as possible, Denise would stand at the kitchen window, cup of coffee in one hand, the other arm bent at the elbow, knuckles on her hip, in a pose Mars never saw anyone strike other than a pregnant woman. She stared out the window at grass they both knew was too long and getting longer. She'd take a sip of coffee, glance over at Mars, then put the cup down on the kitchen counter too hard.

About three weeks after getting the mower, Mars had stayed downtown on an investigation for almost thirty-six hours. When he finally broke away and headed home in a department squad car, he remembered that *The Fabulous Baker Boys* had opened the previous week. He'd asked Denise if she'd wanted to go, and she'd said maybe. Which meant no. He still had adrenaline going from the investigation and decided that going to the movie would be a good transition between work and home.

Three hours later, pulling into his driveway, it was impossible not to notice that the grass had been cut. His worst fears were realized when he hit the remote and the opening garage door revealed the hand mover sitting in a place of honor against the garage wall. Leaving the squad on the driveway, he went into the garage, approaching the mower cautiously. It looked unused, which meant nothing. Denise was fully capable of cleaning a mower spotless after cutting down a rain forest.

He'd walked slowly into the kitchen from the garage, trying to think of a legitimate reason for being indignant. Denise was on the phone, she turned slightly as he entered, didn't acknowledge him and kept talking.

The only thing that felt right to say was the truth. When Denise hung up the phone, Mars said, "I'm never going to cut the grass. And neither are you—at least while you're pregnant. I'll talk to that kid who lives the other side of Olsen's. I'll have him come every weekend."

So Bunny Palmer's lawn was a particular revelation for Mars. He was still staring at it when a handsome young dark-haired, brown-skinned guy emerged from a vine-covered arch. He was followed by a gleaming-brown miniature dachshund who yapped fiercely at Mars.

"Mr. Bahr? I am Fay-leap."

"Phillipe?" Mars repeated, holding out his hand.

"Yes, Fay-leap Gare-in. Bunny said she would be a bit late. That I should get you a drink." He turned to the dog who was circling Mars, still yapping fiercely. "Geronimo! No way to speak to your mommy's guest."

Phillipe Guerin led Mars across the lawn to the front door. "Okay if I walk on this?" Mars said, worried about spoiling the perfection of the lawn's patterned cut.

"Oh, yes," Phillipe said. "Grass should be walked on, don't you think? Won't take me but a minute to put it in order again."

"You take care of the lawn?"

"The lawn, the garden, the pool, the silver. And I cut Bunny's hair."

The lawn, the garden, the pool, and the silver. The wrong side of Cary Street Road was looking pretty good to Mars.

The lawn, however, paled in comparison to the interior of Bunny Palmer's house. It was filled with original hanging art, small and large pieces of sculpture, pottery, china, and a spontaneous mix of antique furniture, each piece of which was a work of art in its own right.

"You do the dusting, too?" Mars asked Phillipe, only half joking.

Phillipe rolled his eyes. "No, thank God. Bunny has a *special* cleaning person who comes in for the housework. I'm very clumsy, really. If I did it, all the china and pottery would be gone. Come, this way. I think Bunny would want you to wait in the gallery."

The gallery was at the back of the house, a huge, high-ceilinged room that was starkly modern. "Bunny added the gallery several years ago," Phillipe said, noticing Mars's curiosity. "Now she shows all her own things here—and sometimes things for friends, as well."

Mars walked across the gallery to a large window that faced the back garden. While the gallery was level with the main floor of the house, the property to the rear dropped sharply, so the gallery looked down a full story on the back garden—and on a magnificent black swimming pool.

Phillipe stood next to Mars, looking down on the pool. "Bunny," Phillipe said with pride, "is an artist in all things. It was her idea to paint the pool black." He flipped a switch on the wall, and dim lights came on under the pool's glittering water. "At night," Phillipe said, "with the lights on, the water turns a kind of copper-green color. See the horse . . ." He pointed at a life-size

245

statue of a horse that stood on one side of the pool. "The pool is like the patina on the horse at night."

"Phillipe! You haven't given our guest a drink?"

Mars and Phillipe turned to see Bunny Palmer walking into the gallery. Geronimo sped across the floor toward Bunny, leaping into her arms as she bent toward him, arms outstretched.

Bunny was an attractive middle-aged woman with prematurely gray hair that was drawn loosely back in a knot. Wisps of hair fell around her face in calculated disarray. Her eyes were a clear, bright blue and like her house, her clothes and jewelry were works of art.

She held a hand out to Mars as she said over her shoulder, "A gin and tonic for me, Phillipe. And hold the fruit. Mr. Bahr?"

Mars shook his head. "Nothing for me, thanks. I appreciate your seeing me on short notice."

"Oh, my word," Bunny Palmer said. "It will be my pleasure, I assure you. Gordon said you were investigatin' a murder Hec mighta been involved in. I can tell you the prospect of convictin' Hec of murder—even from the grave—is like scratchin' an itch that's been botherin' a long while." There was something self-mocking and self-consciously ironic in the softness of her southern accent. She sat down on a lounge chair near the window, patting the seat next to her. "Do sit," she said.

Mars sat. Clearly Gordon Ball hadn't gone into any detail about why Mars wanted to talk with Bunny. "I'm going to have to disappoint you," he said. "The murder I'm investigating took place after Hec's death. What I'm interested in talking to you about is anyone you might know—someone who has business credentials, could pass himself off as a venture capitalist—who also had a passionate involvement in the controversy over the Twenty-eighth Virginia regimental flag that was captured at the Battle of Gettysburg. . . ."

Bunny moaned. "Oh, now you have gone and disappointed me. Shoot. I had such hopes we were gonna hang ol' Hec in effigy—preferably from the outstretched tail of Jeb Stuart's horse on Monument Avenue."

It was, Mars thought, an interesting choice of images. He was considering his next question when Phillipe returned with Bunny's drink. "Oh, damn, Phillipe," Bunny said, "I've just had such bad news. Shoulda had you hold the fruit *and* the tonic." Phillipe, who carried a drink for himself, sat down across from them. Mars found himself wondering about Phillipe's role in the household. On the surface, he was prepared to believe there was a romantic relationship between the two, in spite of the age difference. But beneath the surface Mars would swear there was nothing going on. There was affection and mutual dependence between the pair, but he was willing to bet nothing else.

"Tell me why you disliked your brother-in-law so much," Mars said.

"Where to start!" Bunny said, pulling her feet up under her. "The funny thing is, I introduced Hec and Ruth. I met Hec at UVA—Ruth's my older sister, but higher education wasn't her thang...." Bunny's sarcasm was thick and blatantly intentional. "To my own now re-tro-spective amazement, I'd been datin' Hec. Nothin' serious as far as I was concerned, but he did cut quite a figure on campus, and we had some fun. I didn't take his right-wingin' as seriously then as I shoulda. I was actually getting set to cut him loose when Ruth came down to UVA for a weekend and took a fancy to him. To this day, Ruth likes to think my heart was broken. Truth is, only thing that broke my heart was seein' what my only sister became after marrying Hec Macintosh. They got married right after Hec graduated UVA. Hec brought out all kinds of latent crap in Ruth. Bigotry and bein' a snob foremost. Once she was a Macintosh, there was no livin' with Ruth. We've not got along real well since then."

"So you don't see much of Ruth anymore?"

"I said we don't get along real well. Doesn't seem to prevent us from seein' each other on a regular basis. Especially since Hec died. Ruth's kinda been lost since then. She and Hec were happily married—although Lord knows she put up with plenty most women wouldn't have. . . ."

"Such as? . . ."

"Other women, primarily. Ruth pretended it didn't bother her any. It *was* common knowledge. Even on Hec's annual turkey huntin' expeditions, he usually took along a couple chickie babes. Everybody knew that. Ruth said publicly she wished he'd had 'em along on the last trip, mighta saved his life. Only time I ever saw her admit to bein' jealous was over me, actually. I'd had some security problems and changed the locks on the house. Ruth and I have always had keys to each other's houses, so I left a key on the desk at her place after the locks were changed. Hec musta picked it up, 'cause Ruth found it on his key ring, tried it on my house and accused him of all kinds of nonsense. Told me a lot, that did. Told me that Ruth was regularly checking Hec's keys and keepin' pretty close track of what they unlocked—and told me she suspected Hec was seein' me on the side—why else would she have tried the key on a lock to my house? Crazy, of course. I wasn't interested and neither was Hec. Not after all these years. He had a definite predilection for younger women."

"But you and Ruth are still on speaking terms. . . ."

Phillipe said, "Well, not for a while, now. . . ."

Bunny's eyebrows raised and fell and she took a big gulp of her drink. "This is gonna sound real trivial to a sensible man like yourself."

"In my business, nothing is trivial," Mars said.

Bunny glanced at Phillipe, then said, "We had a fallin' out a few weeks ago. Over Phillipe, as it happens. Ruth called me up one afternoon, tellin' me I should read some wild-eyed editorial in the *Washington Times*, which Ruth reads and memorizes on a daily basis. She no sooner finishes lecturin' me on whatever it was that right-winged butt rag was expoundin' about then she says, 'Oh—and I need to borrow Phillipe tomorrow afternoon to do my silver before my holiday reception on Friday.' Jus' like that. I said, 'Number one, if you need to borrow Phillipe, you need to ask him yourself, and I'd recommend askin' him more than twenty-four hours in advance.' Phillipe *does* after all have a busy life apart from everything he does for me. . . ."

"I *did* have a Barbie doll convention in Atlanta that weekend," Phillipe said. "I absolutely couldn't go over to Ruth's for the silver and get to Atlanta on time."

Mars resisted biting on the Barbie doll bait.

Bunny continued. " 'Number two,' I said, 'if you're gonna ask a favor of me, I'd recommend not askin' the favor in the same breath as you go quotin' that right-winged butt rag to me.' Ruth hung up on me. I've hardly talked to her since. But I expect I'll be hearin' from her shortly. She always comes over here for New Year's. So she'll call about that, jus' like nothin' happened."

"And you don't know of anyone in Hec's circle that felt as strongly about the Confederacy as Hec did?"

"Hardly anyone in Hec's circle that didn't have real strong feelin's about the Cause—you been out to Hollywood?"

"Hollywood?" Mars said. "The cemetery near downtown?"

"Exactly," Bunny said. "What we say in Richmond is, 'You haven't *arrived* in Richmond until you've arrived at Hollywood.' And it's true. We care a lot more about the past than we do about the future. Leastwise, it seems that way, sometimes."

"Must have been the cemetery I passed when I was walking by the river earlier."

"That would be it. Well, you want to understand the Cause— or as Hec used to say—*'the Recent Unpleasantness'*—you need to go to Hollywood. To the section where they've buried Confederate soldiers. I swear, there are ghosts about that place."

"But nobody specific you can think of—especially someone who might have been involved in the controversy over the flag to the same degree that Hec was?"

"Other than Ruth herself, no."

249

Her words hung between them. Bunny heard the meaning just after speaking. She stopped cold and looked like she was about to say something, but the phone rang before she spoke. Phillipe picked up the phone, then, holding the receiver to his chest said, "Bunny, it's Ruth for you."

They decided it on the phone. Mars would talk to Ruth at her house after three o'clock. She was going to a reception at the Museum of the Confederacy before then, but planned on being home early.

"You want a tour of the house before you go?" Bunny asked as Mars stood.

"For sure he wants to see my Barbie dolls," Phillipe said.

The Barbie dolls were definitely worth seeing. Phillipe's bedroom was upstairs, above the gallery, overlooking the pool. Apart from the French doors that opened onto a small balcony over the pool, every wall, every table surface was covered with Barbie dolls.

"How many?" Mars asked, incredulous.

"Ohh," Phillipe said, considering. "Not more than five hundred on display. But then, I have twice as many in storage, I should think. Yes, at least twice as many."

"You sell them, trade them?"

"Both. Some, of course, will never leave me. But I travel to conventions perhaps twice a month, and I always buy, trade, and sell at conventions. It's what makes collecting so interesting."

As they walked back down the stairs, Bunny said, "We have a perfect symbiotic relationship, Phillipe and I. You couldn't pay someone to do the sort of thing Phillipe does—much less to do it as perfectly as Phillipe. And yet we're never in each other's way, are we Phillipe? I can be home for days at a time without seeing Phillipe—I don't even hear his phone when it rings. And of course, he travels so much. . . ."

"I'm going to England day after next for a big convention. I'll be gone for more than a week."

"He'll cut my hair just before he leaves, and fortunately, the grass doesn't grow much in January. So, I'll survive," Bunny said. "You gotta c'mon back and see my room. No etchin's or nothin', but I want you to see the frame on my bed. Made out of the wood of the last walnut tree on the Palmer farm, out west on the James River."

As they walked through the house, Mars couldn't help noticing that there was a dog's bed in each room, including a Gucci-upholstered dog bed in a sitting room. Passing through the kitchen, there was a small, granite-topped table maybe eight inches high. Two pewter dog dishes were fitted into precut holes in the granite. Geronimo kept his sharp brown eyes on Mars throughout the house tour, still cradled in Bunny's arms. He watched Mars noticing his beds, his pewter dishes, and gave Mars a look that made clear that touching anything that belonged to Geronimo would be a mistake.

Bunny led Mars to a separate wing at the opposite end of the house from Phillipe's room. Her bedroom walls, carpet, and bedding were shades of pearl grey. The room's centerpiece was an elegant wood headboard behind the bed, cross-cut to show a distinctive grain.

Bunny stared at the bed. "So sad to have lost the walnut trees." She looked up at Mars, an impish expression on her face. "This was the only thing worth havin' I got from my husband. He had this bed made for me as a wedding gift. Gave me hope, it did. Thought when he gave it to me that maybe marryin' him wasn't such a big mistake after all. Two months after the wedding, I figured out that confusin' good taste and good character was a mistake. Kept the bed, divorced the man."

"You've not remarried?" Mars said.

"Oh, my, no. No need these days, is there? Besides, I just don't trust my judgment in men for a minute." She bent her head down and kissed the dachshund's head. "Geronimo excepted, of course. Perfect little gentleman . . ."

Phillipe said, "Unless, of course, one leaves Brie cheese unattended. . . ."

"Don't bring that up," Bunny said. "Darlin' G has only just got his tummy back in order after he ate that hunk of Brie at my last show in the gallery. A tiny tendency toward gluttony aside, I've been happier with Geronimo than I ever was married. My husband was as much a right-winger as Hec. And they were best friends. The first—but not the last—big clue I missed. Only true difference was, my husband didn't have Hec's money."

Mars gave it some thought. "Your husband still around?"

"Lord, no. Can't say where he got to . . ." Bunny's face knotted up a bit. "I *assume* he's still alive, but truth is, I wouldn't know if he wasn't. He left Richmond after the divorce, which was—oh, do I even want to say? Twenty years ago at least. Last I heard, he was out in Phoenix on some land development deal."

As he left, Mars took out a business card, stopping to scribble his home phone below the Homicide Division number. He handed Bunny his card. "Call me if you have any second thoughts about someone who might have been involved with Hec."

Bunny glanced at the card, then dropped it on a silver tray on a hall table. She held her hand out to Mars and said, "So now you go on over to the 'right' side of Cary Street Road. Let me tell you somethin'. Rattlesnakes and cottonmouths come up from the river on that side. Cause no end of trouble. They can't make it across the traffic on Cary Street Road. One of our many advantages. You just be careful over there, is what I'm saying."

CHAPTER

21

From a distance she looked midthirties.

It was her style that gave her age away first. The boxy, short-skirted black suit, the golden bouffant hairdo—nobody had hair that color or shape anymore. After the retro style came reality. As he approached her limousine, having arrived just after Ruth Palmer Macintosh pulled into the circular driveway of her West End Tudor-style house, she pulled down large, heavy-framed sunglasses.

Without the big glasses covering her face you saw havoc. Deep deforming lines. Age alone couldn't have caused that kind of damage, and Mars was sure that Ruth Macintosh wasn't more than a couple years older than Bunny Palmer.

"I bet you're Mr. Bahr," Ruth said, the words all blurred and soft. She held her sunglasses down on the end of her nose, peering at him intently. Her southern drawl was calculated, intentional.

Mars opened his badge, and tipped his head. "Yes. I'm with the Minneapolis Police Department. I appreciate your being willing to see me."

She flopped a hand at him in dismissal, "Spare me all the bureaucratic courtesy, *puh-leeze*. C'mon in. I am starvin'. Don't know what's happening in this town anymore when a gal goes to a reception and there's not a single ham biscuit to be had. A de*cline* in standards, I can tell you. No ham biscuits is the absolute bitter end of civilization as I have known it."

She walked briskly toward her front door as the navy blue Lincoln Town Car pulled silently away. She left the door open, and Mars followed her into a large, formal foyer. She dropped her dark glasses and a small, hard alligator purse on a Louis XIV chest in front of a hall mirror. She faced the mirror, poking at the corner of her lips, which gleamed with an oily shade of coral lipstick.

Bending, Ruth lifted one leg to pull off a pump which, when removed, looked absurdly high. With both shoes off, Ruth lost four inches of height. She was tiny, even smaller than her sister who Mars would have described as being small. He'd thought all along that if Ruth Palmer Macintosh had been involved in Beck's murder she'd have to have an accomplice to handle the physical side of things. Seeing her—especially seeing her with her shoes off—confirmed that fact.

"I'm gonna have to see what I can scare up to eat or I will surely perish," she said. "We can talk in the kitchen good as any-where."

The kitchen was bigger than Mars's entire apartment by a fac-tor of four. It gleamed like a high-tech factory, fully equipped with all the latest gadgets and appliances. Ruth moved with surprising authority in the kitchen. At first sight, Mars would have predicted she was a woman who got cooked for. But she seemed real clear about what she wanted and where to find it. From the stainless steel Subzero refrigerator she removed a covered glass dish that she placed on a center island counter. "Sit with me while I eat. . . ." She turned toward him as if surprised by a thought. "You want somethin'?"

Mars shook his head, "No, thanks."

Ruth didn't pay much attention to his answer. She opened a couple closets, pulled a folding step stool from the second closet, and climbed up to open a high cupboard. From the cupboard she lifted a bottle of Chivas Regal. The bottle looked half her height as she carried it back to the counter, a heavy tumbler in her other hand. She put both the bottle and the tumbler on the counter, opened a drawer, taking out a fork, then sat down across from Mars. She removed the cover from the glass dish, poured a tumblerful of scotch, and began spearing what looked to be tuna-fish salad from the bowl.

"Doesn't pay to keep live-in help, anymore," she said. "More trouble than they're worth. Hec insisted on having people, but since he's been gone—well, now I got a gal that comes in to cook, do the heavy cleanin'. And she knows to keep somethin' in the fridge for me."

Ruth had balanced her stockinged feet on a chair rung, her skirt hiked up well over her knees, a stocking-top held by a garter showing just below the hem. Her small legs were shapely. The longer Mars looked at her, the more he saw about her that was attractive—in spite of her ravaged face. She was—well, the word that came to mind was *glamorous*. And sensual, in the way that a face and body that's suffered too many years of good scotch and bad sex can be sensual.

Drinking long from the tumbler, she said, "Bunny says you're here about Hec."

"I'm here about a murder that took place in Minneapolis recently. We have reason to believe that the suspect had a particular interest in the Twenty-eighth Virginia's regimental flag that was captured on the third day of the Battle of Gettysburg. . . ."

"How you figure?" she said, not looking at him.

"There was a series of numbers written on the vic's arm. They correlate to events associated with the captured flag."

"Wellll," she said, "you *are* clever."

"I don't know about clever," Mars said. "I think our suspect left footprints on purpose."

"And Hec? What's a dead man got to do with these numbers?"

"Only that someone like Hec would be the perfect suspect.

Someone who looked like a serious businessperson, passionate about getting the flag back—any of Hec's friends fit that bill?"

Ruth shrugged, twisting her tumbler on the counter. "No one willin' to actually *do* something about getting the flag back." She picked the glass up, then set it down hard on the counter. "Hec was what was called a stand-up guy. A man who had the courage of his convictions and all that. These days, you can't even get the boys over at the Commonwealth Club to say what they're thinking out loud, much less take action. They all act like someone might be recording what they're saying. They try and say things with their eyes, giving your arm a little squeeze—but passion? You did say passion? Well, after Hec, there's no passion left. Least, not that I've been able to find."

"You ever meet Junior Boosey?"

Ruth rolled her eyes. "He was around some. Hec's business. Nothing to do with me." She paused, then said, "Junior had the passion, all right, just didn't have much else to go with it. Not to say he was dumb. Heard Hec say more than once the boy had a good head on his shoulders. But no exposure to anything that would take him past being a hillbilly. You looking for someone who could pass as a businessman, Junior's not your trick."

It seemed to Mars that Ruth knew an awful lot about Junior. "How about Phil Stern—or any of the other ROFers—you meet any of them?"

"I met Phil. He came over on ROF business every now and again. A wussie. A politician, not a patriot. You want to know the truth, Hec didn't have much time for him." She snorted. "You're looking for a murderer, I wouldn't spend much time on any of those ROF boys."

Mars rose to go. Ruth was a waste of time. As he left, he said, "Thought I'd take a run out to Hollywood. Hec buried there?"

Ruth gave him a look that was hard to understand. As if Mars had asked something inappropriate and deeply personal. For a moment he thought she wasn't going to answer him. Then, her voice cold, she said, "No. Not Hollywood. Hec wasn't the kind of man you could pile dirt on."

There's never been agreement as to the number of hills on which the city of Richmond is built. Whether the number is seven, eight, or nine, what is agreed is that the hill on which Hollywood Cemetery lies provides an unparalleled view of the Richmond skyline to the east and of the James River, which makes a graceful curve below Hollywood just west of downtown Richmond.

It was to Hollywood that the first casualty of the War Between the States was brought to rest. And it was to Hollywood that more than eighteen thousand Confederate soldiers, both officers and enlisted men, were laid to ground.

The forty-plus-acre property is heavily wooded—in part by holly trees from which the site takes its name—and lushly landscaped. The landscape shows no evidence of human dominance; there is a careless decadence to the site that suits its purpose. There are weeds and untrimmed foliage. In the fall there are unraked leaves. In the heavy, killing heat of summer the ground is covered with dead magnolia blossoms.

But it is the ornate and intensely emotional monuments that give the cemetery its singular character. The cast-iron dog standing guard at a child's grave. A family site clustered with stone tree stumps. Jefferson Davis's statue staring out at his son's tombstone, his daughter's grave overwatched by a life-sized winged angel. The dramatic wrought-iron Gothic-Victorian structure that shrouds President James Monroe's tomb.

Driving back toward town and Hollywood, Mars ran into an early rush hour. It took him about twenty minutes to get to Hollywood, and by the time he parked the car, the sun was dropping. He stopped in at the Gothic chapel that served as the cemetery's office and picked up a guidebook.

He walked casually at first, falling under the cemetery's spell in the late afternoon light. He walked to the Presidents' Circle to see Monroe's and Tyler's graves and began to walk to the Jefferson Davis site before deciding he wanted to concentrate on the opposite end of the cemetery where there were Confederate monuments. As he turned, walking in the opposite direction, he noticed a stark, elegant, ground-level grave that seemed altogether different from everything else he'd seen. There was a stone surround within which a simple tablet lay. Under the names and dates, the inscription read Oh, Mercy, I've Had a Gracious Plenty. Mars laughed out loud. For Mars, the epitaph summed up perfectly the difference between Minnesotans and Virginians. He would put money on the fact that you could visit every grave in Minnesota and not find anything close to that mortal insouciance.

Mars found his way along Midvale to West Vale Avenue, which would intersect with Confederate Avenue. He set off at a slow jog in the direction of Confederate Avenue, looking off to his right and back, toward the river, where the Confederate officers' section was sited. There'd be no time for that. He wanted to spend what remaining daylight he had in the section where the Confederate Monument had been built and where the graves of the Gettysburg dead were located.

As he merged onto Confederate Avenue, a massive stone pyramid was visible. Mars stopped, flipping pages in the guidebook. The ninety-foot structure, constructed of rough-hewn Richmond granite, unsecured with mortar, had been completed in 1869. The monument's enormous cost had been borne at a time when the South was impoverished in the war's wake.

Mars walked slightly north and east toward the graves of the Confederates who'd lost their lives at Gettysburg. Their journey here had been labored. First unburied, then buried in a mass grave, they had not come home to Hollywood until 1872. He walked slowly over the site, remembering what Bunny Palmer had said about ghosts. He saw no shadowy figures, but the air was thick with dead passions.

Far to the right, near a fence that was the northernmost

boundary of the cemetery, was a solitary monument. Curious, Mars approached the memorial. It was forlorn in its isolation and in its proximity to a busy road that ran just the other side of the fence. It was almost as if the monument was in exile, uncomforted by the cemetery's deep atmosphere of shared purpose. Mars fumbled in the guidebook to find the statue, but in the gathering dark, it was almost impossible to locate where he was.

When he found what he was looking for, it took his breath away. It read, "General George E. Pickett, 1825–1875."

George E. Pickett. The Confederate general who led the infamous Pickett's Charge on the third day of the Battle of Gettysburg. The general whose ranks included the Twenty-eighth Virginia. It was during Pickett's Charge that the Twenty-eighth Virginia had lost their regimental colors to the First Minnesota Volunteers.

Mars closed the guidebook, circling the Pickett memorial. He was thinking about what Keegan had said. About their killer wanting to complete the ritual of death at a place that would have special significance.

This, Mars was certain, would be that place.

CHAPTER

22

Mars saw the television crew by the podium at gate 37 at Minneapolis–St. Paul International Airport moments before they saw him. But it wasn't until they saw him that Mars realized he was their target.

He heard the reporter, Wayne Feiss, say to the cameraman, who'd been sitting on an equipment case, "That's him. In the navy blue jacket with the tan carry-on. Let's get going." By the time they caught up with him, the camera was running and Mars was caught in the glare of the camera's auxiliary lights.

"Mr. Bahr!" Feiss called, his voice ringing with false moral authority. "Mr. Bahr—Wayne Feiss with the Channel Twelve Eye-Watch Team. Mr. Bahr, can you tell me if you've been traveling at taxpayer expense. . . ."

Mars stopped, dropping his carry-on case to the floor. He knew the drill. Knew that what the reporter wanted was for Mars to keep walking away from the camera, like a fugitive, head down, ignoring their questions. So he came to a full stop and turned, facing the reporter and the camera.

"I have been traveling on police business."

Dropping the microphone from his face, Feiss said, "We don't want to hold you up. You can keep walking. We'll follow."

Mars settled into an at-ease position. "I'm not going to do that. It'll make me look bad. I'm staying put until you've got your interview on tape. We stop talking, I start walking, and you put the camera back on—I'll stop and stay stopped. We'll both be here for a long time. Which would make me unhappy."

Feiss scowled. Then he signaled his cameraman to turn on the camera again. Feiss said, his voice doubly authoritative to compensate for his loss of ground, "Mr. Bahr, you have acknowledged that you have been out of the city at taxpayer expense. Is that correct?"

Mars fixed Feiss with a look that was between the two of them. "I have been out of town on police business."

The booming voice again. "Mr. Bahr, will you tell us where you've been," and before Mars could answer, Feiss added, "and will you please confirm or deny that you were in a resort area in the Southeast?"

"I will confirm that I was out of town on police business. Any details regarding that business will be released by the department's public information office, *if* and *when* the PIO determines doing so is in the public interest. It is not our practice to release details regarding specific investigations until a public need-to-know purpose has been identified."

"Mr. Bahr, you arrived on flight three-twelve from Chicago. Will you acknowledge that by using a connecting flight you have disguised your true point of departure?"

Mars couldn't stop himself. He screwed his face into an expression of contempt and disbelief. "*'My true point of departure'?* C'mon, Wayne. That just sounds dumb. My travel was scheduled by the department's administrative division. They pick flights based on cost and schedules."

"You are denying that you flew first class?"

"I flew for free in first class, Wayne. I had abdominal surgery a little over a week ago, and out of consideration, the department pooled frequent-flyer miles to get me a first-class ticket. It didn't cost the department anything."

"Other than the cost of tickets the department will have to

buy, rather than get free by redeeming those miles for other travel." Feiss looked particularly self-satisfied on this point.

"Wayne, have you tried to redeem frequent-flyer miles lately? Almost by definition, when the department needs to schedule airline travel it does so on short notice. Nine times out of ten, the travel is covered by a blackout period. Bottom line is, the department has a pile of miles it hasn't been able to use. The miles that were used for my ticket were miles that were about to expire." Mars shook his head in impatience, knowing as he did so that being impatient wouldn't get him anything. "These are all questions the PIO could and would answer if you bothered to ask. Anything else?"

Still looking smug, Feiss said, "Our sources tell us that regardless of the circumstances of your travel, the investigation itself is bogus. 'Busywork' is the term our source used. Busywork to conceal the fact that the department is wasting tax dollars to support an elite unit within the Homicide Division that is underworked and overpaid. How many uncleared cases are you working on right now, Special Detective?"

Mars sighed. "Our caseload is the lowest—in terms of number of cases—that it has been since the First Response Unit was formed. But as any seasoned police beat reporter could tell you, ten cases can take less time than a single case. It always depends on the facts of any particular case how much time, how many resources are going to be needed to clear—"

Feiss interrupted him. "Will you at least confirm that the investigation from which you are just returning is widely considered to involve a suicide rather than murder?"

"See above responses," Mars said, picking up his carry-on. "We about done here?"

As the camera lights went off and Mars walked away, he heard Feiss say to the cameraman, "We need to go down and cover baggage. If he had golf clubs, he's not gonna pick 'em up tonight.

But if there are clubs down there with his name on them, we can get a shot of that."

Without looking back, Mars called out, "Your source at the Police Union should have told you. I don't golf—not here or anywhere else."

Nettie's back was to him when he entered the squad room. She glanced around, caught sight of him, and turned.

"Where's the suntan?"

"Pretty much what the television crew that met me at the airport wanted to know."

Nettie groaned. "I should have warned you. I had a call from the Police Union, asking where you were. Like, when have they ever cared? I gave them a very ambiguous answer. But then they wanted to know when you'd be back. I told them tonight."

"Don't worry about it, Nettie. What's going on here? Any more hanging victims with Beck's number?"

"Nothing. And the chief has been doing some follow-up on the last teletype that got sent. He's saying he thinks the three are all there is at this point. But the big news is . . ." She turned. "Got this late this afternoon. Tried to get hold of you in Richmond, but you were already in the air."

She had a large manila envelope with exotic postage. She pulled out a sheaf of pages and a piece of cardboard to which was stapled a couple of plastic envelopes.

"Sheep news from across the pond," Nettie said. She rifled through the report, stopped, tracing lines as she read, then began to nod. "Here it is, down in the summary section on this page." She passed the report over to Mars.

It was what they wanted. The lab in Bradford, England, confirmed that the fabric sample from Beck's noose included fibers that matched Herdwick sheep wool produced on a Yorkshire farm.

Mars read out loud: " 'The materials used in the construction of this fabric are consistent with fabric woven from wool produced by the Herdwick breed sheep currently bred on Thwaite Farms in west Yorkshire. Microscopic analysis was made by a binocular-zoom surgical microscope with a magnification power of two-ten. Chemical analysis was not conducted on samples provided as microscopic analysis was judged to be conclusive. It was further concluded that the age of the sample material is contemporary. While the weave pattern and wool source are consistent with nineteenth- and early twentieth-century flag materials, damage to the fiber's scaling suggests a bleaching process was used to enhance a white or cream fabric. Such a process would not be consistent with fabric processing prior to 1960. Furthermore, microscopic analysis suggests that thread used to sew the seam in the sample provided was of a polyurethane type, again, not used in thread production prior to the 1960s. Chemical analysis of conclusions with respect to the age of the sample provided are available if requested.' "

"Hot damn," Mars said.

"*And,*" Nettie said, "I got some harebrained clerk at Quality Flag Fabrics to fax me their customer list for that fabric."

"Boosey or Macintosh on the list?"

Nettie shook her head. "Couple West Virginia addresses, though. Probably figures that Boosey and Macintosh wouldn't use their own names for a mailing."

Mars flipped through the full report, stopping briefly under the section headed "Age Analysis." He stopped cold when he read, "There is microscopic staining of the fabric sample determined to be related to fragments of berry seeds found in the fabric. Given the positioning of the fragments, it is judged that the seed fragments were introduced by the individual sewing the seam in the fabric sample."

"You have the fax from the fabric place handy?"

Nettie handed over the fax. "What?" she said.

He traced down the list, looking for Green Springs. Nothing.

But his eye stopped at a Darlene Jessup who had a post office box address in East Hill, West Virginia. If Mars remembered the map of West Virginia he'd used on the trip, East Hill would have been the closest town of any size to Green Springs.

"Shit." Mars slapped his head. "Boosey's sister's name wasn't in the Feebie's file, and I didn't ask when I talked to her. *Shit!*"

"You're thinking the sister ordered the fabric, made the noose?"

"More than thinking." He pointed to the age analysis section. "They note the presence of berry seeds in the fabric. When I talked to Boosey's sister, her toddler was eating dried berries." Mars sat forward, rubbing his temples. Then he turned back to Nettie.

"Is there any way you can get me a phone number for an Esso station in Green Springs?"

Nettie looked at him. "It's almost midnight in West Virginia, Mars." She saw his face, and shrugged. "You have your travel expense receipts with you?"

Nettie had the number for the Best Esso service station in Green Springs, West Virginia, in five minutes. As Mars dialed the number, he tried to remember if the old guy in the baseball cap and wool jacket had a name. It would make it simpler if Mars could ask for the guy by name, but nothing came to mind.

It was a moot issue. Mars recognized the old guy's voice as soon as he picked up.

"Esso." He sounded wide awake.

"I'm Marshall Bahr. Sorry to bother you so late, but I bought gas at your station a couple days ago . . ."

"Two point three."

"Pardon?"

"You bought two point three gallons. Put it on a credit card. Noticed the name. Parked bad and asked a lot of questions."

Mars saw an opportunity. "You got it in one."

"Always do," the old guy said.

"I appreciated the directions you gave to Junior's place. But I need to talk to his sister again, and find I don't have her name. I was wondering if you? . . ."

"You a cop?" the old guy said.

Mars said, "You got it in one again."

"Married name Jessup," the old guy said. "Darlene Boosey married Wayne Jessup."

Within three hours of Mars's confirming that Junior Boosey's sister's name was Darlene Jessup, Gordon Ball and Mars had worked out what Ball would need to get a search warrant on Jessup's double wide and Junior's Airstream. Ball had cautioned Mars that if the search didn't yield anything definitive, the best they could hope for was to get Junior to say something that would give them a clue who he might be working with. Ball had made contact with county authorities in Green Springs who would support an arrest, just in case Junior stepped in it. And Ball promised Mars that if Junior wasn't taken into custody, surveillance would be in place immediately.

After talking to Ball, Mars said to Nettie, "Put that one in the plus column. Remember that case in Ohio? Where they did DNA analysis on some kind of vegetation at the crime scene? Don't know if that's a possibility with these berry seeds, but it's worth a try. At the very least, we can match them visually to the fragments in the fabric."

Mars got up and started pacing. He looked at his watch. At best it would be another ten, twelve hours before he'd hear from Ball. He looked at the white board, seven names now in the column to the right of the seventeen names of the First Minnesota Volunteers who'd died at Gettysburg.

Nettie said, "Mars, I'm beat."

"Get out of here. Depending on what we hear back from Ball, tomorrow could be chaos. Get some sleep while you can."

"What about you?"

"I'll be out of here in fifteen minutes."

After Nettie left, Mars remembered something he'd thought about when he'd put the suspect profile together. He'd thought it likely that their suspect would disassociate himself from the flag controversy in advance of beginning the killings.

Now that they were pretty confident that the three hangings they knew about were the only three hangings that had taken place, they had a starting point. Which meant Mars could check people who'd been involved in the flag controversy who had dropped out or become inactive prior to the first killing.

Mars went through Keegan's files again to see if there was anything on Hec Macintosh, Junior Boosey, or Phil Stern that referred to individuals dropping out of the group. Macintosh had been forced out of the ROFers, but had continued a more damaging association with the Pure Blood Boys. Other than that, Mars didn't find anything. Maybe Keegan was right. Maybe their suspect was a guy who'd never joined up, who'd kept his nose clean.

His eyes were starting to get heavy. Mars carried Macintosh's file back to the lounge, bunched his parka on one end of the couch, and lay down. As he read through the file in detail he shook his head in regret. Macintosh would have been the perfect suspect. But there was absolutely no one who fit their invisible-man profile. Mars got back up, unable to sleep, and walked back into the squad room. He stood, staring, in front of the white board.

No question about it. They were making progress. But it was impossible to feel comfortable with where they were. The first time Mars could expect to take a deep breath would be when they'd identified all the target victims and had them under protection.

Before heading back to the apartment, Mars picked up the full report on the fabric analysis. Under the report was a thin file labeled Twenty-eighth Virginia/19 Dead. Mars flipped it open. It was a file Nettie had started as she began the process of identifying any of the nineteen members of the twenty-eighth Virginia who'd died at Gettysburg who had been hanged.

Mars sat down on the edge of his desk, reading what Nettie had pulled together. They knew almost nothing about these men. Nettie's information—as far as she'd gone—was scant. She had one page that listed the names of the nineteen. She'd begun individual sheets for two of those, but had little information filled in, other than birth dates, a marriage date for one. He held the file in his hand for a moment. If he had trouble getting to sleep, he knew he'd regret not having it with him. So he dropped the file on top of the fabric analysis report and headed out.

He was at the intersection of Portland and Eleventh Street when he became conscious of a small point of green light deep within his consciousness. He pulled over and concentrated. Nothing came. The light flickered. On instinct, he picked up the file on the dead Virginians, flipping on the dome light.

He looked twice at the birth date for Algernon Broaddus. Broaddus had been born on May 11, 1843. Was Mars remembering correctly that Gaylord Rowe had been hanged on May 11, 1999? If he was remembering correctly, were the two dates a coincidence?

Mars switched off the dome light and pulled a U-turn on Portland, driving the wrong way on the one-way street as he headed back to city hall.

He didn't take his jacket off as he entered the squad room. He went straight to the white board. He'd remembered right. Gaylord Rowe died on May 11, 1999.

Mars's hand trembled slightly as he flipped to the only other page that contained a birth date. Purvis Graham Jr. had been born on January 2, 1845. Of the two remaining hanging death dates— for Beck and the Salina, Kansas, victim—neither death date matched January 2. But without knowing the death dates for the other names on the board, he couldn't be sure. The only way Mars could rule out that the May 11 match between Rowe's death and Algernon Broaddus's birth was a coincidence was to come up with as many birth dates for the remaining names of the nineteen Twenty-eighth Virginians as he could, and see if any of those birth dates matched Beck's or the Salina victim's death date.

Still in his jacket, Mars sat down at his computer. He fiddled around with the Yahoo and Google search engines, cursing himself for being too reliant on Nettie to handle this kind of thing. After a few false starts he found a Web site for the Virginia Historical Society. That site allowed Mars to enter a search date for documents going back as far as the sixteenth century. It was simple enough to enter the name, specify a death record—which he felt pretty sure would include a date of birth—and limit the search to July 1863. George E. Whitman had been born on October 9, 1837; Mars noted the date next to Whitman's name on Nettie's list, but he couldn't match it to Beck's death date of December 6 or the June 3, 1998, Salina hanging.

An hour and three names later, it was Frederick James Olm's birth date that matched Beck's death date of December 6. The next name Mars checked, Gideon Walsh, showed a birth date of June 3.

He'd matched the death dates of all three known hanging victims to birth dates for three of the nineteen dead Virginians.

His sleep-deprived brain struggled for the obvious conclusion: by identifying birth dates for all nineteen of the dead Virginians, they'd know when the remaining target victims would be at risk. Knowing that would make all the difference.

Just before dawn he'd found birthdates for all nineteen of the Virginians who'd died at Gettysburg. He stared, numb with fatigue, at the array of dates. What he saw jolted him into full consciousness.

Boyle Keegan's voice was fuzzy when he answered Mars's call. Mars could hear Keegan yawning softly and moving about as he listened to what Mars had to say.

"It's a break," Keegan said, his voice still thick with sleep, but now charged with oxygen. "It gives us a way of managing this thing. Fax me the dates, will you? I'll see that they get out immediately to all the jurisdictions where we've identified targeted victims. We're going to need to pull together a task force meeting—can Minneapolis host? Some hands are going to need to be held to keep this thing on track. We'll want all the jurisdictions that have a victim or a target, the chiefs that have been involved, the FBI satellite offices—"

Mars said, "I'm not sure we want to pull those guys in to Minneapolis now."

"Not on the target dates," Keegan said, "I'm talking about getting this done in the next few days."

"That's the problem," Mars said. "We've got a target date coming up in four days. And we haven't identified all the target victims yet."

For sure Mars woke Linda VanCleve.

"Linda, it's Mars Bahr. What's going on? I thought we were going to have researchers working shifts to identify our target victims. I got back from Richmond last night, and I haven't seen anybody."

Linda VanCleve may have been sleeping when he called, but she managed to give Mars a sharp reply.

"It's been difficult, the time of year and all. We should be able to go to shifts after New Year's." Her voice was intentionally unresponsive.

"Jesus fucking christ, Linda! This isn't recruiting hall monitor volunteers. People could die while we put this information together. I thought you understood that. And why, if you're having problems finding people to work, haven't you told someone? We could have brought in people from other states, if necessary. We can't just sit on our hands while we wait for people to come back from Hawaii, or wherever. You need to fucking communicate if you're not able to do what you said you'd do, when you said you'd do it—"

"Oh, I love *this*," Linda hissed. "*You* lecturing *me* on proper communications. Do you want to explain when you intended to let me know that you'd brought in the legal beagles to return the flag to Virginia? After all the effort we've put out to help? Including Christmas *Fucking* Day, to borrow your language?"

For a moment Mars was too angry to speak. Controlling himself he said, "That's what this is about? Keeping the flag in the basement of the History Center? That's more important to you than saving the lives of innocent people?"

Her response was clipped. "I'm sorry you see it that way. I thought we'd worked pretty effectively together until now. Which is why I felt so betrayed when the center's attorney in the AG's office told me what you were up to. I even had the impression that we'd gone above and beyond the call of duty to try and—how did you put it—keep innocent people alive."

"You've done a lot. It's been appreciated. But doing a lot shouldn't be confused with doing everything that needs to be done. And right now, we have to identify the targeted victims fast. Because we've gotten a break in the case that indicates one of them is scheduled to die in four days. And if giving the flag back to Virginia—even on a temporary basis—increases their chances of staying alive, it seems to me to be more important to do that than to waste time and energy throwing a hissy fit over who gets the flag."

"Maybe, Mars, you should spend some time thinking about what was important to the innocent men of the First Minnesota who died at Gettysburg."

Mars lost it. He was tired, he was scared, and Linda VanCleve was making him crazy.

"Put it in a can and eat it with a fork, Linda. Read your own documents on what was important to the innocent men of the First Minnesota. What they cared about was the Union. They did *not* go to war, they did *not* risk their lives, so you could keep a flag in a drawer in the basement. And consider this: If we lose one of the First Minnesota's descendents in four days' time because keeping the flag in your basement is more important to you than saving their lives, I'm not going to be too concerned about letting any number of people know what your priorities are. You can be over here with your researchers by—" Mars glanced at his watch, startling himself. It was eight o'clock in the morning. "You're over here with your researchers by ten, or I'll find somebody else who can do the job. And I can promise you won't like the consequences if it comes to that."

Mars slammed down the receiver and blew air. When he turned around, Nettie and Glenn Gjerde were standing behind him in slack-jawed amazement.

Nettie said, "I didn't know you felt that way. That you felt that strongly about giving the flag back to Virginia."

Mars jammed his hands into his pants pockets. "Neither did I. Until just now." He nodded toward the white board. "I figured something out last night about the schedule for the hangings. We've got four days to complete the target victim identification."

To Glenn he said, "I assume you bring glad tidings."

Glenn pulled up a chair and sat down. "Based on what I just heard, I'm not feeling all that great about what I've got to say."

"C'mon, Glenn. It won't be the first time you've told me something I didn't want to hear."

"I've spent a fair amount of time with John Yanch—Yanch is the attorney in the AG's office that handles History Center business."

"He's the guy who issued that convoluted opinion justifying why Minnesota was entitled to keep the flag?"

"The same," Glenn said. "But like it or not, Mars, Yanch is a first-class lawyer. And he's saying no federal court is going to order Minnesota to return the flag to Virginia. The federal court is gonna say this is a state issue that needs to be resolved in state courts. Which pretty much puts a lid on it. A Virginia court can order Minnesota to return the flag, but you don't need me to tell you what Minnesota is gonna do with that order."

Mars tossed his cigarette box on his desk. It had been beaten up pretty bad in the past twenty-four hours. "The fact is, Glenn, right now, I don't have time to work this issue. Like you heard me say, we've got four days to complete our target victim identification—less than that. We need to have the victims identified in the next forty-eight hours so we can get protection in place. Maybe if the flag had gone back a week ago, it might have made a difference. Right now . . ." Mars shrugged. "Right now I figure we've missed our chance to return the flag and have that make a difference."

Mars dropped down in the chair next to the chief's desk.

"Developments," he said.

The chief sat back, fixing his eyes on Mars.

Mars talked through what had happened with the fabric evidence and the target dates. The chief's eyebrows went up in response to what Mars was saying, but he stayed quiet.

When Mars stopped, the chief said, "Sounds like we need to have a status call with our colleagues in other jurisdictions."

"That's what I wanted to talk about. Keegan's suggesting a task force meeting in Minneapolis. But that can't happen until we complete the target victim identification and have protection in place in advance of the next target date—January fourth. Ideally, I'd like to get the victim identification completed in the next forty-eight hours, which takes us to New Year's Eve. If we could get the task force meeting in place on January second, we'd have time to contact all the jurisdictions with target victims and everybody attending would have time to get back to their own jurisdictions well in advance of the fourth. And they'd be fully briefed, we'd be better coordinated. Thing is, can we pull off a meeting here on that kind of notice—three days from now? Our resources are pretty well tapped out in the division. Can your office handle arrangements for the task force meeting?"

The chief gave Mars a nod. "Consider it done."

Boyle Keegan arrived shortly before noon. He was too hyped to stay in Washington, running the administrative end of the show. "Everything's in line there," he said, "I need to be on this end. Target victim identification is where it's at now. Can't we get more people working this thing?"

"We considered it," Mars said. "Decided the best way to manage quality control—and maintain confidentiality—was to have the same group working the research, supervised by people close to the investigation. The last thing we want to do is make a mistake and either miss someone or identify the wrong person. Of course, we made the decision to keep the research here before we knew the target dates. Now it's really too late to rethink that decision. It would just take resources away from the effort to train new people."

Mars sighed. He was tired and wanting to get over to see Chris, who'd returned with Denise the previous night. And there wasn't much he could do in the squad room until they completed target victim identification.

He rubbed the heels of both hands across his face. "Our biggest problem is turning out to be coming up with accurate current address information, once we've identified the target victim." He blinked and stared over at the white board. His brain was making a buzzing sound inside his skull.

Keegan said, "Shit, Mars. The Bureau can run those checks with both hands tied behind our backs. Have your people feed the Bureau the information on the target victims as soon as they have a name. Then your people can get back to doing the family line research. Should speed the process up no end."

Keegan's suggestion took a lot of pressure off. Mars should have thought of it himself, but his brain was showing serious signs of burnout. Relief washed over him now that completing the target victim identification process looked to be a sure thing. Relief was quickly followed by profound sleepiness. Mars picked up the phone to call Chris.

"Dad! Can you come over? I want to set the computer up."

"You're welcome."

Mars could hear Chris's embarrassment in the silence that followed. Then Chris said, "I'm sorry. I thanked Mom. I would have asked for one, but I thought it cost too much."

"It did cost too much. But your mother and I agreed you'd earned one. Okay that it's not a dog?"

Chris's voice resumed its buoyancy. "I named it Spot. And I can get software that'll make it bark every time I turn it on."

"Just so it doesn't get muddy paws and shed hair."

"So can you come over?"

"Yeah. But I can stay just long enough to get the computer set up. Then I've gotta get some sleep."

Denise's expression was grim as Mars walked in. She was trying to dump a cardboard box full of Styrofoam mailing peanuts into a plastic trash bag. From where Mars stood, it looked like her success rate was significantly under 50 percent. Chris was on the couch, hand over his mouth, working hard to control laughter, with about the same success as Denise was having with the Styrofoam peanuts.

Gulping back laughter, he said, "Mom? If you'd gotten me a dog, it wouldn't have been wrapped in all that plastic stuff."

"That," Denise said, straightening up, "is the best argument for a dog you've come up with." She looked at Mars. "I've been trying to get rid of these things for the past twenty minutes, and so far I've got a lot more on the floor than in the bag."

This statement broke through the remaining shreds of Mars's and Chris's self-control. The truth was that more of the Styrofoam peanuts had, through the miracle of static electricity, stuck to Denise's clothes and hair than had fallen to the floor.

"*What,*" she said, hands on her hips, a plastic peanut hanging artfully from her elbow, "is so funny?"

Mars pulled his coat off and started to help Denise. It was roughly like herding cats. Within seconds, the electricity that had been generated when he'd removed his jacket was sucking peanuts out of the box and onto his pants and face. The peanuts clung to his hands as he tried to shovel them into the bag.

Rolling with laughter, Chris said, "Mom? Know what we should do? We should just put you and Dad in plastic bags."

CHAPTER
23

It was becoming clear that the secondary casualty of the investigation was sleep.

After leaving Chris and Denise, Mars slept for less than four hours when, once again, he'd awakened with a start. And with the certainty that falling back to sleep wasn't going to happen.

There was just too much going on and too much that needed to be thought through. He wanted to confirm their progress on the target victim identification, look at the plans for the task force meeting that Nettie had worked out with the chief's office. And he wanted to make another pass over files for anything he might have missed.

The dark quiet of the squad room had served him well the previous night. He headed back downtown.

Mars was almost relieved to find no one in the squad room other than researchers. And they were zombies, hypnotized by the screens they'd been staring at for hours. He talked briefly to the lead researcher who confirmed they were closing in on the last five target descendents. Then Mars scooped up files and headed back to the lounge.

He went first to Hec Macintosh's file. His gut was telling him there had to be some connection there that would lead them to Hec's silent partner. But there was nothing that fit. No one who had been involved who fit the profile. Especially no one who had been involved and then dropped out in advance of the hangings. He went to Nettie's file on the nineteen Virginians who'd died at Gettysburg. She'd found cause of death for all but two—and none of the seventeen she had identified involved hangings. That fact hit him hard. It was their best chance for figuring out a connection to a suspect, and it wasn't looking good.

He went back over news clippings on the flag controversy, hoping for a name that had been missed. Marshall Sherman, General Pickett, Phil Stern, John Lee . . .

Mars stopped at Lee's name. *What?* He looked at Phil Stern's name. Then he heard Phil Stern's voice saying, 'Hector *Lee* Macintosh.'

What? John Lee had been the last member of the Twenty-eighth Virginia to carry the flag before it was captured at Gettysburg—but he'd *survived*. And the South was full of Lees. The possibility that John Lee of Gettysburg was related to Hector Lee Macintosh was probably less than the possibility that the names were a coincidence.

There was a way of checking. Mars went back to his computer, back to the Virginia Historical Society's Web site. He worked through the screens he'd used to identify the birthdates of the nineteen Virginians who'd died at Gettysburg. He entered "John Lee" and selected death record. Fulfilling his expectations, endless screens of names scrolled before him.

He stared, then went back and filled in a date field for one year after Gettysburg. What if John Lee had died of wounds following Gettysburg? The screen reported the deaths of eleven John Lees in the year after Gettysburg. There were no Macintosh names associated with any of the eleven.

Mars exhaled deeply. He needed to rethink his approach. There had to be a simpler way of zeroing in on John Lee of Pickett's Charge. Which gave him an idea. He went to newspaper records and entered five search words: "John," "Lee," "Gettysburg," "Pickett," and "death."

A newspaper obituary flashed on the screen. The article included the bearded face of a man identified as John Lee. The obituary noted that Mr. Lee had fought in the Twenty-eighth Virginia, the Army of Northern Virginia and had survived Pickett's Charge at Gettysburg. John Lee had died two years after Gettysburg, but no cause of death had been listed. The only thing the article told Mars that he didn't know was the name of Lee's only child. A daughter, named Thalia Marie.

At this point he had two choices. He could go back and search for more information on John Lee's death or he could track the daughter's line to see if he could find a Macintosh connection. He went for Thalia Marie.

In moments a list of newspaper headlines appeared. An engagement announcement was the first to catch Mars's eye. On July 14, 1879, Thalia Marie Lee, daughter of John Lee, deceased, and Marie Lee Harris, was betrothed to George M. Macintosh of Richmond, Virginia.

It was only half a neural synapse from Thalia Marie's engagement announcement to Mars's next question.

And minutes later to an answer that rang bells and sent chills up and down Mars's spine.

The newspaper account of Hec Macintosh's death told Mars everything he needed to know. Hec had gone up to his cabin west of Green Springs to hunt wild turkeys. He'd gone alone, the article noted, which probably cost him his life. When he didn't return to Richmond as expected, Ruth Palmer Macintosh called the sheriff's office near Green Springs. The sheriff and his deputy found the cabin door open, a trail of blood from the door into the woods. Inside the cabin was a blood-covered chair and a table on which gun-cleaning equipment and materials were spread out. And an almost empty bottle of bourbon. On the floor was a rifle, its trigger, trigger grip, and butt covered in blood. Lab testing confirmed the blood was Hec Macintosh's.

No one thought Hec Macintosh killed himself. He was a man who enjoyed life and believed himself to be superior to any challenge. The scenario everyone accepted was that Hec had cleaned his rifle while he was drunk and shot himself in the process. Probably shot himself in the face, looking down the barrel. Then had staggered out, screaming, into the woods. Where he'd been picked apart by critters.

The part that interested Mars was that Hector Lee Macintosh's body had never been recovered. Mars pushed back from the computer with a deep sense of accomplishment. He was remembering Ruth Palmer Macintosh's face when he'd asked her if Hec had been buried at Hollywood. He was remembering Phil Stern describing Junior at Hec's funeral. How Junior hadn't been upset.

For the first time in this investigation, Mars knew who he was looking for.

A half hour after she came in, Nettie found Confederate army pension records that indicated John Lee had hanged himself two years after Gettysburg. Not that Mars needed anything else to convince himself that Hector Lee Macintosh was their phantom suspect. But it was nice and neat, which they hadn't had a lot of.

He'd half expected the chief and Keegan would view it more as a hallucination than a revelation, but that hadn't happened. Both of them—maybe especially Keegan—listened quietly to Mars's reasoning. They had a few questions, but they were prepared to accept that it was probable that Macintosh's death had been staged and that Macintosh was their suspect. Keegan immediately began contacts with the Bureau to set the Bureau's fugitive search team in motion. He planned on going back himself immediately after the task force meeting.

Keegan had said, "Macintosh could hole up for a while with a stash of cash and get by, but to conduct an operation like this, he has to have access to funding. I just can't believe he's accessing assets in any direct way, or that his widow—if you'll pardon the expression—is giving him money directly. Ruth Palmer Macintosh driving up to some West Virginia backwater to hand Hec a bag of cash? I don't think so."

Nettie said, "That's where you think he'd be? West Virginia?"

"No place better for him to hide," Keegan said. "He knows the Appalachians. He was a good woodsman, a good hunter, a world-class fly fisherman by all accounts. He probably set up some kind of base before he staged his death. And I can't see Hec driving down to Richmond to get money. He was a well-known man about town. Somebody's helping him. I'd put money on Junior Boosey, but Junior doesn't explain the money connection—so there's still somebody else out there who's working with Hec."

Looking at the chief, Mars said, "I agree with what Keegan says about Hec staying clear of his wife's house in Richmond. All the same, I think we need to ask the Richmond police to set up a stakeout around Hec's wife's house."

CHAPTER

24

Mars knew as soon as he heard Gordon Ball's voice that bad news was next.

"You couldn't find Junior?" Mars said.

Ball's words were slow and pained. "Worse than that. We found Junior. Just like you said, in the Airstream. We're asking him about his whereabouts on the three dates we've got for hangings, and Junior says, 'I need to take a crap.' I checked the can out myself, Mars. Thinking maybe he was gonna go for a gun or try and get out a window. There were no weapons, and the only window was this horizontal vent just below the ceiling. No way he was getting out through that. So we let him go. Something else. I mean, this guy was ready for us. He had a tape recorder running in the bathroom. His voice, saying stuff like, 'I'll be right there. Give me a minute.' Five minutes go by, and when we open the door, he's gone . . ."

"Geez, Gordon, you didn't make him keep the door open . . ."

"You ever been in an Airstream can? Especially the little Airstreams? If the door had been open, Junior wouldn't have been able to sit on the john. And we heard him talking—the tape recorder. He's been expecting something like this to happen."

"Sorry, Gordon. No doubt about it, he was waiting for somebody to show up. Made his day. I was just—"

"I know. Believe me, I know. When we went in, the whole

282

fucking floor was up. The kid had made a trapdoor out of the entire floor. He'd put struts in a tunnel under the floor that supported the shower and the can. The tunnel—if you can believe this—was more than five hundred feet long. It came out in the woods behind the trailer. By the time we got into the bathroom—which was no easy trick, because when he lifted the floor it propped up against the door—he was long gone. And I don't need to tell you what it's like trying to hunt down a fugitive in the Appalachian woods. We've got a serious problem."

"Be sure to have your guys look for a place in the woods where a vehicle may be parked . . . and Gordon? Do we have surveillance on Ruth Macintosh's house yet? If they were in this together—and I still believe someone else had to be involved—he may try to make contact with Ruth. Go for a wiretap, if you can. How we doing on a search warrant for the trailer and his sister's house?"

"Forthcoming. We'll do the search before we leave here. And we haven't said anything to the sister yet about what's goin' on. So hopefully she isn't in there flushin' stuff down the crapper. Mars—there's one other thing. And it's problematic. When we were talking with Junior, asking him about his whereabouts on the three dates. The June third hanging date . . ."

"Yeah?"

"He laughed at us. Said he was in the county jail for breaking in to the Esso station in Green Springs."

Which, Mars thought, explained why the old guy had always been more than willing to tell Mars anything he wanted to know about Junior.

"I don't think that's much of a problem, Gordon. I've never thought Junior was actually doing the killings. My guess, he uses his computer to locate the victims, maybe does some surveillance—I think his biggest role is to be a link between Hec and Ruth. I think he's the conduit for getting money from Ruth to Hec. I just can't figure how that works. Let's hope the surveillance on Ruth's house tells us something. If Junior's on the run, he may need to be in touch with her."

Ball said, "One thing I'm worried about. Junior making contact with Hec. Letting him know that we're onto him. I've been thinking about what you said—about Hec going kind of wild if he thinks there's a chance we'll catch him before he finishes the job."

Mars stared at nothing in particular before he said, "My thoughts are running on the same line—the one thing we've got going for us is that you didn't know about Hec when you were at Junior's. There isn't any way you could have said anything that tipped Junior to that."

"That's true," Ball said, still sounding worried.

Mars didn't feel much better about it. He updated Ball on what they knew about the target dates and the task force meeting Keegan had asked Minneapolis to host.

"We're trying to get it scheduled ASAP—but it can't happen until we complete the target victim identifications. So, you'll be hearing from us."

The next call from Gordon Ball confirmed Junior's involvement in the murders, even if it didn't resolve how far Junior's involvement went or a connection to Hec Macintosh.

The search warrant had yielded fabric samples from Darlene Jessup's house—Junior's sister—that visually matched the fabric used in the nooses, and Ball's people had taken dried berries from the house. They'd not yet had time to complete an analysis of Junior's computer files, but just looking at cache files on the computer, they'd identified a number of sites where Junior could have traced descendents of the surviving First Minnesota Volunteers. Of particular interest was a book on knot tying that Ball had found on Junior's bookshelves.

"I glanced at his books," Mars said. "But I didn't notice that one."

"Real easy to miss," Ball said. "The book on knots was on the shelf backwards. Pages out, spine back. Looked like a blank spine until you took it off the shelf."

Mars shook his head. "This kid can think. What's the chance his sister is involved in this—beyond doing the sewing for Junior?"

"Ohhh, I suppose that's possible. But not likely. She was genuinely upset by our going through the house—but not defensive. Not like she thought we were gonna find anything. Her big concern was somebody paying her for the stuff we took out. Particularly the fabric. Said it was real expensive and she'd paid for it and Junior owed her. We're checking out her husband—but that doesn't look real promising. He's not around much. Has a job over in one of the coal companies about seventy miles from Green Springs, comes home every other weekend. Sounds like a pretty straight arrow."

CHAPTER

25

Every city has a 494 strip. In the Twin Cities, 494 is the south and west section of a ring road that encompasses the outer perimeters of Minneapolis and St. Paul. A primary commercial artery in the cities, its increasingly clogged traffic is the result of its being the feeder road to the Minneapolis–St. Paul International Airport and to the burgeoning suburbs to the south and west of Minneapolis's first-tier suburbs. But it was when the Mall of America—a monument to the power and passions of American consumers—opened in 1992 that development along 494 grew exponentially. And new hotels led the list of new development along the 494 strip.

On January 2, more than fifty law enforcement officers from around the country gathered in a sublevel meeting room at the Airport Sheraton, less than a mile from the airport and located on a 494 frontage road. If you'd asked the theoretical question, can you get fifty people together from multiple agencies and jurisdictions in four days' time—right after the New Year's holiday—everybody's first answer would have been a solid no. But Minneapolis had something going for it in getting the meeting scheduled fast. Nobody wanted a victim dying on their watch now that they had been alerted to the risk.

In addition to the chief, Mars, Nettie, Glenn Gjerde from the Hennepin County Attorney's Office, Linda VanCleve, and Tee Tucker, there were chiefs of police from sixteen jurisdictions in the investigation, investigators accompanying the chiefs, attorneys from the U.S. Attorney's Office in Minneapolis, local FBI investigators, and Boyle Keegan. Gordon Ball had sent a junior officer since Ball was unwilling to leave Richmond until they'd found Junior Boosey.

As Mars looked around the room, he wished Joey Beck was there. To see what he'd started, to know that something good might yet come of his dad's death. Mars glanced at three FBI agents standing together near the coffeepot. They'd made little effort to mingle and a lot of effort to look bored by the proceedings. On an individual basis, Mars didn't have anything against FBI agents. He'd worked with more than one who'd been top-notch investigators and who'd made substantive contributions to cases. Part of the problem came from the Bureau's hiring practices. It had in recent years made a practice of hiring young attorneys without much street experience as investigators. And too often the attorneys thought the law degree gave them a leg up over other law enforcement professionals. Arrogance doesn't get you anywhere in an investigation, and more than once an arrogant FBI agent had caused serious problems. From where Mars stood, the three young suits by the coffeepot looked arrogant. Except when Boyle Keegan was within sight. Their deference to Boyle was obvious, even from the opposite side of the room.

The task force meeting began with a go-around where each of the attendees introduced himself or herself and explained their connection to the case. Then Mars was up. He gave a chronological presentation of the case, but spent most of his time on target victim identification. That was, after all, what made the local jurisdictions' collective hearts beat faster. And there were the still unanswered questions about who the final three victims were.

The funny thing was, the missing victims made sense to Mars and Keegan. The missing victims were Hec's wild card. A target that he controlled. A target that he could use to confuse and confound anyone that had figured out his methodology. It was just one more example of the cunning built into his strategy. Mars was sure that Macintosh had used the same elegant means of selecting the last three victims that he'd used in selecting the first sixteen. But what that elegant means was had not yet come to light.

Hec would have been pleased to see the effect his missing three victims had on those attending the task force meeting. They ignored the fact that they had names of target victims in their own jurisdictions and the dates on which those target victims would be at risk, protesting vigorously that anything less than 100 percent certainty was unacceptable.

In frustration, Keegan rose. "Look," he said. "Consider yourselves lucky. It's not impossible that one or more of Macintosh's last three victims would be in your jurisdiction—but it's not likely. You're the ones who know who the targeted victims are and when they're going to be at risk. It's much more likely that we've got someone out there where the jurisdiction hasn't been notified."

Keegan's word quieted the group, but Mars could tell they weren't comfortable with having anything less than an airtight assurance that there wouldn't be another victim on their watch.

A chief of police from Watertown, South Dakota, rose. "Let's see if I've got this straight. You've got nineteen target dates for the hangings—based on the birth dates of the nineteen guys from Virginia who died at Gettysburg. That right?"

Mars nodded, waiting for his point.

"And what you're saying is, of the sixteen identified target victims, three are already dead. Leaving thirteen who are at risk on all nineteen dates—or just the sixteen dates where no hangings have occurred yet?"

"I think," Mars said, "we can be pretty confident Macintosh isn't going to hang more than one victim on the same date. His point is to honor all nineteen members of the Twenty-eighth Virginia who died—and all those birth dates are different."

"So," the Watertown chief concluded, "our job is to protect identified victims within our respective jurisdictions on the sixteen dates."

"You got it in one," Mars said.

The Watertown chief looked around the room. "Well," he said, "I guess I can live with that. Even if, somewhere out there, there're three guys who can't."

The room erupted in laughter.

"Exactly," Mars said. It was what he and Keegan had been saying, but having it come from somebody other than the two of them helped. Mars hated to throw a monkey wrench into the improved atmosphere, but it had to be said.

"But remember what we've been saying all along. Confidentiality is critical. If Macintosh becomes aware that we know what he's doing, and when he's going to do it—if Macintosh thinks there's a chance we'll catch up with him before he completes his mission, we think that's when he'll use his wild cards."

Linda VanCleve followed Mars's presentation with an overview of the historical controversy. VanCleve made the story of the First Minnesota Volunteers's capture of the flag a compelling narrative, but Mars was irritated by the amount of time she spent justifying the History Center's retention of the flag. Who had a right to have the flag wasn't at issue here, but Linda VanCleve had put more effort into winning hearts and minds for her cause than explaining how the deaths that had brought them together related to the captured flag. VanCleve and Mars were a long way from achieving anything like reconciliation.

After VanCleve's presentation, Gordon Ball's delegate from Richmond, along with an FBI agent leading the Fugitive Task Force, gave a presentation on Junior Boosey and Hec Macintosh and the status of the search to find the two men. "Like a needle in a haystack," was the unoriginal but correct conclusion of the Feebie agent. All the same, it was useful for the attending jurisdictions to attach faces and personalities to the previously amorphous perpetrators.

Mars came forward again after the perpetrator presentation had been completed. He paused for a moment, taking a long gulp from the can of Coke he'd balanced on the podium. "What we want to do now is talk about how we can protect targeted victims in your jurisdictions."

The room stirred; investigators sat forward with pens poised for note taking.

"As we've advised in previous communications, from what we know about the hanging here in Minneapolis and the hangings in Kansas and Wisconsin, Macintosh moved on the victim in a very calculated manner. Our belief is that he chooses a time based on specific knowledge regarding when the victim will be alone and on what the victim's specific interests are. In Minneapolis, our victim was in dire financial straights. He needed capital badly. His situation had been covered in business publications in the Twin Cities media. We believe the perpetrator researched the victim and identified the victim's Achilles' heel. Then he contacted the victim, indicating an interest in investing capital, and asking for confidentiality. He met with the victim, they came to an oral agreement, and then he does something like pulling out a hip flask, proposing a toast. The flask—or whatever—has been heavily spiked with barbiturates—something that has been confirmed by the medical exam. The hanging takes place when the victim's ability to resist has been compromised.

"Wisconsin and Kansas have just opened homicide investigations in their hanging cases, so we don't yet know for sure if this scenario matches with their victims. But we know enough to be reasonably sure that Macintosh is using a tailor-made approach based on what he has determined is the victim's special interest, need, or concern."

An investigator from Upstate New York raised his hand. "So, as far as what you feel it would be effective for us to do? . . ."

Mars glanced at the chief before answering. "You all need to evaluate your targeted victims' risk individually and make your own judgments. At a minimum, speaking for myself, I'd meet with the potential victim and explain the situation based on the fraud scenario we distributed earlier. We don't want to start a panic. We don't think anybody's gonna be wakened in their beds at night. We're pretty confident they're going to receive a contact from a stranger, from somebody suggesting they can support—with money, expertise, whatever—something in which the targeted victim has a strong interest. The stranger will want to meet, and that meeting will be under circumstances where the perp can be confident he will be alone with the victim. So, number one. Your targeted victims should be advised to be extremely cautious regarding any contacts from strangers and to be in touch with law enforcement immediately if they are contacted. Number two, my guess is the perp is not only doing research on victims but is conducting extensive surveillance on the victims before making the contact. So your victims should be alert to the repeated appearance of strangers or vehicles."

The chief was the last item on the agenda. He covered interagency communications and coordination, indicating it had been agreed that the Minneapolis Police Department would act as lead agency. The Coffeepot Three exchanged disgruntled expressions at this, but said nothing.

Then the chief reviewed support that would be provided to each of the local police departments on target dates. No less than a dozen FBI field agents would be in place, undercover, around each targeted victim. All airports, rental car agencies, and bus and train stations would be covered to identify any suspects that met Macintosh or Boosey's descriptions. The chief looked over his glasses at the room. "I should say that we're not expecting public transportation to be used. Our suspect has resources to provide himself with a vehicle, and he has the time to get himself from wherever he is to where he needs to be on the target date. A vehicle gives him much more flexibility and makes him much harder for us to track. Gives him more anonymity, especially as he can afford to change vehicles from time to time."

Concluding, the chief said, "Any questions?" The room was silent. "Our hope and expectation is that January four will produce an arrest, not another hanging. And I thank you all for coming to assure that end." His eyes covered the room. "And Happy New Year."

Mars, Nettie, and Boyle Keegan stayed around the squad room after midnight on January 4. The plan was that task force members would be advised by phone as soon as Macintosh made his initial contact with a targeted victim. That call would be followed by a conference call for all task force members as soon as Macintosh was—fingers crossed—arrested.

Nobody expected to get the call about Macintosh making a contact with the target before morning. It just wouldn't make sense to approach a target anytime other than during daylight hours. All the same, Mars, Nettie, and Keegan couldn't stay away. They hunkered down in the lounge, talking aimlessly, occasionally watching television, and wandering off, one at a time. They took turns napping on the couch, which brought forth curses from Keegan.

"Every time I start to fall asleep, this thing bucks," he said, rolling off the couch on all fours and crawling on the floor to figure out the problem.

"That's been happening for years," Nettie said. "Nothing short of a new couch is gonna change that."

Keegan stood up, carefully selected months' old magazines of the desired thickness from the coffee table and dropping down again, slid the magazines under the leg.

Gingerly, he balanced himself on the couch. No rocking. He smiled broadly at Mars and Nettie, raising both arms over his head. "Oh, ye of little faith! I solve murders, I heal the crippled! And now I sleep." He sank down on the couch, and said, "If we ever bag this case—which admittedly is a pretty dubious possibility—I'm going to see to it that the Minneapolis PD Homicide Division gets new lounge furniture. That's a promise."

He woke, abruptly, at three. "I'm trying to decide," he said, "if I'm still on duty."

Mars raised his head. He'd fallen into a doze sitting in a chair. He blinked and looked at Keegan. "In my experience," he said "we're always on duty."

"Yes," Keegan said. "But there's on duty and there's *on duty*. If what I am right now is *on duty*, then it wouldn't be appropriate to pour myself a vodka on the rocks from the bottle in my briefcase. There's enough for three drinks, if we can decide that none of us is *on duty*."

"Drink up," Mars said. "Me, I'm going in search of an Atlanta cocktail."

"An Atlanta cocktail?" Keegan said.

Nettie yawned and rebunched her coat under her head. "He's gonna get a Coke. My turn on the couch yet?"

Mars went down the stairs to the vending machines. City hall was stone silent. It was an odd feeling. To be on the edge of the biggest homicide investigation of his career and to have nothing to do. To know that as he walked the corridors of city hall in the dead of night, Hector Lee Macintosh could be waiting for the dawn of light, poised, ready to move again. While Mars was getting a Coke, the FBI's premier forensic analyst was fixing furniture and pouring himself a vodka on the rocks, and Nettie was sacked out on the lounge couch.

"What's wrong with this picture?" Mars mumbled to himself as he fed the Coke machine quarters.

At 6:00 A.M. Mars said, "Al's Breakfast is open. Macintosh isn't going to call anyone before eight, nine o'clock. Let's go for breakfast and get back here by seven. I'll have my calls here forwarded to my cell phone."

It was something to do.

Al's Breakfast was in Dinkytown, an approximately four-block-square cluster of squat buildings just north of the university's East Bank campus. Al's was an intrinsic part of the university's culture and one of the few fixtures of that culture that hadn't changed much in fifty years. It was short on comfort and quiet, and long on atmosphere and attitude. A guy with a good wingspan—Michael Jordan, say—could stand in the center of Al's single aisle and touch Al's two walls. Because essentially, that's what Al's was—an aisle, with a narrow grill on one wall, a counter, and maybe a dozen stools along the counter.

On a summer morning when the U was in session, there'd be a line out the door waiting for a stool. Once you made it in—no matter how hot it had been outside—you'd get hit with a blast of heat that had texture. If you were there with someone, you didn't think about getting two stools together. You just took the first stool that was available and hooked up again after breakfast. It wasn't like you could have a conversation with someone while you were at Al's, anyway. Mars and Chris went to Al's occasionally, but they never went when they had something specific to talk about. The noise level obliterated conversation. Eating breakfast at Al's was more like going to a performance, with the audience all lined up on the stools. The show was Al's staff cooking, taking orders, being rude to customers—sometimes in a friendly way, sometimes not.

At 6:15 A.M. on January 4, with the university on winter break and the temperature at four degrees Fahrenheit, Mars was able to pull the squad into a space directly opposite Al's front door. The three of them walked in without a wait and took stools together at the far end of the counter. There were four other customers at the counter, and to Mars's eye, they were a perfect microcosm of Al's clientele: a street person, doubtless enjoying Al's renowned largesse; a couple in jeans, with identical high-volume tightly curled shoulder-length hair; and a notably sedate, middle-aged guy who was chewing blueberry pancakes very slowly.

Nettie, who was sitting on the opposite side of Keegan from Mars, leaned across Keegan and whispered, "The president of the University."

Keegan's brows tightened. "Who?"

Nettie continued to whisper, giving her head a delicate tip in the direction of the blueberry pancake eater. "The president of the university. He came up from the University of Texas—like two years ago. From what I've seen of him, he has almost no personality. Except that he's made a big deal out of being a pancake aficionado. Not, as far as I'm concerned, an acceptable substitute for actually having a personality."

Keegan smiled wickedly. "I'm thinking," he said, "that it would be amusing if your pancake-eating president with the personality deficit was in fact one of our missing three victims, and that fellow"—Keegan tipped his head in the direction of the street person—"was Hec Macintosh in disguise."

"I'm thinking," Nettie said, "that sleep deprivation is making some of us silly."

"Sleep deprivation," Mars said, "and vodka."

By 10:00 A.M. they'd been back in the squad room for almost three hours. Mars was getting uneasy and Keegan had stopped being silly. The chief had come by twice, the second time with news that he had called other chiefs of police. There was nothing, anywhere. And everyone was getting nervous.

Mars wouldn't have said it out loud, but he would have preferred a death to nothing. Nothing happening threw all their assumptions about Macintosh and his strategy into question. Nothing happening meant they'd spend too much time on the phone trying to explain to other jurisdictions what was going on. Which wasn't easy, given that they didn't know themselves.

Better one death than to risk all the remaining targeted victims, was how Mars felt.

Nettie said, "What we'd talked about before—that if Macintosh realized we knew what he was doing—that he'd pitch the plan, go wild. Do you think that's happened?"

Mars and Keegan looked at each other. Then both shook their heads. Keegan said, "What Macintosh knows at this point is that the cops are onto Junior. And that Junior has escaped. I don't see how he gets from that to we know he's alive, that we know who he's targeting . . ."

Mars said, just remembering, "Ruth knows about the numbers. I told her when I was there. Before I knew Hec was still alive."

"Yes," Keegan said, a bit impatient, "she knows we know the numbers relate to the Twenty-eighth Virginia flag—at least, that's what I gathered from what you said, Mars. That doesn't mean she knows we know about the dead survivors' target descendents—much less who and where those descendents are. And he doesn't know we know about the dates. Right?"

Mars nodded. "Probably not."

"I was thinking," Nettie said. "Macintosh started these killings almost two years ago. But he didn't hang a victim last January fourth. Maybe he hangs on those nineteen dates, but he's not going in chronological order. He kills when he has the information he needs to select the victim, he works on a regional basis—I don't know, something like that."

Keegan groaned. "She's right. Hadn't focused on that at all. He could do one a year, two a year—any of the dates. Damn. This could go on past my lifetime." He looked at his watch, then snapped his fingers. "Something else. We've had cameras set up at Gettysburg since the twenty-eighth. I could get those tapes and—"

"No," Mars said. "I haven't told you yet. When I was in Richmond, I went out to Hollywood Cemetery. The Confederate soldiers who died at Gettysburg are buried there. There's a big pyramid memorial to the Confederacy, a monument to General Pickett—when I saw it, I thought, if Macintosh is doing some kind of ritual to mark the killings, this is where it'd be."

Keegan slapped his hand flat on the desk. "Exactly the right place."

"I didn't see anything that looked like something Macintosh would have done, as part of a ritual," Mars said, "but it was almost dark. I meant to call Ball and ask him to go out to the cemetery during the day and check it out. Slipped my mind completely."

Without a victim contact by 10:00 P.M., the task force conference call was moved up.

Mars dreaded the call, but it was even worse than he'd expected. In preparing what he was going to say, he realized they'd oversold the certainty of an attempted killing on the fourth. What they should have emphasized to the task force was that January fourth was the first day that identified victims were at risk. Instead, they'd sold January 4 as a sure thing. So much for hindsight.

The jurisdictions that had spent the whole day at full alert were frustrated. Worse, everyone was losing confidence in Mars's analysis of Macintosh's MO. What they wanted—and you could hear it in the tone of their voices—was the sure thing.

Mars apologized for the false alarm, then said what should have been said with more emphasis when they'd met on January 2: there was no certainty that Macintosh would make a move on any of the targeted dates. The only thing that was certain was that they needed to be ready on the targeted dates.

They sat together in silence after the conference call, until Mars said, "Nettie? When's the next date?"

Nettie flipped pages in a file. "February eighth."

A simultaneous sigh rose from the chief, Keegan, Mars, and Nettie. The chief stood up. "Well, I guess that means we can all get a good night's sleep, for a change. That's the good news." He looked at Mars. "I don't want you beating yourself up over this. I'm the guy who sold today as D day at the task force meeting. You're the one that's made sense out of this whole thing—the three of you together, but Mars, you especially." Keegan and Nettie piped up with words of support. It only made Mars feel worse.

Losing the confidence and support of the task force was nothing short of a disaster, and they all knew it.

The chief went home and Keegan went back to his hotel to pack.

"I think the best thing I can do now," he said, "is to pitch in with the field agents looking for Junior and Hec. I'll plan on being back here shortly before February eighth. Wouldn't want to miss breakfast at Al's while we wait out the task force call."

Mars and Nettie sat in silence for maybe fifteen minutes after Keegan left.

Nettie said, "What do you want me to do next?"

Mars bent forward, dropping his elbows to his knees, cupping his hands over the lower half of his face. He looked up at Nettie and moved his hands. "Did you get hold of Gordon Ball's secretary? About his going out to Hollywood to see if there's any evidence of ritual? . . ."

Nettie nodded. "She said he'd get to it as soon as he could. He's out of Richmond right now, working with some of the Feebies in West Virginia. Should be back to us sometime tomorrow." She looked closely at Mars. "Should I ask her to have someone else assigned to do it?" Nettie's voice was almost gentle.

Mars looked at her. "No. Gordon will know what to look for without knowing what he's looking for. One other thing."

"What?" Her voice was still gentle.

"I *hate* it when you're nice. You make me feel like an invalid."

"So stop moping around like you are an invalid," Nettie said. "That's better."

"There's got to be something we can do . . ."

"Tee Tucker ever get back to us on anything about the dead survivors that might explain why one of them would have more than one descendent targeted? I asked him Christmas Day."

Nettie shook her head and made a note on her pad. "I'll call him first thing tomorrow. Struck me as the kind of guy you need to keep after." She doodled aimlessly for a minute, then stood up. "I'm gonna follow the chief's lead and head home. You should get some sleep, Mars."

"You're being nice, again."

"Get your ass out of here, Mars."

CHAPTER
26

The ringing phone wakened Mars.

He'd slept so hard his right arm was numb. He knocked the receiver off the hook before retrieving it with his functioning left hand.

"Mars Bahr?" the voice said. Quiet, confident.

"Yeah," Mars said, trying to sound awake, not sure of the time.

"I have something to say."

"Who's calling?" Mars looked at the caller ID screen. It was a long-distance call, area code 302. He stretched for his jacket, hung over a chair near the bed, fumbling in the inside pocket for a pen. He didn't take time to find paper and he didn't want to risk losing the number on the ID system, so he wrote the number on the wall.

"If you pay attention to what I have to say, you'll know who I am . . ."

Then the voice began a carefully cadenced recital of the familiar words:

> " 'Mine eyes have seen the glory of the coming of the
> Lord;' "

There was a long, purposeful pause before the voice said,

" 'He is trampling out the vintage where the grapes of
        wrath are stored;' "

Again, the long purposeful pause, then,

" 'He has loosed the fateful lightning of his terrible, swift
        sword;
        His truth is marching on.' "

Then, intensifying, becoming almost intimate, the voice said,
"Now, here's the part that will be of the greatest interest to
you. . . ."

" 'I have seen Him in the watch-fires of a hundred circling
        camps;' "

The voice said, "We'll talk again." And the line went dead.

Mars was back in the squad room by 6:00 A.M. He called Nettie and Evelyn and asked them both to get down to city hall as soon
as they could. He was hoping that Evelyn's experience in analyzing poetry could be put to use in interpreting the hymn's lyrics.
Then he called Boyle Keegan at his hotel.

"Don't leave. Macintosh called me at five-fifteen this morning."

Evelyn stared at the lyrics of "The Battle Hymn of the Republic"
that Nettie had printed out from a Web site.

"Tell me everything you know about the song," Mars said.

Still staring at the pages, Evelyn said. "Not a lot. Written by
Julia Ward Howe, the lyrics, that is. Isn't the tune from 'John
Brown's Body'? I can't remember for sure. It was more or less the
Union's anthem."

Nettie said, "Why would Hec Macintosh use a Union song?
Why not Dixie'?"

"That's the question," Keegan said.

Mars said, "Union anthem or not, I think the words fit what Macintosh has been doing. The words have this godlike authority and sense of purpose . . ."

"Omniscient point of view, is what us pointy-headed academics would call it," Evelyn said.

"Exactly," Mars said.

"There's one thing," Evelyn said. "Not a big thing, but given what you said about how he paused after each line . . ."

"What?" Mars said.

Evelyn held the page up, pointing. "You've drawn a line under each line as he recited it, and after each line there was a long pause, right?"

Mars nodded.

"Okay. The lines he recited are from the first stanza of the Hymn. I think it's generally considered that there are four lines in each stanza—but he's combined the last line of the stanza—'His truth is marching on'—with the third line. Given that he was so precise about pausing after each of the first two lines, it's curious. And then, he skips the chorus—you know—the 'Glory, Glory, Hallelujah' bit—and moves to the first line of the second stanza, telling you that line is going to be of particular interest. It just seems to me that how he's putting the lines together is curious. That may be more significant that the words themselves. But I agree with Mars: Macintosh sees himself as being the first person singular 'I' and 'mine' of the lyrics. And by doing that, he's aligning himself with Christ. The thing that was really notable about the Hymn—the thing that did and does drive southerners crazy about the song—is that it puts Christ squarely in the Union's camp. In using the Hymn for this message, Macintosh is coopting the Union's claim of righteousness. The guy's a megalomaniac."

Keegan gave a wry smile to Evelyn. "Anytime you want to kick over your traces and leave the pointy-headed academics in the dust, say the word. I could put you to work in the profiling section at Quantico."

Mars turned to Nettie. "We got anything on the phone number yet?"

Nettie glanced at her watch. "Waiting on the phone company."

"That's the other thing," Evelyn said. "Why did he call Mars? Why take the risk, calling from a phone where the number isn't blocked?"

Keegan said, "It all ties back to your description of Macintosh as a megalomaniac. He has a point to prove. It's a catch-me-if-you-can taunt. Adds to his sense of superiority, to the thrill of what he's doing. Putting down us feds is where it's at for him."

Mars got up and walked over to the white board. He drew a box on the small section of the board that wasn't covered with notations on the dead survivors and their descendents.

Writing, he said, "Here's what I think is most important to finding Macintosh."

Mars made a little star with the marker, then wrote, "Everything he does has significance. Nothing is random or without meaning. No detail of those ninety seconds at Gettysburg when the flag was captured has gone unnoticed."

Mars looked at each of them. "So," he said, "What are we missing?"

Immediately, Nettie said, "Sherman and Lee."

They all looked at her. Keegan said, "Two Confederate generals?"

Nettie shook her head. "No. Marshall Sherman of the First Minnesota who captured the flag, and John Lee, the guy from the twenty-eighth Virginia—Macintosh's ancestor—who lost the flag to Sherman. There's nothing about them in what we're doing. Nothing on Sherman because he never married, never had children. And nothing on Lee because he died after Gettysburg. He's not one of the nineteen members of the Twenty-eighth Virginia who died at Gettysburg, so we didn't include his birth date in target dates for hangings."

Mars said, "I think Nettie's nailed it. John Lee might have survived Gettysburg physically—but he lost the flag, he lost his soul, and he was Hec Macintosh's ancestor. His birth date is gonna be one of the nineteen. And Hec would have wanted to have found a way to tie this thing to Sherman. The question is, how?"

Keegan said, "With the three missing descendents, Macintosh created a wild card for his target victims. With Lee, he's created a wild card for the target dates. This guy's a genius."

Mars said to Nettie, "Where's the photo of Sherman?"

Nettie wheeled on her chair to a file cabinet. She wheeled back with the book Mars had read in the hospital. Flipping through it, she found the picture of Sherman posed in front of the captured flag, and passed the opened book to Mars.

Mars looked at the picture of the handsome, virile man. If you'd described him as a ladies' man, no one would have disagreed. He held the book open to each of them, and said, "Even in the 1860s, you didn't need to be married to father a child. Nettie, we need to find Sherman's bastards and Lee's birth date."

By early afternoon the phone company had confirmed that Macintosh had called from a hotel in Wilmington, Delaware. Mars spoke with the hotel manager who could tell them nothing of any use, other than the guest to whose room the call had been charged had checked out at 6:30 A.M., Eastern Time, that morning.

"Right after he talked to me," Mars said.

Nettie called out to him. "Mars!"

He looked over at her. Her face was ashen.

"John Lee was born on January fifth, 1840."

Mars covered his eyes with one hand. "No wonder he didn't move yesterday. Today's date trumped the fourth."

* * *

The hanging body of Willes E. Corrigan—the thirteen numbers inscribed on Corrigan's right arm—was recovered from a boat shed on the Chesapeake Bay. His name was one of the sixteen targeted descendents, so they could assume he was not one of the three missing targets. What Mars couldn't understand was how the Wilmington Police Department had failed to protect him.

"He left to go down to his boat around seven-thirty this morning, same as always," the sergeant assigned to cover Corrigan said. "He told us yesterday nobody had contacted him yet, and nobody can reach him when he's down at his boat. We told him to check back with us when he got back to town. And this not being a target date . . ."

Mars sat in silence after the call. Wilmington was blameless. Macintosh must have known enough about Corrigan's habits to be sure Corrigan would be alone in the boat shed, so he'd skipped making a preliminary contact. Was Macintosh starting to be more reckless? For sure Macintosh's wild card date had served him well.

Just when Mars thought things couldn't get much worse, Gordon Ball called.

"Something extraordinary has happened," Gordon Ball said, sounding shell-shocked. "I think the simplest way to tell you about this is to start at the beginning. And let me warn you. All I can do as of this moment is tell you what happened. I'm not anywhere near knowing what any of this means."

"Just tell me," Mars said.

Ball drew a deep breath. "I got a call from Bunny Palmer mid-morning. Asked if I'd send someone out to her house. She'd started upstairs to check on something her houseboy had asked her about—he's in London—and she thought she heard a toilet flush in the bathroom in his room. Scared the hell out of her. She was gonna dial nine-one-one, but she was afraid if she did that, a goon squad would arrive and come barreling into the house, breaking china and all. Mars, you've been in the house, you know how she's got artwork and what-not all over. . . ."

Mars nodded, too absorbed in what Ball was saying to remember to speak out loud.

"Anyway," Ball said, "I would have gone out myself, but I was gonna go over to Hollywood, check out the Confederate graves and monuments. So I asked one of the burglary investigators to run on out. Tell you the truth, thought it was probably nothing. Squirrels on the roof, or whatever. Damndest thing, the guy who went out didn't even think to pack his gun. Just pulled on a jacket and got in an unmarked squad, drove out to Bunny's. He gets there, and Bunny's standing out by the driveway. Didn't want to be in the house. They both go back in, and he starts up the stairs, calls out, 'Hello? Anyone upstairs?' Nothing. So he calls out his name, identifies himself as a police investigator. At that point, he hears footsteps, then a big crash. He goes up to the room, opens the door, and sees that someone's gone right through the French doors, knocking down a shelf of—if you can believe this—*Barbie dolls*—on his way to a little terrace off the room, over the pool. Anyway, he walks out onto the terrace, looks down, and sees a body lying facedown, head and shoulders hanging in the pool. Blood all over everything. Blood and Barbie dolls. The jumper took the curtains with him when he went through the doors, and the dolls must have gotten caught up in the curtains. A couple of dozen dolls are lying all around the body, floating in the pool. Most surreal crime scene you are ever going to see. We have digital crime-scene photos. They're being E-mailed to you as we speak."

Mars interrupted. "The body, Gordon. Who was it?"

"Thought you would know without being told. It was Junior Boosey."

Mars, Nettie, and Keegan huddled together in front of her computer as the file with the digital crime-scene photos opened. It was slow, dropping inch by inch from the top of each photo to the bottom. When the first photo was at midpoint, there was a pristine image of Bunny Palmer's garden on the far side of the pool. Its variegated green depths, with stone paths leading into darkness, seemed impossibly romantic.

"It's lovely," Nettie said, turning toward Mars. "You saw the garden when you were there?"

Mars nodded, but didn't take his eyes from the screen. The image continued to drop. The first hint of tragedy was a discoloration that muted the glittering black water of the pool. Nettie squinted. "The pool is filled with black water?"

"No. The interior of the pool is painted black."

The reflection on the pool's water changed as the image moved from shadow to sunlight. The sun made clear that the discoloration in the water was red. Blood red.

They continued to stare as fragments of Barbie dolls began to take shape. Some floating faceup, an arm raised as if in a salute, others facedown, their elaborate costumes splayed about them on the water. A miniature chorus-girl leg appeared, its foot clad in a sequined, spike-heeled sandal. Bridal Barbie's smile was indefatigable, but her white dress had absorbed the red of the water.

Then Junior Boosey's face, distorted by the prism of the water, began to appear in the bottom third of the picture. His body from the shoulders down lay flat on the pool's edge, arms and legs at sickening angles, possible only when bones under the flesh are broken. A river of pink streamed into the water from his mouth.

Mars, Nettie, and Keegan sat silent in front of the computer screen for minutes.

"You're sure it's Junior?" Nettie said.

"It's Junior all right. It wasn't a dumb move. He was trying to jump to the pool. Another couple feet and he would have made it. By the time the Richmond cop got back downstairs and out to the back, Junior would have been long gone."

Nettie shook her head. "Do you have the faintest idea why Junior would have been in Bunny Palmer's house?"

Mars didn't answer right away. The odd thing was, something about it did make sense. Mars just wasn't sure yet what it was. "Not now," Mars said. "Need time to rethink everything I know about Bunny, Phillipe, Ruth, and Junior."

"You think Bunny and Phillipe may be involved?"

Mars shook his head slowly. "Only by association. Neither has any motive to be involved in the hangings. Phillipe doesn't have a malevolent bone in his body, and his only passion is Barbie Dolls. Bunny's got no sympathy for the flag nuts. And she's the one who called the police when she heard the noise in Phillipe's bedroom. But it's clear they've been used. I just need to figure out how."

The answers started to come as he thought it through. He needed to talk to Ball again.

Ball wasn't available, and Mars couldn't wait to talk to him. He called Bunny Palmer, being certain she'd be able to answer his questions.

Bunny sounded shaken. Which reminded Mars that she probably still had the bloody body of a dead stranger lying in her back garden.

"Sorry to hear about your problem this morning, Bunny."

"My God," she said, "you have any idea what that young man was doin' in my house?"

"An idea is all I have at this point. And I'm sorry to bother you, but there's something I'd like to know, and you're the quickest way I have of finding an answer. You feeling up to talking a bit?"

"Talking is better than sittin' around thinking about what's out back."

"Did Ruth know Phillipe was going to be in London this week?"

"Sure, she did. Whenever we talked she asked about Phillipe. She always had some little thing she wanted him to do."

"And she still has a key to your house?"

He could hear Bunny considering his question, and he could tell from her voice when she answered that she understood why he asked.

"Ruth and I have always had keys to each other's houses. Think I told you that when you were here."

"And Bunny—does Ruth know what happened to Junior Boosey?"

"Yes," Bunny said. "She called not an hour ago. Of course I told her what was going on."

Which meant that if Hec Macintosh didn't already know that Junior was dead, he would know soon.

Nettie sat up straight and pulled back over to the computer. "You want to look at the other photos?"

Keegan shook his head. Mars had surprised himself by feeling a kind of sadness at Junior's death. He recognized the emotion from back when he'd investigated drug homicides. You'd come across these young black guys, intelligence glittering from their eyes. Young men who—given half a chance—could have done just about anything they'd put their minds to. Junior was the first white-trash character he'd run into who'd had the same kind of misdirected intelligence. The image on the computer screen was painful. He didn't need—or want—to see any more.

"Not now," he said.

Instead Mars talked through with Keegan and Nettie what he was thinking about.

"Hec's wife, Ruth, always had live-in help—until after Hec 'died.' Which means she had a lot of privacy. By choice. And she knew when Phillipe was at Bunny Palmer's and when he wasn't. Ruth Macintosh had a key to Bunny's house. Which means Hec could have a key to Bunny's house. And I don't have any doubt that Hec and Junior would have thought through where they could hide out if they needed to. With the layout of Bunny Palmer's house, I think Hec Macintosh would see it as a perfect

309

safe house. Bunny's living area—the area of the house she frequents—is in an opposite wing from the room where Junior Boosey was discovered. And apart from formal gatherings, Bunny doesn't often have casual visitors."

There was no response to what Mars said, so he continued. "I'm also willing to bet that Bunny's house was the drop point for Ruth to leave money for Junior. Then Junior would get the money to Hec. Don't know that we'll ever be able to prove that's how it worked, but I can't believe Ruth would have driven up to West Virginia with cash or that they'd risk mailing large amounts of cash. And having Hec or Junior go to Ruth's house would be too risky.

"My guess is Hec has a place somewhere in the mountains—within hiking distance for Junior. Junior got there after he came out of the tunnel. I think it's an open question if Hec was there, but I'd guess that's where Junior picked up a vehicle."

They were quiet until Mars rose, patting himself down. "Damnation," he said. "I'm out of cigarettes." He dropped his hands to his side and sucked air. "Not the only thing I'm out of."

CHAPTER
27

The first thing on Mars's mind when he woke the morning of January 6 was that Gordon Ball had said he hadn't gone out to Bunny Palmer's house when she'd called about the intruder because he was going out to Hollywood. But Gordon hadn't said anything about what he'd found at Hollywood.

It was an hour later in Richmond. With the Boosey death on his desk, Ball might be in early. Mars dialed, got a wrong number, thought about it and dialed again.

"Hate to push—but did you have a chance to get out to Hollywood?" Mars asked when Ball picked up.

"Yeah. I was there when I got paged about Junior. Sorry, I meant to say. But this thing with Boosey . . ."

"You didn't find anything around the Confederate monument that looks like it could be tied to Hec's ritual?"

"There was something. Not sure—but there's been some defacing on the base of Pickett's monument."

"Like what?"

Ball was silent for a moment, then he said, "There were three vertical marks. Looked at them real close. They were carved." Ball hesitated, then sounded sheepish. "Truth is, I got the call about Junior just then. I did think about the three hangings. Maybe a long shot, but . . ."

"Gordon? You don't know this yet. There's been another

hanging—yesterday. Near the Chesapeake Bay." Mars's head spun as he tried to sift through the ideas that were popping in his brain. "Gordon, what time were you at Hollywood? Be as precise as you can."

"Well, I left my office right around ten-thirty. Got caught up for a few minutes in a couple of issues as I was leaving—guess I was out of the building no later than, say, eleven. I would have been at Hollywood no later than eleven-thirty."

"I don't know drive times in your area, but tell me. The Wilmington police said it would have taken Macintosh about an hour—tops—to get from where he was in Wilmington at seven-thirty A.M. to the boathouse on Chesapeake Bay where the body was recovered. So let's say he's there at eight-thirty and spends an hour hanging the victim. Could Macintosh have gotten from the bay to Hollywood in a couple hours?"

Ball's line was silent for a moment. "It's going to depend, of course, on where he was on the bay. If he was an hour from Wilmington, I'd guess he was pretty far north. Make it from there to Hollywood in a couple hours? Damn near impossible. And traffic in that area is a bitch. He'd have to go over the toll bridge, then through Newport News, back up to Richmond—again, depending on exactly where he was on the bay. My guess is he wouldn't want to take a ferry, so I think the smart guess is he'd go to the bridge. I suppose it's possible, Mars. But I don't think it's likely."

Mars thought about what Ball was saying. He put that together with the thought that it was unlikely that Macintosh would want to carve on the Pickett monument in broad daylight.

"Gordon," he said, "could you send someone out to Hollywood to check the Pickett monument again?"

It didn't take Ball any time at all to say, "To see if Hec carved a fourth mark on the monument between the time I was there yesterday and now?"

"You got it in one," Mars said.

* * *

He found Nettie and Linda VanCleve in the lounge, piles of paper stacked on the floor in front of them.

Mars and Linda each started at the sight of the other. Nettie started talking as if the tension in the air didn't exist.

"I'm glad you're here. I wanted to run something by you that Linda and I have worked out on what you so elegantly referred to as Sherman's bastards. It's a big assumption—but not entirely off the wall. And it's all we've got, so . . ." Nettie turned toward Linda. "Tell him what you found."

Being careful not to meet his eyes, VanCleve said, "What we did was to check St. Paul birth records for the period of 1865 through 1893, which was the period Sherman owned and operated a boardinghouse in St. Paul. What we were looking for was a birth to an unmarried woman with a resident address that matched that of the boardinghouse . . ."

Mars unintentionally raised an eyebrow, signaling skepticism. Noticing his response, VanCleve's voice tightened, and she spoke faster. "We had a bit more to go on than that. I personally reviewed the correspondence we had on file for Sherman. There was very little that he'd written, other than business correspondence. But there were two letters addressed to Sherman written in a woman's hand, dated August eleven, 1866, and October nine, 1866. As it happens, I'd read both letters previously, when we were looking for any evidence of Sherman's connection to the flag after its capture. I hadn't thought much about them—at least in terms of representing an intimate relationship between Sherman and the correspondent. But when I read them again, it struck me that the tone was self-consciously formal and there were several very ambiguous references. What I thought on rereading the letters was that the first could well be a letter announcing the birth of a child, and the second was a letter thanking Sherman for his continued consideration . . ."

"The woman's name?" Mars said.

"The mother's name on the birth certificate was Colleen Johnson. We did find a marriage license for her dated three years later, when she married a Richard Peter. There isn't a full signature on the correspondence to Sherman, just a *C* followed by a period. But the date of birth for Colleen Johnson's son was August ninth, 1866—two days prior to the letter that could be interpreted as a birth announcement."

"Something else," Nettie said. "Sherman sold insurance after he lost his leg and left the First Minnesota. Commerce Department records indicate that a life insurance policy in the amount of five hundred dollars was issued to a Colleen Johnson in late September of 1866. The beneficiary was Johnson's son. We can't establish that it was Sherman who purchased the policy on her behalf, but . . ."

"But it fits," Mars said. He stepped forward, giving them a joint hug. "Not even close to off the wall. The question now: How long to get to the living descendents of Colleen Johnson Peter's son?"

"We're on the second generation past the son now," VanCleve said. "Another six to eight hours—maybe."

Mars had just turned to leave the lounge when a division secretary approached him.

"Mars? Gordon Ball on your line."

Mars felt his pulse accelerate as he took the phone.

"Gordon?" He couldn't bring himself to ask. He just held his breath.

"Four marks, Mars."

Mars closed his eyes and exhaled.

"I'm setting up undercover surveillance on Hollywood now," Ball said. "It'll be in place twenty-four-seven for as long as necessary. This is great news, Mars. It gives us a real shot."

"Good news, bad news, Gordon. To get our shot, someone needs to die."

Mars looked over his shoulder. The division secretary was signaling him again.

"Long distance holding for you," she mouthed.

"Gotta go, Gordon. I'll be back to you shortly."

Before picking up the second call, Mars looked at the ID screen. Area code 906. A light chill ran down his spine. He jotted down the ten-digit number and passed it to the secretary. "Get a location on this number right away. We've got the recorder on this line?"

When the secretary nodded, Mars picked up.

"A change in plan," the voice said.

Macintosh's smooth confidence was gone. There was an emotional vibrato in his voice. It sounded like he was working hard to maintain control.

He knows about Junior, Mars thought.

Immediately Macintosh began.

> " 'With a glory in His bosom that transfigures you and me;
> As he died to make men holy, let us die to make men free
> While God is marching on.' "

The last phrase was hissed in a voice overtaken by rage.

Then the line went dead.

Keegan, Nettie, VanCleve, and Mars pored over the copy of "The Battle Hymn of the Republic." They found the three lines that Macintosh had quoted. They were the final three lines of the final stanza.

Keegan said, "He's gone from the first four lines of the Hymn to the final three lines—except in the final three lines he's included the emblematic phrase—'While God is marching on.' In the first stanza, the emblematic phrase, 'His truth is marching on,' was omitted. What is he saying?"

Nettie, staring at the Hymn, traced down the lines, her lips moving but silent.

"It's what Evelyn said. That how he's choosing the lines is more important than the words themselves." She turned the pages of the Hymn around, facing them, while she moved an index finger from line to line.

"It's not complicated. If you count the lines in each of the six stanzas—excluding the emblematic phrase—you have eighteen lines. If you include the final emblematic phrase—'While God is marching on'—you've got nineteen lines." She looked at them. "Is there any doubt why he'd select nineteen lines—and why he'd want to end with 'While God is marching on?' And his message in the first call—three lines when we had three deaths, followed by a line in which Mars would have 'particular interest'—was 'I've killed three of the targets, I'm about to kill the fourth.' "

Keegan said, "And in the second call, by quoting the final three lines, he's telling us there are going to be three more victims. And like he said: a change in plan. For some reason he's skipping targeted victims five through sixteen and going for victims seventeen, eighteen, and nineteen."

"Do any of us," Mars said, "have any doubt who he intends those final three victims to be? Or why? Junior's death has raised the possibility Hec won't complete his message. He's covered Lee's birth date with the Willes Corrigan hanging. He's starting on Sherman's descendents, and I'm betting there are going to be three of them. If nothing else, those are the targets he wants to be sure he takes out."

Keegan ran his fingers through his hair. "The one thing we've got going for us. He doesn't know what we know. He doesn't know we're close to identifying his final targets."

Nettie and VanCleve rose simultaneously. "If we really push, we can have one within the next four hours."

Mars shook his head slowly. "According to what we found out

316

about the phone number and based on what happened in Delaware, Hec's next victim is in the Marquette, Michigan area. That person has one, maybe two hours to live. It's too late to save him. The best we can do is save the other two."

CHAPTER
28

The police in Waring, Michigan, found Harry Mickelson's body when they went to his office to set up protection.

They'd gone out to his house first. Three squads, sirens on, lights flashing. That had scared Mrs. Mickelson because Harry was late coming home. When she saw the police cars she thought they were there because Harry had been in an accident.

Sirens on, lights flashing, the squads had turned around and headed back downtown. The security guard at the front desk in Harry's building said Harry had left the building two hours earlier. One of the cops thought to check the parking lot. After seven o'clock on this cold January night, the darkened lot was deserted. Except for Harry Mickelson's blue Chevy. When the cop shone his long-handled, big-headed flash into Harry's powder blue Chevy Celebrity, Harry's bug-eyed, powder blue face had stared back at him.

When they opened the car, what happened was obvious. Someone had been waiting for Harry in the Chevy's backseat. Harry's keys were lying on the floor of the front seat, so the killer had slipped the noose over Harry's head before Harry had a chance to start the car.

Then Harry made a mistake. His hands were free, so if he'd been thinking, he could have laid on the horn. But Harry had been too surprised to think. He'd acted reflexively. He'd brought both hands up to his neck, to pull the noose back. The middle three fingers on each hand had big blood blisters at the tips, just above where the noose had tightened.

The springs on the backside of the driver's seat had popped from where the killer's feet had pushed in for traction. The long end of the noose hung over the back of the seat, stained red from rubbing the killer's palms raw.

The thirteen numbers had been written on Harry Mickelson's forehead.

Mars and Keegan stared at the crime-scene photos of Mickelson's death on the computer screen.

"Well," Keegan said, "this pretty much wraps it. He's gone off the rails. Junior's death was probably the precipitating factor. What he'll do next is anybody's guess. We've just got to hope he'll stick to his plan and go back to Hollywood before he goes out after the next two."

"But not before we get there," Mars said.

There were no flights to Richmond the night Harry Mickelson died, but the chief signed off on a charter flight without blinking. By the time Mars and Keegan got to Hollywood, Gordon Ball and maybe two dozen other officers were waiting for him in the dark along the outside wall of the Gothic chapel.

"How many marks on Pickett's statue?" Mars said as soon as he saw Ball.

"Same as before," Ball said, holding up his right hand, four fingers extended.

Mars looked at his watch, pushing the stem to light the face. It was just before 4:00 A.M. "Like I said, if Macintosh left the Upper Peninsula of Michigan at, say, six o'clock last night, the *earliest* he could be here would be around eight o'clock this morning. . . ."

"Agreed," Ball said. "But I also agree with you that it made sense to come on out tonight just in case. And nobody really expects him to show up in daylight, regardless of when he gets back in town. So this gives us a chance to set up operations, get a feel for what we'll be dealing with tonight. And we've got the lights set up over on the fence by the statue and on the trees around the monument." Ball looked at his watch. "Still waiting for the canine patrol." Then he turned in a slow circle, looking at the sky. "Perfect conditions now. Clear as a bell. Warm front coming in that will fog things up by sunset."

"What time does the cemetery close to the public?" Keegan asked.

"Five-thirty," Ball said. "Macintosh is gonna come in over the fence. I'd put money on it. Doesn't draw attention to himself, the fence is directly behind the Pickett monument—perfect set up for him."

Mars glanced around, then looked again. He took Ball by the arm and led him away from the others. "Am I imagining things, or is that Phil Stern standing back there with a bunch of guys that aren't in uniform?"

Ball made a face. "I was going to tell you. News about Junior got back to some of the ROFers. Stern called and talked to one of my sergeants—a guy Phil knows personally. My sergeant used bad judgment. Told him pretty much what was going on. Stern wanted to help out, offered to bring four other guys with him. By the time I came on the scene, they were already here . . ."

Mars shook his head. "It's a mistake, Gordon. This needs to be a tight operation, these guys—even if you can trust them—aren't trained to handle a situation like this."

"Look, Mars, we'll only use them for perimeter observation. Let me be candid here. Number one, we've got over forty acres to keep under close observation. We've got walkie-talkies on everybody, but even so, it stretches our resources. I could bring in the national guard, or some other jurisdictions, but frankly, I trust Stern's guys more than some of the guys I could bring in. Remember, there are still people in Virginia who'd consider Hec Macintosh to be a hero. Number two, Phil's guys are motivated. They feel like this is their only chance to redeem their cause. This operation goes down without their demonstrating that they stand against what Macintosh's been up to, and they know they're doomed. Can't say as I blame them. . . ."

Mars shook his head again. "We're on your ground, Gordon. I can't tell you what to do. But I think it's a mistake."

According to plan, the group moved into covert positions just before sunrise. Mars, who apart from dozing off briefly on the plane, hadn't slept in almost forty-eight hours, sacked out in the back of an unmarked van parked downhill from the cemetery. He slept more soundly than he should have, waking just after noon when Gordon Ball climbed into the van.

"Sorry to wake you."

Mars sat up, stretching, stiff all over from deep sleep on a hard surface. "I should be awake."

They sat together in silence for a few moments before Ball said, "You hungry? We've got sandwiches, drinks, over in the chapel."

"There's a john in the chapel?"

"Fully equipped."

The van moved slowly up the hill, parking close to the front entrance of the chapel. Mars and Ball were inside in two quick steps. Mars immediately bumped into Phil Stern.

Stern held out his hand. "Good to see you again—glad to have a chance to say how sorry I am how this has worked out. We appreciate getting an opportunity to help out."

Mars shook Stern's hand, but said little. Time crawled for the rest of the afternoon. Cell phone activity had been restricted in the event that Macintosh used a scanner. All police radio activity had been scripted earlier to exclude any mention of a watch for Macintosh at Hollywood or anywhere else in the city. Officers patrolling the cemetery as tourists and mourners came in and out of the chapel as they changed shifts.

Gloom gathered before the sun had set. Gordon had called the weather right. Warm air came up the river, hit the high, cold ground of Hollywood, and thickened into fog. There was enough of a breeze to keep the fog shifting, but the eerie light added to the building tension.

Mars and Ball stood together in the darkened chapel. Lights had been turned off after sunset. Except for a couple of infrared lights that had been plugged in at floor level and allowed careful movement within the chapel, there was total darkness. Mars and Gordon stood together at a window facing in the direction of the monument until almost nine o'clock. Then they put on dark, hooded jackets and walked out to take their positions.

Ball said, "You still sure this is gonna happen tonight?"

Mars said, "We'd better hope it does. It's pretty obvious Hec has been coming back here directly after each of the murders. If he doesn't show up now, I think we can assume he's gone on a rampage to take down the final two Sherman descendents as quickly as he can."

"What's the status of those two?"

"They've been located, so I'm pretty sure we can protect them. Problem is, by now, Hec probably thinks it's possible we know who he's after. That's been part of the thrill for him. So he's going to be prepared to run if something doesn't seem right around the victims. We could lose him, even if we can save the targets. The one thing I'm pretty sure he doesn't know is that we know he comes back here after the murders. This is our best shot at a quick capture."

Before they separated, Mars said, "Gordon, when Hec shows—before you give the signal for the lights to go on—give me a heads-up on the walkie-talkie. I want to know as soon as you're sure it's Macintosh."

Mars was positioned in a small clump of bushes that allowed him a view of both Pickett's monument and the pyramid. *Would* have allowed him a view if the fog hadn't limited his vision to perhaps two feet in front of his own face. He began to worry that Macintosh could slip in and out of the cemetery without being seen. Thinking about it, he realized an advantage of having decided to wait to close the net until Hec chipped the fifth line on the base of Pickett's statue was that they could hear that happening.

Mars had called Ball before leaving Minneapolis to propose the Hollywood stakeout. Gordon had been quick to see the opportunity. But they'd had considerable discussion about when to close the net on Hec if he did show up. Mars and Gordon both leaned toward taking him as soon as he showed up. But the chief of police in Waring, Michigan, had been in contact with Ball as soon as he heard about the plan. He'd begged that Macintosh not be taken until the fifth line had been chiseled.

Ball and Mars understood why; it would be a significant piece of evidence in the overall investigation and particularly in Waring's case against Macintosh for Harry Mickelson's murder. Mars was comfortable that they had plenty of evidence against Hec without the fifth line. And he was pretty sure Hec Mcintosh would have been dealt with by another jurisdiction long before Waring took its case to court. But there was something poetic in letting Hec chisel the fifth line seconds before he was apprehended. As long as the stakeout seemed secure, Mars agreed to go along.

Mars's walkie-talkie flashed, signaling that he needed to turn on his earphones.

Gordon Ball's thoughts had been running along similar lines. "Mars," he said, his voice hushed. "I'm thinking we might not see Hec at all when he comes in—but if we hear him chiseling on the base, I'm gonna treat that as a sighting and give the signal to turn the lights on."

"Good idea," Mars said. "Something else. Didn't you say you scented the dogs to the bloodied noose from Waring?"

"Right."

"Make contact with the dog handlers. Tell them if the dogs get restless, if their hackles go up, to let us know. The dogs will smell Hec a long time before we see or hear him."

And they did.

Mars's walkie-talkie flashed shortly after 11:00 P.M.

"The dogs are restless," Ball's voice whispered.

"Oookay," Mars said. "You see anything yet?"

"No. But the dog that responded first was just down the fence from Pickett's monument. My guess is he's gonna come over the fence. Which is a smart move. Visibility being what it is, the fence gives him a guide right up to the statue."

"I'll wait to hear from you."

"Mars? The one thing I regret about not being able to make a visual sighting?"

"What's that, Gordon."

"When I saw him—when I spotted Hec—I was gonna call you and say, 'Dead Man Walking.' "

If there was a more chilling sound than the echo of a chisel striking against stone in a cemetery on a night when nothing could be seen, Mars didn't know what it was. Shivering, he waited for Gordon Ball to give the signal for the light switch to be thrown. But he still wasn't prepared when it came.

"Lights!" Ball screamed, and what seemed like a million watts of brilliance flashed, the switches making loud, clacking sounds as an accompaniment.

The damnedest thing was, even with the powerful lights, all you could see in the fog was dark forms of people, with statues in the background casting darker shadows. The figure by Pickett's monument forced itself upright, then stood frozen for a moment. Until the dogs started after him. Then the figure ran, not toward

324

the fence but to the left, away from the dogs, toward the river, in the direction of the pyramid.

Mars ran in the direction of the pyramid, but men coming over the fence were closer to the fugitive by a hundred yards. The fugitive hesitated for just a moment. The dogs were almost on him. Then, with a leap, he started to scramble up the rocky ledges of the monument, his feet slipping, then finding footing as he moved higher. Out of reach of the frantic dogs below, the man began climbing slowly higher. Just below him, two men started up the pyramid in pursuit.

Gordon Ball was in a hell of a position. Without being certain it *was* Hec Macintosh, he was reluctant to order fire. The two men below took action on their own. They scrambled up opposite sides of the monument, approaching the figure laterally, slowly closing the distance between them. Within seconds the two men were within arm's reach of the fugitive.

Mars heard the noise before he saw the side of the monument start to collapse. It was almost like a groan, then rocks began cascading in a racketing roar.

The dogs were back and away from the avalanche in a flash.

The three men on the monument went down with the falling rocks.

CHAPTER
29

Mars stayed in Richmond after Hec Macintosh and Phil Stern died at Hollywood Cemetery. The third man on the monument, a ROF associate of Stern's, was in the hospital in critical condition. He'd probably live, though walking again might not be an option.

The chief ordered Mars to be the city's representative at Stern's funeral and personally made reservations for Mars at the Jefferson, an old, elegant hotel with wonderful restaurants.

After filing reports on the incident, Mars spent most of the second day in Richmond working with Nettie and Dana Levy by phone to put together a press kit on the investigation. To Dana, he said, "I don't want us puffing ourselves up as the big heroes. Credit all around. Especially to Gordon and the ROF people—and to Boyle Keegan in Quantico. Go real heavy on the cooperation we received from all nineteen jurisdictions."

Ball had set Mars up in a first-class office in the police department, assigning a shrewd, sarcastic black woman as an administrative assistant. Made Mars feel right at home. He called Nettie to advise her that she could be replaced.

"I can't talk," she said.

"What's going on?"

"New furniture for the lounge. Just got delivered. Huge leather couch, matching club chairs, ottoman. I may give up my apartment and just move into the lounge."

"Where the hell did that come from?"

"Keegan. He promised. Don't you remember? This stuff was in the office of some deputy director at the FBI. When he retired, the new guy wanted new furniture. The Feebies who were involved in the Macintosh investigation pitched in to pay the freight to deliver it to us. There's a catch, though."

"Which is?"

"Keegan sent a plaque that has to be displayed on the lounge door."

"Let me guess. 'The Boyle Keegan Lounge.' "

"You got it in one."

He was reviewing the final version of the press kit that Dana had faxed to him when Ball knocked on Mars's half-open door and walked in, closing the door behind him.

"Just when you thought you were out of the woods . . ."

Mars groaned. "What now? What could possibly go wrong now?"

Ball looked Mars in the eye. "Mary Katherine Stern is here. Over in my office. She has a favor to ask you."

"Phil's wife?"

Ball shrugged. "Widow, to be precise. You can be thankful she didn't bring the four kids along. The oldest is nine."

"What is it—what's the favor?"

"You'd better talk to Mary Katherine."

By the time Mars got to Ball's office he'd figured it out, more or less. And it made him sick to his stomach.

Mary Katherine Stern was in her early thirties, pretty in an unspectacular way. Working hard to maintain her composure. Mars came in behind her, flinching at the sight of her straight back.

"I'm Marshall Bahr of the Minneapolis Police Department," he said, gently touching her shoulder. He was about to add, 'I'm sorry for your loss.' But he heard how it would sound before he

327

said it. Heard it echoing from all the times he'd said it before. Always meaning it, but this time, like all the other times, it just wasn't enough.

So instead he said, "I'll do whatever I can to get the flag for display at Phil's service."

Back in his office, he sat behind the desk for a long time, feet up, thinking. Then he called Dana Levy.

"How'd the press kit look?" she asked, thinking that's why he called.

"The kit is fine. Perfect. But I need you to do something—two things, actually."

"Shoot."

"Can you get at least one of the papers—preferably both the *Strib* and the *Pioneer Press-Dispatch*—to run the story tomorrow?"

"Oh, geez, Mars. This is a big story—I don't think there's any way they can be ready to go by—"

"It's really important, Dana. Really important. You can do it. I know you can."

"You said two things."

"I'm going to transmit a digital photo of Mary Katherine Stern and her four kids. Phil Stern's widow. I'd like that photo, along with a sidebar on her request to have the flag displayed at Phil's funeral, to run with the article."

He could hear Dana grin. "This is starting to sound doable, Mars. The funeral is when?"

"Three days."

Dana said, "I need to get off the horn with you to make some last-minute changes to the press kit. Get that picture to me *now*. When I've got that, I'll get in touch with the front-page editors at both papers. Let them know the kit is coming over. And I may just drop a hint to each that the other paper is already working the story."

After hanging up with Dana, Mars called Linda VanCleve. He guessed she picked up only because she didn't recognize the phone number.

"I need you to do something, Linda."

"I just bet you do," she said. But there was something in her voice that didn't sound as bad as he'd been expecting.

"The widow of the Recover Our Flag guy who died at Hollywood Cemetery has requested that the flag—and I don't mean the Stars and Stripes—be displayed at his funeral. Three days from tomorrow."

"Oh, Mars, there's no way. Just from a conservatorship standpoint it's not possible, not to mention doing something like this on that timetable. . . ."

"I think you should know, Linda. Sometime within the next twenty-four to forty-eight hours, one or both of the Twin City newspapers are going to be running a story about what happened at Hollywood on the front page of their papers. And they know that Mary Katherine Stern has asked that the flag be displayed at her husband's funeral. You can talk conservatorship and humidity and ultraviolet light damage all you want. But you're smart enough to know how that's gonna sound under these circumstances. It won't be good for you and it won't be good for the History Center."

The line was quiet, then Linda VanCleve said, "I'll call you back."

The morning of Phil Stern's funeral was cool, dry, and overcast. Perfect conditions for displaying a 137-year-old flag with minimal risk of exposure to the elements.

The flag had been air transported from the Twin Cities to Richmond on the governor's personal jet. Accompanying the flag were Linda VanCleve, two nationally recognized Civil War flag conservators, and four members of the First Minnesota reenactors who were in full-dress Civil War uniform regalia. The four reenactors would present the flag to four members of the Twenty-eighth Virginia reenactors, who in turn would drape the flag over a specially constructed cotton cloth that had been laid on top of Phil Stern's casket. The 3M Corporation was providing a special plastic cover that would deflect ultraviolet rays without obstructing a view of the flag.

When the flag had been placed on the casket, the eight reenactors would jointly serve as pallbearers.

After the service, Mars and Linda VanCleve stood on the steps of the church together, watching the flag and the casket as they were loaded into a glass-topped hearse.

"You're not going to the cemetery with the flag?" Mars said.

Linda shook her head, avoiding looking at Mars. "I'm going over to the Virginia Historical Society. We're having a meeting to agree on how to share the flag over the next five years. My bottom line is, it can only be displayed in Virginia as part of a historical exhibit that tells the story of the First Minnesota and the Twenty-eighth Virginia." She turned toward Mars, without looking at him, keeping her eyes on the departing hearse. "I need to ask you this. If we'd given the flag back when you'd asked, would that guy in Michigan still be alive?"

Mars kept his eyes on the hearse too, letting moments pass before he said, "Hard to say. Fifty-fifty whether Macintosh would have stopped. My guess is he was into what he was doing by then and getting the flag back wouldn't have made any difference." He looked down at her. "So you're going to work on sharing the flag for the next five years. And after that?"

"Oh, I don't know, Mars. Don't ask. This is more than anybody would have hoped for until . . ."

"Until four days ago," Mars said. He nodded toward the hearse. "You're okay with this, then?"

"More than okay. It's damn wonderful. And you were right. It beats the hell out of keeping the flag in the basement."

The picture that appeared on the front page of every major American newspaper the next day was an overhead shot of the eight reenactors carrying the flag-draped casket up the steps of the church. Mary Katherine Stern and her four children followed.

It would have been hard to beat the headline that ran in *USA Today*: "Suicide Investigation Saves Fourteen Lives."

CHAPTER

30

For the second time in less than two weeks, Mars came back to Minneapolis from Richmond on a late-night flight and headed straight from the airport to see Chris.

"Before you go in to see Chris," Denise said, "I should tell you . . ."

Mars turned to look at her. She shrugged. "He's taking care of the neighbor's dog for two weeks. The dog is with him in his bedroom. Just didn't want you to jump out of your skin when you went in."

Chris wasn't visible when Mars went into the bedroom. All Mars could see on the bed was an immense mound of brown, white, and black fur. The mound was on its back, four legs that could have supported a grand piano, splayed in the air. A deep, rattling snore rose from the mound. Mars walked quietly around to the side of the bed where a sleeping Chris was partially visible. Mars extended a hand to touch Chris's hair. The motion woke the mound, who sprang sideways with a loud snort. Freed by the dog's move, Chris opened his eyes.

"Dad! You're home! I thought you weren't coming back till tomorrow."

"Wasn't sure I could get home tonight, so didn't want to get your hopes up. But I always planned on trying to get home tonight." Mars found a place on the side of the bed and sat down. He reached over and scratched the dog's head. "What's his name?"

"She. Penelope. She's a St. Bernard."

Penelope didn't seem particularly interested in her name, but she did decide that if conversation was taking place, she wanted to be in the center of things. She rose, shaking violently, then stepped half over Chris before dropping down. Immobilized and gasping, Chris said, "She's real cuddly."

"Cuddly could kill you. So. You finally got your dog."

"Only for two weeks. Till the Castwalls get home."

"Yeah, but two weeks with Penelope is like the equivalent of two months with any other dog. So if you take care of her six weeks out of every year, you've got a whole dog. I'm glad your mom decided it was okay."

"The Castwalls are paying me fifteen dollars a day, so it'll be three hundred and sixty dollars. It'd cost them, like, thirty dollars a day to put her in a kennel. Mom said I could do it if I saved one hundred and eighty for soccer camp next summer and ninety for my college savings. I get to keep ninety for myself." Chris grinned, thinking about something. "Penny drools a lot. She *totally* slimed Mom. We were in the kitchen, and Penny'd just taken a big drink of water. When she shook her head, all the drool hanging off her lips went all over Mom's pants."

"And Mom didn't blow up?"

Chris's smile widened. "Mom didn't know it happened. But I heard her saying later she wondered what she'd gotten all over her pants."

They grinned at each other. Silent conspirators in the Land of Neat. Mars scratched Penelope's head, and the dog rolled her eyes back at Mars, panting with pleasure.

"You know who she reminds me of?" Mars said.

Chris lifted his head and squinted at the dog. "Who?"

"That weird actress, model, whatever. The one with real

blond hair—kind of a cartoonish sex bomb. Can't remember her name—Anna Nicole Smith. Penny's got that same big-girl voluptuous look as Anna Nicole Smith. And a real short nose."

"Does Anna Nicole Smith drool?"

"Probably."

They sat quiet for a bit, each rubbing a different part of the dog. Then Chris said, "I've put all the newspaper articles about what happened at the cemetery in a scrapbook. You wanna see it?"

"I do—but not tonight. Let's look at it this weekend."

"So you got everybody, right?"

Mars thought about it. "There's still an issue about Hec Macintosh's wife. She says all she knew he was doing was planning a way of getting the flag back. Maybe, maybe not. It will be just about impossible to prove what she did know. Glenn will take a look at it, but I doubt we'll take any action. Hard case to prove, different jurisdictions . . ."

"I wanted to see the flag again before they took it away. It was our flag, Dad. Why did we have to give it back?"

"We didn't have to. It was the right thing to do. I didn't start out thinking that, but I guess I think so now. Sharing it, anyway. You'll still get a chance to see it."

"Why did you change your mind?"

"I think mostly it was reading about the Battle of Gettysburg. One of the things that really struck me was how much respect both sides had for each other. Gettysburg was the bloodiest battle of the war—I don't remember exactly, but thousands of men died. And there was regret on both sides over what they had to do as soldiers. I started to feel like it just didn't honor what those guys did for us to still be fighting about a flag. I wouldn't feel that way if the Virginians wanted to fly the flag in public as a symbol of the Confederacy. But all they want is to have the flag in an exhibit that'll be part of the history of the battle."

"If we share it—that would sort of be like saying the war's over . . ."

334

"You got it in one."

"Number three, Dad. Probably number one, too."

"What?"

"You've been saying 'You've got it in one' *a lot*. Number three. And you should think of something else to say. Number one."

Three months to the day after Frank Beck had been hanged, Mars picked up Chris and Evelyn for dinner at Restaurant Alma.

It had been Chris's idea to take Evelyn out for dinner the evening she was leaving for England. Evelyn and Chris had an easy friendship that had begun with Mars's hospitalization. They had maintained the friendship separate from Mars. Mars had begun by being uncomfortable at the prospect of Chris being hurt if Evelyn dropped out of his life, but the more he saw the two of them together, the more confident he was that Evelyn and Chris could be trusted to manage their friendship without Mars's intervention.

And Chris and Evelyn shared a passion for food in general and chocolate in particular that had become an unbreakable bond.

What Mars hadn't worked through was how Evelyn's leaving made him feel. A small hollow feeling emerged somewhere between his heart and his gut when she'd set her departure date. It took up more space every day. So, when Chris suggested the farewell dinner, Mars immediately thought of Alma's, hoping a happy evening with good food would fill the hollow spot.

"Would the young gentleman like a kiddy cocktail?" The waitress smiled at Chris.

The young gentleman barely contained his disdain. "*No*. I want a fat Coke."

As the waitress walked away, Chris said, "Dad? Remember when Gloria asked me to go with her?"

Mars nodded. "Yeah. And neither one of us could figure out what 'going with' someone meant when you were eight years old."

"Well," Chris said, "going with Gloria was like that," he jerked his head in the direction of the departing waitress. "Going with Gloria was a kiddy cocktail."

Evelyn said, "He's gonna do great on the analogy section of the SATs."

After dropping Chris off, Mars took Evelyn to the airport. They didn't talk until they took the exit to the airport approach road. Then Evelyn said, "I can't imagine writing to you. But I don't want you to think that means you won't be on my mind."

The funny thing was, Mars understood exactly what she meant. "But you'll write to Chris."

Evelyn said, "Of course."

Hoping it sounded only half-serious, Mars said, "Not even a postcard? No words, just the postcard?"

"That I could do."

Back at the apartment, Mars turned on the television, sound off. Then he went into the kitchen, got a can of Coke, and walked back into the living room, watching the silent screen. The news was on, and the face on the screen looked familiar. The woman was elaborately made-up, and even with the sound off, it was obvious she was mighty pleased to be on the evening news.

A tag line appeared under her image on the screen. As soon as he saw it, Mars remembered why she looked familiar. He turned the mute off and listened to the last few seconds of the interview. Then he made a phone call and left the apartment, driving downtown to city hall.

He stopped in at the property room and picked up the box, which they had waiting for him. He carried it back up to the department, relieved to find the squad room empty. Dropping the box on his desk, he dug around until he found what he was looking for. Then he made another phone call, punched buttons on the automated response system, and wrote down the recorded message.

After he'd compared what he'd written with what he'd found in the box, a big grin broke out on his face.

Sleeping that night wasn't an option, so he stopped by a Video Update on his way back to the apartment and picked up three videos, *Pulp Fiction, The Insider,* and—what the hell—*The Sound of Music.* Looking at the times for each of the films on the back of the boxes, he calculated they'd get him through to a reasonable hour the next morning when he could make the last phone call.

He got to the Dunn Brothers on the corner of Sixth Avenue and University Southeast ahead of Joey Beck. He was annoying himself by not being able to stop humming the melody to "Climb Every Mountain." And he was antsy. Playing with the cigarette box nonstop.

"Mr. Bahr," Joey said, a big grin on his face. "I was really glad to get your call. Mom and I've been talking about calling you. We want you to know how much we appreciate what you did."

Mars held up a hand. "Not why I wanted to get together. Fact is, we should be thanking you. If you hadn't pushed, Macintosh would have kept going until he was finished. I called because—" Mars reached into his pocket, pulling out a white envelope.

"Because of this. I was watching television last night and heard something that I connected to the case." Mars held up the white envelope, then pushed it across the table to Joey.

Looking puzzled, Joey opened the envelope. He took out the pink Powerball ticket and the slip of paper on which Mars had written the winning Powerball numbers for the December 7 Powerball drawing.

Joey's face was blank as he looked at the ticket and Mars's numbers. Then he said, "Where'd you get this?"

"It was taken with your dad's possessions by the officer on the scene when your dad died. I'd looked at the tickets early on—thinking the numbers on the tickets might have been related to the numbers on your dad's arm. Your dad bought the ticket at the convenience store just across the street from the Dachota maybe an hour before he died. I'd interviewed the clerk during the investigation, and I recognized her on the television news last night. They were doing a story on a Powerball jackpot that hadn't been claimed."

Joey put his hand to his mouth and slowly shook his head. "I just can't believe this." He looked up at Mars. "Do you know what this would have meant to my dad?"

"It would still mean a lot to him to know that you and your mom were provided for, Joey."

The story ran on the front page of the *Strib*, above the fold, with a picture of Mona and Joey Beck holding a big mock-up of a Powerball jackpot check. The headline read, "Dead Man's Lucky Legacy."

The story's angle was what interested Mars. The Beck family was using the proceeds of the win to pay off Frank Beck's investors. Joey was quoted as saying he was happy there'd be enough left to allow his mother to live comfortably.

When he was asked if he was disappointed that finding the lucky ticket hadn't left him a wealthy man, Joey'd said, "I can make my own luck."

"Got it in one," Mars said out loud.

AUTHOR'S NOTE

Fact and imagination are mixed with abandon in *The Dead Survivors*. As imagination is the larger part of the whole, it is easiest to begin by stating facts.

As of this writing, there is a heated controversy happening between Virginia and Minnesota over Minnesota's possession of the Twenty-eighth Virginia's regimental flag. That flag was captured during the Civil War on the final day of the Battle of Gettysburg by Marshall Sherman of the legendary First Minnesota Volunteers. By most accounts, John Lee was the last member of the Twenty-eighth Virginia to carry the regiment's colors before the flag was captured. Because of the important role played by these individuals at a critical juncture in the battle, I chose to use their real names.

All other names of soldiers associated with the First Minnesota and the Twenty-eighth Virginia and their descendents are fictional. It is especially important to note that personal details with respect to Sherman and Lee are fiction: there is no evidence that Marshall Sherman fathered a child, that John Lee hanged himself two years after Gettysburg, or that John Lee fathered a daughter who married a man named Macintosh.

While the Twenty-eighth Virginia's regimental flag is held in a secure area at the Minnesota Historical Society's History Center in St. Paul, Minnesota, all History Center personnel in *The Dead Survivors* are fictional, as are all characters in the book.

Jack Blanton, in addition to being my trusted first reader, provided invaluable assistance and incomparable hospitality in orienting me to the charms and curiosities of Richmond in general and Hollywood Cemetery in particular. Luis Patton's collecting and gardening talents inspired several scenes set in Richmond. My dear cousin, Barbara Kuske, was the perfect companion for a visit to the Gettysburg National Battlefield; who else would think reading every inscription on Gettysburg's more than 1300 monuments, memorials, and markers was a perfect way to spend summer afternoons? June Gornitzka, Carol Beglau, Delores Henehan, Helen Lifson, and Edie Johnson continue to provide important support.

Ian Sumner, honorary librarian of the Flag Institute, East Yorkshire, England, made helpful suggestions regarding sources for fabric used in Civil War Confederate flags. Richard Poole of the British Wool Marketing Board, Bradford, England, told me the true story of wool research conducted in 1995 to identify the crew of a British ship sunk off the U.S. coast during the Revolutionary War. This is a story that merits a mystery all its own; I have plundered selected details of Mr. Poole's tale for my own purposes in *The Dead Survivors*.

To enter the historical archives of the Civil War is to follow Alice down the Rabbit's Hole. I did eventually emerge, dazed, and with particular appreciation for four books: *The Last Full Measure: The Life and Death of the First Minnesota Volunteers* by Richard Moe; *For Cause & Comrade: Why Men Fought in the Civil War* by James M. McPherson; *Minnesota in the Civil War*, edited by Kenneth Carley; and *April 1865: The Month That Saved America*, by Jay Winik. Articles on the flag controversy in *The Washington Post* by Kathy Sawyer and *The St. Paul Pioneer Press* by Nick Coleman were of great value.

To end with the beginning, I've had great luck in my agent

and editor—respectively, Jane Jordan Browne and Kelley Ragland. As with all people who are good at what they do, their associates are first-rate and include Scott Mendel, Benjamin Sevier, Linda McFall, Deborah Miller, Janie McAdams, and Yamil Anglada.